THE
DOORSTEP GIRLS

Val Wood

D0588641

CORGI BOOKS

THE DOORSTEP GIRLS
A CORGI BOOK : 9780552150316

Originally published in Great Britain by Bantam Press,
a division of Transworld Publishers

PRINTING HISTORY
Bantam Press edition published 2002
Corgi edition published 2003

18 20 19 17

Set in 11/12pt New Baskerville by
Kestrel Data, Exeter, Devon.

Black Swan Books are published by Transworld Publishers,
61–63 Uxbridge Road, London W5 5SA,
a division of The Random House Group Ltd.

Addresses for Random House Group Ltd companies outside the
UK can be found at: www.randomhouse.co.uk
The Random House Group Ltd Reg. No. 954009.

Printed and bound in Great Britain by
CPI Cox & Wyman, Reading, RG1 8EX

The Random House Group Limited supports The Forest Stewardship
Council (FSC), the leading international forest certification organisation.
All our titles that are printed on Greenpeace approved FSC certified paper
carry the FSC logo. Our paper procurement policy can be found at:
www.rbooks.co.uk/environment

To my family with love

ACKNOWLEDGEMENTS

Books for general reading:

Confessions of an English Opium Eater, Thomas De Quincey, 1822.
History of the Town and Port of Hull, James Joseph Sheehan, 1866.
Victorian Women, Joan Perkin, 1993. John Murray Ltd.
Living and Dying: a picture of Hull in the Nineteenth Century, Bernard Foster.

My thanks to Catherine for reading the manuscript and to Peter and Ruth for their support and encouragement.

CHAPTER ONE

The two girls sat side by side on the doorstep, their knees drawn up and chins resting in their hands. They both stared vacantly into space without speaking. It was midsummer in 1848, and the dank and narrow court was humid and sticky. It stank of putrid decay, sewage, and of seed oil and blubber drifting in from the mills situated close by along the river Hull. The ground beneath their bare feet was unpaved and muddy yet they chose to sit outside on the stone slab, with their cotton skirts tucked under them, rather than be indoors; they had both been inside mill walls since six o'clock that morning and it was now seven o'clock in the evening.

'I'm hungry,' Ruby muttered. 'I've had nowt to eat since this morning and that was onny a bit o' bread.' Her face was pinched and white, and made more colourless by the contrast of her dark hair, which strayed from beneath her cotton cap and across her forehead.

'Did you take no dinner to work?' Grace asked, and when Ruby shook her head, said anxiously, 'Shall I ask Ma if she's got any broth to spare?'

She knew that although there was little food in her own house, there would be none at all at Ruby's.

They both looked up and turned their heads as they heard a rumble of cartwheels coming down the narrow alley into the court. 'Who's this then?' Grace murmured.

'Dunno, but they'll have a job getting that cart down here,' Ruby said as a wooden cart, piled high with odd pieces of furniture, came into view and scraped against the walls of the alley in an attempt to push itself through. 'Watch out for that brickwork,' she called out. 'You'll have 'landlord after you if you damage it.'

They heard a snort of derision and they both laughed as, with a grinding and grating, the cart was sent with a violent shove into the court. A man and a youth of about eighteen manhandled the contents in a valiant attempt to keep the furniture, a table, three chairs and a pendulum clock, from crashing to the ground. A woman walking behind the cart screeched at them to be careful and although the man glared at Ruby and Grace as if it was their fault that the furniture was falling, the youth winked and smiled, and the two girls turned to each other and raised their eyebrows.

'You moving in opposite?' Ruby asked. 'To Mrs Roger's old place?' The house across from where they were sitting had the door and both downstairs and upstairs windows boarded up.

'Well, just look at that,' the woman complained, ignoring Ruby's question and staring at the boarded door. 'They said it would be open! How are we supposed to get in?'

'Don't worry, Ma,' the youth said. 'I've got a crowbar about me somewhere.'

'No need,' Grace interrupted. 'My ma's got a key.'

The woman turned to her. 'Then let's be having it. We can't stand here all night!'

'Landlord boarded it up,' Ruby disclosed as Grace rose to her feet and went inside her door. 'Vagrants kept moving in. Let down 'tone of neighbourhood, you know!' but, as the woman didn't smile or comment, added cheerfully, 'Not that they stayed long. 'Place was overrun wi' rats and mice.'

The woman grimaced in distaste, but then turned as Lizzie Sheppard, Grace's mother, came out holding an iron key in her hand. 'Tek no notice of her,' she said. 'Sanitary men have been and put poison down. There'll be none there now, onny dead ones anyway.'

She pursed her lips as the woman shuddered and pulled her shawl closer around her shoulders. Lizzie said sharply, 'Been used to summat better, have you? Well, you'll have to put up wi' it till your fortune turns.'

She handed over the key. The woman took it without a word and moved away, but the youth came towards them. 'Thanks.' He touched his cap. 'I'm Daniel Hanson and they're my ma and da. They're a bit put out.' He lowered his voice. 'This is 'third move we've had in six months.'

'How come? Didn't you pay 'rent?' Ruby asked, looking up at him from the doorstep, whilst

11

Grace leaned in the doorway, her fair head on one side as she scrutinized the newcomer.

He shook his head. 'No, it wasn't that. But my da's lost his job and Ma can't settle.' He grimaced. 'He's a joiner and he's lost his fingers on his right hand.'

'That was careless.' Grace's mother folded her arms across her thin chest. She wore a large sacking apron over her dark skirt and a man's cap on her head. Like her daughter, she was fair, but her hair, scraped back into a bun, was intermingled with strands of white. 'How did he manage that?'

'He was showing an apprentice how to saw a piece of timber and was holding it steady for him. He was distracted for a minute and 'lad sawed right over his hand.'

'Didn't 'company pay him owt? If it wasn't his fault?' Ruby asked boldly. 'Sometimes they do.'

Daniel was interrupted in his answer by his mother calling to him. 'Daniel! Don't stand there gossiping like an old woman. Come and help your da with this furniture.'

'Nosy beggars,' she muttered as Daniel came across and lifted one end of the table. He and his father manoeuvred it through the door. 'I hope you didn't tell 'em all our business?'

'Course I didn't. Anyway, what's there to tell? Everybody round here is down on their luck, we're no different from anybody else!'

'Huh! Don't class me with 'likes of folk round here!' His mother's mouth turned down. 'And if they get a whiff that your da got some benefit from his accident, we'll have all 'beggars from Hull after us.'

Daniel's father spoke for the first time. 'In another couple o' months there'll be nowt of it left anyway,' he muttered. 'So we shan't have to worry about folks knowing owt.'

'I'll be earning soon, Da,' Daniel assured him. 'Then we'll be all right. We'll soon be set up again. We just have to hang on till then.'

His mother looked around the small dark room. 'What a comedown. I never thought I'd be brought to this. When I think of my nice little house!'

'Shut up will you, woman,' her husband bellowed in a sudden burst of frustration. 'It wasn't my fault, it was that stupid lad's.'

'I never said it was your fault!' his wife retaliated. 'But you should have been watching him.'

'Think I did this on purpose?' He shook his injured hand at her. Only his thumb and swollen stumps of fingers below the knuckles were left, and she turned away.

'Can you get 'board off 'window?' she muttered. 'Let's get some light in here.'

'I'll do it. Will you help me, Da?' Daniel reached for his tool bag and crowbar inside it.

'Aye.' His father's voice was low and despondent. 'From craftsman to labourer in ten seconds. That's all it teks.'

'We'll be all right,' Daniel again assured him as they forced the board off the window. 'You teach me all you know and as soon as I'm out of my time I'll be earning good money. Then,' he wrenched at the board over the broken door, 'as soon as I've made a bit o' money, we'll get set up in business. You can talk to 'customers and look after accounts and I'll do 'woodwork.'

He spoke with such confidence that his father was almost reassured, until he returned indoors and saw his wife staring out of the window with a look of horror on her face. 'Just look! I don't believe what I'm seeing!'

Her husband and son gazed past her through the cracked and dirty glass.

'It's a pig,' she croaked. 'A filthy stinking pig.'

'She's let that blasted pig out again.' Ruby scrambled to her feet as the snuffling sow came towards them. 'I swear I'll kill it and have it for breakfast.'

'You can't.' Grace moved further back into the doorway. 'It's having piglets. Ma!' she called urgently into the house. 'Mrs Peck's pig is out again.'

Her mother appeared with a broom and brandishing it furiously she swept the grunting sow back to the high wall which enclosed the court, and towards a dilapidated wooden structure, barely big enough for a dog, let alone a pregnant sow. Against this wall and at one side of the pigpen was a water pump and at the other side was the privy which served the twelve houses in the court. The ground below the broken door of the privy seeped with foul and stagnant water and flies and mosquitoes hovered about it.

'Well at least she's not keeping it inside 'house any more,' she muttered, though her face

14

showed no distaste, either for the grunting sow or for the stench emanating from the privy, so inured was she to her surroundings.

'No, but she's got chickens inside,' Ruby groused. 'They scratch about under her table and there's mess all over 'doorstep!' Ruby lived with her mother and younger brother in an upstairs room above the ground-floor room which housed Mrs Peck and her husband, six children, a dog, chickens and the pregnant sow which had now been turned out to graze in the rubbish-strewn court.

'She should get back to 'countryside where she belongs if she wants to keep pigs and chickens,' Lizzie Sheppard grumbled. 'It's bad enough trying to keep 'place clean without 'mess of stinking livestock. And they attract vermin,' she added. 'I can hear rats scratching every night.'

'Her husband can't get work in 'country,' Grace volunteered. 'She told me so herself. You know, that day when she gave us an egg.'

'Aye,' her mother muttered as she went back indoors. 'I remember the egg, but do I have to be grateful for ever?'

'Hello, Jamie!' Ruby called to a youth appearing out of a house at the top end of the court. He was yawning and in his hand he had a slice of pie.

'Hello, Jamie,' Grace said hesitantly.

He came across to them, then sniffed at the aroma drifting from the Sheppards' doorway. 'Mm, your ma's cooking summat good, Gracie.'

'Fish stew. My da brought some fish heads from off 'dock.'

Ruby swallowed and licked her lips. 'What you eating, Jamie?'

'Beef pie.' He took a bite, then handed the remainder to her. 'Do you want it?'

'Thanks.' She tried not to appear too eager, but she was salivating so hard, and the sight of food and the savoury smell of fish and onions from Grace's house was almost too much to bear.

'What's happening over yonder?' He nodded towards the house where the Hansons had moved in. 'New folks?'

'Their name's Hanson.' Grace offered the information. 'Mr and Mrs, and their son Daniel. Mr Hanson's lost his fingers in an accident. He was a joiner.'

'Mm. How old is he? Daniel Hanson?'

'About 'same as you.' Ruby spoke with her mouth full. 'Not as handsome though!'

'Well, no. Of course not!' Jamie laughed as he spoke, but he sounded confident that what Ruby said in jest was true. He was tall and slimly built, fair-haired with pale blue eyes. He didn't have the pinched and hungry look of most people living in this area. These folk never had quite enough to eat and certainly wouldn't be inclined to give away a slice of beef pie. He was also quite well dressed and although the frock coat he wore was large on him, having come from a bigger man, it wasn't threadbare but only a little worn around the cuffs and collar.

'He's got a nice face, though,' Grace said. 'And he smiles a lot.'

'Must be a bit simple then,' Jamie said lazily. 'There's nowt much to smile about, is there?'

'No, I suppose not,' Grace agreed, downcast. 'Not for most people.'

'Except for them as is rich and not allus hungry.' Ruby licked her lips to catch the last crumb. 'Thanks for 'pie, Jamie.'

'It's all right,' he said. 'You can pay me back when you get your wages.'

Ruby's mouth dropped open. 'Are you joking?' she said huskily. 'My wages are spoken for – I owe –'

'He's joking, Ruby. You are, aren't you, Jamie?' Grace pleaded. 'Say that you are!'

He gave a sudden laugh. 'Aye.' He slouched against the window sill and gazed at her in a way which made her feel vaguely uncomfortable, and then from her to Ruby. 'Course I am. But I might call in 'debt one day.'

Ruby let out a sigh of relief. 'If ever you're desperate for a piece o' pie, Jamie,' she grinned, 'just you call on me.'

'Supper's ready, Grace. Come on in.' Grace's mother called from inside the house.

'Is there enough to spare for Ruby, Ma?' Though Grace asked her mother, she glanced at her father, who was sitting by the low fire.

Bob Sheppard looked up. 'Lass is earning money, same as you. Can't she buy her own food?' He spoke brusquely but Grace knew very well that he wouldn't turn Ruby away.

'She pays 'rent out of her wages, Da, you know that she does. And she keeps young Freddie as well as her ma.'

Her father grunted, but her mother called out through the open door. 'See if you've a bit o' bread at home, Ruby, and you can have a bowl o' soup to dip it in.'

Ruby appeared in the doorway. 'I know we haven't, Aunt Lizzie. I ate 'last piece this morning afore I went out.'

'So what's Freddie had to eat all day?' Lizzie paused with the iron saucepan in her hand. The pan was heavy, but Lizzie, who hired herself out as a washerwoman to the people in the big houses in the town, was strong, with muscular arms.

Ruby knew that Freddie wouldn't have had anything to eat, but she didn't answer and watched as Grace's mother poured the thin soup into three bowls which were already on the table. Ruby eyed them. 'I'm not tekking yours, am I?'

'No.' Lizzie shook her head. 'I've had my dinner already. 'Cook at High Street where I've been today, she allus does plenty of food on washday. Now tomorow, when I go to 'house in Albion Street, 'cook there is that mean she onny gives enough to feed a sparrow. Go on, sit down. There's not much but it'll fill a corner.'

'I don't know what I'd do without you and Mr Sheppard,' Ruby said gratefully. 'Ma just can't seem to manage.'

Bob Sheppard slurped his soup and dipped a thick slice of bread into it. 'If she didn't spend money on 'poppy and her pipe, she'd be able to,' he muttered, glancing at his wife who raised her eyebrows at him, and Ruby nodded in agreement. It was acknowledged by everyone who knew Ruby's mother, Bessie, that she was totally dependent on the opium which she bought raw and grated, and then mixed with herbs or leaves if she had no money for tobacco. She was never seen without her short clay pipe in her mouth. If she couldn't afford to buy the raw, she dosed herself with laudanum bought from the grocer which was ready mixed with wine or spirits.

'Somebody's been to your house today.' Lizzie stooped to place a small piece of wood on the fire. Being on the ground floor they had the luxury of a hearth, unlike the upstairs room where Ruby and her family lived. Although they could say they were lucky to have a roof over their heads, the ceiling above them was so rotten that a gaping hole showed through to the attic.

'Who?' Ruby was startled. 'Not 'debt collector?'

'A family,' she replied. 'A man, wife and three bairns. I saw them come this afternoon, but I didn't see them go out again.' She gave Ruby an intense glance. 'Mebbe they're still there.'

Ruby pushed her chair back. 'Thanks for 'soup, Aunt Lizzie. I'd better go and see what's going on.'

Although Lizzie Sheppard wasn't her real aunt, Ruby had always called her such. She had known the Sheppards most of her young life and she and Grace were inseparable. Once, so she had been told, Grace's mother and her own mother, Bessie Robson, had been good friends too. But they no longer spoke, and no-one knew why.

The house in which they lived was at the end of the court, and nearest to the wall which separated this court from the one beyond. The wall was almost as high as the houses, thus blocking out any light or air. Sunshine never reached down here and although today, being summer, the sun had been bright in the sky, the residents of Middle Court had not been aware of it.

Ruby climbed the broken stairs, and, when she came to their small landing, saw that a rickety wooden ladder had been placed against the wall. Attached to the ladder was a piece of rope which had been pushed through the partially open trapdoor in the ceiling. She looked up and thought that she could hear whispering.

She opened the door of their room. 'Ma! Why's that ladder here?'

Her mother was sitting on a ragged mattress with her shawl and a thin blanket wrapped around her. The room felt cold and damp in spite of the heat outside. She gave Ruby a nervous smile which showed that several front teeth were missing but where the gap perfectly accommodated her clay pipe.

'I've made us some money,' she wheezed, and tapped the side of her nose. 'You'll be pleased wi' me, Ruby.'

'What have you done now, Ma? What have you sold? Not that we've owt left to sell!'

Her mother crooked her finger for Ruby to come nearer. When Ruby was near enough to hear a whisper, Bessie pointed up at the ceiling. 'I've got us some lodgers,' she croaked. 'They're living upstairs.'

CHAPTER TWO

'Living upstairs! What do you mean, living upstairs? There's no floor upstairs!' Ruby stared at her mother and then up at the broken ceiling. 'Besides, what's 'landlord going to say?'

'He'll not find out, 'rent man never comes up here. He's too scared o' tummelling down 'steps.' Her mother gave a satisfied grin and chewed on her unlit pipe. 'And 'chap up yonder – Mr Blake – he's found a bit o' planking and put that down for them to walk and lie down on.'

'Somebody'll see that ladder!' Ruby insisted. 'You'll have us turned out, then what'll we do?'

'Nobody'll see it. I'll keep 'front door shut, and folks upstairs won't say owt. They've nowhere else to go.'

There was no reasoning with her, and Ruby sank onto the mattress and put her hands to her head. 'Front door won't shut, Ma,' she said, even though knowing she was defeated. 'Hinge is hanging off.'

Ruby never ever left the rent money with her mother, for she knew she would rush to spend it on her addiction as soon as Ruby had left the house to go to work. The rent collector called on a Sunday when Ruby was at home, and if there was any money left after buying bread and potatoes and paying off some of the debts which they owed, he took it. They were always in arrears, and, try as she might, she could never catch up with the payments.

'I'm charging a shilling a week,' her mother wheedled. 'They're ever so grateful.' She looked at her daughter pleadingly and held out her hand. There were a few coppers in her palm. 'You can have these, Ruby. I saved 'em for you.'

Ruby took the coins. I can buy bread, she wavered, and short of climbing the ladder and telling the people to leave, I can't think what else to do. Ma will have spent the rest of the shilling, so we can't give it back. And they must be desperate, she decided, to be grateful to live in a cold damp loft with rotten beams and gaping holes in the roof.

'Where's Freddie? Has he eaten today?'

Her mother dropped her gaze. 'He's out. He might have got a job.'

'How can he get a job? He's onny just eight.' In spite of her lack of education Ruby knew the factory law. When her brother was nine, then he could apply for a job just as she had done when she had reached that age. 'Anyway, he's skin and bone. Who'd tek him on?'

Her mother had a shifty look about her. What was she up to? She glanced up at Ruby. 'I do my best, Ruby,' she whined. 'I do my best for all of us. I can't help it if I'm not well enough to work myself.'

'Freddie!' Ruby persisted. She had heard her mother's story of ill health so often that it no longer raised any sympathy. 'Where is he?'

'A man came to 'house this morning. He'd seen Freddie out in 'street and said that he was just 'sort of bright lad that a friend of his was looking for. So Freddie's gone with him, and if this man's friend teks to him then he'll bind him as an apprentice. He said he was old enough at eight.'

'But who was he? You let him go wi' a stranger! To do what, Ma?'

'He'll get fed and clothed and looked after, though he won't be able to come home.' Her mother shuffled around on her bed of old rags and coats. 'We shan't have to buy so much food if he's not here.'

'Ma!' Ruby screeched. 'Doing what?'

'Didn't I say?' Her mother's mouth worked nervously. 'As a chimney sweep's lad!'

Ruby lay down and curled herself into a ball with her head on her knees. She was so tired and weary, and now this. 'Ma! How could you? You know he's not strong. He could get stuck up a chimney and never get out!'

'No,' her mother said eagerly. 'That's what I said to this man that came, and he said that because Freddie was so small there was no fear o' that. That's why he would be just perfect for this job. And he said he would be working in 'countryside in big houses so he'll get plenty o' fresh air.'

She waited a moment before adding, 'And he said that if his friend took him on, then he'd pay us ten shilliings.'

23

Ruby lifted her head and gazed at her mother. 'You'd sell Freddie for ten shillings?'

'What else can I do?' Her mother took her pipe out of her mouth and laid it on the bed. She took hold of Ruby's hand. 'Don't be angry wi' me, Ruby. I'm doing my best. If we'd a man about we'd manage better. If you'd onny find some nice young fella in work who'd look after us.'

'Like my da, you mean, who went off with a fancy piece? And like our Josh who you sent off to sea as an apprentice and we've never seen since. Oh, yes.' Ruby nodded her head vigorously. 'That's just what we need, a man about the place to keep us in little luxuries, like hot dinners now and again or a pair of boots that don't leak, and mebbe a room with a fire so's we could keep warm.'

She started to weep. 'I'm fifteen years old, Ma, and I feel like an old woman.'

But she wiped her eyes and with the few coins clutched in her hand went out to buy old bread from the baker. In the shop window was one small meat pie with a bluebottle buzzing round it. 'I'll give you a penny for that pie,' she said, handing over a penny for the bread. 'It's got a fly on it.'

The baker flicked the fly away then wiped the top of the pie with his floury fingers. 'It would have been tuppence to anybody who hadn't seen it,' he said. 'Here, tek it.' He wrapped a piece of paper around the pie and handed it to her, waving away her offer of a penny. 'I saw your ma earlier,' he said, and gave a knowing nod. 'She was coming out of apothecary's yonder.'

Ruby's heart sank. 'Thanks,' she muttered and taking her purchases she hurried across the street to the chemist's shop. There was no-one else in the shop but the chemist in a loose brown coat with his back to her, lifting down a stone jar from the shelf. 'Mr Cooke,' she said diffidently. 'Mr Cooke, I'd be obliged if you didn't give my ma any more medication.'

He raised his eyebrows. 'If she asks for it and has the money to pay for it, then I'm obliged to sell it to her.' He shook his head at Ruby. 'If I don't, she'll go elsewhere and may be given something totally unsuitable.'

Ruby's mouth trembled. 'We've barely enough money for food,' she began.

'I know,' he murmured. 'I do understand. But it's too late, your mother has to have an opiate, she's taken it since she was a child. She can't give it up now.'

Ruby turned away, tears pricking her eyes, but the chemist called her back. 'I've only given her a small bottle of Black Drop. It's mild, just a solution in wine and won't hurt her, only calm her down. You could even take it yourself.' He reached across to a drawer and took out some coins. 'Here.' He handed her a sixpence and a penny. 'Your mother paid me too much. I was going to keep it until next time.'

She thanked him and left. Take it myself, she mused. Perhaps I should. It's supposed to reduce depression. Then she gave herself a mental shake. Don't be so stupid, Ruby. Don't start on that downward path. She knew that her mother had given her laudanum when she was a child, as

25

she had given it to Freddie when he was a baby. Most mothers gave it to their children to ensure that they slept all day whilst they were out at work. Then the mothers were often so tired themselves, after a long day at the factory or fish dock, that a cordial laced with laudanum was given to the children in the evening so that they would sleep, and the mothers could get some sleep themselves.

It was Grace's mother who had weaned Ruby off it. She had been seven and still remembered the quarrel between Aunt Lizzie and her mother, when Aunt Lizzie had snatched the bottle from Ruby's little hand and smashed it to the ground. 'You'll kill her,' she'd shouted. 'Just as you killed those other bairns.' And it was then that Ruby had discovered that there had been other children, brothers or sisters, who hadn't survived.

As she crossed the street towards home, she saw Freddie walking hand in hand with a stranger who was very well dressed for these parts. She called out and ran towards him.

'Ruby!' the child shouted excitedly. 'I'm starting work! I've had my dinner and – this is Mr Jonas. He's just given Ma ten shillings so's that I can start straight away.'

Ruby stared at the man in the frock coat. He inclined his head towards her, but didn't take off his top hat. So, whilst her back was turned the deed was done! Freddie had been sold and probably already her mother was smoking her pipe and taking an extra dose of Black Drop to celebrate her good fortune.

'How shall I know where to find Freddie?' she asked Mr Jonas. 'In case owt happens and we need to be in touch with him. And to know if he's all right,' she added, not liking the look of the man.

Mr Jonas looked surprised at the question, as if he hadn't ever been asked it before. He fished in his waistcoat pocket and brought out a card which he handed to her. 'Get in touch with me in the case of emergency or death and I will contact Freddie's employer. Do not disturb me for anything trivial as I am an extremely busy man.'

Ruby looked at the card. It was grubby and bent at the edges as if it had been in his pocket a long time, and, as she glanced at Mr Jonas now, he didn't seem to be quite as prosperous as she had first thought. His hat was rather battered, his black frock coat had a tinge of green and was crumpled as if it had been slept in, and his fingernails were extremely dirty.

'It's not you, then?' she asked pertinently. 'You're not 'chimney sweep?'

'Certainly not,' he replied huffily. 'I am an agent. I search out suitable people for employment.'

'Wouldn't you rather come back home, Freddie?' she asked her brother. 'You're too young to work.'

'Too late, young woman,' Jonas interrupted. 'The contract is signed and the money paid over to his mother. And he's not too young, he's had his eighth birthday I understand.' He took hold of Freddie's arm. 'He comes with me.'

'I'll be all right, Ruby,' Freddie called as he was

marched away, though she thought she now saw doubt in his young eyes. 'Don't worry about me.'

Ruby was concerned, she was fond of her brother and didn't like to think of him going to live with strangers, but she ran as fast as she could back towards Middle Court and was just in time to catch her mother scurrying out of the alley and into the street. 'Come on, Ma,' she demanded. 'Hand it over.'

Her mother clutched her black shawl around her throat. She looks like a wizened old crow, Ruby thought. Her face, which Bessie always maintained had been beautiful in her youth, was wrinkled and pallid and her once dark hair was now mostly white. 'Hand what over?' she croaked. 'I haven't got a penny on me, honest to God, Ruby. I haven't.'

Ruby stood her ground and beckoned with her fingers for her mother to hand over the money she had taken from Mr Jonas. 'It's mine,' her mother whined. 'It's for my son. Nowt to do wi' you!'

'Give it here,' Ruby insisted. 'It can go towards 'rent and I can get my boots mended, my feet get soaked whenever it rains.' The last time it had rained, when the court was flooded with water, she had carried her boots in her hand until she reached the footpath out in the street. She had dried her toes on her skirt hem and, although her feet were cold, at least her boots were dry. There was nothing worse, she had reasoned, than wearing wet boots all day.

Her mother fished in her skirt pocket and took out five shillings and gave it to Ruby.

'And the rest, Ma. Another five!'

'I'm going to 'butcher's,' she muttered petulantly. 'I need some money.'

Ruby kept her hand out. 'And what will you buy at 'butcher's?' she asked. 'A nice joint o' meat? A mutton chop?'

Her mother nodded eagerly. 'Yes! Yes, that's it.'

'And where will you cook it, Ma? Seeing as we've no fire!'

Her mother looked confused for a moment, then said, 'Ah!' She gazed around her as if searching for inspiration. 'Well, I'll buy summat already cooked. That's it! That's what I'll do.'

'Give me 'rest of money, Ma,' Ruby said wearily. 'I've got a meat pie here that we can have for our supper. Come on, I'm tired, I want to go to bed.'

Reluctantly, Bessie handed over the remaining five shillings. Ruby took it, then, in a fit of pity for her mother, gave her the penny which the chemist had given back to her. 'Go get yourself a glass of ale,' she said. 'Then come home and we'll share 'pie.'

'You're not a bad lass, Ruby,' her mother said. 'Don't you want a glass?'

Ruby considered, then handed over the six-pence. 'Aye, why not! Borrow a jug from Tap and Barrel and we'll both have some.'

CHAPTER THREE

'Come on, Jamie, get moving. Time you were on your way.'

'Yes. Yes. All right.' Jamie heard his mother's urging voice, but didn't hurry and continued to gaze at his reflection in the piece of broken mirror which hung by the door, then retied the yellow kerchief around his neck.

'That's mine!' his mother admonished. 'You little thief!'

'I'm onny borrowing it, Nell. Keep your hair on. Besides,' he added, 'it wasn't yours in 'first place.'

'Yes it was. Somebody give me it.'

'Instead of money? You were short-changed. It's onny a bit o' cheap cotton.'

His mother shrugged. 'I liked 'colour. Besides, it was that or nowt.'

'I keep telling you, you should tek money first, make sure they've got it.' He turned away from the mirror to look at his mother. 'You should leave 'bargaining to me, you're far too trusting, that's your trouble.'

'Not like you, eh, Jamie? Go on, get off. Drum up some business.'

Jamie laughed and left his mother to gaze in the mirror as he had just done. She saw a similar version of his face, the same light blue eyes and full mouth, but where his features were strong and angular, hers were rounded and feminine. 'He must tek after his father, whoever he was,' she murmured, brushing powdered rouge on her cheeks and carmine on her lips. 'A man o' business, I shouldn't wonder.'

Nell had succumbed to the blandishments of an older man when she was fourteen. He had given her a bracelet and gifts of money to ensure her discretion, for he was a friend of her parents and didn't want them to find out about his liaison with their daughter. As she found the experience not unpleasant and the money very welcome, for she was fond of pretty clothes, she decided that it was an easy enough way of making a living and much more congenial than working in a factory or on the fish dock as she was doing. She found plenty of customers, for she was attractive and willing, and she told her parents that she had changed her job and was working night shifts at a seed mill.

Inevitably she fell pregnant, was discovered and turned out of the house by her father. She suffered great hardship for many years as she tried to make a living for herself and her child, Jamie. When he was a baby he slept all night with the help of laudanum, but as he grew older he had to fend for himself during the night hours when she was at work. She had a miscarriage when Jamie was two and bled profusely, but after that she never again became pregnant.

When Jamie reached thirteen, he confronted her. 'You're doing it all wrong, Ma,' he said. 'You should be more particular. Tradesmen and businessmen are the ones wi' regular money. Not seamen or common labouring types who onny spend on a Saturday night after they've got their wages.'

He was right of course, trade was generally slack during the week, but Sunday mornings she was always exhausted and spent the day in bed. But how would she attract businessmen? She was much thinner than she had been in her younger days and her clothes were shabby and torn. She looked what she was, a destitute street woman.

'Leave it to me,' Jamie had said before he went off to the Market Place. He came back a few hours later and shook her awake. Under his arm he had a black and red cotton dress trimmed with lace at the neck and hem, an embroidered shawl, and a jacket for himself. She didn't ask how he had acquired them, for he often brought things home that he couldn't have obtained honestly.

'This is what you must do,' he'd said. 'Get dressed now, no – not in these,' as she'd reached for the new finery, 'and find a customer. Charge as much as you think he can afford. Then,' he'd shaken a finger at her, 'in 'morning you must go to 'public baths. It'll cost a penny but you'll get a clean towel and soap in with 'price of hot water. Wash your hair – you used to have lovely hair, Ma,' and she nodded, for she did, thick and fair and curly. He winked. 'Then we're in business.'

'What you talking about, Jamie?' she'd asked. 'How can *we* be in business?'

'I'm going to choose your customers,' he grinned. 'I've been observing folks coming and going and I know 'best places to catch 'em, and it's not walking up and down outside inns and public houses like a common drab.'

She was unsure to begin with, but she'd trusted him and it had worked. He approached, not single men walking alone, but groups of men, coming out from their banks or places of business, and in a sly whisper told them that he knew of a very presentable lady who was most obliging. There was much guffawing and loud banter as they refused his offer and walked away, but there was always one, or sometimes two, who would turn their heads and catch his eye. He would nod and place his finger on his lips to denote secrecy, and then sit on the nearest steps or wall and await their hurried return to arrange an assignation.

He was often given a copper for his trouble and when the time and place were arranged, he would race off to the nearest clean and private establishment where they were discreet about such matters, and book a room for an hour.

As time went on, his mother's customers became regular, her income was steady and they eventually were able to afford a ground-floor room of their own instead of having to share with others. Although Middle Court was hardly luxurious, the rent was cheap and the neighbours minded their own business.

Jamie had no other regular job, but he carried messages about the town and was known to be discreet. He delivered packages and parcels and even joints of meat for the butcher and boxes of groceries for the grocer, both of whom also happened to be his mother's customers. He was his own master, beholden to no-one, and always had money in his pocket. But he was adamant about one thing, and that was that his mother should never bring men home.

He sat now on the steps of the bank in the warm summer evening and watched as people hurried home from their places of work. Through shop windows he saw shop girls with weary faces, and drapers folding rolls of cloth and rearranging their displays. Factory workers trudged along the street towards homes where there would be little comfort, and he was glad of his good fortune that he and his mother could choose their working hours. They didn't have to be up before dawn broke through the skies, but were usually just tumbling into their beds.

He saw Ruby come out of the chemist's shop and hurry across the street to a man with a small boy. Curiously he observed her as she spoke to the man. 'Surely!' he muttered. 'Not Ruby?' but then he saw that the small boy was her brother. He watched as Ruby herself watched the man walk away and Freddie constantly turn around to wave, and his natural inquisitiveness made him want to know what was happening. He followed Ruby as she raced towards home and greeted her mother as she came out from the alley, saw money change hands and her mother scurry off towards the Tap and Barrel.

They've come into money, he mused. I wonder how? And it was then that a process of thought began and he saw Ruby in a different light.

When Daniel Hanson pushed the cart down the alleyway and saw the two girls sitting side by side on the doorstep, he was immediately struck by their closeness, their obvious easy companionship. At first he thought that perhaps they were sisters, even though they were dissimilar: one so dark and lively, who looked as if she might have been plump had she had sufficient to eat, the other fair and slender, with fine accentuated cheekbones and an air of fragility. But then he reasoned that they were not sisters, for the fair one, whom he now knew to be Grace, entered her house whilst Ruby stayed outside until invited in.

He helped to unpack the box containing their few belongings, but kept glancing towards the uncurtained window and across the court towards Grace's house.

'Don't keep looking out there,' his mother grumbled. 'And don't think of getting friendly with them lasses! Dirty little trollops. No better than they should be, I reckon.'

'That's not fair, Ma,' he protested. 'They're probably just back from work.'

'Well, they're not shop girls, that's a fact. Not wearing those old rags.' Had Mrs Hanson had a daughter, being a shop girl would have been an ambition she would have actively encouraged.

35

He saw Ruby come out of Grace's house and go to the end of the court, and, by peering from the side of the window, watched her go through another doorway. So that's where she lives, he thought. So the two girls are friends. A little later, as he glanced out at the darkening court, a youth of about his own age sauntered by. He was whistling as he went towards the alleyway and adjusting the yellow kerchief around his neck. Daniel perked up. He seemed a merry sort of fellow. He had a jaunty step and an air of confidence about him, which was quite unusual in this bleak and dilapidated area.

'I can't get this fire to burn. 'Wood must be damp.' His mother's voice interrupted his thoughts.

'It's not damp,' he said. 'It was under cover at 'wood yard. Here, let me do it.' He knelt down on the rough bricks which had been laid to keep the occupants' feet clear of the earth floor. They were laid haphazardly and in the gaps between them, damp soil oozed out.

He blew vigorously at the smouldering wood in the hearth. 'It's not drawing. Do you think 'chimney stack is blocked up with soot, Da?'

'There's mebbe a fireplace upstairs.' His father drew himself up from the chair where he had been sitting in deep melancholy. 'It's probably been shut off to keep draught out.'

'Go on and look then,' his wife urged. 'There's nobody up there. But look sharp about it otherwise there'll be no pot o' tea tonight.'

Daniel was halfway up the stairs when he stopped, his father almost cannoning into him.

'What a stink, Da.' He held his hand over his nose. 'That's not just damp!'

His father too put his hand over his lower face. 'It's privy! It'll not have been emptied. I bet it's seeping under 'floor.' He screwed up his face and muttered despairingly, 'God! What have we come to? I never ever thought – '

'We'll be out of it soon, Da.' Daniel lowered his hand from his face but dared not take a breath, the stench was so overpowering. 'If it's 'privy, why is it worse up here?' He took further steps up the broken staircase towards the closed door of the upstairs room, which had a piece of timber battened across it to keep out vagrants or other such persons who were seeking shelter and unable to pay for it.

'I'll fetch 'crowbar.' His father turned and went downstairs and opened the outer door to let in some air.

'Door's locked,' Daniel told him when he returned. 'We've no key.'

'Shan't need one.' His father, awkwardly, because of his damaged hand, applied the crowbar and wrenched off the board. 'Put your foot against it. These houses weren't built to last.'

'Are you sure, Da?' Daniel was hesitant about damaging other people's property.

'I'll do it. 'Landlord who owns this place should be made to live in it.' His father's tone was bitter and he handed Daniel the crowbar and aimed a kick at the door, which splintered. He kicked again, viciously this time as if he was kicking the landlord's head, the panels fell in and they stepped inside.

The room was dark, the window being boarded up from the outside. At first they couldn't see anything as the only light was coming from the doorway, but the stench was intolerable and they kept their hands over their noses. As their eyes became accustomed to the gloom, they saw that the only furniture was a battered wooden chair and a small table, with a pile of rags heaped in the corner. Daniel baulked at the odour and turned to go out. If the chimney was blocked then it would have to stay blocked, he couldn't stay a moment longer without taking a breath.

His father laid a hand on his arm to detain him. 'Daniel!' he whispered. 'Wait.' He stepped slowly and cautiously towards the corner of the room where the rags lay, and where now could be seen the decaying remains of dead rats.

He put his boot against the rags and hesitantly nudged them, then jumped back in alarm as if he had been bitten. He turned to Daniel, a look of horror on his face. 'Better fetch 'constable. There's a body under here.'

CHAPTER FOUR

'Who do you think she was, Ma?' Grace and her mother watched from the window, first the constable and parish officer arriving at the Hansons', and then the carters who brought out a body on a wooden stretcher. The sheet covering the body slipped as the men manoeuvred the stretcher through the narrow doorway and they saw a glimpse of a woman's skirt and bare foot.

Her mother shook her head. 'Some poor soul with nowhere to go.' She sighed. 'She's out of her misery now, anyway.'

'Somebody must be missing her.' Grace was almost in tears. 'She must be somebody's daughter or sister. Or mother,' she added, for they couldn't tell the age of the woman by the glimpse they had of her.

Her mother turned away from the window. 'She might not be from these parts. She could have come from another district looking for work. Or mebbe been turned out by her family. Who knows?' She gave a cynical grunt. 'She wouldn't have chosen to live in this sewer anyway, not if she'd had any other choice.'

Grace continued to gaze at the darkening court. Daniel Hanson came out of the house and leaned against the wall. His face was pale and he kept running his hand through his brown hair in an abstracted way. I wonder if it was Daniel who found the body? she thought. And where was it? She glanced at the upstairs room opposite. The boards had been knocked out and from the broken window a torn curtain fluttered.

Daniel saw her and signalled to her to come across. 'Not a good start, is it?' he began. 'Finding a body on 'day we move in! Ma's having a fit inside.' He indicated with a slight movement of his head towards the doorway.

'Who was it?' Grace asked in a low voice. 'I hope it wasn't anybody we know.'

'It was a woman.' He grimaced. 'She'd been there a week or two, I reckon. She must have hidden in 'cupboard when she heard sanitary men coming in. They'd been to put poison down for 'rats.' He glanced at her and decided not to explain anything further.

'Landlord will be in trouble for sealing up 'window, I expect,' Grace said in a low voice. 'His men should have checked first to make sure there was nobody inside. She might have been knocking and we didn't hear!' Her voice broke. 'It doesn't bear thinking about.'

'Do you fancy a walk?' he asked suddenly. 'I could do with getting out of here for a bit.'

'All right,' she agreed. 'I'll just get my shawl.' The sun was down and a breeze had sprung up, dispelling the sultry air.

'I'll not have to be long,' she said, when she

came back and followed him down the alleyway and towards the street. 'I've to be up at five o'clock.'

'Where do you work?' he asked.

'Cotton mill.'

'Are you a weaver? Or a spinner?'

'No!' She gave a grim laugh. 'Neither of those. Wish I was. I fetch and carry, sweep 'floors, wash down 'frames, shift 'bales, fill 'bobbins, do whatever I'm asked. I'm one of 'old hands, been there since I was a bairn.'

It was his turn to laugh. 'You're onny a bairn now!'

'I'm not,' she said. 'I'm fifteen.'

She looked younger. She was slight, with small hands and feet and a heart-shaped face, her eyebrows darker than her fair hair. Eyebrows which had a coating of white dust on them, as did the tip of her nose.

They came out into the busy street. Shops were still open to allow the factory and mill workers to buy their provisions and the inns and taverns were already crowded with people.

'How long have you lived in Middle Court?' he asked.

She glanced up at him. 'I don't remember ever living anywhere else.'

'Really? It's a dump! How can you stand it?'

She shrugged. 'We've no money to live anywhere else. Besides, 'landlord knows that my ma and da will allus pay 'rent. Da says we must pay 'rent even before we eat.'

They walked on, away from the overcrowded courts and alleyways which spilled over to the banks of the river Hull, and towards the pleasant square of Jarrett Street and John Street.

'Well, I don't intend staying there.' Daniel's face was set. 'We've hit hard times now, but as soon as I'm out of my apprenticeship, then I'll get a job and we'll up sticks and be off.'

'Where will you go?' She was curious. She had never even thought that the option of moving house was open to her or her parents.

'Where the work is. But I shan't live in a cesspit like Middle Court! Those houses should be pulled down. No,' he said decidedly. 'There has to be something better and I shall work towards it.'

'I must get back,' she said, suddenly anxious at the lateness of the hour. 'If I sleep late in 'morning, I shall lose wages.' She was also secretly alarmed at what he had said about pulling down the houses in Middle Court. Where would they live if that happened? No-one would give them another room such as they had now, with a hearth and a window, and a door that wasn't broken, and a proper bed on legs, not just an old mattress like Ruby and her mother and brother slept on. Not without paying extra rent, they wouldn't, and even with her mother's, father's, and her own wages, they couldn't afford more than the two shillings and sixpence which was what they paid now. Whatever was he thinking of?

Some rubbish, paper and a piece of cardboard, blew in front of them and Daniel kicked it with his boot, but Grace bent down and picked up the cardboard and turned it over in her hand.

'What do you want with that?' he asked.

'It'll line 'sole of my boot,' she said. 'I've got a hole in one of them.'

He said nothing, but glanced down at her feet. Her boots were shabby and worn and he saw that the leather had come away from the sole. The cardboard, he thought, would do nothing to keep the rain out. 'Will you come for a walk on Sunday?' he asked. 'I generally go down towards 'river.'

She pulled a face. 'To 'river Hull, do you mean?'

'No! Of course not. It's foul. Everybody throws rubbish in there, including 'butchers and 'night-soil men. I once saw a dead pig floating in it and some little bairns were trying to lasso it and drag it out! No, I meant down to 'estuary – to 'Humber. There's always a breeze and you can watch 'ships coming in and going out.'

'All right,' she agreed. She had been down to the Humber many times with her father when she was a child, but not lately. Her father now-adays slept most of Sundays, especially if he had been drinking the night before.

His Saturday-night drinking was the one thing guaranteed to put her mother into a state of anger. But Grace's father insisted that it wasn't his fault. He had to have a drink. The labourers' wages were paid out in one of the inns close to the docks and they were expected to buy ale there once they were paid. If he didn't, he said, then his employment couldn't be depended upon, as the employers and publicans were hand in glove.

It was almost dark as they approached the first court and blackness confronted them in the narrow alleyway leading to Middle Court. 'Are you scared?' he asked, and she didn't like to admit that she was and that she usually raced down the alley if she was alone. 'Do you want to take my arm?'

She hesitated. Once, several years before, when she had approached the alley, Jamie had seen her and offered her his arm too. But he had put his arm around her waist, to protect her, he'd said, only his hand had strayed under her shawl and found its way towards her developing breasts. She'd felt very strange and a little frightened and she'd pushed him away and run off. His laughter had echoed after her and since then she had been careful not to be alone with him.

'I'm all right,' she murmured, but he walked in front of her and held his hand out behind him so that she could hold it if she wanted to, so she felt quite reassured.

Her mother and father were already in bed when she opened the door to their room. Her father was asleep. She could hear the gentle *pht, pht*, sound that he always made. 'You're late, Grace,' her mother chastised her. 'You'll not get up in 'morning and you know I've to be at work for five.'

'Sorry, Ma. I've been for a walk with Daniel Hanson.' She slipped out of her boots and took off her skirt and shirt and climbed into the bed next to her mother. 'Ma!' she said, after a few minutes.

'Mm?' Her mother responded sleepily. 'What?'

44

'Have you ever thought that you'd like to live somewhere else? Instead of Middle Court, I mean?'

'Huh! Every night in my dreams,' her mother murmured. 'Why?'

Grace sighed. 'Oh, nothing really.' She looked up at the ceiling. Sometimes, if they had had a good fire, if her father had found plenty of kindling or even a piece of coal that had dropped off a coal waggon, she would watch the dancing shadows flickering on the ceiling as she lay in bed. But tonight the fire had burnt to ash and the room was in darkness, the only light filtering in from the uncurtained window. She thought of Daniel and his determined tone of voice saying that he wouldn't be staying here. 'I just wondered, that's all.'

'What's he like?' Her mother's voice was muffled from beneath the blanket. 'This Daniel Hanson?'

'He's nice,' she said softly. He wasn't as handsome as Jamie, his features were stronger, and he didn't give her those strange stirrings that Jamie did when sometimes she caught him looking at her. But she thought him honest and straightforward, as if he would only say what he meant and believed in. He had nice eyes too, grey with long lashes. She wrapped her arms around herself and slid further beneath the blanket. 'I think he could be a friend. Like Ruby,' she added.

Her mother gave a little chuckle. 'Ah, Gracie,' she said softly. 'You're still just a bairn.'

Grace was puzzled. That was what Daniel had

said. But she wasn't. She was a grown woman with a job and wages. What did they mean?

Both her mother and then her father had shaken her to rouse her before they left the house the next morning. Her mother was working at a house in Albion Street and the domestic staff there liked to have an early start. Her father had to walk towards the dock on the other side of town to his work as a labourer and so he was off early too, but Grace fell asleep again and was only awakened by Ruby banging on the door.

'Come on,' she urged. 'We're late!'

Grace scrambled out of bed. She was usually the one to waken Ruby. She pulled on her skirt and shirt and slipped her bare feet into her boots. There was no time for a rinse under the pump this morning, nor time for anything to eat, but she tore a piece of bread from the loaf which her mother had left on the table, put the bread back into the bread crock in case the mice got it, locked the door and hid the key in the usual place under a stone, and raced after Ruby.

There really wasn't any need to lock the door as they had no possessions worth stealing, but, as her mother frequently pointed out, they wouldn't want to come home to find that somebody else had moved in and neither did she really trust the family living in the room upstairs.

Ruby's mother, Bessie, on days when she wasn't sleeping in her bed, sat on the doorstep with her pipe in her mouth, watching the comings and goings of her neighbours in the court. She knew who was in and who was out, who was working and who wasn't, what kind of work

46

they did, and whether they owed their rent, and she knew the bailiffs by name.

Ruby had been late up that morning and didn't leave the house until nearly six o'clock. Bessie waited until she was sure that her daughter had left the court and was on her way to work, then rolled off her mattress and onto the floor. She lifted first one corner of the mattress and peered under it, and then the other. Then she pulled it out to the middle of the room and lifted and peered under the other side. She could see nothing but grey dust, but nevertheless she wriggled beneath, lifting it as best she could until she reached the middle. Coughing and spluttering she wormed her way out again.

'So what's she done with it? She's hidden it somewhere. She's never tekken it to work! Young varmint. That was my money!'

She gazed around the empty room. There was nowhere else Ruby could have hidden the money. There was no cupboard, and the fireplace had been blocked off years before, so she hadn't put it up there. Bet she's given it to Grace's ma to look after, she deliberated. She'd know that owd skinflint wouldn't spend it. She put her shawl around her head, went down the stairs and looked out into the court.

Dare I go in? she thought. I know where they keep 'key. But then! She hesitated. Them new folks opposite might see me. She peered across to the Hansons' house. Young lad'll have gone to work, but mister won't have and I don't know about her. She seems a bit snooty but she'll soon change. Come down in 'world if she's got to live in this hovel.

As she stood meditating, the Hansons' door opened and Mr Hanson came out and stood on the doorstep. He coughed and spat, glanced around and saw her and briefly nodded. He put his hand into his jacket pocket and brought out a pipe, then from the other pocket a wad of tobacco.

Bessie perked up. That was a large wad of baccy. She could usually only afford a screw of scraps from the bottom of the tobacco tin which, if the tobacco merchant was feeling generous, he would sell to her cheap. She wandered across to him. 'G'morning. Bad job about that woman. Would've given you a fright, shouldn't wonder?'

He nodded. 'Aye.' He pulled out strands of tobacco with his left hand whilst awkwardly balancing the pipe with his fingerless right.

'Do you want a hand wi' that?'

He glared at her. 'No! I can manage.'

'Accident at work, wasn't it?' she persisted, ignoring or unaware of his irritation. 'Hope you got some recompense? By!' She sniffed appreciatively. 'That smells like good baccy.'

'It is.' He tamped down into the bowl but didn't light the tobacco. 'It's my last wad. Got to last me a lifetime.' He thrust the pipe towards her. 'Here,' he said. 'Tek a sniff at that, missus.'

She looked askance at him. What was the good of that? You could take a sniff at the baker's shop but it didn't make you less hungry. There were some mean, parsimonious folk about and here, it seemed, was one of them.

Bessie wandered back to her own doorstep. 'Can't go into 'Sheppards' house while he's hanging about,' she muttered into her shawl. 'And I bet his missus is looking out of 'window. Nosy old cow.'

She sat down on the step and thought about her money, which, she considered, had been stolen from her, and by her own daughter. She looked over at the house opposite where Jamie and his mother, Nell, lived. The door was firmly shut and there was no sound from within. There was a curtain at the window, the only house in the court that was curtained, and that too was drawn.

'It's a disgrace,' she muttered between her few clenched teeth as she sucked on the empty pipe. 'Not right for a young fella like that to be playing 'pander for his mother.'

There was not much that Bessie missed, even though she was often addled with opium, and she had no objection to Nell making a living in the best way she could, for wasn't she still a pretty woman who was only using her charms to her advantage? But Bessie had, beneath her own cunning and duplicity, a thin and hidden layer of respectability, and a sense of seemliness of what was right and proper, and Jamie procuring for his mother wasn't, in her opinion, at all decent.

She heard a rattle behind her and Mrs Peck came out from her door, followed by a clutch of squawking hens and a dog which ran outside and lifted its leg against the pump. Behind her, as Bessie peered into her room, two children sat by a low fire. Mrs Peck was a small woman, similar in size to Bessie but younger in age, and she too was wearing a black shawl over a dress which had perhaps once been grey, but was now of an indeterminate colour. On her head she wore a handmade tucked and pleated bonnet, the kind that countrywomen wore.

The two women exchanged greetings. 'I'm just going to let 'pig out,' Mrs Peck remarked. 'I don't suppose you've any scraps o' dinner for her?'

Bessie snorted. 'I've barely enough to feed missen, let alone your pig!'

'It's a worry.' Mrs Peck rubbed her chin. 'Perhaps we shouldn't have brought her with us, but I was sure that I'd be able to get leftovers from 'neighbours or baker. And I've no grain for 'hens either.'

'By heck, missus, what sort of place do you come from if you expect luxuries like that? Folks round here are half starved most of 'time.' Bessie eased herself up from the doorstep. 'Best thing you can do is kill yon pig and wring hens' necks. At least you'd have a few good dinners.'

'Why, I can't do that!' Mrs Peck was shocked. 'That's not good husbandry. I'd have no eggs and, besides, sow will drop her litter any time and I'll sell piglets on when they're big enough.'

'Well, why didn't you stop where you was?' Bessie was flabbergasted. 'You could have done that in 'country!'

'But we were turned out!' Mrs Peck's bottom lip trembled. 'It was a tied farm cottage and there was no work on 'land for Mr Peck. That's reason we came to Hull, so's he could find some other job. I never wanted to come. Never would have come of my own accord. Why would I? There's nowt here for likes of me who's lived all of my life in 'country.'

'And has he found work?' Bessie asked, already knowing the answer.

Her neighbour shook her head. 'No, not yet. A month we've been here and he's not earned a penny. We've applied to Guardians, but they wouldn't give us owt 'cos Hull's not our legal living place. We've been to vagrant office and they give us a loaf o' bread and a screw o' tea for 'bairns and said we should apply to 'workhouse. But I'll not do that,' she said fiercely. 'I'll starve first.'

'That you will,' Bessie said sagely. She had had a taste of both starvation and the workhouse when her husband had gone off and left her pregnant and with two children. It wasn't until her eldest son had gone to sea and she had found work scrubbing floors, that she was able to leave the workhouse and find a cheap room here in Middle Court.

'Try Sculcoates Guardians,' Bessie called after Mrs Peck as she made her way towards the pigpen. 'We're just on 'edge of 'boundary. You might get summat from them,' and though she saw a small ray of hope in Mrs Peck's face, she knew that the hope would probably not be realized.

She was feeling hungry, the morning was getting on and she hadn't yet eaten anything. She and Ruby had dined well last night on the

51

meat pie and bread and the jug of ale, and there was a crust left if Ruby hadn't eaten it before she went out.

At least my little lad will have had some fodder this morning. She thought of Freddie as she puffed her way upstairs. 'Bet he had a nice slice of beef and a cup o' tea afore he set off for work,' she muttered to herself as she frequently did when she was alone. 'I must ask missus downstairs where she thinks he might have gone in 'country. There'll be lots of big houses, I expect. That's where all 'toffs go once they've made their money out of us in 'town.'

There wasn't any bread, and she fumbled in her skirt pocket for some of the change left over from the sixpence Ruby had given her. There were two pennies, and she sat down for a moment to consider. Should she buy a penny loaf? Ruby would be so pleased with her if she did. Or should she go to the apothecary's and buy a tincture? She gave a shiver and pulled her shawl closer to her. It was warmer outside than it was in. She looked at her hands and saw the tremor in them. It was there more often than not these days.

'I'll go to apothecary,' she decided. 'No I won't! Not to Mr Cooke anyway. He diddled me yesterday, I'm sure of it. Charged me too much, and', she groused as she pulled on her old boots, 'he onny gave me cordial. Huh! Thinks I don't know 'difference! No, I'll go to 'grocer for a pennorth o' loddy. That'll set me up for 'day and I'll buy a penny loaf as well.'

She came out of her room and looked up as

she heard the scrape of the trapdoor above her. A man's head peered out.

'Don't come out yet,' Bessie croaked in a hoarse whisper. 'Missus downstairs'll see you. She's just gone out to see to 'pig.'

'Can't help that.' Mr Blake pulled on the rope that held the ladder and hauled it towards him. 'I'm fair busting for privy and so are 'bairns. 'Pail's overflowing and we can't wait any longer.'

He climbed halfway down and then reached up the ladder to take a wooden pail with stinking slops from his wife, who was leaning down from the trapdoor. As he took it from her some of the contents spilled out onto the floor.

'Privy's not been emptied for weeks,' Bessie commented and watched as Mrs Blake and then two children climbed down.

'Where's 'other babby?' she asked.

'Sick,' Mrs Blake said wearily. 'I've left him sleeping.'

'He can't crawl out, can he?' Bessie gazed up at the open trapdoor and pondered that the child would break his head if he fell out.

Mrs Blake shook her head. 'He's not got 'strength, poor little mite. I'm just off to 'vagrant office to beg for some milk for him.' Her mouth turned down. 'If I don't get some soon, then he'll not last 'week out.'

Bessie fingered the two coins in her pocket. She was desperate for her laudanum, the trembling in her limbs was increasing by the minute and, if she didn't get relief soon, she'd be screaming. She hesitated, then pulled out a penny. 'Here, missus. Tek this. Go fetch 'bairn some milk.'

'God bless you, lady.' Mrs Blake's gratitude was reward enough. 'That shilling we gave you for 'rent was our last, but we had to find shelter or we'd have finished up in 'gutter. Somebody above must have directed us to you.'

'Well, I don't know about that,' Bessie mumbled. ''Cos I was on my beam end when you gave me that shilling.'

'Where's your young bairn this morning?' Mrs Blake called as she went down the stairs. 'Has he got a job of work?'

Bessie's face creased with pain. She'd have to hurry to get her dose of loddy, she could feel her body shaking and her fingers tingling. She nodded. 'Aye,' she croaked. 'He has. I've sold him to 'chimney sweep.'

CHAPTER FIVE

Wincomlee and Cleveland Street, the streets which ran on either side of the river Hull, were thronging with hundreds of workers making their way home. Factories, tin works, cotton and seed mills all spewed forth a crush of humanity from their gates, tipping them out in much the same way as the machines on which they had been working had tipped out an end product of machine parts, metal sheets, cotton, or oil.

Some of the women, and more especially the children, seemed to have little energy with which to drag themselves back to the place from where they had started that morning. The sun was just up as they had set out and was just going down as they returned, and for most of them that was the only glimpse of the summer that they would have. The exception to this routine drudgery was Sunday, when they didn't work and could choose whether to spend their weary day in bed, or clean their dwelling rooms, or, if they were so inclined, could do their washing so that they might have a clean garment of clothing for the following week.

Many of the men spent their Sundays in the

company of the innkeepers, for on a Saturday they received their meagre salary, and some, if their womenfolk were not lying in wait for them by the factory gate, would divert from their normal way home and take another route towards the alehouse, and not go home at all that night.

But there were also others who would count out their wages, reckon the rent and the cost of candles or coal and a bowl of soup and bread for wives and children, and know with a despairing certainty that the numbers didn't add up.

'I didn't tell you, did I, Grace – about Freddie?'

'What about him?' Grace didn't look up at Ruby as they trudged away from the cotton mill, for she was concentrating on her feet. The sole of her left boot had worn through and she could feel the rough ground scraping on the ball of her foot. She hoped that her mother hadn't thrown away the piece of cardboard that she had found. She would mend the boot just as soon as she arrived home.

'Ma's sold him to 'chimney sweep. Got ten bob, all found.'

'What?' Grace hadn't really been listening. 'What did you say?'

'Ma. She got ten shillings for Freddie. He's apprenticed to a chimney sweep.'

Grace stopped suddenly and was roughly barged into by someone in the crowd behind her. 'They paid her?' she said incredulously and winced as the person behind her trod on her heel. 'But what does it mean?'

'It means he can't come home. 'Sweep owns

him. He teaches him his trade and feeds him and everything.' She took a deep breath and said in a choked voice, 'I've been thinking about him all day, wondering if he's all right. He's onny eight, poor bairn, but 'chap who took him said he was old enough to be a sweep's lad.' She rubbed her eyes and muttered, 'Ma cried in bed last night, first time I've ever known her do that. She said she did it for him, so's he'd have a trade.'

'He's onny a year younger than we were when we started work.' Grace took Ruby's arm to comfort her as they walked on.

'Yes, but we came home at night, didn't we? And we were only supposed to work eight hours. Freddie could be working for longer than that if he's got a hard taskmaster.'

'Try not to worry.' Grace stepped back as a chaise drawn by a bay horse came out of the mill gates and clattered towards them. 'Those toffs in 'big houses will want their fires lit early, he'll probably come down 'chimney by dinnertime and have 'rest of 'day off.'

'Do you think so?' Ruby was momentarily distracted by the two men sitting in the chaise. They seemed to be taking particular note of the workers as they passed them by. 'I heard a rumour today,' she said absently. 'There's been a directors' meeting. Somebody's resigned.'

'Oh?' Grace glanced across to the other side of the road. Someone in the crowd was waving in their direction. She waved back. 'Look,' she nudged Ruby. 'There's Daniel. I went for a walk with him last night. He was upset about that woman's body that they found upstairs.'

'My ma said that she'd seen a woman go in one night a couple of weeks ago,' Ruby said, 'but she didn't tell anybody in case they fetched a constable to turn her out. She never saw her again and thought she must have left.'

Grace shuddered. 'It makes me feel sick. Poor woman. She must have been in a bad way to go in an empty house on her own.'

'He's coming across.' Ruby watched as Daniel dodged the crowds and the horses and waggons that were coming in both directions.

Grace smiled. 'Do you like him, Ruby? I do. He's asked me to go down to 'Humber with him tomorrow, just for a walk, you know.'

'Has he!' Ruby put on a knowing look.

Grace blushed. 'Silly!' she said, and dug her elbow into Ruby's ribs.

'I'd best come with you, then,' Ruby sighed. 'You're onny a bairn, you need somebody to look after you.'

'I'm not a bairn,' Grace objected. 'Why does everybody keep saying I am? I'm 'same age as you. But yes, do come, Ruby,' she agreed. 'It should be fun!'

Daniel joined them. 'Good evening, ladies,' he bantered. 'Are you taking the air?'

'We are.' Ruby joined in the humour. 'We've had a stroll in 'country and taken tea with my Lady Bountiful and are now wending our way home where we shall partake of supper!'

He grinned. 'Prepared by your cook, no doubt?'

'Oh, yes.' Ruby clasped her hands together.

'We shall have a bowl of turtle soup, a little delicacy of fish—'

'A morsel of boiled chicken followed by cold ham,' Grace broke in and ran her tongue around her lips.

'Oh, stop!' Ruby bent over and clutched her hands to her middle. 'What must it be like not to be allus hungry?'

Daniel glanced at her and then at Grace. There was a question in his eyes. 'Do you not get enough to eat?'

'Does anybody?' Ruby said dismally. 'I know that Grace's ma manages somehow to put food on 'table every day, but we don't.' Then she brightened. 'But we had a meat pie last night and I've got enough money to buy food for tonight.' She raised her eyebrows significantly at Grace. 'With Freddie's money and my wages, we can have a feast.'

'Don't forget 'rent,' Grace urged.

'I won't,' Ruby declared. 'I never do. I'm too scared of us being turned out by 'landlord.'

Ruby left them and walked on towards the Market Place to buy a meat pie and bread. She always bought ready-cooked food, having no means of cooking in their room. One thing she longed for was a room with a fire, not only for the heat which it threw out but for the possibility of hot food. She remembered clearly one winter's night some years before, arriving home from work to find her mother had lit a fire in the corner of the room. She had smelt the burning wood as she ran up the stairs and saw her mother poking with a stick amongst damp wood and scraps of burning paper, which were singeing the floorboards.

She had seen the despair and confusion on her mother's face, and at the age of twelve had decided that she would take control of the household from then on.

'Is Ruby very poor?' Daniel asked as he and Grace walked home, cutting through the warren of streets which lay behind the dock in the centre of Hull. 'Doesn't her mother work?'

'She can afford a room, but not with a hearth and her mother doesn't have a job of work. She runs errands for people I think, and earns a copper or two that way.' She didn't add, for she was very loyal to Ruby and her mother, that Bessie Robson spent anything she earned on laudanum.

'I've been at your mill today,' Daniel said. 'My boss sent me to repair some of 'equipment.' He looked pleased with himself. 'He said it was a job I was well capable of and he didn't need to send one of 'time-served lads.'

'Oh, I wish I'd seen you,' Grace enthused. 'Though we're not supposed to talk when we're working. But it's such a long day that sometimes we do, when nobody's looking,' she confessed.

He nodded. 'I talked to a little Irish girl, she'd started work this week.' He frowned. 'She looked too young to work, but she said she was ten. She lives in the Groves with her father and grandmother. Her mother's dead. Died of cholera, she said.'

'Poor little bairn,' Grace murmured. 'I've seen some of the Irish waiting for 'ferry to take them across 'river. Some of them haven't any boots.'

She looked down at her own feet and thought how lucky she was, at least she was shod, even though her boots were worn.

'I'm glad it's Sunday tomorrow.' She looked up at him. 'Are we still going for a walk?' She wanted to remind him in case he'd forgotten.

'Of course. You still want to, don't you?' A small crease appeared above his nose. 'It'll be good to get away from Middle Court for an hour or two.'

'I've asked Ruby to come too,' Grace said. 'Is that all right?'

He grinned and teased, 'Scared of coming on your own, are you?'

'No!' She blushed. 'Course I'm not, but Ruby doesn't get many treats.'

'Is she a good friend?'

'My best,' she confided. 'The only one.'

'Oh!' He seemed rather downcast. 'Can I be one? A friend? I'd like to be.'

She lowered her eyes. 'Can a girl have a fellow as a best friend? I allus thought that – '

'What? That there has to be kissing and cuddling and all that?' There was laughter in his voice and she nodded, her head bent, and didn't dare look at him. Her face was burning with embarrassment.

He lowered his head towards her and grinned. 'You can have that instead, if you'd rather!'

'No, no, I didn't mean – ' How he teased. She didn't know how to answer him.

They were approaching the alley which led down to Middle Court. 'I think,' he said softly, 'I think it's best if we're just friends, don't you?

Then you don't have to feel worried about owt – like taking my arm down 'alleyway when you're scared!'

She looked up. So he had known she was scared the other night! He smiled at her and she smiled back, feeling such relief. She knew girls of her age who had regular fellows, and they told such lurid tales of kissing and fondling in dark alleys, and of other things too, which made her heart beat faster and her face grow hot. She knew she wasn't ready for any of that.

'I'd like that,' she said. 'To be friends. To trust you, like I trust Ruby.'

He left her at her door and went towards his own house. He felt good. He'd had a job of work on his own and the mill foreman had been pleased with it, and he was taking Grace for a walk tomorrow. He was glad that Ruby was coming too, for she was very vital and merry and Grace would be less shy if she was there.

He felt a warm glow inside him. He had thought, when he saw Grace that first evening as she sat on her doorstep, that she was going to be special to him. But he felt that he must tread carefully to build up her trust and confidence. She seemed to be so innocent and vulnerable, which appealed to his nature, though he found it curious that she was so, considering her circumstances and her place of work. He had heard the coarseness of some of the women who worked in the mills and factories, and although not all could be classed the same, as many were decent hard-working women, there were others with mouths like sewers and morals likewise.

He pushed open the door of his house and entered the room. It was dark and there was no welcoming fire, only half-burnt pieces of wood in the hearth. 'Ma!' He peered into the gloom and saw his mother sitting motionless in a chair. 'What's up? No fire?'

'I can't get it to light. There's no draught.'

'Chimney'll want sweeping, I expect.' He dropped his tool bag on the floor. 'Where's Da?'

'Don't know.' She answered in a flat montone. 'He's been out all day.'

'What's for supper?' He looked round for a sign of food prepared but there was none. 'Shall I try to light 'fire?'

'If you like.' She didn't move from her position in the chair, which disturbed him as usually she bustled around when he or his father returned from work, slicing bread or making tea. 'Your father went to 'alehouse this morning. Tap and Barrel,' she added as if the name was of significance. 'He was still there at dinnertime.'

'What you telling me, Ma?' He looked up from the hearth where he was trying to blow some breath onto blackened smouldering sticks and saw her put her hand to her eyes.

'I'm telling you that he's taken a pocketful o' money and is treating everybody in 'inn. He's everybody's friend and while he's buying they're all listening to his tale of woe.'

'How do you know?' He straightened up. The wood wouldn't burn, he'd have to start again with a fresh bundle. As he glanced at his mother's grim expression, it struck him that he couldn't ever remember seeing her smile, not really smile, as if she was happy inside.

'Cos I went looking for him, that's how I know.' She shivered and pulled her shawl around her shoulders. 'He called me a pettifogging shrew and ordered me home. Me!' Her voice became shrill and indignant. 'And I'm the one who's had to give up everything cos of his accident!'

'It's not been easy for him either, Ma.' Daniel tried to be conciliatory. 'He's allus been used to working.'

'Aye, well he's not working now. He's throwing all our money at 'landlord's apron.'

He heard noises out in the court. Loud voices and somebody singing. He opened the door. His father was being held up by his armpits by two men who were almost as drunk as he was. His legs seemed to be made of rubber and he swayed downwards from the waist. He saw Daniel and exclaimed, 'This is my boy,' he slurred. 'Chip off 'block, he is. Teks after me.' He swung his head upwards to try to focus on his companions, who were staring mindlessly at Daniel. 'Not after his ma.'

He swung towards Daniel, and his two friends swung with him so that they made a tableau of figures leaning into each other. 'Your ma's going to have summat to say,' he blathered. 'She'll be as surly as a bear.' He waved his finger to his lips. 'She's a dowly woman, your ma, onny don't tell her I said so. Now then.' He hiccuped. 'I won't be long, I've just got to set my friends home.'

The door opened behind Daniel and his mother stood there. Her mouth was in a tight

64

line and her face was rigid. Daniel wondered how she could soften it to speak, and she didn't, she spoke through her teeth, her lips barely moving. She stepped out of the doorway and pointed with a straight arm towards it. 'Get inside,' she hissed at her husband. 'You're drunk.'

He narrowed his eyes and peered at her. 'You're right!' he said, as if he was surprised at her discernment. 'I am! And I'm going to be drunk tomorrow and 'day after, and 'day after that as well. I've got me some friends, haven't I, lads?' He looked blearily at his companions, who were swaying and lurching by his side. They both nodded and both closed their eyes as if they were about to drop off to sleep.

Daniel stepped forward and urged the two men home. 'Come on,' he said. 'Time you were off. Your supper'll be waiting, I expect.'

They both stared at him hopefully and his mother made derisive noises behind him. 'If they've got homes to go to,' she grunted. 'They look like a couple o' tramps to me.' She drew herself up indignantly and glanced scathingly around at the other houses in the court. 'What a showing up! In front of this lot as well!'

'Come on, lads,' Daniel urged them again. 'I'll see you to 'top of 'street.'

They both nodded agreeably and Daniel thought that this had probably been the best day of their lives. As if to confirm his thoughts, one of the men slurred, 'By, it's been right grand, we've had ale and baccy and a slice o' pie. Landlord sent us off when yon fellow ran out o' money.'

Daniel heard his mother's hiss of breath and

he pushed the men towards the alley. If his father had spent all of his money, then his mother was going to be very hard to live with. He sent the men on their way and when they reached the street they looked about them as if they didn't know where they were. He hesitated for a moment, wondering if he should ask them in which direction they lived, but then decided against it. His priority now, he surmised, was saving his inebriated and spendthrift father from his mother's wrath.

CHAPTER SIX

The two men in the open chaise glanced down at the throng of workers as they passed them. 'Disreputable crowd, aren't they?' Edward Newmarch said to his brother. 'They look as if they haven't had a bath in weeks.'

'They maybe can't afford a bath,' Martin admonished. 'They won't have facilities in their homes. They'd have to use the public baths.'

'Even so.' Edward looked down at two young girls walking together arm in arm. 'Cleanliness next to godliness.'

His brother gave a wry smile. 'And what, may I ask, would you know about that?'

'I go to church every Sunday!' Edward protested. 'I sit through the parson's boring sermon, that's penance without a doubt.'

'But you don't listen, you're too occupied making sheep's eyes at May Gregory!'

'It's my only chance of seeing her.' Edward expertly manoeuvred the chaise between a brewer's dray and a hawker's cart. Itinerant pie-sellers were standing in the road shouting of the excellent qualities of their wares to the passing crowd, and one held up his tray towards the two men. The horse and chaise brushed past him and he jumped back, losing some of his pies which he hastily picked up from the road and replaced on the tray.

'Her father keeps her under lock and key! I'm twenty-six, it's high time I was settled with a comely little wife.' And her father is rich and influential, he added beneath his breath.

'Ask Mother to arrange a soireé and invite the Gregorys. She'd like that.' Martin glanced over his shoulder at the pie man, who was shaking his fist at them. 'She likes giving parties.'

'That's a good idea.' Edward flicked the reins and urged the horse on in a trot as they left the busy town and its crowds, and drove west along the long road towards their home in the village of Anlaby. 'And perhaps May's cousin Georgiana could be persuaded to come too.' He started to whistle artlessly, and Martin shrugged but said nothing.

There were only eighteen months between the brothers, yet their personalities and characters were totally different. Martin, the elder, was thoughtful and steady in nature, sometimes roused to anger over injustice, and always willing to consider another's point of view. His appearance, though considered handsome, was unpretentious: he was clean-shaven around a firm chin, and his thick dark hair was often tousled as he ran his fingers through it while he considered issues or dilemmas. He was not aware of, nor did he attach the same importance to style as Edward, who had his hair cut in the latest mode and his sideburns finely trimmed down to his jawline, where they met with his well-groomed beard. His opinion was that he was usually right on most matters.

'Imagine Emerson resigning,' Edward commented after a while. 'Silly old fool!'

'Not a fool at all,' Martin retaliated. 'He's highly principled, and he's anxious about the workers who are going to get their hours cut.'

'They won't thank him for it.' Edward waved a thumb back in the direction they had come from. 'Not that dissolute crowd. All they'll be worried about is whether they've money for their ale and baccy.'

Martin felt irritation growing inside him. 'And whether they can put bread on the table or pay their rent.'

Edward gave a sudden laugh. 'Did you hear about Bradley? It was reported in the *Packet* that the last typhus outbreak started in one of his properties. He's refused to do any improvements as he said that next door to it there's a fish smokehouse, a piggery and a slaughterhouse! Quite right too, why should he spend good money on property like that?'

Martin gave an exclamation. 'And the place has an open sewer running alongside it! And Bradley didn't happen to mention, I suppose, that he also owns the building which houses the slaughterhouse?'

'Well, he's a businessman, isn't he?'

'He makes his money out of poor people who pay him rent for living in these disease-ridden hovels without privy or drains!'

'Did you notice those two girls that we passed back there?' Edward changed the subject. His brother got on his high horse sometimes, he was as bad as Emerson with his high-flown ideals.

Martin shook his head and Edward went on. 'I just wondered – well, they probably work at the mill, but if the workers are as poor as you seem to think they are, do you think – well, do you suppose that they make a living in any other way?'

'Like what? There isn't any work for women and children, they're all scrambling for the same jobs. They either work on the fish docks or in the factories and mills.' He knew very well what his brother was getting at, but he didn't rise to the bait. It was indeed time that Edward was married with a wife to satisfy his needs.

They pulled into the drive of their home, where they lived with their parents. Edward breathed in a deep silent breath. He had seen the two mill girls several times before, and each time he had experienced an odd hankering to get to know them. One was dark-haired and vivacious, with a carefree spirited laugh unlike that of any young lady whom he knew socially. The other was fair and almost ethereal, so slight that he imagined a breath of breeze would blow her away. He had even looked for them one evening, strolling in the darker side of the town, where he thought they might live.

But he didn't find them, and he had his pocketbook and a silk handkerchief filched from his pocket for his trouble. He did, however, come across a youth who chased after the thief who had stolen his belongings, but unfortunately didn't catch him. The young man whispered on his return that if he was in the area for any particular purpose then he could probably assist him, being a resident of the district.

Edward bluffed that he had lost his way and the youth had nodded agreeably and said he quite understood, but that if by chance he should venture that way again and fancied a little female company, then he knew someone who was very discreet and obliging.

Edward had smiled condescendingly and lied that he was a happily married man, but had felt a stirring of desire as the youth had described the woman as being bonny and buxom. 'A little older than yourself, sir, and she would expect nothing more than payment for her – er, services. No seeking out your place of business or home. A discreet arrangement only,' he'd whispered, close to Edward's ear. 'One from which you would both benefit.'

He'd touched his hat, and with long white fingers adjusted the scarf at his neck and taken his departure, not staying to barter or extol the virtues of the woman further. Edward deliberated that he might return. He had never been with a prostitute, but he was a man with strong desires and inclinations, and his courtship of May Gregory seemed doomed never to begin.

Daniel closed the door behind him the next morning and heaved a sigh. He was glad to be out of the oppressive atmosphere within, his father nursing a sore head and his mother tight-lipped and not speaking. As he had put his father to bed the previous evening, his mother had reached into a cupboard where they stored their few dishes and plates. From a cup she had taken something and put it into her skirt pocket. She had turned around and seen Daniel watching, and had fixed him with a warning stare which said, in no uncertain terms, don't ask questions!

When he had gone to his bed in the corner of the room, he had turned his face to the wall away from his parents, as was his habit, and heard the chink of coins as his mother undressed. He had felt a sense of relief that she had had the foresight to hide away some of his father's money and that there was at least some left. It was obvious that his father wouldn't get his hands on it.

Grace came out from her door and waved to him. 'I'm ready,' she called. 'I'll just go and fetch Ruby.' She was dressed in a clean grey skirt and bodice, and a different shawl from the one she wore for work. Her hair was loosely tied with a thin ribbon in the nape of her neck and her cheeks had a soft glow to them, as if she had just been scrubbed.

Ruby came out from her door. She was wearing the same clothes as previously, but she had let her dark hair fall loose to her waist and hadn't fastened it. 'I've been waiting on 'rent man,' she said. 'But he hasn't been yet.' She looked anxiously at Grace. 'I don't know what to do. I don't want to miss him. You'd better go on without me.'

'Oh, no,' Grace said. 'Leave it with my ma, she'll look out for him and pay it for you.'

Daniel wanted to ask why Ruby's mother couldn't pay the agent, but he had seen a glance pass between the girls and guessed that there must be a reason. He also realized that the money his mother had hidden in the cupboard was probably their rent money. He bit his lip. He had always felt secure when his father was working. Their rent was always paid and there was always food on the table. Now he realized that their fortunes had changed for the worse. Calculating how long it was before his apprenticeship ended and he became a journeyman, he knew with a growing despondency that it was some considerable time yet.

'Daniel?'

He blinked. Grace was speaking to him, standing before him with a smile on her lips. 'You were gone away,' she said softly.

'Sorry,' he said. 'I was just thinking of something.'

'Bet your da has a sore head this morning,' Ruby said gaily as she returned from giving the rent money into the care of Lizzie Sheppard. 'I saw him come back with his pals last night.'

'Yes.' Daniel saw no point in denying it. 'He's sleeping it off. Ma's none too pleased with him,' he added with a wry grin.

'My da gets the broom whacked round him if he comes home worse for drink,' Grace confessed, and they all laughed innocently at the influence that alcohol had over their lives.

Out of the court and in the streets, the day was

hot. The girls took off their shawls and carried them and Daniel unfastened his shirt neck. Grace put her face up to the sun and basked in its warmth. 'If we could only catch the heat and put it in a basket to take home,' she said, and Daniel, looking at her, wanted to kiss her warm flushed cheek.

Ruby glanced at him and caught his expression and gave a little smile, yet felt jealous too. How would it be, she thought, to have a man look at me like that? I've had them look at me in other ways, where their eyes have told me what they wanted, but I've never had such a look as that.

They came out of the cluster of rooming houses and courts which ran into and behind Sykes Street and Mason Street, and crossed over Charlotte Street which led towards the river Hull. They skirted the eastern side of the Old Dock which was, as always, crowded with ships of all nations.

They crossed the town and came to the Holy Trinity church where they waited whilst Grace sat on a wall and adjusted the cardboard in her boot, and then continued down the long street of the Market Place, where tramps slept at the feet of King William's golden statue. In Queen Street, scavenging dogs sniffed around the butchers' shambles, and both Ruby and Grace wrinkled their noses at the smell of blood in the gutter and stepped over the scraps of raw meat which littered the pathway as they passed.

As they approached the new Corporation Pier which had been built on the site of the breakwater jetty, the heat dispersed, the air became bracing and they felt the cooling breeze and breathed in the fresher, salty smell of the flowing waters of the Humber. People were leaning over the railings to watch the choppy sparkling estuary, thronging with steamers and sailing ships. Coggy boats were bobbing on the water, which men were plying for their pleasure as well as transport.

'Oh, my feet!' Ruby eased off her boots. 'I'd forgotten how far it was to 'pier.'

'Oh, but it's lovely!' Grace leaned on the railings and let the breeze catch her hair and whip around her skirt. 'And look at all the ships. Where do you think they're going?'

Daniel leaned on the rail next to her. 'Well, that's a timber barge heading back towards 'river Trent.' He pointed with his hand. 'And that's a shrimp boat – they'll have brought in a catch from Paull, just up 'river, I expect. Hey, watch out!' He and other onlookers gave a warning shout as two youths in a coggy boat, inexperienced judging by the way they were handling the oars, almost tipped over into the water. 'My,' he exclaimed. 'That was nearly a tragedy.'

They looked down into the water. It was deep. There had been many a drowning, both accidental and deliberate, along the Humber shore.

Daniel turned his back on the river and leaning on the railing he gazed across towards Queen Street and the Vittoria Hotel. 'If I'd enough money I'd treat you both to a glass of ale,' he said.

'It's my birthday tomorrow!' Ruby said. 'I'm going to pretend that it's today.'

'Oh, so it is, Ruby,' Grace exclaimed. 'Yes, let's say it's today!'

'In that case – ' Daniel felt deep into his pocket and pulled out a few coins. 'Let's see if I've enough for us to share a tankard.'

'I've got tuppence.' Grace put her hand in her skirt pocket, and Ruby, looking dubious, said, 'I've got a bit of change, but I was going to use it to buy supper.'

'Oh no, you can't pay if it's your birthday.' Daniel took a penny from Grace and added it to his own coins. 'There, we have enough for us to share.' He smiled from one to the other and placing himself in the middle of them, put his arms around their shoulders. 'Come on. Let's go to 'Vittoria and celebrate.'

The two girls sat on a bench outside the hotel and basked in the sunshine, whilst Daniel went inside and presently came out with a brimming tankard. 'There you are, Ruby. You must take 'first drink. How old will you be tomorrow – or today?' he asked.

Ruby took a deep drink. 'Sixteen.' She laughed and wiped away a moustache of creamy froth from her lips. 'Grown up!'

'Happy birthday, Ruby.' Grace took the tankard from her and raised it in a salute before drinking. She sighed and handed the tankard to Daniel. 'This is 'best day of my life.'

'And mine,' Ruby added fervently.

Daniel took a draught and then leant across and kissed Ruby on the cheek. 'Happy birthday,

Ruby! May you have lots of them and all you wish for.' Then he turned towards Grace. 'You too, Grace.' His eyes met hers and she shyly looked down and blushed as he kissed her too.

CHAPTER SEVEN

The sun shone relentlessly throughout the rest of July and the whole of August. The water levels in the open drains and sewers went down, uncovering the stagnant and offensive filth and rotting animal matter at the bottom. The muck garths where the night soil was deposited started to steam and were in imminent danger of exploding, much to the dismay and consternation of the numerous residents who lived in close proximity.

Daniel searched out the sanitary officer in order to complain that the privy in Middle Court hadn't been emptied in weeks, and a harassed office worker said that he would pass the message on. But no-one came and the stench got worse.

Mill and factory workers sweltered. Grace and Ruby worked barefoot at the mill with their skirts tied up around their knees, constantly swilling and mopping the floors to keep down the fine cotton dust.

There was rumour that the mill was losing money, yet the workers didn't believe it as they saw the directors and managers coming and going in their smart carriages and chaises.

Grace had her sixteenth birthday and, although it would normally have passed without incident, Daniel had insisted on taking her and Ruby to the Zoological Gardens which were to be opened free to the public without the usual admittance charge on the following Sunday.

This was the Sunday nearest to her birthday and her mother said that she would come too, but then decided at the last minute that the long walk out of the town and along the Spring Bank would be too much for her as it was so hot. But also, Sunday was her only day of rest, and when she had finished the chores of cleaning their room, drawing water from the pump and doing the washing, she would treat herself to a glass of ale then lie down on the bed and sleep for an hour.

But Grace's father had said he would like to go with them, for there was to be a balloon ascent which he was keen to see. There were seven acres of gardens and lakes to walk around. Deer were kept in a special enclosed area and ostrich ran with their peculiar stiff-necked gait. Gaily coloured parrots flew from the trees above them and shrieked raucously in protest at the crowds below.

Ladies in domed white dresses and beribboned poke bonnets shielded their faces from the sun with lacy parasols as they strolled on the grass, and Ruby and Grace looked at them in awe and envy. Debonair young men in dark frock coats and narrow trousers, and brightly coloured waistcoats, lifted their top hats as they passed ladies of their acquaintance, whilst others clip-clopped around the broad pathways in their gigs, broughams or landaus.

They heard a sudden shout and an explosion, and looked up to see the balloon and basket rising into the sky and figures inside the basket waving to those below. 'Imagine that!' Grace's father exclaimed. 'Imagine that! Fancy being up in 'sky like that, flying like a bird,' and he put his hand up in the air and waved as so many others were doing.

'This is 'next best day of my life,' Grace said as they walked home in the evening. 'Thank you so much for taking us, Daniel.'

That evening a storm broke. The air had become heavier and hotter throughout the day, then the skies darkened and those who were out hurried home, even whilst praying for rain to ease the oppressive sultry atmosphere. Thunder rumbled threateningly and lightning flashes illuminated the sky.

The rain came as most people were in their beds and those who were not ran for cover. The deluge found every loose roof tile, every broken window. It cascaded off gutters and spouts, and Ruby and her mother sat with a blanket over their heads as the rain poured in through the ceiling, and listened to the shrieks of the Blake family who were taking the brunt of it in the loft above them.

Grace and her parents were dry in their ground-floor room, though the rain ran hissing down the chimney and put out the fire. Her father got out of bed and peered through the window to see the torrent running off the roofs of the houses opposite, where there were no gutters, and swilling down the walls and into the undrained court, filling it with muddy water.

'We're on ground level,' he muttered. 'If it gets any worse it'll come under 'door, there's nowhere else for it to go.'

Grace and her mother got up from the bed and together the three of them moved as much as they could from the floor and put it on the table: their boots, the rag rug from the hearth, and the small sacks of potatoes, onions and barley which were kept in a corner of the room.

That night as the population did their best to sleep in spite of the racket overhead, the drains and gulleys filled up and overflowed into the streets, the flood bringing with it all manner of debris. Some of the poorer housing didn't have any drains, and those who lived below street level got out of bed and found they were paddling in dirty water up to their knees.

A report was given in the local paper of the dire neglect of the poor and the bad housing conditions in which they had to live, emphasizing that something must be done before the filth which abounded in these mean streets caused a major epidemic.

Nothing was done, though promises were made by councillors, doctors, and those eminent residents who professed to be concerned. The poor didn't know of the promises, for few of them could read, and those who could didn't believe what they had read, for they had seen and heard it all before. What was the use of complaining, they complained to one another, for who would listen to such as them?

In September, the mill foreman called the first of the workers to be put on short time. Ruby was amongst them; she was older than Grace by a month.

'Please!' she begged him. 'I really need this work. I'm 'only wage earner at home, my ma can't work—'

'Sorry, Ruby,' he said. 'If it was up to me – but I've got my orders. I've to put single lasses on short time. Married women and bairns get priority.'

''Cos they earn less!' she said bitterly.

He nodded. 'That's about 'strength of it,' he said in a low voice. 'Directors call it compassionate grounds, but we know better, don't we?'

'I don't know what I can do,' she wailed to Grace as they walked home that night. 'I can't manage as it is. We've spent Freddie's money and I'm still behind with 'rent. Four days' work! I want to weep.'

Grace was silent for a moment. If Ruby had been put on short time, then she would be next. But her circumstances were not so precarious as Ruby's. Both her mother and father worked and although their wages were not high, they earned enough between the three of them to feed and clothe themselves and pay the rent.

'Best try 'Kingston Mill,' she said eventually, speaking of the other cotton mill. 'Perhaps they'd take you on full-time.'

Ruby sighed and shook her head. 'I heard

they've plenty of labour. They onny want trained operatives. Why didn't we learn spinning or weaving, Grace?' There were tears in her eyes. 'We'd have a proper trade by now.'

'I know!' Grace tucked her arm into Ruby's. 'But nobody said. Nobody told us when we were bairns that that's what we should do.'

Ruby swallowed away her tears and sniffed. 'Well, at least our Freddie is learning a trade. He'll be a master sweep by 'time he's finished.'

Grace looked dubious, but patted Ruby's hand and said, 'Yes, of course he will, and won't we all be proud of him?'

The foreman at the Kingston Cotton Mill refused Ruby when she applied. 'But you're in work already,' he frowned. 'You're lucky to have four days. Times are hard, you know. If you'd been trained, that would have been a different matter. We're having to bring experienced people from other towns, Manchester and places like that.'

She turned away. Times are hard! He was telling *her* that, as if she didn't know!

'What's up, Ruby?' Jamie called to her from the other side of the street as she came back into the town. He ran over to her. 'Why aren't you at work?'

'Oh, I just thought I'd tek a bit of a holiday!' she said with sarcasm. 'Such a nice day it's a shame to be indoors.'

'You've been put on short time?' He wrinkled his forehead. 'You should have learned a trade!'

'Don't you start,' she said sharply. 'I know what I should have done, but I didn't and it's too late now!'

'Too late for some things, yes, but not too late for others.' He looked at her quizzically and gave a little smile.

'Like what?' she said abruptly. 'Not what I think you're suggesting! Come off it, Jamie, I'm not that desperate.'

'Not yet you're not. But what if you were?'

'It's a job I can do without, thanks very much. I don't fancy standing on street corners in 'middle of winter!'

'You wouldn't have to,' he said, looking straight at her. 'I've got an idea.'

'Then keep it and stuff it in your boots to keep your feet dry,' she muttered angrily and turned away, intending to cross over the road away from him.

He grabbed her arm. 'Just let me tell you,' he urged.

She shook him off. 'Go away!' she shouted. 'I've told you, I'm not that desperate. When I am, I'll come back and then you can tell me!'

She hurried off, tears streaming down her face. 'Damn your eyes, Jamie,' she muttered. 'Just who do you think I am?'

'Cheerio then, Ruby,' she heard him calling after her. 'Be seeing you!'

Grace and another batch of workers were put onto short hours the following week. Four days of work, twelve hours each day. 'What else can we do?' she asked Ruby. 'There must be something.'

'Fish dock,' Ruby said. 'I heard they were wanting women to fillet and gut.'

Grace blenched. 'I don't think I could do that.' She looked at her hands, which were small and white. 'I'd never be able to handle those big fishes.'

But they tried and were turned away by the forewoman, who laughed at them. 'Sorry, me dears, but you'd never last a week. You've not got enough brawn on you.'

Ruby tried for a job in one of the inns serving ale, but she only lasted one night and was sacked for throwing a jug of ale over a customer who had put his hand up her skirt.

A month later, as November approached and the weather turned colder, they were put onto three days work and Grace's father was also put onto short time at the docks.

There was despondency in the whole of the town. So many workers had been given shorter hours that everyone was suffering. Rents were not being paid, people were being threatened with eviction and shopkeepers were losing trade as no-one could afford to buy their goods. Some of the traders went out of business as their customers who had been given credit could not afford to pay off their debts.

Lizzie Sheppard sprained her back. She came home from her work one afternoon and went straight to bed. 'I lifted a pail o' water, same as I allus do,' she grimaced to Grace, who was at home on one of her non-working days. 'And I felt it go. Mebbe if I rest today it'll be all right by 'morning. I've a big wash to do tomorrow in Albion Street.'

'I'll see to 'supper, Ma,' Grace assured her. 'You just stay there.'

Her father was at home also and he looked

anxiously at his wife lying in the bed. 'Things'll be desperate, Lizzie, if you can't go to work.' His work had been cut to three days a week, the same as Grace's.

'It's nowt,' she said, but drew in a breath through her teeth as the pain bit into her back and down her legs. 'I'll be fine.'

Grace took a bucket to the pump for water and kicked away some of the rubbish which had blown against the wall. She pumped half a bucket of water for she knew she couldn't carry a full one, unlike her mother who normally could carry two heavy buckets without any trouble at all.

The water slopped over her feet as she struggled back to the house. She arrived at her door as Daniel came into the court.

'Hello, Grace.' He didn't stop as he usually did, and he wasn't wearing his usual cheerful expression.

'You all right, Daniel?' She waited, one hand on her hip.

He pursed his lips and shrugged. 'Suppose so. Yes,' and went to his own door. 'And you?' He asked almost as if it was an afterthought, and she felt as if she had done something wrong.

'Ma's hurt her back. She's gone to bed.'

'Oh!' His face this time showed concern. 'Is she bad?'

She nodded. 'She's in pain. She said she'll be all right by 'morning – but I don't know.'

He put his tool bag down on the doorstep and came across to her. 'There's no good news any-where. Workers are being laid off, traders going out of business. What a life.' He folded his arms across his chest. 'I'm sick of it!' He was very downcast, not his usual self at all.

'Has something happened to you?' she said anxiously. 'You haven't been laid off?'

'No, I won't be laid off. I onny earn a pittance anyway, being an apprentice, but my boss is worried because he's lost orders through two of his customers going bankrupt.'

'Oh!' She hadn't thought of employers being in difficulties. She thought it was only the poor who were suffering.

'But it's not just that.' He scuffed the toe of his boot along the ground. 'It's them!' He inclined his head towards his door. 'Ma and Da. They're forever at each other's throats. I swear they wait until I get home to start arguing. It's sending me mad.'

'What are they arguing about?'

'Money! Or 'lack of it. Da won't try for any other kind of work. He says he's a craftsman and won't do menial jobs.'

'He's not been hungry then?' Grace commented.

He gave an ironic grin. 'Not yet! But it won't be long.'

'Doesn't your ma work?'

Daniel shook his head. 'She's never had to. She thinks she shouldn't. They're both so proud, you see.'

He seemed so miserable that she wanted to hug him, the way she would have hugged Ruby. 'But you're not?'

He looked at her in surprise. 'Proud? Me? No, I'm not. I'd do anything to earn a crust if I had to.' His eyes pierced hers. 'I might have to, if things don't improve.'

'But you're bound, aren't you?'

He scratched the dark unshaven hair on his chin. 'Mmm. I am. But I might ask to be released. I need to earn some money, Grace. Things are getting desperate.'

CHAPTER EIGHT

Edward Newmarch had had several formal meetings with Miss Gregory. The first was when his mother had arranged a supper and invited the Gregory family to attend. He and his brother were then asked to a concert at the Gregorys' home, and there had been an occasion when he had requested that Miss Gregory and her cousin Georgiana might accompany him on a carriage drive towards Hesslewood and along the Humber bank.

Now he was to ask Mr Gregory formally if he might pay court to his daughter with a view to marriage. Edward had thought long and critically about the prospect. May Gregory, at eighteen, was pert and pretty, small and fair-haired, with blue eyes and a snub nose. She was the only child of her parents, used to taking her mother's place at formal functions if that lady was unwell or otherwise occupied. She could play the piano-forte and sing passably in tune, and was schooled to make light conversation at the luncheon or supper table. She was therefore very suitable and desirable as a wife, and had many admirers.

She did not, however, set Edward's heart on fire. But perhaps that is as well, he mused, as he rode towards her home. I would not consider that it is advisable to have a great passion when choosing a wife. It would cloud one's judgement when assessing her worth in becoming a suitable companion in marriage, a good mother and an able household administrator. Affection, he contemplated, was something which would undoubtedly grow over the years. And if I am candid, he pondered, gratification is one thing, but I don't feel that I am a man who would be aroused to intense emotion or be totally enraptured.

He regarded himself as being very sensible and clear-headed over the proposed alliance with May Gregory, and if she irritated him a little with her girlish prattle and kittenish behaviour, why, he thought, she is only young and will grow up to be sensible under my influence. And it is possible that there might even be something in me that is not altogether pleasing to her. Though I doubt that, he had mused, staring into the mirror and smoothing his sideburns and neat beard. She always gazes at me quite adoringly whenever we meet.

He was interviewed by her father, a brusque, straight-speaking man, whom Edward had met at board meetings before being introduced to his daughter. Montague Gregory was a substantial shareholder in both cotton mills and other major businesses in the town. He was a member of the Dock Board and a director of a private bank. He enquired of Edward's prospects and knew already of his father's fortune, and appeared to be satisfied on both scores.

'Good luck then, Newmarch.' He shook Edward's hand. 'Of course if May doesn't want you – and she might not, for she knows her own mind, I'll say that for my daughter – then I'm afraid you'll be disappointed. But her mother thinks well of you so you might already be under consideration, you know what ladies are like in these matters.'

Edward, on taking his leave of Mr Gregory, and awaiting May's arrival in the withdrawing room, considered reluctantly that he didn't know what ladies were like in these situations, and that perhaps it wasn't a question of him choosing Miss Gregory as a suitable marriage partner, but of himself or some other suitor being the chosen one.

His composure therefore was a trifle shaky when May came into the room and he stammered out his proposal in an agitated manner. This annoyed him but appeared to please May, as she took his hand and sweetly said, 'Dear Edward. Please don't be nervous. I have already considered my answer, should you propose, and I shall be so very willing to marry you.'

And so that was it. He rode away feeling pleased with the outcome, but aware also that perhaps his future wife wasn't going to be quite as malleable as he had imagined.

The marriage was to be the following spring. 'So much more pleasant,' Mrs Gregory gushed to Edward's mother. 'The winter is so dreary, when all one wishes to do is to stay indoors where it is warm and cosy, with the curtains drawn and fires blazing. I do not even wish to travel abroad to warmer climes.' Mrs Newmarch agreed most decidedly and so the date was set for April.

'Just as well to wait,' Martin agreed as he and Edward drove away from the mill the next evening. 'Business is a little tricky at the moment, and perhaps by April we shall be running normally again. You'll want to take some time off at any rate after the wedding!'

They were both under-managers at the cotton mill, their father having bought them twenty shares each at one hundred pounds a share. He had then requested of his friend, Joseph Ryland, the chief manager of the company, that he might give his sons an involvement in the day-to-day running of the business. Charles Newmarch had bought the maximum of one hundred shares and was determined to see a good return for his outlay. He had always been an industrious man and expected his sons to be the same.

Martin was conscientious and diligent and carefully watched the price of cotton and the production line, but Edward disliked the trade intensely. He hated the fine dust which pervaded every part of the mill, he railed against the commitment of having to be there every morning at nine thirty when he would have preferred to be in bed, and he had no interest whatsoever in the fluctuating cotton market or the conditions of the workforce.

He took out a handkerchief now and blew his nose to clear the dust from his nostrils. 'Damned cotton,' he muttered, but his brother didn't answer and slowed the horse to allow some workers to hurry across the road in front of them.

Edward looked up. There were those two girls again, walking arm in arm. He turned sideways to see them and the dark-haired one lifted her head and gave him a half-smile. Her shawl slipped to her shoulders and he saw that her hair was thick and shiny and plaited into a knot behind her neck.

He nodded to her, and thought that no doubt she would know who he was and he wanted to know her name too. He had looked for her previously, walking through the mill as if on some mission, determining that if he saw her he would pause and say a few words. Not long enough to stop her from working of course, but to ascertain, as a manager naturally would if he was interested in his employees, how long she had been at the mill, and, importantly, what her name was. It had slipped his memory that he was newly affianced to Miss Gregory.

But she wasn't there and neither was her friend. He went up and down all the floors in the mill block to look for them, and to the warehouse and the scutching floor, though he didn't stay long in there on account of the dust. Nor did they appear to be there the following day, and on enquiring of the foreman if they were short-handed, the man looked at him in surprise and said, 'Why yes, sir! As you know we had to cut some of 'workers down to three days a week in order to meet costs.'

'Indeed we did,' Edward had hastily concurred. 'But let us hope that business soon picks up and we can have them back to normal hours again.'

'Aye, sir.' The foreman fixed his gaze on him. 'They'd be glad of that. You maybe wouldn't know it, but there's great hardship out there in 'streets.'

Edward had fallen silent for a moment, then asked, 'What do they do? Those people who are put on short time, I mean?'

The foreman gave a grim laugh. 'They starve, sir!'

'Not their fault, I suppose.' Ruby stared after the brothers. A lantern swung as the chaise rolled away in front of her and Grace as they walked home.

'What isn't? Who?'

'Newmarch brothers! They can't help being rich any more than we can help being poor.'

'No,' Grace agreed. 'It all depends on where you were born and who your parents are. It's funny,' she considered. 'I never felt poor until I went on short time. Then my da did too and now Ma has had to take today off cos of her back. She couldn't get out of bed this morning, so she'll lose a day's wages. We allus had sufficient money before, enough for 'rent, enough for food.' She frowned. 'And now we haven't.'

'I couldn't pay 'rent man yesterday,' Ruby admitted. 'I pretended I wasn't in and let him knock. What are we going to do, Grace?' She started to weep. 'I don't know what to do!'

Grace shook her head. She felt numb. Her ma and da had always looked after their finances and maybe they had had worries and not told her, but now everything was going wrong. And not just for her family and Ruby, but everyone they knew. Daniel was talking about giving up his apprenticeship because his parents had spent all of their money, at least Mr Hanson had. Mrs Peck's sow had died after giving birth to six dead piglets and someone had stolen her hens when she was out. The Blake family who had lived in Bessie Robson's loft had come down after the big storm and were now living on the landing, rent-free.

'It's not fair,' she said suddenly. 'It's just not fair! Surely somebody can help us? The weavers and spinners get a bit of support when they come out of work, they've got a union or something. But we get nothing! Even 'vagrant office won't help us, not if we've got a roof over our heads. We've got to be really destitute before they'll give us as much as a loaf of bread!' Her face flushed and her eyes flashed. 'It's just not fair!'

Ruby stared at her, then gave a surprised gasp. 'Heavens, Grace! I've never seen you in such a state afore. It's allus me that gets into a temper, not you!'

'I know,' she said fiercely. 'But I'm that mad! Something should be done, Ruby. We're flesh and blood, we feel hungry – and cold in winter! Should we go barefoot because we can't afford to buy a pair o' boots? God helps them who help themselves, have you heard that? It's what my da is allus saying. Well, what I want to know is, how can we help ourselves when we're so far down we can't get up? All we want is a chance to work, to earn money to pay our rent and buy food.'

She pointed down the road where the chaise carrying the Newmarch brothers had now disappeared into the darkness. 'We don't ask for riches to buy a carriage or fancy clothes, we just want enough to keep us from 'workhouse door!'

Ruby wiped away her tears and gave a watery grin. 'I'll get you a soapbox, Gracie, and you can go to Dock Green on Sunday with 'other agitators.'

Grace stopped and took hold of Ruby's arm. 'I'm not an agitator! But I think I've been asleep and I've just woken up.' She stared at her friend. 'I want my rights! How can I get them?'

'Rights!' Ruby shook back her hair and gave a shout of derision. 'Rights! We're sixteen, Grace, and we're women. We have no rights!'

'There has to be something.' Grace's fingers pinched Ruby's arm in her fervour and she winced.

'Ow!' Ruby shook Grace's hand off. 'There's nothing we can do,' she said. 'Heaven knows I've been begging at 'vagrant office often enough and I've been to 'Guardians and there's nowt for such as us, onny 'workhouse if things get too bad, and we've been in there, my ma and me, onny I don't remember much about that, thank God.'

'Well, maybe I will go to Dock Green next Sunday,' Grace pronounced. 'I'd like to know what other folks think.'

Ruby didn't answer. Across the street, coming out of their alley, was Nell, Jamie's mother. She stopped for a moment beneath the street lamp and Ruby saw that she was wearing a warm cloak, and beneath it the hem of a red dress flounced provocatively. Behind her came Jamie. He spotted the two girls and gave a cheery wave. He was wearing a heavy topcoat and had a muffler around his neck.

Ruby shivered and pulled her shawl closer about her. Winter was almost upon them. The fog was drifting in from the river and the air felt dank and cold. She would sleep in all of her clothes tonight to try and keep warm. She hung back and watched Jamie and Nell until they turned at the corner of the street.

'Trouble is, Grace,' she murmured, following her friend down the narrow dark passage towards home, 'we're in 'wrong sort of job.'

CHAPTER NINE

Ruby came down the stairs the next morning and found Mrs Peck's door wide open. Mr and Mrs Peck, the children and the dog were gathered outside in the court, with their few belongings stacked onto a rickety old handcart.

'Say goodbye to your ma for me,' Mrs Peck said to Ruby. 'We're off back to 'country.'

'Oh!' Ruby glanced from her to Mr Peck, who stared at her but didn't speak. 'Will it be better there? I thought there wasn't any work!'

'There isn't,' replied Mrs Peck. 'But if we're going to starve then we'd rather starve among our own folk, than here in Hull.'

'Will you find somewhere to live?'

Mrs Peck shook her head. 'Mebbe not. Hedge bottom more'n likely, but we'll throw ourselves onto 'mercy of 'parish until 'summer and then Mr Peck'll get work harvesting.'

Mr Peck pushed his cap to the back of his head. 'Aye,' he nodded, and Ruby realized that that was the first word she had ever heard him utter.

'Good luck, then,' she said and watched as they

went in procession out of the court and towards the alley.

Mrs Peck stopped and turned around. 'If you see 'rent man,' she called, 'tell him to tell 'landlord we're sorry about arrears. We'd have paid if we could.'

Ruby raised her hand in reply. 'I'll tell him,' she muttered. 'If I see him, which I hope I won't.'

She went back inside and looked around the newly vacated room. It was completely empty, but swept clean. Mrs Peck was or had been a good housekeeper – even the hearth was swept clear of ash.

'Mmm,' Ruby pondered and stared hard at the empty hearth, then on a sudden impulse hurried out of doors again, past Grace's house where it had been her intention to call, for she and Grace were not working today, up the alley, through the other court and out into the street towards the banks of the river Hull. She returned half an hour later with her arms full of driftwood and twigs and a precious piece of coal which she had found in the middle of the road. Several people had seen it fall off a coal waggon and there was a sudden rush forward, but Ruby had sprinted past the others, the first to reach the precious black nugget, scooped it up and victoriously dropped it into her pocket.

'Now then, how do I light a fire? I've never done one afore.' She knelt by the hearth in the downstairs room. 'I don't want to waste this kindling. I think I need a bit o' newspaper. I'd better go and ask Aunt Lizzie or Grace. They'll know.'

She knocked on the door of the Sheppards' room and, on opening the door, saw that unusually they had no fire, though it was laid ready. Lizzie Sheppard was in bed, Grace was crouched over a bucket, peeling potatoes, and Bob Sheppard was sitting by the unlit fire reading an old and torn newspaper.

'Pecks have left,' Ruby said gleefully. 'They've gone back to 'country. I'm going to make a fire in their room so Ma and me can get warm.'

Bob Sheppard put down his paper. 'Won't 'rent man be coming to lock up?'

Ruby shook her head. 'He doesn't know they've gone. She said would I tell him she was sorry about 'arrears.'

Mr Sheppard tutted. 'It's not right. Folks should pay their debts.'

'With what?' His wife spoke from her bed. 'Wi' a dead porker? Poor folks never stood a chance. They'll do better wi' their own kind.'

'That's what Mrs Peck said,' Ruby agreed. 'But now I want to make a fire before anybody comes. Onny, I don't know how and I don't want to waste 'wood. Why haven't you got a fire?' she asked.

'Saving fuel!' Grace looked up, a knife poised in her hand. 'We'll light it later when we want to cook.'

'Ah,' Ruby said. 'Yes, of course. Well, I want to be warm now. Will you help me, Grace?'

Grace took her cold red hands out of the bucket of water and dried them on a scrap of cloth, then shook them to get the circulation going.

'Where did you get 'kindling from?' she asked as they went back towards Ruby's house. She'd begged a sheet of her father's newspaper and a lucifer to light it, for Ruby had neither.

'I went to 'river bank. As soon as Mrs Peck said they were going, I decided we'd move downstairs and have a fire. Just for today,' she added earnestly. 'We can't stop. Can't afford 'extra rent.'

Grace gave a sudden peal of laughter. 'What?' Ruby asked. 'What's funny?'

'You!' Grace said with a wide grin. 'You can't afford 'rent upstairs either. You said you hadn't paid 'agent.'

'No more I haven't!' Ruby said. 'So why are you laughing? Oh!' She too gave a grin. 'I see! So we might as well stay downstairs which we can't afford as stay upstairs which we can't afford either!'

'My da would have a fit if we couldn't pay our rent.' Grace blew on the blue and yellow flame that was curling around the newspaper and wood. 'You heard him. He's allus paid his debts. There, I think it's caught.'

Ruby looked shamefaced. 'Tell him it's onny for today if he says owt.'

Grace nodded. 'Well, you might just as well stay there until 'rent man comes. What's 'use in leaving it empty?'

'Will you help me downstairs with 'mattress then, Grace? It'll be easier with 'two of us.'

They stepped between the legs of the Blake family, who were huddled on the landing, and went into the Robsons' room. Bessie was lying on the mattress with the blanket and the old coats and rags on top of her, but she quickly rolled off and gathered them together on being told that there was a fire awaiting her downstairs.

'Sorry, Mr Blake, Mrs Blake. Would you mind shifting for a minute while we move this mattress?'

The Blakes scrambled to their feet. 'Is your room going to be empty then, Ruby?' Mrs Blake asked. 'Cos if so . . .'

'Yes, you move in,' Ruby said generously. 'But if we get turned out then we'll have to come back up.'

They slid the straw-filled mattress down the stairs, then stopped and giggled as it caught on the splintered treads halfway down and they couldn't shift it. Mr Blake came down to help them and they manhandled it into the room.

Bessie was standing close to the fire with a huge beam on her face. 'Oh, Ruby! What a clever lass. However did you manage it? A proper blaze!' She put her hands towards the flame, and Mr Blake too came and opened his palms in front of it.

'Thanks, Ruby,' he said, before going back upstairs to move their few belongings off the landing and into the comfort of an empty room.

Ruby and her mother were there for three weeks before they were found out. Each time the rent man came, they pressed themselves into a corner on the window wall where he couldn't see them as he peered through the glass, and would see only a low fire and a mattress on the floor. Mr Blake had managed to fix a wooden bolt on the door, and though the agent hammered and called, no-one answered.

But then he arrived early one morning when Ruby was on her knees lighting the fire, and her mother had gone to the privy and left the house door open.

'Ruby!' he said, coming into the room. 'What are you doing here? Where's Mrs Peck?'

'She's left, Mr Stevens.' She rocked back onto her heels and looked up at him. He was a short shabby-looking man of middle years. 'She said to say how sorry she was that they couldn't pay 'arrears, and would you tell 'landlord. They've gone back home to 'country.'

'Have they?' He folded his arms in front of him and turned as Bessie came through the front door. On seeing the early-morning caller, she spun round and scuttled out again.

'And you and your ma have moved in?'

'Well, it seemed a pity not to use it when it was empty,' Ruby confessed. She stood up. 'I've never lived in a room that had a fire, Mr Stevens, and it's lovely to be warm. I've been gathering wood from 'riverbank every day, but you've got to get there early or there's none left.'

'Are you not working?'

'Three days,' she said. 'There's onny enough money for food.' She put her hand into her skirt pocket and brought out three pennies. 'I work Monday, Friday and Saturday.' She held out her hand. 'You can tek this if you want. Today's

Wednesday, we'll manage till Saturday when I get paid.'

He waved her hand away. 'So your room'll be empty, is it?' His eyes stared into hers and she looked away and didn't answer.

'I'll have to come back, you know that?' His voice was quiet but not threatening. 'And 'landlord might send 'bailiffs.'

'Ha!' She gave a grim laugh and gazed around the room. 'There's onny 'mattress and an old blanket left and I doubt they'd want them. They'll be full o' fleas.'

'You and your ma could go to prison, Ruby. People do. Non-payment of debts.'

'Where do you live, Mr Stevens?' she asked.

He frowned. 'In lodgings. Why?'

She sighed and pushed back a lock of hair. 'I just wondered, that's all. You've been coming here all this time and we don't know owt about you.'

'There's nothing to know,' he said, turning towards the door. 'I get up in a morning, do this job, and go to bed at night. That's my life.' He nodded to her. 'Bye, Ruby.'

It's a rotten job, he thought, as he picked his way down the alley. Trying to extract money from people who haven't got any, to give to people who have. He called in at his office and filled in a report to the effect that the Peck family had left the district owing arrears of rent, and that Mrs Robson and her daughter were no longer living in the upstairs room.

The house appeared to be empty, he wrote, and was in urgent need of repair before anyone else could safely live in it. Tiles were missing from the roof and the stairs were unsound. The house, he added, would probably be condemned if the Corporation Sanitary Committee should see its condition. He knew that they wouldn't see it, for the owner had friends in many places.

He handed the report to the chief clerk and placed on his desk the leather bag which he used to collect the rent money. This morning it was empty as he hadn't been any further than Middle Court. The chief clerk looked at him and frowned. 'What's this, Stevens?' he said tersely. 'You haven't finished!'

'Yes, I have,' he said, 'I've finished for good,' and walked out of the door.

'Da!' Grace put down the newspaper which she had been reading. 'It says here that somebody has just been given some silver plate for their services to charity. So who paid for that?'

'Corporation,' he replied grimly. 'They've plenty o' money. Hull is a rich town, with poor people,' he added.

'So why don't they give some of that money to the poor?'

Her father shrugged.

'And who's this Henry Vincent that they keep mentioning in 'newspaper?'

'Vincent! His name's allus cropping up. He's a Radical – a Chartist. Came to Hull to speak, oh, eight or nine years ago.'

'Speak about what?'

'The poor. He said that Poor Law wasn't working. I went to hear him,' he continued. 'Three thousand people were there on Dock Green and they all cheered him.' He put his chin in his hands and sighed. 'Fat lot of good it did anybody!'

'But at least he was speaking for us, Da. He was speaking for 'poor when we can't speak for ourselves.'

Her father looked up at her. 'We can speak for ourselves,' he claimed. 'Trouble is, if we do then we're branded as troublemakers. Vincent spoke up for women too,' he added. 'Said they should have a voice. Your ma agreed wi' that!'

Grace gave a sigh. 'Oh, I wish I could have heard him.'

'There was another fellow there,' her father reminisced. 'I remember him even more than Vincent. He lived in 'lunatic ward at Hull workhouse. Word got around that he wasn't mad but had been put there by 'authorities for speaking his mind. They made out that he was deluded so they locked him up! Anyway, somebody got him out for this meeting and put him on 'same platform as Vincent. Poor bloke! Samuel, that was his name, he could hardly talk to begin with, but when he did – ' He shook his head. 'He warned us, told us of what was happening, said it wasn't right that young bairns had to work long hours in factories, and poor folk were in 'workhouse through no fault of their own. He had an educated voice so he knew what he was talking about. We're nothing, he said. Just sweepings in 'gutter. I'll allus remember those words.'

He fell silent and Grace waited for him to continue. He cleared his throat but his voice was husky as he went on, 'And he was right, that's what we are. We're of no account, Gracie. No account at all. We're in this pit and we'll never get out.'

Grace glanced around the room which was home and saw it as if for the first time. Bare walls, with here and there the bricks showing through where the plaster had fallen off. The earth floor made hard by their feet tramping on it. A stone slab for a hearth and a few pieces of wood and coal, waiting to be lit. Her mother, who was now back at work, kept the room clean with the aid of a besom, and always had, until recently, a pan of soup bubbling on the fire.

A pit, that was what her father called their home! She frowned. Daniel had called the court a sewer too. I must have had my eyes shut. But then, I've never had anything else. I've grown up accepting things as they are, just as Ruby has never had a room with a fire before. So, she pondered. Could we have something better? And what do we do to get it?

'Do these people, these Radicals, still speak at Dock Green?' she asked.

He got up from his chair, stretched and reached for his jacket and scarf. The room was getting cold. 'Aye, most Sundays. There's allus somebody spouting. Gets it off their chests I suppose, even if it doesn't do any good.'

She gazed at him. He'd always been a good father, taking her out for walks when she was little whilst her mother got on with the washing or cleaning the house, and he always answered her questions, no matter how trivial.

'I'd like to go, Da. To Dock Green! Will you come with me?'

CHAPTER TEN

'Do you want to come, Ruby? I'm going to Dock Green with my da.'

'For what?' Ruby was crouched by the low fire with her shawl wrapped around her shoulders. Her mother was sitting on the mattress with her arms across her chest and her hands tucked under her armpits. She was shivering and rocking, her head and shoulders moving backwards and forwards.

'I'm going to listen to 'speakers.'

'There'll be nobody there. It's raining – and it's cold! No thanks, I'll stop here by 'fire.' She glanced at her mother. 'Besides, I have to keep an eye on Ma,' she said in a low voice. 'She'd not had any loddy for a couple o' days and I bought her some yesterday when I got my wages. She took it straight away instead of waiting till this morning and has been awake all night, jigging and dancing and talking all sorts of nonsense. Now she's suffering for it.'

'Oh I am suffering!' Bessie heard Ruby's last few words. 'Nobody knows how I suffer. Such pain in me head and belly,' she groaned. 'Too much spirit in it. You should have got me raw Turkish, Ruby. That's 'best you can buy.'

Ruby gave a snort. 'We don't have money for Turkish, Ma! It's eight pounds a pound! When did you last have any of that?' She turned to Grace, misery etching lines on her face. 'I'm sick of this, Grace. I'm at my wits' end.'

'What's your ma talking about?' Grace frowned. 'I thought 'laudanum made her feel better.'

Ruby sighed. 'It does for a bit, but 'loddy that you buy from 'grocer is mixed with spirit, so you can get drunk on it. And she didn't take just a spoonful but drank it straight out of 'bottle!'

'I'm sorry, Ruby,' Grace said. 'So you won't come?'

Ruby shook her head. 'No. You go, and see who's putting 'world to rights.' She gave a wry smile. 'And if they've got any answers, send 'em to me!'

'Poor Ruby.' Grace told her father about Bessie as they walked down the road towards the town. 'Do you think her ma will ever be cured of taking opium?'

Her father glanced down at her. 'No, course she won't. If she stops taking it she'll see 'world as it really is and she won't like it.'

'It's hard for Ruby, though. They could spend that loddy money on food.'

'Aye, it's hard on 'lass, I agree, but Bessie takes it to forget. Life seems better and brighter when you eat a grain of opium.'

She looked up in astonishment. 'Does it? How do you know? Have you taken it, Da?'

He hunched down into his jacket so that his face was half hidden from her. 'Aye, a few times in 'past, but not any more.'

'So how did you stop?' This was a revelation to her. She'd never seen either of her parents taking opium, not even when her mother had been in pain with her sprained back.

He lifted his head and stared straight ahead. 'Your ma. She stopped me. Weaned me off it. It hadn't got hold,' he said. 'I wasn't dependent on it. Not like Bessie. It was too late for her.' He seemed about to say something more, but then thought better of it and simply cleared his throat.

There were other people, mostly men, who were walking from the Market Place, down Castle Street and towards Dock Green. This was an open place where meetings were held, where Trinity House schoolboys played their games and where every October at the Hull Fair, the showmen put up their entertainment of swings and whirligigs, menageries and circuses. There too on the outer perimeter, the gypsies pitched their camps.

Today, though, it was quiet. The rain and cold had deterred the crowds from their Sunday walk and a chance of laughter and discussion with the speakers who stood on boxes and gave their opinion on the world as they saw it.

But there was one man who was exhorting everyone to repent, for the world was coming to an end. They heard his voice bellowing across the grassy area and they approached to listen. 'It may be too late if you wait,' he shouted.

'Tomorrow will be too late! Today may be too late! Repent now of your sins.'

He looked down at Grace. 'You, child! You might not think you have been sinful, but we sin from the moment we are born. Come!' He held out his hand towards her. 'Come. Repent now before it is too late!'

Grace stared up at him. 'But I haven't done anything,' she called back, ·and her father glanced at her and grinned. 'And anyway, I'm not a child. I'm a woman. I work for a living.'

A man standing on a small platform close by heard her, and shouted to the people who were standing near. 'Isn't this what I have been saying?' He called to Grace. 'Come here, child! How long have you been working?' he asked as she drew near. 'And what kind of work?'

'I'm not a child,' she repeated. 'I'm sixteen and I've been working since I was nine at Hull Flax and Cotton Mill!'

'Come up,' he said, 'so that everyone can hear you.' The speaker put his hand out to her to step onto the platform, and, almost without thinking, she did so.

'How did you feel, starting work so young?'

Grace pondered. Seven years. It seemed such a long time ago. 'I remember that I missed my ma,' she said. 'And I was very tired at 'end of each day.'

'What kind of work did you do that an adult couldn't?'

'Well, I could get into small places, like under 'machinery to get rid of 'dust, which a grown-up person couldn't. You had to be very small to squash underneath.' She gave a little shudder as she remembered the whirring of the machines above her.

'And how long was your day?' he pressed persuasively,

'Oh, only eight hours,' she said, sure of her facts. 'Until I was thirteen, then I could work twelve. We were only allowed to work those hours. I think there's a law. But I can work longer now.' Her face dropped. 'At least – I could, but we've been put on short time.'

'Of course you have,' he said triumphantly. 'And do you know why?' His gaze went from Grace to encompass the crowd below, which had grown considerably since Grace had come onto the platform. 'I'll tell you why.' He raised his forefinger towards them. 'This young woman – who is no longer a child – has been put on short time because children, such as she was just a few short years ago, can do the work cheaper!'

He waited a few moments for maximum effect, then raised his voice and shouted. 'Is it right? Is it right that children should be expected to work for eight hours out of a twenty-four-hour day, when they should be home with their mothers or playing with their toys?'

Grace looked at him and held up her hand to speak. The man frowned momentarily, put off his stride, but then raised his eyebrows in permission.

'I didn't have any toys,' she said. 'My ma and da couldn't afford shop toys.' She glanced down at her father, 'But they made me a peg doll when I was little.'

The speaker lifted his arms and stretched out his hands as if Grace had confirmed all that he had said. Then his voice thundered. 'Things must change! We must rebel against these factory and mill owners who exploit our children. We must demand a proper wage for adult workers so that they don't have to send their children to work to put food into their mouths . . .'

As Grace looked across the grassy area, she drew in a sharp breath. Strolling along and listening to some of the speakers, she saw, in the company of a lady, one of the Newmarch brothers, a manager of the mill where she worked. Suppose he saw her! Suppose he heard the demands of this speaker who had brought her onto his platform. Just suppose he linked her with him and she lost her job altogether!

'Excuse me,' she whispered to the speaker, 'I have to go,' and she stepped down from the platform.

'Come away, Da.' She took her father's arm and pulled him along. 'Come away.'

'What's up?' he asked. 'You were doing right well up there.'

'I saw somebody – a manager of 'mill. I didn't want him to see me, he might have thought I was a troublemaker.'

'Aye,' he said thoughtfully. 'He might.'

Martin Newmarch had seen Grace, although he didn't recognize her immediately until she was pointed out.

'Look at that girl,' his companion laughed. 'She's starting young as a speaker.' She indicated the platform. 'That's what I like to see, young women who are thinking for themselves.'

'Georgiana!' he remonstrated, and narrowed his eyes to look where she was pointing. 'She's a child. What can she know of anything?'

'Perhaps her parents have taught her well, mine did.'

They walked towards the platform, and saw the girl step down. 'I think she works for our company,' he said. 'Yes, I'm sure that she does.'

She arched her eyebrows, but not in a coquettish manner for that was not Georgiana Gregory's style. She was merely teasing him. 'You said she was a child! So how is it that you remember her from all of the hundreds of workers that you employ? What has she done for you to mark her out?'

'It was Edward,' he said, speaking of his brother. 'He noticed that girl and her friend as they walked home from the mill. They're always together,' he explained, awkwardly. 'One dark, one fair, and they always walk arm in arm.'

'How very observant of Edward.' She turned and looked at Martin quizzically. 'Strange, I never thought of him as the type of man who would notice mill girls.'

'You are so very bold, Georgiana!' Lightly he mocked. 'I know of no other young woman who would speak so plainly.'

'But that is because I know that, unlike some gentlemen, I cannot shock you.' She put up her umbrella as the rain started again and held it over them both, tucking her free arm into his.

'If you married me,' he persuaded, 'you could always speak your mind.'

'But I would lose my independence.' Then she added flippantly, 'Besides, you don't love me!'

'I am fond of you, Georgiana, you know that very well, and I know also that you would have no patience with a lovesick man who is all hearts and flowers! But that apart, you would have as much independence, more, in fact, with me than you do now under your uncle's guardianship. We would suit each other, I am sure of it.'

She sighed. 'I dislike intensely being under anyone's benefaction, but you, Martin, are dependent on your father at present, are you not?'

'If I married I would receive a settlement, and I am doing well at the company. You would have no fears for your future, I am the elder son. Come,' he said quickly. 'Where is your chaise? The rain is getting heavier.'

They hurried across the field, others doing likewise, as the sky became blacker, and he handed her into her aunt's chaise. 'Think about what I have said, Georgiana. You are stifled living in your aunt's house.'

'That is why I escape to stay with May from time to time,' she agreed. 'Goodbye, Martin. It was most fortunate that we met. We will meet again soon, I have no doubt.'

The chaise pulled away and she settled back against the cushions. He's nice enough, she thought, shaking the wetness from her cloak, a thoughtful man and considerate, but rather self-restrained. She sighed. But I'm poor and poor beggars can't be choosers. And especially not women.

Her parents had died in an accident when their carriage had overturned and fallen down a ravine whilst travelling in Cheshire. Her father had never been very good with money matters and had left her only a small legacy. Her uncle, Montague Gregory, her father's brother and father of May, had generously become Georgiana's guardian and benefactor, but had stipulated that she should live with his sister, for companionship.

She never had been able to comprehend how a ten-year-old child could be a suitable companion for a fifty-year-old maiden lady, but she was not consulted. It was decided, and whether her aunt Clarissa had been consulted in the matter either, Georgiana never knew. Aunt Clarissa too was dependent on her brother for her comforts, which included the use of the carriage in which Georgiana was now travelling. The brougham, though rather old-fashioned, was at least keeping her dry, she mused. It was better than having to walk as others were doing. She saw people scurrying along with their heads down. There was that girl! She called to the driver to stop just past her and a man who was hurrying alongside her.

'Can I take you somewhere?' she called to them. 'There is room if we squash up.'

The girl stared up at her, then glanced at the man with her. 'It's all right, miss,' he said. 'Thank you all 'same. You won't be going our way.' The rain was running down his face and neck and the girl's shawl was soaked.

'Oh do get in,' Georgiana urged, opening the

door. 'I can drop you off. Where do you want to be?'

'Thank you. George Street please, miss.' The girl climbed in followed by, Georgiana guessed, her father. 'We can walk from there.'

'George Street,' Georgiana called up to the driver. 'Do you know where that is?'

'Yes, Miss Gregory,' he said sullenly and muttered, 'It's miles out of our way.'

'Are you sure that's near enough?' she asked the couple. 'Don't take any notice of the coachie. Is that where you live?'

'No, miss.' The man had taken off his cap as he entered the chaise and she saw that he was as fair as his daughter, though his hair was thinning on top. He touched his forehead. 'Beggin' your pardon, miss, but you wouldn't want to come to where we live.'

'Why not?' she asked bluntly. 'Would I be shocked by the conditions?'

He nodded. 'Aye, I reckon so. It'll not be what you're used to.'

'Then I would not wish to offend you by imposing my disposition upon you, though I assure you I am not easily shocked! We shall travel to George Street, it will save you some distance at least.'

She turned to the girl. 'I saw you at Dock Green, I think. Weren't you speaking on a platform?'

The girl swallowed and seemed nervous. 'I wasn't really speaking, miss. I was asked some questions, that's why I was on 'platform.'

'Ah! A pity.' Georgiana smiled to put her at her

ease. 'I thought you were a young Radical.'

'Grace isn't a Radical, miss,' her father began.

'I don't know what it means,' Grace interposed. 'The speaker was asking about my work and how old I was when I started.'

'And how old were you and where do you work?' Georgiana asked.

'I was nine, miss, and I work at Hull Flax and Cotton Mill.'

Georgiana nodded. So Martin was right. I wonder what her friend looks like, for this girl is beautiful in spite of her shabby clothes. Her eyes are such a deep blue and her skin so fine it's almost transparent. She appears so fragile, yet I would stake my allowance that she is not.

'Are you a weaver or a spinner?'

Grace smiled. 'Everybody asks me that, miss, and I'm neither. I do whatever I'm asked.'

'I'm sure you do it well, whatever you're asked to do,' Georgiana said. 'I have a friend who works there, but I'm sure he doesn't work as hard as you.' She paused. 'I come quite often to Dock Green to hear the speakers. I hoped when I saw you today that you were going to speak on women's issues. I belong to an organization which helps the cause of women's independence. If you are at all interested we could perhaps meet again. Maybe after winter is over? No-one wants to stand out in the rain listening to others, no matter how interesting.'

The carriage slowed and the driver called down, 'This is George Street, Miss Gregory. Do them folks want to get out?'

'Thank you, miss,' Grace's father said as he opened the door. 'Most civil of you.'

'Thank you, miss.' Grace bobbed her knee as she stood in the cobbled road. 'You're very kind.'

Georgiana nodded and the vehicle moved on. 'I'm not at all kind,' she murmured as she settled back again. 'But I am very curious about you, young Grace. Very curious.'

CHAPTER ELEVEN

Ruby was as despondent as she had ever been. She was hungry and she was cold. The fire was low and she didn't have the energy to walk to the riverbank to find more kindling. Her mother had kept her awake most of the night with her ramblings, and now in desperation she had sent her out with their last few coins to buy another dose of laudanum. It'll mebbe calm her down if she has a drop more, she thought.

Her mother had scurried out, finding a rush of energy which Ruby envied, and promising that she wouldn't spend it all on her loddy, but would bring back some day-old bread as well. Ruby sighed. She would believe that when she saw it clutched in her hand.

A shrill whistling came from the court and then a sharp rap on the door. Ruby felt a rapid palpitation in her chest; she was forever expecting the landlord's agent to come back demanding overdue rent. Well, there wasn't any.

'Ruby!' Jamie's cheerful voice sounded from outside the door. 'It's onny me!'

'Door's open,' she called. 'Come on in.'

Jamie put his head round the door and grinned. 'Saw your ma go out. Thought you might like a bit o' company.' He brought his hand from behind his back. 'And a bit o' cake!'

'Oh, Jamie. Thank you!' Eagerly she took it from him. 'You're an angel.'

'Is that 'best you can do for a fire?' he asked. 'You need some coal.'

'I need a miracle, more like,' she said, her spirit lightening as she tasted the sweetness of the cake in her mouth.

'I'll get you a miracle.' He turned to go out again. 'Don't go away.'

She was licking the crumbs from her fingers when he returned with a few lumps of coal in a paper bag and a bundle of twigs under his arm. 'There, that'll soon get it going.' He glanced around the room. 'It's a bit cosier than upstairs I suppose, but you've no chair? No table?'

'Luxuries!' she commented, running her tongue around her lips to catch the last vestige of sugar. 'Ma sold those years ago.'

'Have you heard owt about your Freddie?' he asked as he put the coal and twigs on the fire, then sat down on the mattress beside her.

'No,' she sighed. 'Agent said we hadn't to bother him unless it was an emergency.'

'Hmm.' Jamie looked thoughtful. 'Poor little chap. I wonder where he is? It would be good to buy him back, wouldn't it?'

Ruby felt hot tears pricking her eyelids. 'I can't imagine we'll ever see him again.'

'If you could just get more regular work, and

better paid,' he murmured, 'then you could save to get him back.'

'If only,' she began, and laughed. A dry cynical laugh. 'How could I ever save? There is nothing, nothing but poverty ahead. It's all I've ever known. I don't long for riches – I wouldn't know what to do with them, but it'd be nice to have enough to eat, to have a decent pair of boots for my feet, and a fire like this every day.'

He nodded and took hold of her hand, gazing into the now blazing fire. 'You could,' he said after a moment's hesitation. 'You could.'

She shook her head. 'Don't, Jamie. Don't tempt me. I'm feeling so low that I might just fall.'

He remained silent and gently squeezed her hand, then said, 'I wish you'd come over and see what my ma has.' He paused, and continued softly, 'She has clothes and furniture. We eat every day. And she's nowhere near as beautiful as you, Ruby. When she was young, she had to take whoever came along. Then I made her become more choosy, to go up a notch with 'men she took.'

'My ma disapproves of what you do,' she told him.

'But not what my ma does?'

'No. Odd that, isn't it?'

'Nell's getting past it now.' He sighed and pursed his lips. 'She gets tired. I'd like her to stop but she won't, she's got regular clients who she likes.'

'Who she likes!' Ruby was astonished.

'Yes,' he nodded. 'She says she doesn't want to

let them down. Not until somebody younger comes along who can take over from her.'

'Oh! I see!' Ruby leaned backwards and appraised him. 'You're softening me up.'

He grinned. 'I know how successful you could be, Ruby.' He put his arm around her. 'Let me tell you what *I* want.'

She shrugged his arm away. 'I'll not do it, Jamie.'

'Waiting for a knight in shining armour?' he sneered. 'Somebody who'll value your virginity and virtue?'

She had a sudden mental picture of Daniel, and the expression on his face as he'd looked at Grace. 'Maybe,' she murmured. But not Daniel. He's committed, even though Grace doesn't know it. 'Go on, then. What is it that you want?'

'I want – I want to have a team of women who'll work for me. I'll make sure they onny get decent men, no roughnecks, and, eventually, I'd like my own place where 'women would feel safe and men would come to them.'

'A brothel!' It was her turn to sneer. 'Don't include me, thanks!'

'Not a brothel!' he snapped back. 'A nice house, warm and with good curtains and cushions and suchlike.'

She was silent. Curtains and cushions, and warm. It was appealing. Clothes too, maybe, not the rags she was wearing now. Perhaps she could be coaxed. But the men! What would they be like? What would they expect from me? She gave a shudder and then sighed. Why would I ever hope for romance in my life? My mother never had it. Nobody I know ever did. Nobody around here or at the mill. So why don't I accept? Why not?

'So why not, Ruby?' Jamie's voice was soft in her ear. 'You could mebbe run it eventually. Be in charge, you and Nell. I'd look after 'finances.'

'Have you got anybody special, Jamie?' she asked curiously. She'd never seen him with anyone.

'Me? No!' He gave a sly grin. 'I'll tek my pick when I'm set up.' He saw the look on her face. 'Onny, not wi' you, Ruby. No, you're my friend. It wouldn't be right.'

No, it wouldn't. And somehow she was reassured by his pledge.

'Will you think about it?' he coaxed. 'You see, I'd need somebody reliable. Somebody I could trust.'

'But you haven't got anywhere yet. No house. No women.'

'Teks time, Ruby.' He pinched her cheek. 'We'd have to start slowly. First thing I'd do is set you up wi' somebody decent – seeing as it'd be your first time. It would be 'first time, wouldn't it?' he asked anxiously.

She nodded and whispered, 'Yes.'

'Ah!' He breathed out a soft sigh. Twice as much then, for first-timer. He began to feel an expectant thrill about preparing her, choosing the right person, somebody who would appreciate her youth, her innocence, let alone her beauty.

'You're ready, I know, Ruby.' He leaned

towards her and kissed her cheek, flushed from the fire. 'I'm onny sorry that it can't be me. But like I say, it wouldn't be right.'

'I haven't said yes!' She was suddenly defiant. 'But I'll think on it.'

'Here.' He jumped to his feet and put his hand in his pocket. 'Tek this.' He put a shilling in her hand. 'Just to show that I'd look after you, Ruby.'

She stood up and stared at the coin. 'A shilling! I can't take all that.'

'Course you can! There's more where that came from.'

'But – your ma – '

'No. That's mine. That's my cut from what she earns.' His eyes pierced hers. 'I find her work, then tek a percentage.'

It sounded so businesslike that for a moment she forgot just what it was that his mother did to earn her living.

'Like I say, Jamie. I'll think about it.'

He nodded. 'Like I say, Ruby. I think you're ready.'

She watched him through the window as he walked jauntily across the court and into his own house, then glanced down at the coin in her hand. No. I'm not ready. But I am hungry.

She rinsed her hands and face under the pump and dried herself with a fairly clean rag. Then she smoothed her thick hair and went out shopping. She bought a hot meat pie and a fresh new loaf, a jug of ale and two potatoes which she intended putting into the hot coals. If the fire kept in they would be cooked by the evening. She looked for her mother in the Market Place but didn't see her, and with a sinking feeling guessed that she would be ensconced in an alehouse with some of her cronies, where they would stay until asked to leave.

The smell of the gravy was tantalizing as it spilled onto her fingers, and as soon as she arrived home she bit into the pie and tore into the bread. She saved half of the pie for her mother, and then guiltily realized that she had eaten more than half the loaf. She took a long draught of ale from the jug and wiped her mouth with the back of her hand. I've still got some change, she thought, I'll go back to 'bakers for another penny loaf.

She belched and heaved a satisfied sigh. Perfect! There will never be another meal as good as that, not ever!

There was another knock on the door, politer than the sharp rap which Jamie had given, and she got to her feet and peered out of the window. Daniel! Her heart gave a sudden lurch. Strange that she had only thought of him a short time ago. She opened the door. 'Come in.'

'Am I bothering you?' he asked. 'Is your ma in?'

'No, she's out. Did you want to speak to her?'

'No. No!' He seemed flustered. 'I was hoping that she wouldn't be – in, I mean.' His glance took in the room. 'I thought you lived upstairs?'

'We did.' He's got such a nice face, she thought. Such kind eyes. Trustworthy, that's what you would say about him. 'But we had 'chance of coming down when 'Pecks moved out.'

'It'll be more rent, I expect?'

'I expect it will be.' She looked at him directly. No point in lying. When she and her ma were thrown out into the street, everybody would know about it anyway. ' 'Landlord doesn't know we're here.'

He stared at her, his grey eyes blank. 'What – ? Oh!' Enlightenment gathered on his face and he took a breath. 'You're fearless, aren't you, Ruby? Daring!'

'No!' she protested. 'Brash, more like, and when 'landlord comes I'll tremble in my boots.' She looked down at her bare feet. She never wore her boots on a Sunday, saving the leather for work days. 'If my boots last long enough, that is!'

'That's what I mean.' He gave a wry grin at her joke. 'You don't let things get you down. You seem to rise above your difficulties.'

'Don't believe that, Daniel! It isn't true. It's just that I don't let my troubles show.' She invited him to sit down next to her on the mattress by the fire. What would he think if I told him that I'm considering changing my line of work? Would he chat to me in this friendly manner if I told him I was going to work on the streets?

She watched his mouth as he was speaking. Full lips which turned up at the corners. I've never been kissed on the mouth, she thought. Daniel kissed me on the cheek when it was my birthday. She touched the place as she remembered. That was 'first time as well. She gave a small sigh, but he kissed Grace too, and it wasn't her birthday.

'And so, I've got to make a decision,' he said, and she realized that she hadn't heard a word he'd been saying. 'But I need to talk it over with somebody who isn't involved with me or my family. Somebody who can think logically and say whether I'm being a fool or not. I went to Grace's house, only she's out and I just have to get it off my chest, so I came to you. I hope you don't mind, Ruby? I'm sure you've got more than enough worries of your own.'

So I was second choice, she pondered. Grace was out. She nodded. Well, so be it. 'Can you go over 'basic facts again?' she hedged. 'So that it's clear in my mind.'

'Yes, I was probably rambling, not making sense.' He shifted uncomfortably and crossed his legs.

He's used to sitting on a chair, Ruby supposed. Mattresses are made for lying on, and she considered how it would be to lie with someone like Daniel, with his arms wrapped around her, so that she felt safe and secure.

'Fact is,' he continued, 'I've got two more years before I finish my apprenticeship. Two years before I start earning any kind of reasonable wage.'

How wonderful, she thought. To have that to look forward to. 'Yes – and?'

'Well, I need to earn money now. Da can't, Ma won't, and we've no money left.'

'Can't your da do labouring work?' Ruby didn't mention his mother. Mrs Hanson never spoke to anyone in the court, and she expected that the woman was too proud to do menial tasks such as washing or ironing to earn a living.

'Well, yes! Of course he could,' he answered irritably. 'Only he won't. Says he worked his apprenticeship to become a craftsman.' He gazed into the fire. 'So, I'm going to have to give mine up so that I can earn a living.'

She drew in a breath. 'What? Give up your apprenticeship? Is that allowed?'

He shrugged. 'I'll be breaking a contract. But nobody can stop me. It just means that I'll never be a master craftsman.'

'But what will you do? What kind of work?'

'I've been down to 'docks to look around. There's some foreign ships who are allus on lookout for general dogsbodies. Men who can handle tools and do repair jobs whilst they're at sea.' His expression dropped to one of misery. 'There's some that's not that particular if they don't see proven indentures.'

'It seems a waste,' she murmured. 'If you've onny got two years to go. Why don't you tell your ma and da that that's what you're going to do, then mebbe they'll come to their senses and try to get work.'

He shook his head. 'Ma will have a screaming fit and blame Da for his accident, and Da will be humiliated at having to look for labouring work. I can't put him through that.'

'They've been lucky then, haven't they?' she said, and thought that his father and mother deserved all the misery that came to them. 'Not everybody has had their good fortune.'

'I know,' he sighed. 'Does your ma work?'

'Not any more. She allus did. Sometimes she runs errands for 'traders. But,' she bit her lip and swallowed hard, 'she can't be relied on any more so I've had to tell 'em not to ask her and not to give her any money.'

She saw the question in his eyes, a question that he was too well mannered to ask. At least he's been well brought up, she mused, his parents haven't failed in that respect. 'She has a habit, you see,' she confided. 'She's addicted to opium and spends everything she has to get it.'

'Can't she give it up, or reduce 'amount she takes? I understand it's safe in small doses. It's 'finest thing for pain, they say.'

Ruby shook her head. 'So she can't work.' She ended the conversation. She knew what the final result would be for her mother and she didn't want to discuss it.

'What do you think, then, Ruby? Should I give up my trade for a chance to earn money now?'

She pondered and sighed. 'I've got a similar decision to make, Daniel. I can give up at 'mill.' She laughed grimly. 'Unless, like my boots, it gives up on me first – and I can take on this other work that I've been offered where I'll earn more money but where there's no future.'

He frowned. 'What kind of work?'

'Degrading.' She felt the muscles in her face tighten at the thought of what was to come.

'Don't do anything you'd be ashamed of, Ruby,' he said softly, and folded his hand over hers. She looked down and saw its strength, and a few nicks and scratches from honest work. Jamie had taken her hand too, not an hour before. His were white, soft and unblemished and he had put a shilling into hers. She lifted her eyes to Daniel's and saw his concern.

'I think, Daniel – I think that we have both already made up our minds.'

CHAPTER TWELVE

'Ruby!' Grace hammered on the door. 'Can I come in?'

'I've never stopped today,' Ruby complained good-humouredly. 'I've had a constant stream of visitors.' She put her hand to her forehead and gave a winsome sigh. 'I'm fair wore out.'

'I must tell you.' Grace dropped onto the mattress. 'Where did you get 'coal?' She stared into the fire, which was giving off a steady heat.

'From Jamie,' Ruby said briefly. 'So what have you got to tell me?'

'Well, my da and me went to Dock Green,' Grace said eagerly. 'And you'll never guess! I went onto one of 'speaker's platforms.'

'You did? Why?'

'I was asked my opinion.' Grace drew herself up and lifted her chin. 'This man kept calling me a child and when I said I wasn't a child, but was a working woman, he asked me to step up on 'platform to answer some questions. Do I look like a child, Ruby?' she asked anxiously. 'I don't feel like one.'

Ruby shook her head. 'I don't think so, but

then – ' She pondered. 'I can't remember us ever being children.'

'Me neither,' Grace agreed. 'Anyway, I was just beginning to get into my stride – and do you know, Ruby, I didn't feel a bit nervous speaking in front of all those folk – when I thought I saw one of 'Newmarch brothers from 'mill. And that', she emphasized, 'did make me feel nervous. I thought if he saw me, I might get finished at work.'

'Why?' Ruby frowned. 'Why would you get finished? It's nowt to do with anybody at work what you do in your free time.'

'It's just that 'speaker was asking when did I start work, and saying that it was wrong that children should be in work at all.' Her eyes widened. 'I didn't want him, Mr Newmarch, to think that I was causing trouble.'

'Which one was it? The good-looking one or – '

'It was the one who allus looks serious.' She gave a grin. 'Not Mr Edward who allus looks over his shoulder at us as he rides past in his carriage.'

'How do you know his name is Edward?' Ruby exclaimed.

'I make it my business to find out.' Grace raised her eyebrows knowingly. 'I ask questions. The other one is called Martin.'

'You're a dark horse, Grace.' Ruby contemplated her. 'Everybody thinks you're such an innocent little angel, and I'm onny one who knows you're not! Anyway, you said you onny *thought* you'd seen one of 'brothers.'

Grace nodded. 'Yes, well, it turned out that I was right because – ' She went on to tell Ruby of the grand lady who had offered them a ride in her carriage. 'She would have brought us all 'way home, Ruby, but my da said onny as far as George Street.'

Her mouth turned down and she looked desolate. 'He didn't want her to see where we lived. She asked if she would be shocked by 'conditions and he told her yes. Isn't that awful?' She turned to Ruby. 'I never thought that Da would be ashamed of where we live. But when we came home I tried to look at it through her eyes, this lady's, and I saw it as it was. The alley and both courts were flooded, cos there's no drain. There was rubbish and straw from Mrs Peck's pigpen floating in 'water and one of Mrs Blake's bairns was peeing in 'middle of it cos he couldn't get across to 'privy.'

They both remained silent and gazed into the fire, then Grace murmured, 'What are we going to do?'

'I know what I'm going to do,' Ruby responded bleakly. 'I don't know what you'll do, Grace, but I'll stand up for you as I hope you'll stand up for me.'

'Well, of course you know that I will!' Grace was astonished that Ruby should even have to ask. 'Haven't we always supported each other?'

'Yes, but you don't know what it is that I'm going to do!'

'Rob a bank? Go to 'mill and demand a full week's work?' Grace gave a small concerned smile. 'Is it something really terrible?'

Ruby looked directly into her eyes. 'You might think so, Grace.' Her voice grew tearful. 'And I should hate to lose your friendship. It's 'onny thing I have that I can depend on.'

'You'll never lose that,' Grace whispered. 'Not ever. Ruby, what is it? Tell me!'

'I'm going to work for Jamie.'

They sat until the fire burned low and the room grew dark, Grace detracting and persuading that Ruby should change her mind, and Ruby insisting that there was no other option open to her.

'Maybe tomorrow we'll be put onto full time,' Grace cajoled, though she doubted it. She had listened to others at work and had heard that the cotton mill wasn't thriving, although the Kingston Mill was doing better.

'I need money now,' Ruby insisted. 'I can't expect to be given handouts. I need to work.' She told of Jamie giving her a shilling.

'A shilling! He could afford to give you a shilling!'

Ruby nodded. 'It's half a week's rent, Grace! Think what he's earning. Or at least what his mother is!'

'So, you'll have to give part of what you earn to Jamie?' Grace said slowly. 'What does he do to justify that?'

Ruby bent her head so that Grace wouldn't see how her eyes flooded, and was glad that the room was dark. 'He finds 'customers,' she whispered, 'so I shan't have to hang around street corners. And he'll know where I am, so I'll allus feel safe. I'll be able to buy food and coal, Grace. Ma will be all right, she won't finish up in 'workhouse. I dread 'thought of that.' She sniffled and sat up. 'Ma,' she gasped. 'Where is she?' She scrambled to her feet. 'She's been out since this morning! Did you see her when you walked back home?'

'No! No, I didn't.' Grace also rose to her feet. 'Come on, we'll go and look for her.'

It was still raining and soon they were soaked through. They looked up and down alleys and courts and peered through inn and alehouse windows. They went to Bessie's favourite alehouse, the Tap and Barrel, but she hadn't been seen there at all that day.

'I saw her this morning,' a man volunteered. 'She was heading towards Whalebone arm in arm with a young fella.'

'She hadn't any money to spend on ale,' Ruby gasped as they ran towards the inn. 'I gave her 'last of our money to buy some loddy. I couldn't shut her up,' she wailed. 'I was sick of hearing her moan. I should never have given it to her. She might be dead and it'll be my fault!'

But she wasn't dead. She was sitting by a blazing fire, with her smouldering pipe clenched between her gappy teeth and a half-full glass of ale on the table in front of her. A man was sitting with her.

'Here she is.' Bessie waved an arm when she saw Ruby. 'Here's our Ruby.' Her voice was slurred. 'I knew she'd come looking for her old ma 'ventually.'

'Where've you been all day?' Ruby was furious, her voice cracking with anger and relief. 'I've been worried sick about you.'

'Don't you worry about me, Ruby, love.' Her

mother took her pipe from her mouth. 'I'll allus survive. I've been here all day, I've had a nice dinner. A few of these.' She lifted her glass, then turned to the man who had risen to his feet. 'You don't know who this is, do you?'

Ruby and Grace, their clothes dripping wet and their hair like sodden rat's tails, stared at the complacent Bessie and her companion. 'Well, I'm glad you've found a friend, Ma.' Ruby's voice was filled with sarcasm. 'I hope he knows he'll have to pay, cos we've no money left.'

The man came towards them. He was stockily built, wore an earring and was dressed like a sea-man, with a short jacket and rough twill trousers. 'You don't know me then, Ruby?' He grinned, and then turned to Grace. 'And this must be little Gracie Sheppard?' His eyes appraised her and she took an immediate dislike to him.

'No, I don't know you. Should I? Do you know him, Grace?'

Grace shook her head. 'No, I don't.'

'You've grown up to be beauties, both of you, haven't they, Ma?'

Bessie took her pipe out of her mouth and gave a toothless grin. Then she gulped a long draught from her glass.

'Ma! What do you mean, Ma?' Ruby gave a sudden deep breath and looked acutely at the stranger. 'You're not – Josh?'

He winked. 'Same,' he said. 'Grown up a bit, have I?'

'I'd say you have,' Ruby answered slowly, and wondered if it could be the same brother who had teased and tormented her. 'But it's been a long time.' She had been nearly eight and Josh twelve when he had left to go to sea, and she hadn't seen him since. 'Eight years,' she said. 'Don't tell me that you haven't been back to 'port of Hull in all of that time.'

Josh looked at her from narrowed eyes. 'You allus had a sharp tongue in your head even when you were a bairn,' he said.

'Have you been back?' she persisted. 'Did you not think to drop us a note and let us know that you were still in 'land of 'living?'

'Seamen don't stop long in a port of call,' he said roughly. 'I've been sailing seas for all those years. It's a hard life.'

'So is stopping at home and starving,' she said acidly. 'Looking at you I reckon you've been well fed all those years.'

He stared at her. 'I'd have sent money, but there was never enough time and you can't trust folks to deliver it.'

'No, you can't,' she said and turned to go out. 'You can't trust anybody. Come on, Grace. We know Ma's going to be all right now that her son's come home. Her eldest son, that is.' She turned back and faced him. 'Ask Ma to tell you of her other son. You remember your brother?' Her voice was bitter. 'Young Freddie? He was just a babby when you left home.'

He looked confused for a moment. 'Ah,' he said. 'Yes! Freddie, I'd forgotten about him. He'll be a big chap now, I suppose?'

'We don't know,' Ruby said from between clenched teeth. 'We don't know anything at all.'

'Ruby!' her mother called from her corner. She

had not taken part in the conversation but had stared steadily at her emptying glass. 'I've told Josh he can stay wi' us tonight. We're going to get a jug of ale and have a bit of a party. To celebrate, you know.'

Ruby gave an hysterical laugh. 'Then he'll have to sleep on your half of 'mattress, 'cos he's not sleeping on mine.' She stared her brother in the face. 'And there'll be no party cos I've to be at work in 'morning.'

'Oh, come on, Ruby.' He gave a persuasive smile, which turned her stomach. 'Take 'day off, you'll not be missed.'

'I'll lose wages,' she growled. 'I can't afford to take time off.'

He felt deep into his pocket. 'Here,' he said. 'Take this shilling for now.' He pressed the coin into her hand. 'There's more where that came from.'

She felt hysteria growing inside her as he repeated Jamie's words. This was the kind of man she would have to deal with if she accepted Jamie's offer. She had seen the lascivious look in his eyes as he'd greeted Grace and she couldn't bear it.

She handed the coin back to him. 'No thanks. We've managed without you for nigh on eight years, we can manage a bit longer.' She looked at her mother, whose head was sinking lower and lower onto the table, and went towards her. 'Come on, Ma. Let's have you home.'

Grace moved forward to help her and together they lifted Bessie from her chair. 'You'd best be getting a room here for the night,' Grace murmured to Josh. 'There's no fire at your mother's house, no food or drink and 'court is flooded up to 'step.'

'And no welcome either, by 'look of it,' he muttered. He cast his eyes over Grace and asked softly, 'What about your place, Gracie? Any welcome there?'

'We're three to a bed already,' she replied sharply. 'I don't think my da would be very pleased. He's a bit particular about who shares his bed.'

Josh grinned. 'That's not what I heard.'

'Don't waste your breath on him, Grace.' Ruby didn't even look at her brother. 'Come on, let's get off home, such as it is.'

'Why were you so hard on him, Ruby?' Grace put an arm around Bessie's waist, as did Ruby, and they hauled her down the steps of the inn and into the street. 'You refused his money!'

'Aye, I did. I remember 'day he went away. He was that cocky and full of himself. He said, "Cheerio. Shan't be seeing you again, not if I can help it anyway." ' She stopped for a minute and took a breath. 'I asked him what would happen to us, to Ma and Freddie and me, and he said he didn't know and didn't much care either. I was onny a bairn and I was frightened. He was allus a bully, but even so I didn't like 'thought of being left alone just with Ma and a young babby.'

They walked on, taking Bessie's full weight for she was asleep on her feet. 'Well, you managed, Ruby, didn't you?' Grace said. 'You didn't need him.'

'No, nor my father either. I vowed then that I

would stand on my own two feet and I have.' But what do I do now, she pondered. Do I accept Jamie's offer and rely on him? I don't like 'idea of it. I suppose I don't really trust him, or any other man for that matter. Daniel, she thought. I'd trust him. 'Oh,' she said. 'I forgot to tell you, Grace. I had another visitor today. Daniel. But he was really looking for you. He has something to tell you.'

CHAPTER THIRTEEN

It was a dark and bitterly cold winter morning when they set out for work the next day.
Bessie was still sleeping and Ruby had left the
remainder of the pie on a tin plate next to
the mattress so that her mother would see it
when she awoke. She ate the last of the bread, for
there would be nothing more until work was over
at six that evening.

Grace's mother and father had gone out
before her and Grace locked the door and hid
the key as usual. Her mother had not felt well,
but made little complaint, save a grimace when
she bent to fasten her boots. Her father was
generally taciturn of a morning and they neither
expected nor received any conversation from
him.

Daniel was coming out of his door at the
same time as Grace, and she greeted him. 'Ruby
said you wanted to see me, Daniel. Will it keep
until tonight?' She noticed that his eyes were
shadowed, as if he hadn't slept well. 'Are you all
right?' she asked.

He hesitated and looked around the court.

Other people were emerging from their doors on their way to work. His own door opened and a man came out. He and his wife and children had taken the tenancy of the room above the Hansons, the one where the body had been found. Ruby too was coming towards them.

'Yes, I'm all right,' he agreed. 'I – er, I was going to ask your opinion on something. I talked to Ruby, though, and I know what I'm going to do.'

She felt a fleeting disappointment that she hadn't been there when he called and that Ruby had. 'Was it important?'

He nodded. 'Yes, but I had to make up my own mind. It's my decision.'

'Sounds worrying,' she said, as Ruby caught up with them.

'Everything's worrying,' Ruby remarked. 'You just don't have to let it get you down, and what's more, when you've made up your mind, stick with it and see it through.'

Grace glanced keenly at Ruby, then walked after her out of the court with Daniel following behind. He left them then, as his workshop was in another direction from theirs.

'Good luck, Daniel,' Ruby called after him.

'What's happening? What's Daniel doing?' Grace watched Daniel's retreating back and saw him raise his hand in response, though he didn't turn around.

'I suspect he's giving up his apprenticeship. That's why he wanted to talk to you and came to me instead.' She glanced at Grace. 'Just as well you were out. You'd have tried to persuade him not to, and I let him talk so that he made up his own mind.'

'He did mention it once before,' Grace said thoughtfully. 'But what will he do if he gives up? There's very little work around anyway.'

'He'll join that elite band of men like my brother did. But I can't think he'll turn out 'same. Daniel's going to sea to save his family,' she grieved. 'Unlike Josh who abandoned his.'

'Oh! Oh, Ruby! That means we might not see him again!'

'Oh, he'll be back, don't worry. He's sweet on you, Grace.' Ruby linked her arm into Grace's. 'He'll be back.'

As they approached Wincomlee they saw work-people, men and women, running towards the warehouses by the river, their clogs clattering on the cobbles. 'Are we late?' Grace pulled at Ruby's arm and they hurried their steps.

'I'm sure we're not!'

Other people were rushing in the same direction, hundreds of them, and they could hear a great commotion of shouts and shrieks. 'Summat's happened.' Grace started to run. 'Somebody's fallen in 'river!'

Pandemonium was rippling through the crowd of onlookers who were gathered at the riverside and staring down into the water below, from where came terrible cries of distress. Men were stretched out at the staithe edge and holding their arms down towards the dark water, and as Grace and Ruby ran towards them, one man pulled off his boots and jumped in and then another did the same.

'Poor bairns! Poor bairns!' a woman shrieked. 'Get them out! Get them out!'

'What's happened? What's happened?' They tried to peer over the heads of the crowd but there was such a crush and it was still dark and the river was black, though they could see a grey shape in the middle and flickering lanterns on the other side.

'It's 'ferry! It's turned over,' another woman told them, her face stricken. 'Folks is drowning! There's some bairns in there. Irish!'

Ruby and Grace stared horrified at each other and ignored the wail of the hooter which was calling them to work. 'What can we do?' Grace pushed her way forward. 'What can we do?'

One of the men who had jumped into the river was swimming towards the overturned boat. He dived beneath and disappeared, then reappeared, holding somebody up from the water. They watched as he swam back to the staithe side. He held up the limp form of a child. 'Get a hook,' he shouted. 'Look sharp. Pull her out.'

Grace looked around. There was a lamp hanging on a warehouse wall and by its light she saw a grappling hook next to it. She rushed to get it. As she dashed back, another man took it from her and kneeling down he leaned precariously towards the river and hooked it into the child's garments, pulling her towards the riverbank.

'I can't lift her,' he gasped. 'Weight's too much, 'pole'll snap. Get a rope!'

Someone threw a rope into the water and the man who had rescued the girl tied it around her.

Grace stood back to make room for the men who were dragging the child from the water. She looked across the narrow river. Someone was hauling a body from under the ferry. Boatmen on the other side were feverishly untying ropes from the wharves to tug off their boats and go to assist. Young men were jumping in the river and trying to help those who were in difficulties, others were rushing towards the Charterhouse steps where a small boat was tied up. What sickened her was the sight of bodies floating in the water, mostly women and children, who had set out for work and been overtaken by disaster.

She turned when she felt a pull on her skirt. It was Ruby, her face ashen and her mouth trembling as she spoke. 'Come away, Grace. We can do nowt here.'

Grace shook her head. 'No. You go. I want to stay. To help if I can.'

Ruby walked away and Grace turned back to the staithe side where a crowd had gathered around the body of the child. She pushed her way through and looked down. The girl was about ten years old, her plaited reddish hair caught with detritus from the river and her blue eyes wide open.

Grace bent down and gently closed her eyelids, removed shreds of green slime from her mouth and touched her cold cheek. 'Does anyone know who she is?' Her voice was choked.

'She'll be from 'Groves if she was on 'ferry,' a voice said. 'Irish more'n likely.'

There had been a murmuring from the crowd

behind her but they started to disperse as one of the foremen from the mill appeared. 'You can do no more. River men are on their way, they'll know what to do. You, you and you.' He pointed to some of the men. 'Stay here to help. Rest of you get to work or you'll lose wages.' He crouched down beside Grace and the girl. 'Do you know any of these people?' Other bodies were being laid out on the staithe side whilst those who had been rescued were weeping and clutching at those near them.

'No. Some of 'em by sight. Can we have some sheets to cover them?' she asked. 'It's not right for them to be laid here like this for all to see. It's not respectful.'

The foreman nodded and called to the women who were walking away, telling them to send back some imperfect cotton sheeting to cover the bodies.

'If I put in a note to say why you're absent, will you stop here?' he asked Grace. 'I have to get back, we've a big consignment of raw cotton coming in from 'docks. I have to be there when it arrives.'

'But what shall I do?' She looked around. Most people had drifted away, leaving one or two women who were comforting those who had been rescued, and a group of men who were organizing the shipping in the river and discussing how best to move the stricken ferry boat and bring out any other victims.

He took a notebook from his pocket and a pencil from behind his ear and handed them to her. 'Make a note of who's who, find out 'names of those who've perished if you can and where they live. We'll have to notify authorities and next of kin.' He pushed his hair back from his forehead and blew out a breath. 'Phew! What a mess.'

'And 'managers of 'mill,' Grace reminded him. 'They'll need to know.'

He stood up. 'As soon as they come in I'll tell 'em, but they'll not be here yet. Mr Emerson allus said there'd be a tragedy on this ferry one day.' He was speaking of the director who had resigned from the board. 'Folks jumping around, not sitting still. 'Boat wasn't stable.'

But it is the quickest way to get across the river, Grace thought. Otherwise the workpeople from the Groves had to walk a fair distance to the North Bridge in order to cross over.

By eight o'clock she had all the names of those who had survived and most of the people who had drowned, including the child, and she didn't know why she felt a sickening certainty that it was the little Irish girl that Daniel had spoken of. She then took it upon herself to requisition a waggon and driver from the mill to take the survivors home for the day, and told them that she would intervene with the mill foreman and ask him not to stop their wages. She had spoken to the constable and sergeant who had arrived and passed on all the details which she had available, and the bodies were taken away.

'By, you've saved us some time, miss,' the sergeant said as she handed the list to him. Then he frowned. 'This child who drowned. How come she was on her own? There's nobody else of that

149

name on this list. Does her ma not work at 'mill as well?'

'I don't know,' Grace answered. 'I've not seen her before.'

'We'll have to inform somebody.' The sergeant looked again at the list and pursed his lips. 'I hate this job sometimes. One of 'worst things is telling a mother her bairn is dead.' He looked at Grace. 'Do you want to come?'

'Come where?' Grace was puzzled. 'To her house, do you mean?' And when he nodded, she said, 'I'm supposed to be at work.'

They all looked up as someone approached them. The constable saluted and Grace dipped her knee. It was Martin Newmarch.

'I came as soon as I heard,' he said to the sergeant. 'Terrible business. How many fatalities?'

'Fourteen, sir,' Grace answered before the sergeant could check the list. 'Twelve of them women and children.'

He shook his head despairingly and gave a soft exclamation. 'Do we know how this catastrophe occurred?'

'We haven't had 'opportunity to establish that as yet, sir.' The sergeant shuffled his feet. 'But there is a possibility that 'ferry was overloaded.'

'There was also some talk that 'passengers were running from one side to the other, sir,' Grace broke in. 'Just having a bit of fun. But then 'boat started to tip.'

He gazed at her. 'Did you see it happen?'

'No, sir, but I've been talking to some of those who were saved.'

He glanced around at the staithe. It was getting lighter now, a thin ray of dawn in the sky. Only boatmen and bargemen who worked the river were there. 'Where are they? The survivors?'

Grace bit her lip. 'They've gone home, sir. I— They were in no fit state to work.'

'Of course. Quite right. Well, Sergeant, I'll leave you and your men to get on with the grim task of telling the relatives – or would you like me to come with you? Most of them would be our workers, I suppose?'

'Some were from Kingston Mill, sir, from up yonder.' Grace nodded up Wincomlee. Both mills had warehouses on either side of the river. 'I've written on 'list where they worked.'

Newmarch put his hand out for the list which the sergeant held. 'You did this?' he asked Grace.

'Yes, sir. 'Foreman asked me if I would.'

'Was there no-one in authority here?' He frowned. 'No-one from either of the mills?'

'It was early, there were only work folk here. Everybody was doing what they could,' Grace protested. 'Men from 'yards, women too. The boatmen tried to put their boats out to save some of them but 'tide was against them. By 'time they got them floated off, it was too late.' She gave a little sob, the enormity of the tragedy suddenly hitting her.

'Yes, yes, I didn't mean – ' he floundered, looking at her. 'I'm quite sure everyone did what they could. But there should have been someone here – one of the managers, to look after the survivors and see they got safely home.'

Grace was silent. No need now to fear any

trouble for using the waggon and driver. Martin Newmarch was feeling guilty that there hadn't been someone in authority to take charge.

The sergeant and his constable touched their foreheads and moved away to talk to the boatmen. Grace seized the opportunity and asked, 'Mr Newmarch? Will it be possible for those who survived and have gone home to be paid their wages? I know it wasn't fault of 'mill owners that 'ferry went over, but those people will badly miss a day's money.'

'I'll look into it,' he said. His mouth twitched slightly. 'And what about you? Will you expect to be paid too?'

She gazed up at him, at his square chin, solemn face and dark eyes. 'I don't expect anything, sir, and I'll go back to work now that I've finished here. But 'foreman did ask me to stay. He said he'd put in a note about why I wasn't at work.'

'Did he?' He continued to gaze down at her and she began to feel uncomfortable under his scrutiny. Then he gave a slight smile. 'Well, he chose very well. What's your name?'

'Grace Sheppard, sir.'

He nodded. 'I think I've seen you before, Miss Sheppard.' His brown eyes seemed to bore into her. 'Now what do you think about coming along with me to comfort those who have lost relatives? A woman's sympathy is always a help, don't you think, and – ' He hesitated. 'A manager of a company often makes people uncomfortable. I don't know why, do you?'

She wasn't sure if he really expected an

answer, but she replied in a candid manner. 'Well, sir, you have their livelihoods in your hands. I expect they're afraid of you.'

He stared at her for a moment, then blinked as if he suddenly remembered who he was, and that it wasn't circumspect to have a discussion out here with a lowly member of his workforce. She saw him visibly stiffen as he said briskly, 'Go inside and tell the foreman that you are coming with me, then meet me at the front entrance in five minutes.'

She dipped her knee and left him. The front entrance! She had never been there before, only through the mill doors at the back of the building. She hurried, thinking it might take her some time to find the foreman, but as luck would have it he was in the mill yard supervising men on a delivery waggon who were unloading bales of raw cotton.

She told him where she was going and he pulled a wry face. 'Mixing wi' management, are we? Get in his good books and he'll be mekking you a supervisor next!'

She hurried away and as she turned a corner to the front of the building she almost collided with Edward Newmarch, who was coming the other way.

'Whoa!' He caught hold of her arm. 'Where are you dashing off to?'

'Beggin' your pardon, sir. To see Mr Martin Newmarch.' Her face flushed. 'I've to meet him at 'front. I'm going with him to see 'bereaved relatives.'

'Ah, very well. Off you go, then.' He looked her

up and down. 'But no rush, he's still in the office.' He nodded to her and she continued on to the front entrance where the chaise, which she and Ruby often saw the Newmarch brothers driving, was waiting by the steps.

If we ride in that, she mused, then that will be the second time I have ridden in a carriage.

'Are you admiring the cab?' Martin Newmarch came up behind her.

'Yes, sir. It's very handsome.' It had a shining black leather hood, which was closed because of the weather, and red painted wheels.

'My brother and I share it.' He opened the door of the cabriolet and invited her to step inside.

'Yes, I've seen you driving it,' she said.

He climbed up at the front and took the reins. 'Do you know how to get to the Groves?' he called to her. 'Most of the people who died seem to live there – did live there,' he corrected himself.

'I know where it is, sir,' she called back and kept the window down so that he could hear her. 'We need to be across 'North Bridge. I'll direct you from there, though we shan't be able to drive down some of 'streets.'

'Oh! Why is that?' He shook the reins and they moved off.

'There'll be no room for 'carriage, sir. Streets will be too narrow. You'll have to find a lad – a boy, to hold 'horse's head.'

She ran her hands across the seat as she was speaking, for she knew he couldn't see her. The seats were covered in a pale blue leather and by the window a brass lantern swung. She sighed. It would be nothing to the Newmarch brothers to drive in such a carriage as this, they did it every day. No walking in the rain and cold for them. She thought of the young lady who had given her and her father a ride in her carriage. She had wanted to let her gaze wander around that too, but was afraid that she would be considered curious.

It wasn't as elegant as this carriage, she decided, but the lady was lovely and wearing such rich-looking clothes. A navy blue dress with a bustle and over it a grey travelling coat trimmed with navy velvet. Grace had noticed her neat leather boots and had self-consciously tucked her own worn boots beneath her skirt.

She sighed again just as Martin Newmarch called to her. 'I'm sorry, I didn't think. Are you feeling uneasy about visiting these people? Would you rather not have come?'

'No, I'm all right, sir. Just sad, especially about the little girl.'

'Yes. She was too young to be at work.'

Grace glanced through the small window which faced the front. She saw the back of his dark hair beneath his top hat and the velvet collar of his coat, and wondered if he really meant it or was only saying it.

They clattered over the old bridge and turned left along the other side of the river Hull, down Cleveland Street which was lined with factories and mills and into Lime Street and towards the Groves.

'I hadn't realized they had to come so far if

they walked,' Martin Newmarch muttered. 'So that's why they use the old ferry.' He slowed the horse to a walk. 'Are we nearly there?' he called to her.

'Just a little further, sir. Turn right here.' They turned into a narrow unmade road and he drew to a halt. Ahead of them was a mass of houses, cramped courts and alleys.

'I can't drive any further,' he said sharply. 'The wheels will get bogged down. Are you sure this is the place?'

'Quite sure, sir.' She opened the door and stepped out. 'Shall I go into this inn and ask if somebody can mind 'horse and carriage?'

He put his hand to his nose. 'Yes, if you will. No, wait. It might not be safe for you to go in alone.'

She looked up at him. 'It's perfectly safe, sir. Are you feeling all right?'

He nodded, keeping his hand to his nose. 'What's that awful smell? It's not whale blubber, I'm used to that now.'

'It'll be 'drain, I expect. Sutton drain runs alongside here. 'Muckgarths run into it.' She gave a laugh. 'If you think it's bad now, sir, you should be here in 'summer. Even 'residents get sick with the smell.'

He stared down at her as she stood below him. His eyes were wide and watery as he strove not to take a breath. 'Be quick then,' he muttered. 'See if you can find someone willing to earn a shilling.'

She was about to say that sixpence would be enough just for holding a horse's head for half an

156

hour, but then decided that if Mr Newmarch had a shilling to spare, someone would count it as their lucky day.

A young boy was sitting on the flagged floor inside the inn doorway. He was poorly and thinly clad for such a cold day, without even a muffler around his neck. His feet were bare and, as he got up so that Grace could pass, she saw that he was also very lame, with one leg much shorter than the other.

'Do you want a job?' she whispered. 'Worth a shilling!'

She saw the amazement on his face, which quickly turned to eagerness. 'You've just to look after a horse and carriage for half an hour. Mek sure nobody messes about with it.'

He nodded and followed her into the street. 'And if 'gentleman asks,' she said in a low voice, 'tell him you're used to hosses.'

'I am,' he whispered in return. 'I go and help feed horses off 'coal waggons. Waggon master gives me a penny. I can't do owt else on account of my leg.'

'Here we are, Mr Newmarch,' she called. 'Here's an experienced lad.'

Martin Newmarch looked doubtfully at the ragged boy, but then jumped down from his seat and told him to fasten the reins to a nearby post and stay with the horse and vehicle. 'If you're not here when we get back,' he said severely, 'I shall search you out. Make no mistake about it.'

The boy grinned. His face was dirty and his hair matted as if it had never been brushed. 'I'll be here, sir. No matter how long you tek.'

'Very well.' Martin looked towards the dark houses which seemed to crowd dejectedly into each other, then looked down at his shiny boots and the muddy road. He turned up his coat collar and glanced at Grace. 'Let's be off then.'

CHAPTER FOURTEEN

They walked in silence down the road, Martin Newmarch picking his way fastidiously to avoid the streams of thick dirty water which were running towards the drain. At the side of the road was an open stagnant ditch, overflowing with fetid liquid which filled the potholes and crevices.

Grace pulled a face. She had heard it was very bad down here. Not only did the residents have to put up with the stench from the factories, the blubber yards and the soot from the mill chimneys, but there were no drains and nowhere to throw dirty water or rubbish. It was worse, she thought, much worse than Middle Court. She wriggled her feet. The cardboard in her boots had gone soggy and she could feel mud squelching between her toes.

'God in heaven!'

She looked up at Mr Newmarch's muttered exclamation. 'Sir?'

He shook his head. 'I can't believe that people have to live like this!'

'We're not there yet, sir,' she said. 'It could be worse.'

'Nonsense,' he replied briskly. 'It can't possibly be any worse.'

But it was. As they turned into the first court where they had been told the little girl had lived, they were confronted by intolerable squalor. Few of the houses had doors as they had been chopped up and burnt for firewood, and the windows were covered over with cardboard or pieces of rag to keep out the cold. The privies had no doors either and were open, not only to the elements but to any passer-by.

They approached one of the houses to make an enquiry, and were hailed by a voice from another open doorway. The sergeant and his constable were there already with the householder, a woman who was holding her apron up to her face.

'This is 'little lass's grandmother, sir.' The sergeant addressed Martin Newmarch. 'Seems that word has got here afore us.'

'I'm so sorry.' Martin walked across to them. 'So very sorry for your loss.'

The woman stared at him as if not comprehending who he was or why he was there. Grace stepped forward. 'Mr Newmarch is a manager of 'mill where your Nancy worked,' she said softly. 'He's come to offer condolences and ask if there's owt he can do to help.'

'Can't bring her back, can he?' the old woman said bitterly. 'For all his wealth, that's one thing he can't do.'

'No,' Grace said. 'No-one can do that.' She hesitated, guessing from the woman's Irish accent that she might be a Catholic. 'Was Nancy a good child?'

'That she was.' The woman's eyes filled with tears. 'Had her First Communion. Went to church this morning before she went to work.'

'Then she's safe in the Lord's hands,' Grace whispered. 'And you'll see her again in heaven.'

The woman nodded and wiped her eyes. 'Come in. Come in.' She beckoned Grace and Mr Newmarch into a small room filled with people who had come to grieve. All the women wore black with black shawls on their heads, and the men too wore dark clothing. On the wall above the hearth, where a low fire burned, was a crucifix.

'This is Nancy's daddy.' The grandmother indicated a young dark-haired man. 'She had no mammy, she died when Nancy was only a weanling. These two are her uncles and these her aunties and cousins.'

Grace heard Martin Newmarch give a slight cough behind her. 'You are very fortunate to have so many relatives to comfort you,' he said diffidently. 'So good of them to come to support you in your grief.'

The woman gave a ghost of a smile and was about to say something, when Nancy's father got to his feet. His eyes were red, the lids swollen as if with weeping. 'They always support us, sir. We support each other. We have to, for no-one else will.' He looked around at the gathering, 'Isn't that right, brothers and sisters? We live together, starve together and comfort each other when our children die. This is our home, such as it is, and you're very welcome to join us in our prayers for Nancy. The priest is on his way and, God bless her, we'll give her a good send-off.'

Martin gazed at the man, who was probably the same age as he was. He had handsome features with long unruly hair but was shabbily dressed, and Martin wondered why he was here, so far from his native land. The railways, he decided, perhaps he or his father came to work on the railways as so many Irish did.

'I regret we cannot stay,' he said. 'There are other families to visit who have also lost loved ones. Are you in work?' he asked abruptly. 'Do you have a trade?'

'Ah! Just at the minute now, I don't. Work for the Irish seems to have dried up. That's why young Nancy was working at the mill, along with her cousins.' He pointed to two young girls of about ten or eleven, who sat with wide frightened eyes close to their mothers. 'They are blessed by the Lord,' he said softly, and crossed himself, as did the women of the group. 'The ferry was full when they came to get on it and were turned away. They'd set off to walk to the mill when they saw the tragedy and returned home.'

Martin nodded. So no wages for them, he thought. What then will they do? How will they pay for the funeral, and the wake? The Irish always have a wake. At least they do for an adult, I don't know about a child. 'Would you come outside for a moment?' he asked, determined to offer the young man money, if he would take it. 'I'd like to have a word.'

Grace shook hands with all the members of the family before following Mr Newmarch and

Nancy's father outside, with the grandmother close behind her.

'Bless you for coming, child.' She pressed Grace's hand. 'You've brought us comfort by your presence.' She put her head on one side. 'But how would I place you now? Beggin' your pardon, but you're not of Mr Newmarch's ilk?'

'No,' Grace agreed. 'I'm not. I'm nobody really. Just one of 'workers from the mill, but Mr Newmarch asked me if I'd come with him.'

'You're nobody, are you? Just like us!' The old woman nodded knowingly. 'Listen to me, child. One day you'll be somebody, but you'll not forget your roots. That I know. God bless you.'

Grace turned away. She was not given to religious beliefs, yet strangely, having come to offer comfort to those bereaved, she felt that somehow, by the woman's blessing, she had received comfort herself.

They visited several other bereaved families in the company of the sergeant and then walked back to the carriage. The boy was still standing by the horse's head and surrounded by a crowd of onlookers, mostly young people, who melted away when they saw the owner approaching.

'They wanted to look inside 'carriage,' the boy said. 'Onny I wouldn't let 'em. Said it was more'n my life was worth!'

'You did well,' Martin said in a subdued tone, and handed Grace a shilling to give him.

'Thank you, sir.' The boy looked down at the coin as if he never really expected to see so much, even though it had been promised. 'Any time you're this way again, just ask for Luke. Everybody knows me.'

'Thank you,' Martin replied. 'But I don't expect to be this way again.'

He looked at Grace. 'Come up to the front beside me,' he said. 'It's not cold, there's a blanket on the seat.'

Grace hid a smile. Mr Newmarch didn't know what the cold was. It wasn't feeling the sharp wind on your face as you rode atop a carriage. It was cold when you had no boots for your feet. It was cold when you had no fire, and water ran down the walls of the room where you lived, and when your mattress and blankets were damp and rain seeped through onto the floor.

She had smelt and felt the damp in that small room where the Irish were gathered, and knew that the neighbours had collected together and generously provided fuel for the fire so that the family could grieve in a little comfort. She had seen the pile of old blankets in a corner of the room and knew that the fifteen or so people, men, women and children, were not visiting their relatives in a time of grief, but that that was where they lived. Every single one of them.

'Tell me,' Martin Newmarch said as they drove away. 'Why did the foreman ask you to stay and help? Did he know of your ability to cope in such circumstances?'

'I don't know, sir.' She had wondered about it herself. 'I've never done anything like that before. Never had to deal with such tragedy.' She pondered. 'I did ask if we could cover up 'bodies, it didn't seem respectful to leave them just lying there. Then he asked me to stop and make a list of everybody.'

'Well, thank you anyway.' He glanced at her. 'You're a very capable young woman.'

'Thank you, sir,' she smiled. At least he didn't call her a child as so many others did.

'I saw you at Dock Green last Sunday,' he said suddenly. 'Why were you there?'

She felt a fleeting sense of dismay, then decided to be quite frank. She could do as she wished on her day off. 'I asked my father to take me to hear the speakers. He was telling me about one of 'speakers who used to come to Hull. Somebody called Vincent who spoke of helping 'poor folks.'

'Vincent! Ah!' He turned again and appraised her. 'And did he, do you think?'

She shook her head. 'I don't think so, Mr Newmarch. Nobody can. There's too many of us.'

'So are you poor?' he asked. 'Does your father not work?'

'He works as a labourer on 'docks, but he's been put onto short time, 'same as me. And my ma has hurt her back which is no good when you're a washerwoman and have to lug pails of water and wet washing about.' She stopped. He hadn't asked for a family report and she hadn't answered his question. 'But we're not as poor as them Irish back at 'Groves. We have a bowl of broth every night, and bread for breakfast, and we manage to pay 'rent every week.'

'I see.' They turned to drive across the bridge. 'And you're on – what? Three days a week?'

'Yes, sir,' she said meekly, and pondered that she had probably said too much. 'Monday, Friday and Saturday.'

He drove on for a while, then said, 'Well, I'll see what I can do about increasing your hours – but I can't promise,' he added hastily. 'It wouldn't be fair to the other workers. But I'll make sure that you get your full wages for today.' He remained silent until they drew up at the mill entrance, when he thanked her for her help. He assisted her down from the high seat and said quietly, 'You could do something better than being a mill girl, you know.'

'I never learned a trade, sir. If I'd known, I could have been a weaver or a spinner.' She gave a deep sigh. 'And it's too late now.'

The whole mill was buzzing over the ferry tragedy. Many of the workpeople knew someone who knew someone who had been on the boat, or who had just missed being on the boat or would have been on the boat if something or other hadn't happened. The management wisely let them talk for half an hour, and then called them to order.

Ruby couldn't concentrate on any of her jobs and was twice rebuked by the foreman. She had left a pail of water in the middle of a walkway where someone had almost fallen over it, and had not finished wiping down one of the frames as she had been requested to do. Then she was seen talking to one of the managers and the foreman thought that she was in trouble over something.

'I'm not!' she claimed. 'Mr Newmarch asked me if I knew anyone on 'ferry boat that sank this morning. I don't know why he stopped to ask me, but he did!'

He had sought her out, she was sure of it. She had looked up and seen him on one of the upper walkways looking down. The next thing, he was by her side. He had a folder under his arm as if he was going about his business, but he stopped to speak and she felt quite embarrassed because, as he questioned her, he stared at her bare feet and ankles.

Grace is such a long time, she thought as she wielded her mop. I wonder if she's gone home? I couldn't have stayed there, not when they were pulling bodies out of the water. She shuddered. Grace has stronger backbone than me.

She saw her later in the morning as Grace came back into the mill, and saw her speak briefly to the foreman. He nodded his head and then pointed her in the direction he wanted her to work. She gave a little wave to Ruby and mouthed that she would see her later, but it was six o'clock before they were able to catch up with each other.

'Where've you been?' Ruby asked as they walked away from the mill. 'I was beginning to think you'd gone home.'

'Home? Why would I have gone home and lost my wages?'

'I thought you might have been upset over

what happened. There'll be an inquiry, won't there?'

'Yes, I expect so,' Grace said slowly. 'Ruby, I've had such a strange day and I am upset and it's just beginning to tell on me.' She put her hand to her forehead. 'I've got such a headache.'

Ruby put her arm through Grace's. 'Do you want to sit down for a minute?'

'Yes, I think I do.' There was a stack of crates outside a warehouse nearby and they went towards it and hoisted themselves up. 'I haven't given myself time to think about all those poor people who died, even though I went to see the relatives. Now the horror of it all is creeping up on me.'

'You went to see 'relatives?' Ruby's eyebrows shot up in astonishment. 'Why was that?'

'First the sergeant and then Mr Newmarch asked me if I'd go with them. 'Sergeant said he hated having to tell of a child's death – and, and I don't know why Mr Newmarch wanted me to go.' She puzzled, a frown on her forehead. 'Something to do with a woman's sympathy, and he said that people were uncomfortable with a company manager around.'

She looked up as the Newmarches' carriage rattled by. Edward Newmarch was driving and he lifted his whip as he passed them. 'I've been in that carriage today,' she pronounced and Ruby stared at her, her mouth open. Grace laughed and felt better. 'I have, honest! I rode inside going towards 'Groves, and on 'outside coming back.'

'Why?' Ruby breathed. 'Why did you do that?'

Grace shook her head. 'Mr Newmarch asked me to. I think he wanted to talk to me.'

'What about?'

'About being poor.' She jumped down from the crates. 'Come on, let's go home. It's been a long day.'

CHAPTER FIFTEEN

'Appalling! Appalling! Appalling!' Martin Newmarch beat his fist on his knees as his brother
drove them out of the mill gates. 'I couldn't
believe the squalor. The mess. The stench! There
were even pigpens in some of the courts that we
passed. And rats! Monstrous!'

'How can people live like that?' Edward
shuddered. 'They can have no sensibilities at all.'

'No. No! You don't understand! They're not
choosing to live that way. There is no other way
for them!'

'Oh, what tosh! They could do something
about it if they wanted to. They don't have to
keep pigs. And they could at least keep clean.'

'A woman threw a pail of dirty water into the
street as we were passing,' Martin went on, 'and
when I remonstrated against her, this young girl
– Grace Sheppard, who went with me – asked
what should the woman have done with it, if
there were no drains to pour it down?' He lifted
his shoulders in exasperation. 'I had no answer
to that.'

He looked down at his boots, which had been

polished that morning and were now caked with mud, in spite of his having scraped them before entering the mill. For the first time in his life he had felt inadequate, imbued with a sense of helplessness as he had viewed those dilapidated houses, the stinking courts and the state of misery in which the people he had visited spent their lives.

'So why did you take the girl with you?' Edward asked. 'What was your motive?'

'She seemed so capable,' he said. 'She was on the staithe side organizing lists of those who had died and those survivors whom she had sent home.' Martin gave a dry laugh. 'She'd even, without a by your leave, sent them home in one of our waggons! But it wasn't because of that.' He took off his top hat and ran his fingers through his hair, letting the wind catch it as if blowing away the day's troubles. 'I thought that she might know what to say to these people, being from the same class, and of course she did, much better than I could.'

Edward nodded but didn't reply, being caught up with his own thoughts. He saw the two girls as they sat on a crate at the side of the road and lifted his whip, knowing that his brother was too engrossed in frustrated anger to notice.

He'd looked for the dark-haired girl again that morning. It was beginning to be an obsession, this searching, hoping to catch a glimpse of her. They'd arrived early at the mill, Martin wanting a prompt start to the day, something or other he needed to do. Edward had been reluctant, he hated to be out so early, but Martin had insisted and, as they shared a chaise, he had had to submit.

But as it turned out, Martin's plans had come to nothing, for on arriving at the mill they were greeted by the news of the tragedy on the river. Martin had set off immediately to the scene and Edward had gone in to calm the workers. It was his own suggestion that they be given time to talk it out, to exchange views on how the disaster had happened and to let out their grief, for many of them would have known the victims.

He'd looked down from one of the upper floors and watched the groups of workers as, after they had finished talking and with much shaking of heads, they started to drift back to their work stations, and it was then that he saw her. He'd hurried down the stairs and caught up with her as she swabbed the floor with her mop.

His eyes were drawn to her bare feet. Her skirts were tied up and he could see her ankles and the fleshy curve of her calves. He looked at her face as he spoke to her, but his glance was constantly shifting back to her naked feet. They were small and white with straight toes and splashed with dirty water from her mop, and he thought that he had never before seen anything so erotic.

He stayed to talk only as long as it was possible without arousing suspicion, but he cursed himself as he walked away, for he had forgotten to ask her name.

'What do you think of her?' The question he asked of Martin was unintentional, emerging as a spontaneous thought.

'What do you mean, what do I think of her?' Martin was irritable and answered sharply. 'I just said that she seemed capable. She's wasted at the mill doing menial tasks, but I have no other thoughts about her. Why should I have?'

Edward shook his head but didn't continue with the conversation. He hadn't meant Grace Sheppard, as Martin had naturally assumed. He had been thinking of the dark girl and her bare feet, not the fair one.

I'll try to arrange a meeting with Emerson, Martin mused. He's always been concerned about the poor, he'll have something to say about the conditions those people are living in. He has some influence, I believe, with the City Fathers. And Georgiana too, she would be interested in what I have to tell her. If, that is, she can tear herself away from the issues of women's rights. He gave a silent grunt. Women like Georgiana don't have any concerns when compared with the wretches I have seen today. And as for the girl, Grace Sheppard . . . Why would Edward ask what I think of her? An odd question. I could make her a supervisor, I suppose. She's competent and steady, but on the other hand . . . He remembered seeing her on the platform at Dock Green. She might make trouble. She would always be on the side of the workers, not the management. I'd bet a sovereign on it.

He gave a slight smile as his thoughts wandered to their meeting on the riverside this morning. Her fair hair had come loose and was blowing in the breeze, and her skirt fluttered about her. She had raised her head as she spoke to him and he was put in mind of a figurehead, sweeping indomitably through a billowing sea at the prow of a sailing ship.

She's as slight as a willow, he mused. So fragile-looking that you would think she would snap in half. She's young, but I reckon she has an inner strength that no-one, not even she, yet knows of. She told me that the workers were afraid of me, or at least of management, because we held their lives in our hands. But she wasn't afraid. She fixed me with those deep blue eyes and without saying the actual words, she showed me that she wasn't.

He took a deep breath. You could be dangerous, Miss Sheppard. You disturb me. So, I'm sorry, but it's back to washing the mill floor.

I have to see her. Edward lashed the horse onward as they reached the open road. She's driving me mad! Or some other woman who can take the passion out of me. For heaven's sake! he silently remonstrated. I'm getting married in a couple of months' time. I have to get this out of my system. I'll frighten poor little May to death if I don't do something about it! I'll go and find that young fellow. He said he knew of an older woman. She'd take the heat out of me. Nothing wrong with that, he reasoned. It's what men do. Can't go upsetting their wives with their demands. As long as the woman was – well – all right. I'd have to take precautions, of course.

A few doubts crept into his mind. He was quite a fastidious man. He liked his shaving tackle laid out properly every morning, his sideburns and beard neatly trimmed, his shoes well polished. Of course he didn't have to do those things himself but he liked to see that they were done. And he wouldn't want misgivings about the cleanliness of any woman he might encounter.

But I'll search him out, he decided. If I can remember where it was that I came across him. Yes. That's what I'll do. Just enquire. And then I'll think about it for a day or two. Give myself a chance to change my mind. But Saturday evening would be a good time and I can say that I'm going to my club.

'I've done it, Grace. I've asked to be released from my indentures.' Daniel's face was white and strained. He had knocked on her door after her mother and father had gone off to work.

'What did your master say? Was he angry?' Grace was anxious for him, he looked so upset.

Daniel nodded. 'He said I was a fool, but he seemed more angry about my father. He said he'd told him that he would give him a labouring job any time he wanted, but that he was totally stubborn and wouldn't accept.'

He sighed. 'He asked me to think it over but I said that I had already. Can I come in?' he continued. 'I want to ask you something.'

She opened the door wider to admit him. There was a low fire burning in the hearth. She had lit it as she wasn't at work that morning, and had decided that she would prepare some broth and cook it ready for the evening when her parents came home. It was the first time that

Daniel had been inside and she invited him to sit down in her father's chair.

'No, thank you. I'd rather stand if you don't mind, but please, you sit.' He took two or three paces about the room and saw that it was neat as a pin, the wooden table scrubbed and the blankets folded tidily.

'I've already got the promise of a ship,' he said bluntly. 'It sails on Friday. I shall be away six or seven months.'

She took a deep breath. 'So long!' she murmured. 'I shall miss you, Daniel.'

'And I shall miss you,' he said softly, and knelt beside the chair and took her hand. 'I know we said that we would just be good friends, but I'm very fond of you, Grace, and I know that I'll think of you all the time I'm away.'

She squeezed his hand. 'Is it too late to change your mind?'

'No.' He shook his head. 'It isn't. My boss said would I go in today and say for certain if I was leaving. He said he wouldn't cancel my contract until then and would give me the option of returning.'

'But you won't?' she said. 'Return, I mean?'

'Only to collect my things. My tool bag and a sack of bits and pieces that I've made since I began my apprenticeship.'

'What did your ma and da say when you told them you were giving up?'

He rose to his feet and stared into the fire, then looked at Grace. 'I haven't told them. I shan't tell them until it's done.'

'But –' she began. 'If your da –'

'No buts,' he said harshly. 'I've decided. And anyway I couldn't stand it if Da was labouring under me. Think of how he would feel, and Ma, she'd never give up grumbling and picking on Da and telling him constantly about what she's had to give up.'

'So what you're really doing is leaving so that they don't have to consider you? They're going to have to make their own decisions on how they'll live?' She shook her head. 'Daniel! You're cutting off your nose to revenge your face! Tell them! Give them a chance to do something before you make 'final decision.'

'No,' he said, and she thought that he was probably just as stubborn as his father was. 'Decision is made.' His mouth turned down. 'I thought that you would understand!'

'I do,' she replied. 'But it doesn't mean that I think what you're doing is right.'

He turned to the door. 'I must go. I'll come back later and bring you this sack of stuff.' He sounded very despondent. 'It's of no value, you can use it for 'fire. Da can get plenty of firewood from 'woodyard. They'll not be without a fire – if they can be bothered to make it,' he muttered.

'You were going to ask me something,' she said. 'What was it?'

'Oh, yes.' He looked down at his boots. 'I wondered, well – that is,' he glanced at her from soft grey eyes. 'I know I'm leaving them in 'lurch, Ma and Da, and it's not because I don't care about them. It's just that I've had enough, I want to do something with my life, Grace. I want to make some mark so that I know that I've lived.'

'Yes,' she whispered. 'I can understand that. So many people disappear without trace, as if they've never been.'

'So what I wondered,' he went on. 'Would you mind keeping an eye on them – Ma and Da?' He gave a slight grin and she knew that the old Daniel was still there, just hidden from view for the moment. 'Listen out to make sure they're not murdering one another!'

She said that she would, but worried about how to prevent such an incident, should it occur. Mrs Hanson never spoke to anybody in the court and Mr Hanson merely passed the time of day, and she wondered, not for the first time, how two such dowly people could have produced a son like Daniel.

Her father arrived home an hour later. 'I've been laid off,' he told her glumly. 'There's no work anywhere. We've been told to report in on Monday, but they can't guarantee owt.'

'Da,' she said urgently. 'Go and try at 'woodyard, Jensons, I think they're called.' She told him about Daniel. 'Only don't say a word to his father if you should see him.'

'I won't,' he said, putting on his coat again. 'And I'll not feel guilty about tekking job either if it's offered. If Hanson's too proud to tek labouring work, there's plenty who are not.' He indicated with his thumb towards the door. 'It's dog eat dog out there.'

She was scrubbing the last of the potatoes and adding them to the water in the iron pan, when Ruby came to the door. She seemed agitated and kept rubbing her hands together. 'Somebody's just been to our house,' she said. 'I kept 'door locked and we peeped out of 'window.'

'Who was it?' Grace lifted the pan with a great effort. It was very heavy but she managed to place it on the trivet over the coals.

'Two men.' Ruby plonked herself down in the chair. 'I hadn't lit 'fire so it would look empty from outside. Ma's made herself scarce, she's going to hang around Tap and Barrel and wait for her pals. She said she knew one of 'men. She said he's a bum-bailiff, one of 'meanest. 'Other one we think is from 'landlord's office. They're checking us out, Grace.' She pressed her fists to her mouth. 'What are we going to do? We'll be turned out onto 'streets.'

Grace put her hand on Ruby's shoulder. 'They might not come again for a bit. Maybe they're just looking to see if 'house is empty. What about 'people upstairs, in your old room?'

'I've warned them.' A tear rolled down Ruby's cheek. 'Mrs Blake said they'd have to go to 'workhouse if they're turned out. They'll be separated, of course. Mr Blake won't be able to go with her and 'bairns.' She stifled a sob. 'What a life, Grace. We're nowt. We might as well be dead as lead 'life we do!'

Grace sat down on the floor next to Ruby's chair and leaned her arm on her friend's lap. 'Daniel is leaving.' She looked up at her. 'He's giving up his apprenticeship and probably taking a ship on Friday.'

'I'm sorry.' Ruby swallowed her tears and spoke in a choked voice. 'I'll miss him.'

Grace nodded. 'Yes,' she said softly. 'So will I, but he feels he has to go.'

Ruby put her hand on Grace's hair and stroked it. It was fine and soft, not thick and heavy like her own. 'If it wasn't for you, Grace, I would've given up long ago. Life's not worth a candle. My ma's an opium addict, our Josh couldn't care a jot for us, and as for poor little Freddie, maybe God knows where he is, for I don't.'

She played with strands of Grace's hair, twining it around her fingers, then said, 'I've come to tell you summat.'

It was a day for confidences, Grace thought. Daniel asking, Ruby telling. She saw the tears running down Ruby's face. 'What is it?' she whispered. 'We've had bad times before and got through them.'

'But not like this,' Ruby cried. 'I've had enough, Grace. I'm frightened. I can't go on any more.'

Grace remained silent and continued to gaze at Ruby, giving her time to compose herself.

'I'm just waiting', Ruby said, 'for Jamie to get up. You know how he and his ma sleep all day.' She took a deep breath and raised her head. 'As soon as I see their curtains open, I'm going to see him. I'm going to tell him that I'm ready.'

'Ready?' Grace whispered.

Ruby nodded. 'I've really made up my mind this time. What's 'point in saving my virginity?

What or who am I saving it for? I'm going to ask Jamie to lend me a shilling or more if he can, then if these men come back I'll give them it for 'rent. I'll make up some story about having just moved in. Then,' she pressed her lips together, 'I'll owe Jamie and I'm committed. There'll be no going back.'

CHAPTER SIXTEEN

Jamie was cock-a-hoop with delight, though he tried not to show it in front of Ruby. She'd seen his mother go out of the house and decided that it was now or never. She'd knocked on his door and been invited in.

'You won't regret it, Ruby,' he kept saying. 'Don't feel bad about it. It's nowt. Doesn't mean owt to men nowadays if women are – you know, not pure. Unless you're out of 'top drawer of course, and that's different. I heard', he bent confidentially towards her, 'that wives of that class onny allow their husbands into their beds in order to get bairns, and when they've got enough – ' He made a dismissive gesture. 'That's it. Poor bloke's got to look elsewhere. But we're not in that class, Ruby, so we don't have to worry. And in a way, we're providing a service, you might say.'

'I don't believe you.' Ruby was critical. 'What about 'Queen? They say it's a proper love affair with her and Prince Albert.'

'Pah! Don't you believe it. Anyway, I'm telling you, Ruby. When you're wearing swanky clothes *and* having a good dinner every day, you'll be glad, you'll know that you made 'right decision.'

'What if – ?' She felt her face flush. 'What if I should get caught – with a babby?'

He pursed his lips and shrugged. 'I think Ma knows somebody who can look after that. It's not summat I've had to deal with. It's a woman's concern, isn't it?'

Of course it is, she thought. Men can turn their backs on that. She thought of her own father, who had gone off when Freddie was just a baby. It was a worry. Her flux was erratic and she'd heard women at work saying that you didn't get pregnant if you didn't have regular bleeding. She gave a deep sigh. I'll just have to deal with that if it comes along.

'Right,' Jamie said. 'I'll give you a shilling for 'rent as we agreed, and here's another shilling to get yourself a bath and some decent clothes.' His eyes appraised her. 'You'd look good in red, Ruby. Something a bit exotic. Go down to 'Market Place. There's a shop there that sells second-hand clothes. Rena's, it's called. It's decent stuff, some of 'actresses from travelling theatres sell their clothes to her. Tell her I sent you and she'll do you a good deal.' He fingered her hair. 'And buy a hairbrush.'

She felt like a white slave as he looked her over and said, 'So you'll owe me two shillings, then I'll want half of what you earn. Agreed?'

She nodded in compliance. What else was there to do? At least the rent would be paid if the men came back, and maybe if she didn't spend all of the shilling on clothes, she could buy some food. *And* she would get her wages on Saturday. A feeling of relief began to surge through her. Never mind that she was nervous and apprehensive of what was to come, she would have money in her hand and food in her belly at last.

'I'll try and get you fixed up for Saturday,' he said. 'But I can't promise. I've got Nell to think of as well.'

'Nell!' she exclaimed. 'Your ma? But you said – you said that she'd had enough. I thought I was to take over from her?'

'Slowly, slowly,' he said and pressed her hand confidentially. 'I don't want her to think she's being pushed out.'

'You mean you haven't told her!' she accused him. 'You haven't told her about your grand scheme?'

'Not yet. But I will. I've got to find 'right time. You wouldn't know it, but she's got a temper on her, has Nell. But I'll tell her,' he assured her. 'I'll tell her soon.'

'Tell her tonight, Jamie,' she begged. 'Please. If it doesn't happen soon I might change my mind.'

He gave her a thin smile and she saw the hardness on his handsome face. 'And how would you pay me back, Ruby, if you did?' He ran his long white fingers around her face and throat. 'Tell me that?'

Daniel held a bulging sack in his hands when he appeared at Grace's door later in the day. 'I've brought you something,' he said. 'A present, and one for Ruby.'

'A present!' she exclaimed. Nobody ever gave presents.

'I know that Christmas has gone and I did try to get these ready in time for that, but we were busy and I wasn't able to.'

'What is it?' she said excitedly. 'Shall I go and get Ruby?'

'I've just seen her go into Jamie's house,' he said, 'so you can give it to her later.' He opened the sack and pulled out a small stool and then another. 'When I first saw you both,' he smiled, 'you were sitting on 'doorstep, and I thought then that what you needed was a stool to sit on. So I made you one each.'

Grace took one of them from him. It was three-legged, like a milking stool, and he apologized. 'It's elm,' he said. 'But there wasn't enough wood to make two square stools with four legs, and as I wanted you both to have the same I decided to make them round with three.'

'They're beautiful,' Grace said softly, over-whelmed by the gift. 'Oh, Daniel, what a craftsman you are and you're giving it up!'

The stools were honed and polished, and finished with such care and symmetry that she couldn't believe that one of them was for her.

Daniel threw the still almost-full sack into a corner. 'Those are just a few things when I was learning 'craft. Nothing of value. As I say, you can use them for firewood.' Then he said he had to go. 'I'm going to confront Ma and Da now,' he said. 'Wish me luck.'

'I do,' she said. 'Thank you, Daniel. Will we see you before Friday? Are you definitely sailing?'

He tightened his lips. 'Yes, I've been to sign this morning. Now there's no going back. Listen out for 'storm across at our house,' he added, as if trying to make light of what was to happen next. 'It'll be heard out at sea.'

As Daniel entered his own door, Grace's father arrived home, jubilant with the news that he had obtained temporary work at the joiner's workshop. 'Master there said that he's waiting for one of his regular men to come back. I guess that must be Hanson. But I can have 'job until he does, and if he doesn't return within two weeks then it's mine full-time.'

Grace heaved a sigh of relief. 'Thank goodness,' she began, and stopped as a shrill ear-piercing shriek erupted from the Hansons' house. 'Daniel's just told them he's leaving!'

A man gave a great roar, and they guessed that it was Mr Hanson berating both his wife and Daniel. They heard another voice which they assumed was Daniel's, and then a crash as something hit the house wall.

'That's 'cooking pot,' Bob Sheppard grinned. 'It'll be 'kettle next, then a boot!'

'How do you know?' Grace asked, alarmed at the thought of violence.

'Never you mind,' her father said. 'I just do!'

Grace's mother arrived home in the midst of the row. 'What's going on across 'road?' she asked. 'Missus got her dander up?'

'Daniel's given up his apprenticeship,' Grace told her. 'He's going to sea. He sails on Friday.'

'Poor lad!' Her mother tutted and was visibly cross. 'He'd not have done that if he'd been mine! I'd have worked day and night to keep him in a craft.' She shook her head. 'Some folks haven't 'sense they were born with.'

'Ma! Da! Why didn't you put me to a trade? I could have been a weaver or a spinner by now.'

'No you couldn't.' Her mother sat down and took off her boots, and turned them over to look at the worn soles. 'When 'cotton mill first opened, they brought weavers and spinners in from Lancashire and 'West Riding. There'd never been a cotton mill in Hull before so nobody had any experience. But they wanted labourers, women and bairns, and that's why when you were old enough you went there.'

'Besides,' her father interrupted, 'spinning and weaving is a family tradition, they're brought up to it in Lancashire, same as coal-mining in 'West Riding. Cotton was new to Hull.'

As he spoke another crash erupted from across the court.

'That's a chair,' her mother reckoned. 'Table'll go over next.'

But the next sound was that of the door crashing and Grace looked out of the window to see Daniel marching towards the alleyway.

'Don't think of going after him,' her mother cautioned, as Grace picked up her shawl. 'He'll need to be by himself until his temper dies down.'

'Daniel hasn't got a temper,' Grace objected. 'He's very steady.'

'He's just had a row with his parents, mebbe 'first ever. They'll all have said things that have been bottled up for months,' her mother reasoned. 'Go to him after a bit when he might want to talk.' She looked directly at Grace. 'Is he special to you, bairn?'

'Why yes! Of course he is,' Grace replied and sounded surprised at the question. 'He's my friend!'

Edward shuffled a pile of papers around his desk. It was almost six o'clock and time for him and Martin to be going home. Martin put his head around the door. 'Aren't you ready? I want to be off.'

'No, you go on.' Edward lifted his head and frowned as if in concentration. 'I've things to clear up here. I'll get a hansom when I'm ready.'

He had dressed soberly that morning and put on a heavy dark overcoat and a grey scarf. The weather was dank and cold and he shivered as he stepped outside. He hunched his shoulders and as he came out of the mill gates he looked about for a hansom cab. One came along quite soon and he hailed it.

'Where to, sir?'

'I don't know the name of the road,' he said. 'But it's somewhere behind the dock, on the north side. Somewhere near New George Street, I think. I'll know it when I see it.'

'Very good, sir.' The cabby raised his whip. 'Just give me a shout when we're there.'

He was so unfamiliar with the area that he didn't recognize any landmarks. They passed crowded inns with lanterns swinging outside and the sound of laughter within, and it crossed his mind that people were not so downtrodden, as

188

the 'do-gooders' would have you believe, that they couldn't enjoy a glass of ale and merriment.

He peered out of the cab window into the gloom. It was raining quite hard now and he was beginning to think that perhaps he would turn around and go home, except that he would change hansoms rather than take the risk of the driver knowing who he was, when he saw the youth he was seeking scurrying along the road.

'Stop here a moment,' he called up to the cabby. 'I'll just ask directions.' He jumped out and called after the youth. 'Hey! You there! Just a moment.' He hurried after him out of the hearing of the driver and hailed him again.

Jamie turned around and recognized the man immediately. He had a good memory for faces and he remembered this one who had pretended that he had lost his way. 'Good evening, sir. Can I be of assistance?'

'Erm, yes. That is, perhaps.' Edward pulled his scarf up around his chin. 'We have met previously, and er, you said that you might be able to arrange erm, a meeting with a certain woman.'

'Did I, sir?' Jamie wrinkled his brow as if trying to recollect. 'A woman? Yes, well, I do know a very agreeable woman, very accommodating, you might say. And discreet,' he added. 'No names or anything like that.'

'Mmm. Mmm.' Edward shuffled nervously. 'Well, I'd erm, I'd like to make her acquaintance. But I'd need to know if she's – well, if she's – ' He let the question hang in the air. 'I'm getting married soon, you see, and I must be sure that everything is all right.'

'If she's clean, you mean, sir? Not diseased?'

'That's it!' Edward was relieved that he didn't have to explain further. 'That's it exactly. I must be sure.'

'Of course you must, sir.' Jamie's voice was smooth and as comforting as butter. 'Can't be too careful. The lady I had in mind is very experienced, sir, but very particular and quite sound in health.' He rubbed his chin thoughtfully. 'But, I'm wondering, seeing as you're to be married and would want to be entirely sure, because of your dear lady wife – I do happen to know of a young virgin. Beautiful, she is and quite untried.'

'A virgin!' Edward breathed. 'Oh, yes indeed.'

'I'd have to persuade her.' Jamie's fingers tapped his lips thoughtfully. 'She's down on her luck just at 'moment and this would be a last resort. But, yes, I'm sure that I can induce her,' he said valiantly. 'For a gentleman such as yourself. It'll cost, though,' he added warningly and named a figure, twice what he would ask for Nell.

'Yes. Yes! Do you want me to pay something on account?'

'Certainly not, sir. Why, you might never see me again! Saturday? Would that be suitable? It'll give me time to persuade her.'

They agreed the day, a time and place and Edward hurried back to his waiting hansom and asked the driver to take him to the Market Place, where he knew he would be able to get another cab.

'Wasn't he able to help you, sir?' the cabby asked.

'No. No, he wasn't.' Edward climbed into the hansom. 'I've decided to leave it for the time being.'

'Oh, dear,' the driver murmured as he drove off. 'That's a wonder. I thought Jamie knew everywhere and everybody around here!'

'This fellow wants a virgin, Ma, and Ruby is willing. At least, she's not willing but she's got no other option.'

'That's my patch!' his mother objected. She'd screamed and shouted at him when he'd told her that Ruby was joining their team. 'I'll not have anybody else tekking over from me.'

'She's not tekking over. When we're set up you'll have 'say on who goes where. This is our big chance, Nell. We could make a lot of money, and you could keep just your specials,' he persuaded. 'You wouldn't have to go out if you didn't want to. Come on,' he said soothingly. 'Trust me. I've never let you down before, have I?'

She conceded that he hadn't, but she didn't trust him entirely, even if he was her own son.

Ruby was quiet as she and Grace met up at Grace's door on Friday morning. She had money in her skirt pocket, for she intended to go to the public baths after they had finished at the mill that evening.

'What's up?' Grace asked. 'Lost your tongue?'

'No. I don't feel in 'mood for chat, that's all.'

191

Grace glanced at her. 'You'd better tell me. Get it off your chest. But not yet, let's wait a minute to say goodbye to Daniel. He leaves this morning.'

'Oh!' Hot tears sprang to Ruby's eyes. 'I haven't thanked him yet for that beautiful stool. Can I leave it at your house, Grace? I'm bothered that Ma will sell it if she's desperate for loddy money.'

Grace nodded, then looked up as Daniel's door opened and he came across to them. 'Have you made it up with your ma and da, Daniel?' She was anxious that there was no bad feeling before he went away.

'With Da, yes. He keeps saying how sorry he is.' Daniel's voice was strained. 'He's just sitting in a chair weeping and I wish he'd get angry rather than that. But Ma won't talk to me. Yesterday she kept on and on about all she'd done for me, all 'sacrifices she'd made. But today she won't speak at all. I'll be glad to get away.'

'We'll miss you, Daniel.' Ruby's voice was choked. 'I hope – I hope – ' She couldn't finish what she was saying and bent her head.

'Hope what, Ruby?' Daniel lifted her chin with his finger and gave her an encouraging smile.

'I hope – that you don't find us changed when you come home again.' Ruby swallowed hard. How to put what she really meant? 'That we can still be friends, no matter what.'

'Of course we can. Why shouldn't we? It'll be summer when I get back, maybe in time for your birthday, Ruby.' He glanced at Grace. 'But I might have gone again by 'time yours comes around, Grace.' He sounded regretful. 'If I get another ship, that is.'

'Where are you going?' Ruby wiped her eyes on her sleeve.

'To 'Baltic,' he said. 'Taking out manufactured goods and bringing in timber for 'raff yards. Your boss from 'cotton mill owns 'company I'm working for,' he added.

'Our boss?' they chorused. 'Who's that?'

'Joseph Rylands,' he said. 'He owns a shipping fleet as well as shares in 'cotton mill. I heard he brings in raw cotton on his own ships.'

They both shook their heads. They'd neither of them ever heard of him. They knew none of the directors or shareholders, only the New-march brothers who were to be seen around the mill and the manager, Mr Staniland, whom they occasionally saw driving away in his chaise.

'We're onny poor ignorant workers,' Grace said, and a note of bitterness sounded in her voice. 'What do we know about anything?'

'We'd better go,' Ruby interrupted. 'We'll be late. God speed, Daniel.' She reached up and kissed his cheek and patted his chin where his beard was growing.

He put his arms out and hugged her. 'Take care of yourself, Ruby. Take care of each other,' he said, as he turned to Grace and kissed her too. 'I'll be thinking of both of you, every day, wondering what you're up to.'

'Oh, don't worry about us, Daniel.' Ruby's tears started to fall again and she sniffed hard. 'We'll be all right. Won't we, Grace?'

Grace nodded. Ruby's tears seemed to be

excessive, she pondered. Is she weeping over Daniel going away or because of what is in front of her? Has she made a commitment to Jamie? She put an arm around Ruby's shoulder. 'Yes,' she replied softly. 'We'll be all right. But come home safe and sound, Daniel. We'll be waiting for you.'

CHAPTER SEVENTEEN

'No work tomorrow, ladies!' The women, including Ruby and Grace, who had been told to
assemble before going home, agreed that the
foreman needn't have sounded so cheerful as he
gave them the news that their work was being cut
to two days. 'Monday and Friday'll be your shift.
Come tomorrow for this week's wages.'

'Why can't we have our wages today if our
hours are being cut?' Grace asked boldly. 'Why
should we have to come back tomorrow if there's
no work for us?'

The other women were of the same mind but
the foreman shrugged. 'Nowt to do wi' me.' He
was newly promoted and, although pleased to be
showing his superiority, he didn't want trouble.
He jeered, 'Tek it up wi' management if you're
not satisfied.'

Grace was furious. 'Right! I will. I'll see Mr
Newmarch.'

'Grace!' Ruby breathed over her shoulder.
'Dare you do that?'

Grace saw that all the other women who
had gathered around were looking towards her

expectantly. 'Yes,' she said defiantly. 'He can't eat me. He can sack me but if I'm only going to have two days' work anyway – ' She shrugged. Two days' work was better than none at all, but it was worth a pittance and she was prepared to take the risk. 'Is anybody coming with me?'

One woman spoke up. 'I'll come. I'm sick o' this. We'll be beggin' in 'streets next.'

'And I'll come,' said another and then another.

'Come on then.' Grace beckoned and a crowd of women followed her out of the mill block, trailed in turn by a straggling group who were not quite brave enough to join the main throng.

'Of course he might have gone home already,' Grace said to Ruby, who had also rushed after her as they marched towards the office block. 'No! There they are. Mr Newmarch! Mr Newmarch!'

The Newmarch brothers were standing in the entrance of the two-storeyed red brick building waiting for their chaise to be brought to them. They both looked up as they heard the call.

'Mr Martin Newmarch, sir,' Grace called, and Ruby let herself be drawn back into the crowd as Grace hurried forward. 'Could you spare a moment, please?'

'What is it?' Martin came out of the recessed opening. 'Is something wrong? Oh!' He recognized her. 'It's Miss Sheppard! What can I do for you?'

'I'm sorry to bother you, sir, you're no doubt on your way home, but – ' She swept an arm to encompass the women behind her. 'We – these women and me have been told that we haven't to come in tomorrow, that we are being put on two days' work.'

'Yes, yes, I'm sorry about that,' he began. 'We realize that there might be hardship but—'

'It's not about that, sir,' Grace cut in. 'If there's no work for us then that can't be helped, but we would like our wages today. We don't want to have to come back tomorrow to get them.'

'I don't understand.' Martin frowned. 'Who said you have to come back tomorrow?'

'Foreman did, sir. He said we had to collect our wages then.'

'Why is that, do you think?' Martin turned to his brother.

'Perhaps the wages haven't been worked out yet.' Edward hazarded a guess and casually brushed away cotton dust from his coat. 'Everybody gets paid on a Saturday.'

'But we're not working on Saturday, Mr Newmarch.' Grace stood her ground. 'So why should we have to come in specially? And it wouldn't take 'clerks more than a few minutes to work out two days' work for fifty women.' Her tone was slightly mocking as she spoke. 'These women know to a penny how much is due to them. They can work it out.'

Martin drew in a deep resigned breath. 'Come with me, Miss Sheppard. I'll see what I can do.' He led her through the wide portico which was decorated with dressed stone, and with a coloured fanlight above the wooden door, and into the office section.

'Mr Staniland. Excuse me!' Martin Newmarch,

she noticed, was as deferential to the manager as she had been to him. He explained the situation and Mr Staniland gazed at her as Martin was speaking.

'And you are one of our workers, are you?' he asked. 'A spokeswoman!'

Grace considered before answering. 'I suppose I could be called a spokeswoman, and yes I am one of your workers, sir. Have been since I was nine years old.'

Mr Staniland raised his eyebrows at this. 'Really! Well, in that case I think the situation can be resolved for you.'

'Not just for me, sir,' she interrupted. 'For all of 'women out there. They need that money, sir. For most of them it'll put bread in their mouths. Tomorrow they'll have to look for other work if they're not coming in to 'mill.'

He nodded. 'It must be hard for them, I agree. Very well. Go up and see the clerks, Newmarch, and perhaps you, Miss – ?'

'Sheppard, sir. Grace Sheppard.'

'Perhaps then, Grace Sheppard, you will ascertain how many women there are so that our calculations are the same?'

She smiled jubilantly and went outside again. She raised her arm in triumph and the women cheered and gathered around her. 'God bless you, Grace,' somebody shouted, and another one bantered, 'Now can you get us an increase and two more days?' 'And a free dinner!' somebody else suggested.

She laughed, the success making her eyes sparkle. 'Don't expect the impossible,' she called back and turned, still with a smile on her face, to find Martin Newmarch behind her.

He looked down at her. 'It's done,' he said. 'The wage clerk will be down in five minutes with their money.'

'Thank you so much, Mr Newmarch.' She beamed at him. 'We're very grateful. You can't possibly know what it means to these women.'

'No,' he said slowly. 'I don't suppose I can. And you, what does it mean to you?'

She hesitated, then said, 'I think it means that I shall look for other work, Mr Newmarch. I can't manage on two days' money.'

'I'm sorry. But I understand.' He studied her. 'If you need a reference you may give my name, but,' he hesitated and pursed his lips, 'if I might make a suggestion. Don't tell a future employer that you have acted as a spokeswoman for your fellow workers.' He gazed at her frankly. 'They might not understand.'

She blinked and contemplated. 'I've always been honest, sir.'

'I'm sure you have.' He gave a slight smile. 'But honesty doesn't always pay. I'm not suggesting you should lie, but be circumspect, Grace. Consider what you do and say.'

She didn't understand what he meant, but she was sure he meant well. As the women suddenly rushed forward as the wage clerk appeared, he put on his top hat, which he had held in his hand, tapped it with his finger and moved away to the waiting chaise.

'What do you make of that?' Edward grinned as he took the reins. 'An agitator!'

'Not a bit of it!' Martin was brusque. 'Nobody else was brave enough to ask for their dues.' He gave a short laugh. 'She told me once before that the workers were afraid of us.' But she isn't, he repeated to himself. Even at the risk of losing her job she'll speak out. I admire that, he admitted, she's got mettle. So rare in a woman, especially in a woman of her class. Yet she looks so angelic, unlike Georgiana, another rare woman but one who has determination and fortitude written all over her.

'What?' he said as Edward finished speaking. 'What did you say?'

'I said that her friend didn't appear to be with her,' Edward murmured. 'They're usually together.'

'Mm!' Martin was non-committal. 'I didn't notice.'

She was conspicuous by her absence, Edward pondered. Perhaps after tomorrow night I shall be able to put her out of my mind.

'I shan't go to 'public baths tonight after all,' Ruby decided. 'I'll go tomorrow seeing as I'm not working. Do you want to come, Grace?' she asked suddenly. 'I've got a spare penny.'

'Ooh, I don't know! Yes! I'll go halves. Why not? What a treat, a warm bath, not a wash by 'fireside!'

Although Grace had the luxury of warming a pan of water over the fire and getting washed in the tin tub by the hearth, Ruby hadn't had that advantage and had only ever washed in cold water drawn from the pump in an iron pail.

The next morning they both set off towards the Humber bank where the baths were situated.

The public baths were newly built, especially for those who had no facilities of their own, but not everyone could afford them. Most people of that district had the priorities of feeding themselves and paying their rent, which came well before the luxury of warm baths. These baths had hot, cold, warm and vaporized water and after much discussion, Ruby and Grace decided that they would have the hot water.

They paid their pennies, were given a towel and a small piece of soap and were shown into separate cubicles. Each contained a large white bath, which a woman was filling with hot water.

Ruby undressed slowly and looked at her tattered clothing. She wore a cotton shift beneath her skirt and shirt and nothing more. She had no stockings, nor had she ever possessed such things.

'Are you in yet, Ruby?' Grace called from the next cubicle. 'It's bliss! Absolute heaven. When I'm rich I'll do this every day!'

Ruby laughed and put a toe into the water. 'It's hot!' she exclaimed. 'Really hot water!' She put the whole of her foot in and then the other and gingerly sat down, holding onto the sides of the bath. Then she lowered herself until she was covered with water and her hair floated about her. 'I'm going to stay here all day,' she pronounced.

An hour later when the water had gone cold and someone had knocked on the cubicle doors and told them that there were others waiting, they emerged clean and shining, their hair washed and their undergarments also washed, for they had taken the opportunity of soaping and rinsing those too and rolling them up into a wet bundle.

Grace had brought a hairbrush which she lent to Ruby and they set off back to the Market Place.

'What must it be like to be a lady of means?' Grace said. 'To be clean and powdered every day.'

'Powdered?' Ruby exclaimed. 'Did you have powder?'

'No, silly, but I know that ladies do. I've seen pictures in newspapers, advertising scented powder.'

'Oh,' Ruby sighed. 'What luxury! Grace?' she said. 'Will you come with me to buy a dress from Rena's? I don't like to go on my own. I'm scared she might guess why I want it. She won't say owt if you're there.'

'Yes, course I will. I'll help you choose.'

It was such a treat for them. Grace enjoyed the pleasure of choosing something for Ruby almost as much as if it was for herself, and Ruby put to the back of her mind why she required a different set of clothes.

'How much have you got to spend?' Rena asked. She was rather a splendid creature, dressed in a bright green embroidered gown which cast a lurid hue to her sharp features.

'A shilling,' Ruby said bravely, having decided that she would cut down on food and buy another shift which she had seen in one of the open drawers. It was cotton and trimmed with lace at the hem.

'A shilling. Mm! Let me see, then – ' Rena perused the rails. 'Yellow perhaps?' She brought out a garish yellow gown with a bustle. She gazed at Ruby. 'Perhaps not. Not your colour, I think.' She looked at Grace. 'It would be more your shade.'

Grace shook her head. 'I'm not buying,' she said. 'Just something for Ruby.'

'Jamie suggested red,' Ruby murmured. 'But I don't want anything too bright.'

'Jamie!' Rena exclaimed. 'You didn't say you were a friend of Jamie's. Well, in that case . . .' She went to another rail covered over with a white sheet, which she removed with a flourish.

'These', she pronounced, 'are for my special customers.'

There were white gowns, pale gold gowns, velvet and moire, floral and plain gowns. Some with bustles, some without. Others had masses of skirt to be worn with a hoop beneath, or were cut slimly with a fishtail to swirl about the ankle.

'My goodness,' Ruby said. 'What to choose?'

Rena gazed at her from hooded eyes. 'Are you about to embark on a new life, my dear?' she asked quietly, and when Ruby nodded, averting her eyes, Rena turned back to the rail. 'Better anyway', she murmured, 'than starving to death.'

Ruby sent a scared glance at Grace, but her face showed no emotion and she too turned to the rail.

'Where do these gowns come from?' Grace asked. It was obvious that they were not brand new, but who would want to be rid of such splendour?

'Actresses, some of them. They have to change their gowns frequently, although', she admitted, 'they don't know that with a little tuck here and a bit of lace there, they sometimes buy their own gowns back a few years later! Then, of course, there are some grand ladies who give their clothes to the poor, only they're far too grand for 'poor to wear, and they sell to me and buy something more suitable for themselves.

'This one,' she said, pulling out a rich red gown. 'Just the thing for you. A simple style that you'll feel comfortable in, but a beautiful shade which will show off your dark hair.'

Ruby fingered the velvet cloth. The skirt was full and the bodice low-cut with a lace fichu at the throat. 'It's beautiful,' she whispered. 'But can I afford it?'

'You can,' Rena said. 'It would normally cost a florin, but I know that you'll come back for another. You can have it for a shilling. And,' she added, 'you can take that shift that you've been admiring and pay me when you've got the money.'

Ruby stood silently. It seemed that the die was cast. There was no going back. She owed Jamie two shillings and some of it was already spent at the baths. 'All right,' she agreed. 'I'll take them.'

A church clock struck three as they walked towards home. 'I'll have to get Ma out of the house,' Ruby said. 'She'll guess what's happening if she sees me dressed up in this finery.' She clutched the brown paper bag which held her future.

'I shouldn't say this, but give her a penny,' Grace suggested. 'She'll not resist going out to spend it. Then you'll be able to change without her knowing. Though she'll find out when you come back home.'

'I shan't mind then,' Ruby admitted. 'Not when it's – not when it's done.'

'I'll come and button you up when she's gone out,' Grace said. 'And brush your hair.'

Ruby bit her bottom lip. 'Jamie said I had to buy a hairbrush,' she remembered.

'Never mind about what Jamie said, I'll lend you mine. It's a bit thin on bristles but it'll do.'

But the hairbrush pulled on Ruby's thick mass of hair, so unlike Grace's baby-fine texture, and she complained loudly. They were both nervous and tense.

'Well, do it yourself then!' Grace flung the brush down and burst into tears.

Ruby put her arms around her. 'Don't cry,' she whispered, her own eyes filling. 'It'll be all right, really it will.'

'I hate to think of you having to do this,' Grace wept. 'It's not right! Why should women have to submit to such humiliation just to earn their keep?'

'Because there's nothing else,' Ruby said softly. 'There isn't another way, except for 'workhouse. It perhaps won't be so bad,' she said hopefully. 'Mebbe it'll be somebody nice.' Though how can he possibly be? she wondered. What sort of a man will take a strange woman? She gave a little shudder. Just as long as he doesn't hurt me. 'Don't worry, Grace,' she reassured her. 'I'll be all right.'

There was a brisk knock on the door and they both jumped. 'Jamie!' Ruby whispered. 'He's come to collect me.'

Grace opened the door to let him in and he gave a low whistle when he saw Ruby. 'Wow, Ruby! You look – ' He exhaled a breath. 'Tremendous.' He shook his head in amazement. 'You're beautiful!' He held out his hand to her. 'You're going to make somebody really happy tonight.'

CHAPTER EIGHTEEN

Edward was nervous. He had announced at home that he was going to his club and wouldn't be in for supper. Nothing unusual in that, he thought, as he dressed in narrow wool trousers and embroidered waistcoat beneath his dark frock coat. I often stay at my club, he contended as he carefully tied a starched lawn cravat. It's not the first time. But he had the suspicion that his mother didn't totally approve of him visiting the club so often, when he was soon to be a married man.

But she had smiled and said indulgently that he must make the most of his freedom, for she was sure that Miss Gregory would want him all to herself once they were married.

'I shall still visit my club, Mama,' he said. 'A man must have some male conversation once in a while.'

'Your father hardly ever goes,' she began.

'But Father locks himself in his library every night. He isn't with you.'

'No,' she sighed. 'That is true. But I had hoped that you young people would want to spend time together.' She smiled. 'But I was always a romantic.'

He bent and kissed her forehead. 'May and I shall spend time together, Mama, but she won't want me always in her pocket. She will have activities of her own to consider.'

They were to take the occupancy of a house in Hessle. May loved the house and its grounds, though she was a little bothered that the air might be damp so near the Humber. 'Not at all,' Edward had declared. 'And you will be able to sit in your room and watch all the river traffic,' for she had delighted in a room at the front of the house which overlooked the river, and declared that if they should take the house, then that would be her sitting room.

It was almost February and the weather was bitterly cold. He put on a heavy greatcoat with a high collar, picked up his top hat and descended the stairs. Martin was crossing the hall and hesitated. 'I'm in two minds whether to come along,' he said, and Edward drew in a breath, 'but, well, perhaps not. If you see Jarvis will you tell him I'll meet him one evening next week? Say Wednesday about seven.'

Edward nodded and relaxed. That was a close shave. 'I might be late,' he said. 'Or I might even stay in town.'

'Theatre, is it? What's on?'

'Oh!' Edward was vague, not wanting to encourage his brother into coming too. 'Music hall or something. Something bawdy anyway!'

'I won't bother then,' Martin said, opening the drawing-room door. 'Not my style. I have

208

some papers to catch up on, in any case.'

Edward drove fast down the road into Hull. He was full of nervous tension and excitement. Hope she's all right, he thought, this girl. Can I be sure she's a virgin? These women have ways of fooling a man. Still, the fellow did say she was untried. A picture of the dark-haired girl from the mill came into his head. Why do I keep thinking of her? I even looked for her in that crowd of women when her friend confronted us, but I didn't see her. She was a beauty too, the fair one, but not my type. Too ethereal. I think Martin was irritated by her. She seemed to have got under his skin.

He drove towards his club which was situated off the High Street, parallel with the river Hull. Glancing along the staithes he caught a glimpse of ships' masts and rigging, for this narrow stretch of the river was the original harbour and was still in constant use, despite the additional docks built over the last three decades.

The High Street was narrow and he whistled a boy to lead the horse into a nearby inn yard where they had good stabling. 'Tell them Newmarch,' he said, giving the boy twopence. 'They know me.'

He went into his club and made a point of greeting several men who were playing cards. He sought out Jarvis, Martin's friend, and gave him the message. 'Have a brandy?' Jarvis asked.

'Yes, but I'll get them. Same for you?'

'Erm, no thanks. I'm just off. Promised I'd be home early.'

Edward tossed back his brandy, ran up the stairs and greeted other people, then slipped down again, through the gaming room, the smoking room and out of the side door. The cold river air tingled in his nostrils as he cut along Scale Lane into the busy street of Lowgate where carriages, hansom cabs and hauliers' carts were trundling past. He hailed a cab. 'New George Street,' he said, for that was where he had arranged to meet the youth, whose name he had forgotten to ask. 'There's an inn called The Ship.'

'Indeed there is, sir.' The cabby clicked his tongue and they moved off. 'And take care of your pocket watch.'

'Damn,' Edward breathed. 'Perhaps I should have said I'd meet him outside. I might be recognized if any of the workers are in there.'

But a figure was waiting outside the inn door, and, as Edward paid off the cabman, he came forward. 'Good evening, sir. It's good to see you. Are you well?'

Edward grunted in reply and Jamie smiled. The fellow was nervous. Well, that made two of them, he thought, for Ruby was positively shaking.

'I'm freezing, Jamie,' she said as she walked alongside him. She'd been cold all the afternoon, especially after coming out of the hot baths. The cold air had struck through her thin garments right to her bones. She hadn't been able to wear her old shift as she'd washed it, and after buying the new one at Rena's, she'd thrown her old one away and seen two poorly clad women pounce on it, grabbing it between them.

The velvet gown was warmer than her cotton skirt and shirt, yet she still trembled. Grace had offered her the loan of her shawl which was in a better condition than her own but she was still cold, right down to her bare toes in her boots.

'I'll get you a brandy when we get to Morrison's,' Jamie promised. 'That'll warm you up.'

'Morrison's? Where's that?'

'It's a sort of rooming house, just off New George Street. Travelling men stay there during the week and at weekends they let rooms out on an hourly basis. It's respectable,' he added.

'Hmm. I'm sure it is,' she muttered and gave another shudder.

It wasn't far and the house was clean. Mrs Morrison led the way upstairs. 'I'll come and collect you if you like, Ruby,' Jamie called after her.

'No.' She turned round from halfway up the stairs. 'It's all right. I'll come back on my own. I'd rather.' She didn't want Jamie ogling her or, worse, asking how it was. 'I know my way.'

The bedroom was small, but to Ruby it seemed like a palace. A bed with a quilted counterpane dominated the room, but there was also a wash-stand with a jug and bowl on it, a towel hanging on a wooden rail, and, best of all, a blazing fire and a hod full of glistening black coal standing next to it.

'Jamie said to give you a drop o' brandy,' Mrs

Morrison said, looking at Ruby with narrowed eyes.

'Not now, thanks.' Ruby refused her offer and wondered who would pay for it, her or Jamie. It wouldn't be free, that was for certain. 'I'll perhaps have one later.'

She wondered if the woman knew why she was here, but it was confirmed that she did when she remarked, 'I'll send 'gentleman up when he arrives. You can get yourself warm while you're waiting. You look frozen stiff.'

Ruby nodded and when Mrs Morrison had closed the door behind her, she drew nearer to the fire, standing as close as she dared without scorching her dress. There was a mirror above the fire and she looked up into it. She saw a pale tense face framed by dark hair which Grace had plaited and coiled in the nape of her neck, and behind her the bed.

She went across to it and tested it with her hands. The springs creaked. Then she sat down on it. Oh, what I wouldn't give just to sleep in it, she thought, without having to demean myself with a stranger, and as the thought entered her head, there came a quiet knock on the door.

Jamie touched his hat as Edward hesitated at the doorway of the house. 'You're expected, sir. But don't worry, the lady of the house is discreet. She won't know you. Even if you had lived next door all your life, which obviously you haven't, she wouldn't know you. Thank you, sir.' He tipped his hat again as Edward pressed a coin into his hand. 'Just pay 'young woman the amount we agreed on and 'landlady for the room.' He nodded and prepared to move away. 'Trust we will meet again. Jamie's the name. Just ask. Everybody knows me.'

'I'm sure they do,' Edward muttered as he followed the woman's fingered direction up the stairs and heard the low strains of Jamie's whistle as she closed the outer door.

'If there's anything you need, sir,' she said. 'A glass of ale or something, I'll just be in my parlour.' She pointed to another door.

He nodded and climbed the uncarpeted stairs. What am I doing here in this shabby decrepit place? For although it seemed fairly clean, as was the landlady, it was in a state of decay, with a frayed curtain at the door and a faint smell of mould pervading the air. I must be mad! For heaven's sake, I'm getting married in a few weeks. He heaved a breath. I'll give the girl a shilling and leave, that's what I'll do. Say I'm feeling unwell. Yes, that's it.

He lifted his hand and with his knuckles gave a soft rap on the door panel. A low voice called, 'Come in,' and he opened the door and stepped inside.

A faded satin counterpane covered the bed, and a girl was sitting on the side of it with her head lowered as if contemplating her folded hands in her lap. The room, at a quick glance, showed it to be as dingy as the rest of the house, but a bright fire was burning in the hearth, which dispersed the aroma of damp. He closed the door behind him, took off his top hat and cleared his throat.

She looked up, turning a pale and nervous face towards him. As she saw who it was, her eyes widened and she put her hands to her mouth in alarm.

'You!' Edward breathed. 'It's you!'

Ruby rose slowly from the bed. 'Mr Newmarch! Sir.' She dipped her knee. 'I wasn't – I mean, I didn't expect – '

He stared at her. 'Nor I you. I – '

'I haven't done anything like this – I mean – ' She felt her face flush with colour. 'It's just that our hours have been cut – ' Her eyes flooded with tears which spilled onto her cheeks. 'And we just can't live – '

'Don't.' He took a step towards her. 'You don't have to explain – not to me.'

She sat down again on the edge of the bed and wiped her tears with her fingertips. She swallowed and looked up at him. 'I'll not say owt – anything, sir, and if you just want to go I shan't mind. It's all right, and I'm not a gossip and nobody knows that I'm here. Onny Jamie – and Grace, I had to tell Grace.'

'Grace?' he said vaguely and looked down at her, feeling his heart pounding. She was beautiful in spite of her cheap and tawdry dress. She wore no rouge or cosmetic, yet, her skin was soft and flawless.

'She's my friend, sir. We share everything, but she's not a gossip either.'

He sat beside her on the bed and put down his hat. 'This is a pretty kettle of fish, isn't it?' He looked at her intently and asked, 'What's your name?'

'Ruby, sir. Ruby Robson.'

Ruby. The name suited her, he thought. It was rich and vibrant. 'So what are we to do, Ruby?' he asked softly and took hold of her hand. 'Seeing as we know each other.'

'I don't know, sir.' She turned luminous dark eyes towards him. 'I'm very frightened,' she confessed.

'Frightened? Of me?' He felt an unaccountable sense of protectiveness towards her vulnerability.

'Of being here. I – I don't know – haven't been with a man before.'

'Never? Surely! A stolen kiss perhaps?' He gazed at her. Yes, she did have an air of innocence, of naivety, but he couldn't believe her. To have taken such a step as she had, she must have had some experience.

She shook her head. 'Life's too wearying, sir. There's no time for pleasure, and no chance of meeting anybody nice.'

He looked down at her hand which he still held. Her fingers were long and the skin pale, and without thinking he stroked them, down to the tips and back. 'I shouldn't be here either,' he began.

'Oh, but gentlemen do,' she excused him, 'so I understand, or that's what Jamie says. He says that their wives don't – or not often.' She swallowed. 'So they have to go to other women,' she finished lamely.

He gave a sudden smile. 'Is that what Jamie says? Well, I'm not married. Not yet, at any rate.' But that is why I'm here, he cogitated. To get this urge out of me before I am married.

'If you want to just leave,' she repeated anxiously, 'I'll understand, though I don't know who'll pay for the room.'

'I'll pay for the room,' he said quickly. 'I booked it, after all.' But do I want to leave? he thought. It won't be right, not now, all desire has gone from me. Yet I want to see her again. He saw the anxiety on her face and impulsively he leant and kissed her cheek. Her lips parted and he longed to kiss those too.

'Ruby,' he said. 'This has been a shock to both of us, meeting here like this.' He took a breath. 'What I suggest is, that I pay you as if everything had gone to plan. I suppose you have to give some money to this Jamie fellow?'

She nodded. 'Half,' she said.

Good God, he thought. She's giving her virginity for a pittance. She must be in dire straits. 'Well,' he said, and bringing out his pocketbook, he extracted some money. 'This is what I agreed with Jamie.' He put the money into her hand, 'and this is for you.' He pressed further coinage into her hand.

'But I can't,' she objected. 'I haven't done anything to earn it.'

I often spend a week at the mill doing absolutely nothing to earn my salary, he thought. And I don't even think about it. Yet she declines to take the money because she hasn't earned it.

'For your trouble,' he persuaded. 'For coming out on such a cold miserable night. But there's a condition.'

Ah, she worried. I might have known.

'I don't want you to say anything to this fellow Jamie or the landlady, about tonight.' He gazed at her as she shook her head in denial of doing such a thing. 'And,' he was sure that he sounded nervous as he made his proposal, 'I would like to see you again, if you are willing. Only not here,' he added quickly. 'Somewhere else. I'll find some other place where neither of us is known.'

She wet her lips with the tip of her tongue. So, he did want to – to be with her, even though she was a virgin and not experienced in this line of work. She considered. Better to lie with him than a complete stranger. And he was a gentleman, after all, with a reputation to consider. If word got out at the mill! She decided. 'All right,' she whispered. 'If you like.'

He gave a little smile. 'If *I* like, Ruby? What about you?'

'I don't have any option, Mr Newmarch. It's 'workhouse otherwise.'

He gave a gasp. He had no idea that things could be so bad. Did she mean it, or was she playing on his sympathy? A glance at her face told him that she wasn't. She wasn't doing this for sheer pleasure, as he was. He placed both his hands about her face and touched her cheek-bones with his fingers. 'I'd like to think you might want to come, Ruby,' he whispered, and kissed her gently on her mouth.

She drew away slightly and lowered her eyes for a second. She hadn't expected kisses. Then she looked up at him. 'Perhaps I might,' she breathed.

He smiled, satisfied now, and she thought that

he was quite handsome and not so superior as he appeared to be at the mill.

'One evening next week? I'll pass you a note saying where and when.' He was suddenly excited and buoyed up at the prospect. He would find somewhere discreet and more comfortable than this establishment. Some private room where they could feel relaxed, perhaps have a bottle of wine or a little supper and not be disturbed. He couldn't take his eyes off her. She was so lovely. There was no wonder that he had thought about her so often.

Again he ran his fingers around her cheeks and down her throat. He wanted to touch her all over, but he didn't want to frighten her.

'So – our secret, Ruby?'

CHAPTER NINETEEN

After Ruby had gone with Jamie, Grace went home and sat on her new stool by the fireside with her chin in her hands. Her mother had gone to the Market Place to find cheap vegetables and bread; there were often bargains to be had on a Saturday night. Her father was reading, by the light of the fire, a newspaper which he had found discarded in the street.

Could I do what Ruby is doing? Grace wondered, and knew instantly that she could not. She didn't think any worse of Ruby for her decision – she understood her situation exactly and that she and her mother were destined for the workhouse if she didn't take this opportunity. But she was angry with Jamie, who she felt was taking an unfair advantage in living off Ruby's and his mother's earnings.

It was dark outside in the court. There were no lights down here. Only in the main street were there lamps lit by coal gas. She heard a noise outside the window. 'Ma?' she called. 'Is that you?'

'No.' A male voice answered. 'It's Tom Hanson. Can I come in for a minute?'

Grace glanced at her father, who nodded and put down his paper. 'Yes. Just a minute.' She went to the door and drew back the bolt. 'Come in.'

Daniel's father looked as if he had been sleeping rough. His clothes were crumpled and his hair was tangled and in disarray. 'I can't find my wife.'

'Can't find her?' Grace repeated. 'Perhaps she's gone shopping.'

He shook his head. 'No, she hasn't. She went off yesterday morning after Daniel had gone and hasn't been back since. And what's more,' he added glumly, 'what bit o' money we had left has gone with her. I've had not a bite to eat since yesterday.'

'Well, we've nowt to spare,' Grace's father spoke up, his voice brisk. 'Teks us all our time to earn a crust to keep body and soul together.'

'I don't know what to do.' Tom Hanson didn't appear to be listening. 'I'll have to go to 'vagrant office, see if they can help me out.'

'You could try getting a job,' Bob Sheppard said harshly. 'Vagrant office won't pay your rent.'

'Well, that's another thing,' their neighbour replied. 'Rent is due on Monday and I just haven't got it.' He stood staring into their fire and repeated, 'I don't know what to do.'

'Don't know what to do about what? Oh!' Lizzie Sheppard struggled in through the door carrying a sack of potatoes. 'I didn't realize it was you.'

'I'm just saying,' Tom Hanson turned to her to tell his woeful tale, 'my wife's gone missing.'

'Aye? Well, I'd have gone missing if I'd a husband who was work-shy,' she wheezed as she dropped the sack.

He gave a gasp and protested, 'I've worked hard all my life, missus.' He showed her his finger stumps. 'But look at these.'

'You've got another hand, haven't you? You can do summat instead of sitting on your backside waiting for sympathy!'

'You're very outspoken, missus,' he began.

'I'm truthful,' Lizzie interrupted and pointed a finger. 'You and your wife have lost a good son because neither of you are willing to face facts. Your fingers are not going to grow back so you've just got to manage without 'em. And', she continued, 'your wife should try and find work. It's not easy, I grant you that, but there's work to be had if she looks.'

Tom Hanson looked at her and then at Bob and Grace. His face flushed, but he said not a word and simply turned and went out of the door.

'Ma!' Grace began.

'I know! I'm harsh. I didn't show him 'milk of human kindness, but if he'd tried to get a job and wasn't able to, I'd have shared a bowl o' soup wi' him. As it is, he hasn't suffered yet, and nor has his wife. Besides,' Lizzie sank onto the bed, 'I'm that weary, onny compassion I've got right now is for me and mine. I could climb into bed and sleep for a fortnight.'

'Lie down then, Ma.' Grace sat down by her mother. 'I'll make you a cup of tea.'

'Hot water, more like.' Her mother sighed as she lay back and closed her eyes. 'We've onny a scraping of leaves left.'

'Where are these jobs that are to be had?' Grace put the kettle onto the fire.

'One of 'houses in 'High Street where I was washing yesterday. They want somebody to scrub floors. I'd do it but my back won't let me.'

'I'll do it,' Grace said. 'I told Mr Newmarch I'd be looking for other work.'

'Mr Newmarch? Sounds familiar. Who's he?' her father asked.

'He's a manager or something at 'mill. I told him I'd be looking for something else as I couldn't manage on short-time work.'

Her mother sat up in bed and stared at her, and her father laughed. 'Well! I bet he was devastated when you told him that,' he said. 'He'll really miss you not being there!'

Grace gave an embarrassed grin and described what had happened at the mill, when she had led the group of women to ask for their wages. 'It was all right,' she said. 'Mr Newmarch was quite understanding about us needing our money.' She gave a little shrug. 'I've spoken with him before,' she explained. 'When I went with him to 'Groves after the accident with 'ferry.'

'You never said that he was there, Grace,' her mother said in astonishment. 'How was that?'

'Didn't think it was important,' she replied.

'Wasn't he the one you saw at Dock Green?' her father questioned. 'When you were worried that he might think you were a troublemaker and give you notice?'

'Yes,' she said. 'He was. But I hadn't met him then and I was nervous. Now that I've met him, I'm not. I think he does care about his workers.' She pondered. 'Not like his brother, Mr Edward. He doesn't seem to care about anybody.'

Bessie Robson had eagerly taken the money which Ruby had given her and set off towards Savile Street, close to the New Dock. It was a long walk but she didn't have enough money to buy what she called real opium, and so she was heading for a reputable grocer, one who knew how to mix raw opium and spirit and could come up with a mixture which was satisfying to an average craving. Twenty-five drops of laudanum was equal to one grain of opium, and one teaspoon held about one hundred drops. Bessie, however, didn't possess a teaspoon, not even a tin one, and so she would take the laudanum straight from the bottle. One gulp, she reckoned, was more or less the same as a teaspoon.

She was panting as she neared the grocer's shop and eager for the sense of well-being which the mixture would give her, but, as she approached the door, panic hit her. The shop was closed, with the blinds drawn.

'His wife's sick,' somebody called out to her. 'He's had to rush home.'

'But I need my loddy!' She turned to the person who had shouted, and recognized her. 'Who else'll be open?'

'Come wi' me, if you like. I'm going to 'Ship, you might get some there.'

'I can't walk that far, Tess,' she said. It was

beyond the direction that she had just come from. 'My legs – '

The woman shrugged. 'Up to you. You can walk with me if you've a mind to. How much money have you got?'

'Not much,' Bessie confessed. 'Onny enough for a small bottle.'

'Tell you what then, Bessie.' Tess came across to her. She was thin as a stick and dressed in dirty rags. Her face was wrinkled and grey so there was no determining her age. 'I've got enough for a jug of ale. You buy 'loddy and I'll buy 'ale and we'll share.'

She leaned towards Bessie, giving a toothless grin, and Bessie backed away. 'All right then, but by heck, Tess, you don't half stink! Where've you been?'

'My old man's locked me out,' she said. 'He said he was sick of me spending his brass on ale and loddy. He's put a bolt on 'door so's I can't get into 'house.'

'So where've you been?'

'You know them pigsties back of New George Street? Well, I slept wi' pigs last night, warmest place I could find. Lots o' straw, roof was sound, sounder than our house anyway. I'd have stayed all day but pig fella came and turned me out.'

Bessie wrinkled her nose. She was used to smells but this stench was appalling. 'Why you going all 'way to 'Ship?' she asked. 'Been thrown out of all the others?'

The woman nodded. 'Aye, that's about 'strength of it. I owe money in all of 'em, so I can't go in.'

'So where've you got money from now?'

Tess grinned again. 'Beggin',' she said. 'If you follow folks for long enough, they'll 'ventually give some money to get rid of you.'

'Specially if you stink,' Bessie muttered.

'Aye,' she answered, with no offence taken. 'Specially then.'

So Bessie turned around and set off back the way she had come, past the cluster of courts and alleyways which bounded her own home territory and towards The Ship. This hostelry served the boatmen and workers from the mills and factories crowding the side of the river Hull.

'You go in and get it, Bessie,' Tess urged. 'They'll not lend me a jug. I never took 'last one back and they might remember.'

Bessie took her money and entered the inn, pushing her way through a crowd of women and children who were waiting outside. The last time she was in here she'd met her son Josh, who'd bought her ale and tobacco and then taken her to the Whalebone Inn where they'd had supper. She remembered little of that evening, didn't even remember getting home and she hadn't seen Josh since. She sighed and muttered, 'That's men all over, but I expect he'll turn up again sometime.'

A river-man that she knew greeted her and passed her a glass of gin which seared her throat as she tossed it back. The landlord served her with a jug of ale but told her that she couldn't take it home and must drink the ale inside. She took a long drink from the jug before calling to

Tess to come in, and they sat in a dark corner just inside the door.

'I need some loddy.' Bessie looked around the room. Sometimes there were foreign seamen who would give an old woman an odd grain of opium or a scraping of tobacco, but there were none in here tonight and everyone else seemed to be counting out their money carefully when paying the landlord. 'What day is it?' she asked. 'Is it Sat'day?'

'Aye, it might be.' Tess took a gulp from the jug. 'How would I know?'

'If it's Sat'day, then folks is spending their wages.' Men were sitting around a table giving out small piles of coinage to others, who then went to the landlord to buy ale or beer. 'Them women outside'll be lucky if there's enough left to buy a bit o' bread.' She took the jug from Tess and drank deeply. 'I remember that all right,' she said. 'Waiting for him to come home and then having to go and look for him so's I could feed 'bairns. Don't you, Tess?'

Tess had been staring at Bessie as she drank. 'No,' she muttered. 'My old man allus brought his wages home, and I never kept any bairns, they all died when they were babbies. Hey,' she grumbled, as Bessie took another deep drink from the jug. 'I bought that! You were going to buy 'loddy.'

Bessie handed over the jug and wiped her mouth with the back of her hand. 'Well, I will, when I see somebody who might have some.' She cast her eyes around the room again and then to the door where a crush of people were entering. 'Ah! Jamie! He might have some.'

She called him over. 'Have you got any loddy? 'Shop was shut when I went. I've got 'money.' She opened her palm to show him.

Jamie grinned. 'So you have, Bessie! And where did you get that?'

'Our Ruby,' she smirked. 'She's a good lass. Looks after her ma. She'll have got her wages today, I expect, so she's treated me.'

He looks pleased with himself, she thought. His ma must be doing good business and he's living off the proceeds. Whoremonger!

'So what kind do you want, Bessie?' He took the coin from her hand and tossed it casually in the air and caught it. 'Ruby will have worked for this, so you'd better spend it wisely. Don't go wasting hard-earned cash!'

He had a satisfied smile on his face and she viewed him suspiciously. She didn't trust him, never had. But she needed her dose. 'Whatever you can get,' she snapped. 'And look sharp about it.'

'All right. All right. Keep your wig on.' He put his hand in his coat pocket and brought out a small bottle. 'It just so happens that I have some here, and you can have it.'

'It's onny a little bottle.' She reached to take it.

He snatched it away. 'Beggars can't be choosers, but this isn't your common or garden cordial,' he said. 'This is 'real stuff. Bought off a foreign ship. It'll give you some great dreams, Bessie. Tek you to places you never knew existed.'

'Tek it,' Tess broke in urgently. 'And don't forget half of it's mine.'

'Fetch us a measure then,' Bessie demanded of him. 'She'll want her full share.'

'Course I will,' Tess bellowed. 'You've shared my ale. That was 'agreement.'

Jamie brought back two measures and carefully poured the contents into each of them, measuring exactly, and handed them to the women. 'Sweet dreams, ladies,' he grinned and winked.

Tess tossed hers back immediately and then took another gulp from the jug, but Bessie put her nose to the measure and gave a sniff. 'It's not 'usual mix,' she said. 'What's it got in it? Brandy? Gin?'

Jamie shook his head. 'Don't know. Didn't ask. I was just told it was 'best to be had.'

Bessie took a sip, then licked her lips. 'Tastes all right.' She took another sip. 'Yes, it's good.' She tossed back the remainder. 'We'll have some more of this sometime, Jamie.'

He nodded. 'I've let you have that cheap, Bessie. Next time it'll cost you more, but you'll soon have plenty of money so you'll be able to afford it.'

'What?' Bessie shook her head to clear it. Laudanum usually calmed her instantly, but now she felt quite light-headed and giddy and Jamie's hair had a silver halo around it. 'Whatcha mean?'

'You mean you don't know?' He affected amazement. 'Ask Ruby, she'll tell you.'

He left them and wandered over to another

group of people. Bessie drained the jug of ale, then watched him through blurred and narrowed eyes. 'What does he mean?' she asked Tess, who was slumped in her chair. 'He's up to summat.' She staggered to her feet. 'I have to go. I'll be seeing you.'

She managed to get to the doorway and was propelled outside by a group of laughing work-men. 'Watch your step, Ma,' and 'One too many, Bessie?' from someone who seemed to know her. She sat down heavily on the step and slumped forward. She could hear voices, and feet tramped around her, but she had no idea whose voices or feet they were or even where she was.

People drifted noisily past her. Laughing women floated above her in flimsy chiffon gowns. Dark-skinned foreign men, wearing turbans and golden slippers, swung silver swords above their heads as they raced on white horses in a starlit sky. Someone bent down to speak to her, but she couldn't understand what he was saying and he shook his head, and walked on. Freddie came towards her and she reached out to touch him. His face was covered in soot and he stretched out a dirty hand to her. Someone pulled him back. It was Josh and he was covered in slimy seaweed.

'Help me,' she called, but her voice came out in a hoarse whisper. 'Ruby! Where are you? Help your poor old ma.'

Ruby walked by. She looked beautiful. She was wearing a red velvet dress which brushed against Bessie as she passed her, and she didn't even look down. 'Ruby!' she cried again, but knew now that Ruby was part of her dream and couldn't hear her.

Someone else bent down towards her. Some devil with a huge grin on his face. 'Come on, Bessie,' the devil said. 'Let's get you home.'

CHAPTER TWENTY

Ruby left the rooming house and hurried towards home. This was not the place for a lone woman to be, so close by the river and in the dark. Perhaps I should have asked Jamie to wait for me, she pondered. She glanced over her shoulder, but then thought that her decision had been for the best. She could decide now what to say to him, for he was sure to ask if she was seeing her client again.

Mr Newmarch! How incredible that it should have been him, and how amazing too that he should remember her when there were so many women workers at the mill. And he wants to see me again! I wonder if he does or if he was just saying that as an excuse to get away without losing face? Well, I'll know come Monday.

She gathered the skirt of her dress around her as she entered the pitch-black alley leading to Middle Court, in case she should brush against the walls and dirty it, and rushed through with her head down. There was no light in the court except for the glimmer through the Sheppards' window which showed they had a low fire, and a flickering light in the room opposite where Daniel's parents lived.

The warm glow in that room indicated that the fire had recently been lit, for she could see quite clearly a dancing flame in the hearth, and someone huddled over it. She glanced in as she passed and saw Mr Hanson sitting hunched with his chin in his hands.

Perhaps he's worrying over Daniel being at sea. He's had no experience, anything could happen. Dear Daniel, I do miss him so. I want to cry when I think of him and I hope, I really hope he doesn't think badly of me when he comes home. I want him always to think well of me. Not that I've done anything to be ashamed of. Not yet. I'm still as I was and I could stay this way. I don't have to go with Mr Newmarch even if he asks me.

She felt the warmth of the coins in her hand. But am I committed to him, just as I am with Jamie? Of course, I could pay Jamie off now if I want to with the money Mr Newmarch has given me, but he'd smell a rat. I know Jamie. He'd suspect I was cutting him out.

She went into their room and took off the dress and carefully wrapped it back in the bag it had come in. Then, lifting the mattress, she slipped it underneath and dressed in her old garments so that her mother wouldn't suspect anything.

There was a commotion at the door and she cautiously opened it. Bessie, either drunk or asleep, was leaning heavily against Jamie.

'I didn't know if you'd be back yet, Ruby.' He winked at her. 'Everything all right?'

'Everything's fine,' she answered briefly. 'What's happened to Ma?'

'I found her outside 'Ship. Thought I'd better bring her home before she froze to death.'

''Ship?' Ruby gave a shudder. She'd walked right past there, she might so easily have been discovered. Though she intended telling her mother of her new life, she wanted to plan what to say and to tell her in her own way.

'Is she drunk?' She put her face close to Bessie's and sniffed. 'What's she had?'

'She was drinking summat out of a bottle,' Jamie said. 'She mebbe bought some loddy from somebody.'

Together they lowered Bessie down on the mattress. She lay there, snoring. 'So?' Jamie said. 'Everything was all right? No problems with your gentleman?'

'None,' Ruby said. 'I'll pay you tomorrow if you don't mind, Jamie. I'm really tired.'

'I'm sure you are, Ruby, but I'll have 'money now. That's 'way I work.' He gave her a thin smile. 'Will you be seeing him again?'

She handed him the exact money that he'd arranged with Mr Newmarch. He counted it and gave her half back. 'I don't know,' she answered. 'I'm not sure I want to continue. It's an ordeal,' she lied. 'Men don't realize.'

'I don't suppose we do.' The expression on his face wasn't distinguishable because of the gloom in the room, but she knew from the tone of his voice that he had expected a different answer.

'But it'll be easy enough next time. And don't forget you still owe me, Ruby.'

'I won't forget,' she said. 'I'll pay you back as soon as I can.'

'I know you will.' She heard the smile in his voice this time and knew that he was banking on her always being in his debt. 'I'll try for somebody for next Saturday, shall I? Or before?'

'I'll let you know, Jamie,' she said. 'When I've made up my mind.'

She hardly slept that night. Her mother tossed around in her sleep and sometimes sat up shouting, calling for Ruby and for Freddie. 'For heaven's sake, Ma,' Ruby cried out in exasperation. 'Be quiet. I'm worn out!'

But even her own broken slumber was peppered with dreams. Images of Mr Newmarch smiling at her and beckoning, and behind him the grinning face of Jamie with his open palm stretched out towards her. There was an obnoxious smell and the sound of someone groaning, and she woke to the sound of her mother retching over the mattress.

She looked around her and remembered the neat room where she had met Mr Newmarch, the proper bed and the bright fire, and she saw now where she was living. She sat up and wept. I have to get out of here. I'll tell Jamie.

'I'm sorry, Ruby,' her mother snivelled. 'Somebody must have given me some bad loddy.'

'Don't tell me, Ma. I don't want to know. Don't give me excuses. If you want to kill yourself, then go ahead.'

'You give me the money, Ruby,' she whimpered. 'If I hadn't had it I couldn't have spent it.'

Ruby gave a laugh which turned into a sob. 'So it's my fault? I might have known! Do you know where I got 'money from, Ma?'

Her mother stared at her. Her face was grey, her eyes bloodshot and her mouth slack and wet. She shook her head. 'Your wages?'

'Not my wages, Ma. I got it from Jamie.' She hadn't intended telling her this way, but she couldn't help herself. 'He lent it to me. I'm going to join his merry band of street women. Last night was my first night.'

She saw the shame dawning in her mother's eyes, and said, 'But nowt happened and I'm not going to explain why, but that's 'life I'm going to live from now on. I want better than what we've got, Ma, and I'm going to have it.'

Grace rose early on the Sunday morning and peered out of the window. It was a dreary dull day but not raining. She riddled the fire and as the ash was still hot, she put a few sticks on top and hoped that they would kindle. She dressed and went outside to the pump and swilled her face, and glanced across at Ruby's house, wondering how she was this morning. I hope she got home all right and that there wasn't any trouble, she thought. Perhaps Jamie brought her home. She looked across at his house but the curtains were firmly drawn. No-one else seemed to be up; all the houses had their doors closed.

Her mother was just rising as she went back inside. The fire was crackling and Grace put more firewood onto the blaze and a piece of coal, then put a half-filled pan of water on top.

'Stay where you are, Ma,' she said, 'and I'll make some gruel seeing as we haven't any tea.'

'No, it's time I was up.' Her mother gave her husband a pinch. 'Come on, get up. It's Sunday, day of rest.'

He grunted and rolled over. 'What am I doing today that I can't do another day?'

'You can go to 'riverbank and see what 'tide has brought in. We need some kindling for a start.'

Bob gave a grin and pulled the blanket over him. 'In that case I can stay abed a bit longer. Look in that sack yonder, Gracie,' he said. 'That one in 'corner.'

'That's Daniel's,' she said. 'He said it was firewood.'

'Not that one.' He pointed a lazy arm. 'T'other one, next to it.'

She opened it up at the neck. 'Firewood!' she exclaimed. 'Loads of it!'

'Aye. Boss said I can tek as much as I need, all 'short bits that they can't use for owt.'

'Put some more on then. Let's have a blaze.' Her mother was delighted. 'We can have hot water for washing and as soon as weather clears up I'll wash all our clothes.'

Grace opened up the other sack which Daniel had given her and told her to use for firewood. She put her hand inside. 'This isn't firewood!' She frowned. 'These are things he's made!'

She pulled out a model of a schooner with a sharply pointed bow, three slender masts intact but bare of sail, the planed deck smooth and level, its hull polished and gleaming. 'Da!' she breathed. 'Look at this.'

Her father got out of bed and padded towards her. 'Firewood!' he blurted out. 'This is a craftsman's work. What's 'lad thinking of, chucking it out?'

Grace put her hand further into the sack and brought out a model of a small building. 'It's a farmhouse,' she said excitedly. 'Look at 'little doors and windows and this is a barn at the end.' The model was of plain wood. It hadn't been painted or polished and she thought that she would like to paint it and put some curtains at the windows.

There were other items, a wooden box, polished and lacquered, the type that a lady might keep her letters or private correspondence in, a wooden doll with arms and legs and a head, but without a face. A toy cart and several peg dolls.

'These are like you used to make me, Da.' She held up a peg doll. 'And Ma and me used to dress them and paint their faces.'

'Aye.' He took it from her. 'But I never made 'em like this. Why, 'lad could make a fortune making toys like this.'

She nodded thoughtfully and put them back in the sack, placing them carefully, rather than throwing them in one on top of another as Daniel had apparently done. Was he angry when he put them in? she wondered. Was he thinking that here was the end of his dream of becoming a master craftsman like his father?

'I'm going to Dock Green,' she announced as they finished their gruel. 'Unless you want me to do anything, Ma?'

Her mother shook her head. 'No, there's nowt, but why are you going there? Is there somebody special speaking?'

'Yes.' Grace got up from the table. 'There is.' Her mother and father looked up expectantly.

'Who?' they chorused.

She gave a sheepish smile and raised her eyebrows. 'Me!'

They both laughed. 'You!'

'Yes.' She picked up the stool that Daniel had made for her. 'Daniel made this for me to sit on, but he won't mind if I stand on it.'

'But what are you going to talk about?' her mother asked.

'Injustice!' she replied defiantly. 'I'm going to ask if folk think it's right that lads should have to give up their chance of a trade because they haven't any money to live on. And is it right that young women should have to become street women in order to eat.'

She saw the shocked look on her parents' faces, then realization dawning on her mother's. 'Not Ruby?' her mother grieved.

'Yes. I probably shouldn't have told you, but you'd find out anyway. She can't keep her mother and herself and pay 'rent on two days' money.'

'She could scrub floors,' her mother protested. 'If I thought that you –'

'I won't,' Grace declared. 'But I'm not as desperate as Ruby is, and I've got you and Da.

238

We can pull together.' She appealed to them. 'She's tried for work. Please don't blame Ruby.'

'No, I won't blame her,' her mother said bitterly. 'But I'll blame her ma. Bessie. She's got a lot to answer for.'

Her father said nothing, but leaned his elbow on the table and rested his chin in his hand. He kept his eyes lowered and Grace wondered why he didn't comment. 'Do you want to come with me, Da?'

'I might,' he murmured.

'I'll come,' her mother determined. 'If I can walk that far. I'll deal wi' hecklers.'

'Hecklers!' Grace was startled. 'Why should there be hecklers?'

'You don't expect everybody to agree with you, do you, girl?' her mother asked. 'There's some folk who make it their business to go around disrupting meetings – stirring up trouble.'

'But I don't want any trouble,' Grace contended. 'I onny want to say what I feel.'

'Then that's what you must do if you think that folks will listen,' her mother agreed. 'Pass me your hairbrush. Let's show 'em that we can be clean and tidy and proud, as well as poor.'

CHAPTER TWENTY-ONE

Grace walked to Dock Green alone. Her mother said she would take her time and come when she was ready, and her father was undecided whether to come at all. There was a nip in the air heralding snow and she remembered the lady who had given her a ride in her carriage, saying that no-one wanted to stand out in the rain to listen to speakers. Well, it wasn't raining, but it was very cold and who would want to stand outside on a winter's day?

But she also knew that the poor would walk anywhere if there was a chance of free entertainment, and often the fresh air of outdoors was preferable to the stale and damp air of their houses.

There were one or two speakers climbing onto their boxes but only a few people wandering around Dock Green, along with some stray dogs sniffing at trees and bushes. She noticed two ladies in voluminous cloaks carrying opened umbrellas over them, even though it wasn't raining. Then, as a chaise drew up at the entrance, they hurried across to it.

The coach driver jumped down from his seat and helped two ladies out, and handed a small box to one of them. The four ladies looked around the area before making their way to a particular spot where they put down the box. Another chaise drew up, and from it descended the same gentlewoman who had previously given Grace and her father a ride towards home.

Grace watched curiously, then followed her as she joined the other ladies, took out a bundle of papers from her reticule, and stepped up onto the box.

She's going to speak, Grace thought, even though there are not many folk here. Then she saw that more people were coming onto the Green, small groups who were obviously together, not poor folk from the town, Grace observed, but well-dressed people. Men in top hats or caps with ear flaps to keep out the cold, and heavy overcoats down to their ankles. The women too were dressed against the cold with wool capes over their wide skirts, and velvet bonnets perched on their heads. Most of them carried black umbrellas.

So who are these people? Grace wondered, and clutching her stool drew closer. What have they to talk about? Surely, judging by their dress, they are respectable and comfortably off? They can have no complaints to speak of.

She put down her stool and stepped on it. I'll tell them, she determined, I'll tell them of difficulties which they cannot imagine as they sit in their fine houses and drive in their carriages.

'My name is Grace Sheppard,' she began, and raised her voice as she saw more people arriving. Shabby, ordinary folk, like herself.

'Why would I choose to stand here on a cold February morning?' she shouted. 'When I could be enjoying the luxury of a straw mattress and a bowl of gruel? Why? Because I want summat better, that's why!

'I'm not yet seventeen, yet I have been working since I was nine years old at 'cotton mill. Eight hours a day I was allowed to work when I was a child, and I was grateful. I was *very* grateful, for it meant that I was helping my parents to pay 'rent and put food into our mouths.'

She was aware of the crowd edging towards her. She was the first of the speakers to find her voice, although there were others now who had placed their boxes strategically around Dock Green. She saw the group of ladies looking towards her and murmuring together. Perhaps they think I'm stealing a march on them, she thought.

'But now,' she continued. 'Now that I'm a grown woman, there's no work for me.' She lifted up her hands. 'I'm not blaming my employers for 'decline in 'cotton industry. But is it right that children should be employed to climb beneath moving machines in order to clean them, to swab down floors, to breathe in 'cotton dust on their poor little chests – for less money than I'd be given for that same work?'

One or two women in the crowd, dressed in cotton skirts and shawls as she was, raised their hands and clapped, and one shouted, 'No, it's not right. They should be given 'same, then we'd all be well off!'

Grace looked at her in dismay. 'That's not 'point,' she contested. 'They shouldn't have to work.'

'I know.' The woman laughed. 'It was a joke, dearie! But how would we manage without our bairns working?'

'Children shouldn't be allowed to work,' Grace emphasized. 'There should be a law against it. And working men and women should be given a decent wage so that their childre' didn't have to work! Why should an apprentice lad be forced to give up 'chance of a trade, because he can't afford to live? And why, as a last resort, should women have to take on night work?' She waited a second for the right impact. 'Yes.' She nodded her head. 'Night work! Out on 'streets selling their bodies for a shilling so that they might feed their families.'

There was a silence for a moment, then someone, a man, shouted, 'Shame! It's a sin! There's no excuse for immoral prostitution.'

Grace put up her hand for silence as women in the crowd heckled him. 'My father would kill me rather than I should take such a step. But what of those women who have no such guidance? Who have no other means of dragging themselves from 'depths of poverty? Starvation *is* a valid excuse.'

She pointed in the direction from where the voice had come. 'I ask – have you ever felt such despair? Have you ever been without food or a blanket to keep you warm, or been unable to pay

243

your rent? Or have you, sir, had 'comfort of a warm bed and the promise of food next morning and so had 'energy to moralize on others less well off than yourself?'

She didn't know where her words were coming from. She seemed to be opening her mouth and they poured out. She only knew, by the murmurings and ripple of conversation running through the crowd, that she had them firmly in her hand, and the man who had spoken so vehemently was silent.

'Rights for women!' A voice called out. 'Equal rights as men. Sisters, is that not what we deserve?'

Heads turned towards the other voice, and Grace looked too. It was the lady from the chaise. 'Our young sister here', she pointed towards Grace, 'has learned at a tender age that women don't have the same rights as men.'

Grace frowned. I wasn't talking about equal rights, I was talking about working children! And why is she calling me sister? How could I possibly be a sister of hers? We're from a different world. Has she ever known poverty?

'Madam,' she called back in reply. 'I don't have equal rights as men. I was a poor child and am now a poor woman. I have no rights at all!'

A great shout rose up, for now most of the crowd were the townspeople of Hull, out-numbering by far the well-dressed element who had obviously come to hear the other speaker. But Grace stepped down from her stool, satisfied with her reception.

'Grace!' Her mother stood there. 'I couldn't

believe it was you up there! Where did you get such learning?'

Grace took her mother's arm, for she seemed tired. It was a long walk from Middle Court to Dock Green. 'It could only have been from your knee, Ma,' she said. 'Yours and Da's, for where else have I been to learn?'

'Nowhere else, it's true,' her mother agreed.

'You taught me to think for myself, Ma. To be honest, and to expect to work for what I need.'

She stopped and looked up at a figure hovering near. It was Martin Newmarch, and a lady was standing beside him.

'Miss Sheppard,' he greeted her. 'Congratulations on your excellent speech!' He raised his eyebrows and she suspected the slight twitch of his lips was humour, though it was gone in a second, as he continued, 'And many thanks for not blaming your former employers for the lack of work.'

Former employers! She took a breath. So her work at the mill was finished. She inclined her head but didn't dip her knee as she once might have done. 'Mr Newmarch.'

He turned to his companion. 'May I introduce Miss Grace Sheppard – Mrs Westwood.'

They both inclined their heads and Grace, not to be outdone, turned to her mother. 'Ma, this is Mr Martin Newmarch, from 'cotton mill. Mr Newmarch and Mrs Westwood, this is my mother, Mrs Elizabeth Sheppard.'

Martin Newmarch made a short bow. 'Mrs Sheppard, you have a very remarkable daughter.'

'Aye,' her mother said proudly. 'That I know.

She's our onny one and I'm glad of it, for she'd tek 'shine off any others that we might have had.'

'You are not of the opinion, then, Mrs Sheppard,' Mrs Westwood spoke in a soft well-modulated voice, 'that the more children parents have, the more money can be earned when they are of age?'

'No, ma'am. I've never thought that.' Lizzie Sheppard gazed squarely at her. 'I didn't bring any bairns into 'world just for them to earn a living, though childre' sometimes come along even when they're not wanted. But there's nowt such as us can do about that. No,' she emphasized. 'We wanted one, or mebbe two that would follow our family line, for continuity's sake you might say.'

Grace stared at her mother. Now she knew for sure where her words and thinking came from. From her parents. From her father who had taught her to read, and from her mother who wasn't afraid to express an opinion.

'You are very fortunate, Mrs Sheppard,' Mrs Westwood remarked, 'to still have your daughter's company. I have a young son and daughter whom I am not allowed to see.'

'Not allowed to see?' Lizzie exclaimed and drew closer to her. 'How's that then?'

'I have left my husband, Mrs Sheppard. He is an extremely cruel and brutal man, and as a punishment for leaving I am banned from seeing my children.' She glanced at Grace. 'That is why I am here today, to support Miss Gregory's campaign for equal rights for women.'

'I didn't realize,' Grace whispered. 'I thought – '

'You thought that only the poor suffered?' Martin Newmarch looked down at her and smiled as she nodded. 'Well, it's probably true that the poor suffer more than most, poverty and hunger must be deplored, but others too can suffer when deprived of home and children.'

'So what did your husband do that you took 'drastic step of leaving?' Lizzie asked. 'It must have been summat bad for you to leave your bairns behind.'

'He beat me in private,' Mrs Westwood said quietly, 'and insulted me in public. That is why I am not afraid of speaking of him now. His character is common knowledge.'

'Well,' Lizzie considered. 'It wouldn't happen with our kind. A beating, yes, and insults, but those sort of men would throw their bairns out after their wives, and be glad to see 'em go.'

'So what would happen to them? These women and their children?'

'Workhouse,' Lizzie replied, matter-of-factly. 'I have— had a friend in such a situation.' Her face seemed to tense. 'It was 'onny place she could go.'

Mrs Westwood shuddered. 'Then I am fortunate indeed that I have good friends who are willing to help me and give me shelter.'

'Have you no family or money of your own?' Lizzie asked curiously. She appeared quite un-embarrassed and not at all intimidated by this well-spoken gentlewoman as they strolled side by side, leaving Grace to fall behind with Martin Newmarch.

'My parents are elderly,' Mrs Westwood said. 'But they are of the opinion that I should have stayed with my husband no matter what his conduct might be. I have no money of my own, what was mine is now my husband's.'

'So what will you do, Grace?' Martin Newmarch murmured to her. 'You said that you would look for other employment.'

'I'll continue with my two days at 'mill until I find something else,' Grace said. 'If I'm still wanted.' She looked up at him, trying to assess his opinion. 'If nobody finds out that I've been speaking against child labour.'

He frowned and glanced quickly at her. 'Do you think that I – ?'

'I don't know, sir,' she said frankly. 'But word will get out eventually. There are some mill workers here today.'

'It won't come from me,' he assured her. 'I am a believer in free speech. That is why I come here. But you must be careful, Grace. You could so easily make enemies.'

The following day, Monday, word was around the mill that the quiet and angelic-looking Grace Sheppard had been on a speaker's box at Dock Green. Whispered conversations buzzed around in odd corners in the weaving shed, the scutching house, the warehouse and eventually the office block.

The foreman beckoned her at the end of the day. 'You're to go and get your wages. Sorry, Grace, but you're up 'crooked path, that's for sure. You're to be finished. You'll not be asked back, not after speaking your mind.'

It had come more quickly than she had anticipated. Not Mr Newmarch, she pondered, but one of my own kind. Perhaps it was unintentional, but people will talk and it must have got back to the management.

It was Martin Newmarch who was waiting to see her in his office, and through another door she saw Edward Newmarch look up from his desk and curiously survey her.

'I'm sorry, Miss Sheppard.' Martin Newmarch was formal, as she expected; there were others within hearing. 'But I regret that we are no longer able to offer you further employment.'

'May I ask why, sir?' she asked, and wondered what the official reason would be.

He gazed at her and there was no expression in his brown eyes. Then he replied, 'We are cutting down on our workforce. The decline in the cotton industry, you know!' There was just a hint of a glimmer in his passive expression as he repeated her own words of the day before.

'The shareholders expect their dividends, of course,' he murmured so that only she could hear, 'so we must make cuts as appropriate.'

She stared at him. Shareholders! Was that why the workers' wages were so low? She longed to ask him, though she knew that she couldn't. How ignorant I am. She swallowed hard. 'Thank you for your explanation, Mr Newmarch. I'm grateful for that.'

She turned away to go out of the office, but he called her back and said in a low voice, 'If you are in any difficulties, Grace, do let me know. I will help if I can.'

She put her chin up. 'Thank you, Mr Newmarch. It's kind of you. But I shan't need any help.'

Ruby was waiting outside for her. 'What's up, Grace? What's happening?'

Ruby had been quiet and tense that morning as they'd walked to work and had said nothing about Saturday night. Grace hadn't seen fit to question her, but had described briefly her own Sunday morning at Dock Green. Now Ruby was jittery and clutched a piece of paper which she kept folding and unfolding.

'I've been finished,' Grace said. 'Management have been told about me speaking at Dock Green. I expect they think I'm making trouble.'

'I'll go and plead for you, Grace. I will. I dare. I think.'

Grace smiled. 'No, it doesn't matter. Anyway, I've seen 'management. Mr Newmarch told me that they're cutting down on staff. Decline of 'cotton industry!'

'Mr Newmarch!' Ruby said nervously. 'Which one?'

'Mr Martin. He's the one that does 'employing and sacking.'

'Ah,' Ruby said softly. 'Yes! Grace,' she muttered. 'I've got summat to tell you.'

She told of her meeting with Edward Newmarch on Saturday night, and of him wanting to see her again. 'I thought he was mebbe saying that just to get away, seeing as I knew him. But he wasn't.' She held up the piece of paper. 'He gave me this this morning. He's arranged a time and place.'

'When?' Grace said. She was almost as apprehensive as Ruby appeared to be.

'Tonight,' she said. 'Nine o'clock.' She clutched Grace's arm. 'I'm frightened, Grace. What's to become of us?'

'Don't be frightened, Ruby.' Grace squeezed Ruby's hand. 'We'll be all right, you and me. Let's just think of it as if we're both starting a new way of life.'

CHAPTER TWENTY-TWO

Ruby again dressed in the red gown, only this time her mother buttoned her up instead of Grace. 'I'm sorry, Ruby,' she kept repeating. 'I've been a bad mother, but I've allus cared about you, and Freddie too.'

Ruby didn't answer. She felt numb, beaten, and, she thought, if Ma had really cared about us I wouldn't be doing this. Nor would I have taken on the responsibility of managing the household when I was little more than a child. She took a deep breath. No. Ma would have worked, just like Grace's mother does. She wasn't prepared to admit, even to herself, that if her mother hadn't been addicted to opium, things would have been so different.

There was a good fire burning in the hearth. Grace had brought some firewood and Ruby had bought a small sack of coal with the money she had left. Her mother shuffled closer to it. 'It's good to have a fire, Ruby,' she said contentedly. 'I've had a nice dinner. Things are looking up. Somebody's smiling down on us at last.'

Ruby gave an exasperated exclamation. She

had bought her mother a meat pie with the money Mr Newmarch had given her, but already Bessie had forgotten how the money had been earned. Oh, what's the use! She picked up the shawl which Grace had again loaned her. I might as well just get it over and done with.

Her mother patted Ruby's hair. 'You look beautiful, Ruby.' She smiled possessively. 'You tek after me, of course. Once I was beautiful too. Now off you go. Be a good girl and be nice to your gentleman, if that's what he is. And don't mix with anybody rough,' she added, 'cos that could be your downfall.'

Ruby sighed and shook her head and opened the door, letting in the cold night air. 'I might be late, Ma. Don't tell anybody where I've gone, especially not Jamie. Do you hear?' she repeated. 'Especially not Jamie.'

'I'll not tell Jamie owt,' her mother replied. 'I'll keep 'door bolted. I'm sure it was Jamie what sold me that bad loddy 'other night.'

Ruby put the shawl over her head as she scurried along the dark streets, skirting the old dock and heading towards St Mary's church where Mr Newmarch had suggested they should meet. As she passed the top of Leadenhall Square, the notorious area of prostitutes and brothels, several men whistled to her and invited her to come and talk to them, but she kept her head down and hurried on. She was breathless by the time she reached the narrow street of Lowgate and saw the tower of the old church looming before her in the darkness.

What if he's not there? she worried. Why didn't

he arrange to meet in an inn? She stepped to one side as a chaise, followed by another, rattled by, and she pressed against the walls of the tower. But he was there. He stepped out of the shadows and said in a low voice, 'Ruby? Is it you?'

'Yes, sir,' she whispered. 'It's me.'

'I'm sorry. I didn't realize it would be so dark.' He came close to her and touched his top hat. 'I didn't want to meet in an inn, my club is too close by.' He gestured towards the High Street, which lay behind the church. 'There may be people who know me.'

'Yes, I understand.' So where are we going? she wondered. We're not staying here. Not by the church. I'll not have that!

'Come.' He took her arm. 'I have booked us a private room at an hotel near the pier. The Vittoria. Perhaps you know it? It's a very respectable place.'

'I know it,' she said softly, and tears sprang to her eyes. It's where I spent the best birthday of my life. It's where I shared a glass of ale with Daniel and Grace. She stifled a sob. Daniel! What would you think of me now?

It was bitterly cold as they walked on, going by the towering Holy Trinity Church, the Market Place and its empty stalls, past the King William statue which glimmered beneath the lamplight, and crossing into Queen Street towards the river Humber. The tide was in and dashed against the wooden jetty and landing slip, throwing up spumes of spray.

Ruby shivered and wrapped her shawl more closely about her. Edward Newmarch looked down at her. 'You're cold! Have you no coat or cloak?'

She gave a small laugh. 'No, sir, I haven't.'

'Then we must get you something to warm you up, a brandy perhaps?'

'That'd be very nice, sir,' Ruby agreed as they walked through the doors of the hotel. And perhaps it will help to ease my nerves, she thought, as she shivered with fright as well as the cold.

A uniformed pageboy took them upstairs and opened a door to a room. 'Supper will be served presently, sir,' he said, as he accepted a coin from Edward and took his coat and hat and hung them up on a coat stand. 'Is there anything else I can bring you?'

'Yes. Two large brandies, some sugar and hot water.'

'For a toddy, sir? I'll do that for you. Yes indeed. It's a very cold night.'

Ruby glanced around the room. There was a blazing fire and two armchairs beside it, several rugs, and a sort of bed, she supposed, or perhaps it was a sofa, half hidden behind a lace curtain. There were flowers on a table and a bottle of red wine and two glasses. She was overawed. It was very grand. So much more so than the rooming house Jamie had taken her to.

'Let me take your shawl,' he said quietly, 'or are you still cold?'

She couldn't stop shivering. 'I'm cold, sir.' She looked up at him. 'And I'm frightened.'

'Still frightened?' His heart began to pound. He wanted her, but he didn't want her to be nervous and tense. If only the boy would hurry up with the brandy. 'Come and sit here by the fire.'

She did as he bid and took off her boots so that she wouldn't dirty the rugs, and, as she sat, there came a discreet knock on the door. The boy entered with the brandies, followed by a maid with a trolley which was covered with a white cloth. The maid removed the covering and they both backed out of the room.

Ruby lifted her head and stared, her eyes widening as she saw the slices of cold beef and ham, and was that chicken? There was a crusty loaf and a slab of rich yellow butter and something in little white dishes. Her stomach churned and she licked her lips. Her shivering eased. If she was to be fed as well as paid for her services, perhaps it wouldn't be such a bad life after all, though she was sure that this wasn't what Jamie had in mind.

Edward passed her the toddy. 'Drink this,' he said. 'It will warm you. Then we'll eat.' He gave a small smile. 'Then perhaps you won't be so nervous.'

She took a sip, and the liquid burned her throat. Brandy wasn't something she was used to. 'You're very kind, sir,' she murmured.

His eyebrows shot up and he laughed. 'No, I'm not! Not one of my acquaintances would ever describe me as kind.'

'Well, I onny speak as I find, sir.' She took another sip and then drained the glass in a gulp. 'That's better.' She stood up from the chair. 'Do you want me to – ' She lifted her hands. 'Or – ?'

He laughed again. 'You are funny, Ruby. Sit down. There's no hurry. We have all night.' He seemed more relaxed now that they were alone. As they had walked through the town he kept glancing about him as if afraid they might be seen. 'Would you like to eat?'

'Oh, yes, please.' She stood up again and he led her to the table and pulled out a chair for her.

He picked up one of the white dishes and passed it to her, asking, 'Would you like to start with potted chicken? Or perhaps a slice of ballotine of pheasant?'

Her eyes became large and luminous. What should she have first?

'Please.' He indicated that she should begin. 'Have whatever you want.' He poured two glasses of wine from the bottle which the boy had opened, placed one in front of Ruby, took a sip from his own and sat back in his chair with a little smile on his face.

'Aren't you going to eat?' she asked as she tucked into the potted chicken which she had spread on a slice of bread, then she reached for a slice of beef. 'It's wonderful,' she mumbled, her mouth half-full.

'Ruby?' He leaned towards her. 'When did you last eat?'

'Today,' she nodded. 'I had a slice of bread before I left for work. Oh, and I took a bite out of a pie I'd bought for my ma's dinner.'

And it's now nine thirty, he pondered, and sighed. Looking at the way she was devouring the food they could be here until midnight, and he decided there and then that he would stay at his club and not go home.

She sat back and gave a little belch, putting her fingers to her mouth. 'If I eat any more I shan't be able to – what I mean is – you'll want to be getting home soon.'

'I know what you mean, Ruby, and I'm not going home tonight.' He stood up, and putting out his hand he pulled her to her feet. 'You can eat again later if you wish,' he said softly. 'And we can have more wine and another table full of food if you are still hungry.' He paused. 'I'm hungry.' He ran his fingers over her cheeks. 'But not for food.'

She moistened her lips with her tongue and his eyes went to her mouth. 'Mr Newmarch,' she whispered. 'I don't know what to do. I told you – I haven't been with a man before.'

He bent and kissed her on the mouth and unbuttoned his waistcoat. This must be savoured, he thought. I mustn't rush her. She's a virgin. Surely unusual in a woman like her. Her lips were soft and he could taste the wine on them. They parted and he gently touched them with his tongue. She gave a small gasp and drew back and he ran his fingers around her mouth, shaping her Cupid's bow and her full lower lip.

'I know what to do,' he whispered. 'You are so beautiful, Ruby. I have never known anyone as lovely as you.' He felt himself slipping into a reverie of avid yearning. He was enamoured and captivated by her, eager and breathless to possess her, but he also wanted to cherish the moment, to savour the tantalizing seduction which was yet to come.

'Take off your dress.' His eyes didn't leave her face as he unfastened his cravat and shirt buttons.

'I can't,' she breathed.

He blinked. 'Why not?'

'I can't undo 'buttons,' she said. 'It's fastened at 'back.'

He tore off his shirt and turned her around, and lifting her hair he bent to kiss the back of her neck and top of her shoulder, then with nervous fingers he started to unfasten the tiny buttons. 'Damn and blast,' he said in an undertone. 'What foolish fashion.' But at least she isn't wearing a hoop as – as – He brushed aside his thoughts of May and concentrated on unfastening the buttons.

'I can do it now,' she said, as he unfastened the dress down to the waist.

'No.' He reached for her again. 'I want to do it.' His eyes were glazed and he ran his tongue around his lips. God! I can't wait. I want her now. But he controlled himself, he knew not how, until all the buttons were undone. He slipped the dress off her shoulders and her arms free from the ruched sleeves, and watched fascinated as the gown fell in folds around her ankles onto the rug.

He gave a deep gasping breath, and then another, and gazed at her with his lips parted. She was not wearing stockings or pantaloons, nor the layers of petticoats he had expected, but was covered only by a flimsy cotton sleeveless shift

259

which came to her knees. Through the thin material he saw her rounded breasts and a dark shadow at the top of her slender thighs.

'Oh, God!' He sank to his knees and put his arms around her legs, feeling the touch of her flesh against his bare chest, whilst she took deep gulping breaths.

'Mr Newmarch, sir – '

'Edward,' he muttered. 'My name is Edward.' He pulled her down towards him and lifted the shift above her head. 'I want to look at you, Ruby. I want to feast my eyes on you.'

She knelt beside him on the rug and he ran his hands around her throat and down to her breasts, touching her nipples, which stood out proud. 'I feel very strange, Mr – Edward,' she said breathlessly. 'Very strange. As if I'm drunk. I think I've had too much wine.'

'No, not too much wine.' He stroked her belly down to the bush of dark hair and she gave little startled jumps and gasps. 'It's desire, Ruby, that you are feeling now.' He pulled her down onto the rug and leaning over her, he murmured, 'Tell me that is what it is, Ruby. Tell me that it is desire!'

CHAPTER TWENTY-THREE

Edward hired a cab to take her home. It was two in the morning and not a fit time, he declared, for her to be out on her own when footpads and ne'er-do-wells were about. He wanted to see her again and had booked the room at the hotel for the coming Friday.

'If I can wait so long, Ruby,' he murmured as he handed her into the cab and promised that next time would be better for her. She sat back against the cushions and although she had been deflowered and her body felt tender, she didn't feel violated, but intoxicated and rather powerful.

He had been tender, which she hadn't expected, but also passionate and demanding, and as she'd cried out as he penetrated her, he had held her in his arms and shouted, 'You're mine now, Ruby. I am the first – there can never be another.'

Before they left the room he had opened his sovereign case and taken out a coin and handed it to her. 'I can't take that, sir.' She had reverted to respect, though she had called him Edward several times during their coupling. 'Nobody would change it for me, they'd think it was stolen.'

He'd emptied his pockets then, and his pocketbook, and given her a handful of coins, silver and bronze, and told her that he would make it up to her on Friday when next they met. She jingled the coins with glee. 'I can pay 'rent now, agent's sure to come,' she murmured as the cab rattled down Lowgate, 'and I shan't want to eat for at least a week after that feast.'

She had eaten a second supper and Edward had watched her in some amusement as she indulged herself, and then had pulled her away from the table and whispered that he found it most erotic to see her gourmandizing so voluptuously. She didn't understand his coaxing blandishments very well.

The cab slowed as it reached Mason Street and the cabbie called down to her. 'Will you be all right from here, miss? I can't get down these narrow streets.'

'Yes, I can manage now. I know my way.'

'I'll wait for a bit if you like, then give me a shout when you're nearly there.'

Edward had given the driver a good tip and told him to see her safely home. He was going to walk down the High Street to his club and didn't seem to be worried about his own safety.

'No, I'll be all right. You get off.' She didn't want to draw attention to herself. There would be some curious comments if she was seen alighting from a cab, especially from someone like Jamie who might be mooching about at this hour.

She cut through several narrow streets until she came to the alley and scooted down it with her shawl wrapped around her head. Oh, suppose Ma's bolted 'door! She had said that she would. I'll have to knock her up and I'll waken all of 'court, she sleeps that heavy.

But the door wasn't bolted, it yielded as she lifted the sneck but there was something preventing her from opening it. She pushed and something malleable moved behind it. 'Is that you, Ruby?' a voice whispered.

'Yes,' she whispered back. 'Who is it? Let me in.'

The door opened. It was Mr Blake from upstairs. 'I've been guarding 'door,' he said in a low voice. 'Your ma was worried about leaving it open, but didn't want to lock it in case she didn't hear you.' It was dark in the entrance and she couldn't see his face and knew that neither could he see hers.

'Bessie said that you'd gone to 'music hall,' he explained. 'And might be late, so I said I'd wait up for you.'

'Oh, Mr Blake. That was good of you. Yes,' she added to the story which she was sure he didn't believe. 'A friend took me for a treat.' She fingered the coins in her hand until she felt a sixpence. 'Look what I found under my seat.' She handed it to him. 'You can have it for being so thoughtful.'

His hand reached out eagerly, then drew back. 'Are you sure? It don't seem fair when you found it.'

'But I've had such a good time, Mr Blake,

and you deserve it. Take it before I change my mind.'

He took it and she felt his smile glow in the darkness. 'Thanks, Ruby. Any time if you go again I'll watch out for you, and keep an eye on your ma as well.'

Grace rose early the next morning, washed, dressed, ate a slice of bread and wrapped her old shawl around her. Her mother had risen wearily from her bed and was dressing.

'I'm going down to that house in 'High Street, Ma. The one that wants somebody to scrub floors.'

Her mother nodded. 'Aye, get there early. It'll show you can get up in a morning.'

It was only just five o'clock and still dark. Her father rolled out of bed and stretched. 'Oh, what a life!' he groaned.

'Be thankful you're in work,' Lizzie said, 'even though you onny get a pittance.'

'Gaffer's known for keeping his workers,' Bob commented. 'If they're reliable and he can trust 'em.'

The streets were already busy with workers hurrying to their places of employment in the seed mills and blubber yards along the river Hull. Grace was now heading in the other direction, still following the line of the river but towards the town and the cobbled High Street. Here the shipping merchants had their offices, and some still had their homes adjacent to the busy waterside.

She cut down one of the staithes which led

to the waterfront and round to the rear of a building, and knocked on a door. A young, sleepy-looking maid opened it and Grace asked to speak to the cook or housekeeper.

'Housekeeper's still abed,' the girl said, 'but Cook will be down in a minute. What is it you want?' she asked curiously. 'We don't need any housemaids and mistress has a lady's maid already.'

Grace shook her head. 'I heard you needed somebody for scrubbing floors. My ma comes to do 'washing here.'

'Lizzie?' the girl said. 'Are you Lizzie's lass?' She opened the door for Grace to enter. 'You'd better come in.'

She took Grace down a flight of steps to the basement area which, in spite of having only one small window, was surprisingly light. It was lit by several oil lamps, and was very warm, the heat coming from an enormous iron cooking range. This was bedecked with several fire-bars, spit racks, basting ladles, a huge copper kettle and a stone salt box, set into the side of the fireplace wall.

'Want a dish o' tea while you're waiting?' the girl asked. 'I've just brewed it ready for Cook. Go on,' she said, seeing Grace's hesitation. 'I've just had one and she won't be down until dead on quarter to six.'

Grace accepted and sipped the strong, scalding tea, so different from their own weak brew at home which was made with as few leaves as possible in order to eke it out.

'You don't look 'sort to be scrubbing floors,'

the maid said chattily. 'I'd have thought you'd be a shop girl or a lady's maid. Where did you work afore?'

'At 'cotton mill,' Grace replied. 'I've worked there since I was nine. But our hours have been cut,' she explained. 'So I decided to look for something else.'

On the stroke of quarter to six the inner door opened and a portly woman in a huge white apron and cap bustled in. By then Grace had finished her tea and was sitting demurely on a hard chair by the kitchen door.

'Now then, Mary, have you got stoked up and 'tea made?' She looked across to Grace. 'And who's this early morning caller?'

Grace stood up. 'I'm Grace Sheppard, Cook. I understand you need some help in 'kitchen.'

'Lizzie's daughter?' The cook looked her over. 'I need somebody strong for scrubbing floors, I'm a scullery maid short. But I don't think you'd do. You look as if a breath o' wind'd blow you over.'

'I'm very strong,' Grace asserted. 'I've been a mill girl for 'last seven years and that was hard work.'

'Aye, so I've heard, and long hours as well? I suppose you've been finished cos you're older?'

'Decline in cotton industry, so I've been told,' she said cautiously. 'There's not so much demand.'

The cook sniffed. 'That's what they say, is it? Well, I'll put you on trial, your ma's a hard worker so mebbe you tek after her. Can you start now?' she demanded.

'Yes.' Grace took off her shawl and rolled up her sleeves. 'I can.'

She was given a coarse brown cotton apron, shown where the pails and scrubbing brushes were and told to scrub the kitchen and pantry floor. 'Can you show me where 'pump is?' she asked Mary. 'Then I'll draw 'water.'

'You can have hot water,' Mary said. 'You don't have to use cold,' and with both hands she unhooked the kettle from over the fire to fill the bucket. 'Besides, we have a lad to draw water for us. We don't do that. He keeps all 'pans and kettles topped up.'

Grace put washing soda in the bucket and was given a slab of soap, and she set to work to scrub the floors.

'Mek sure you wipe suds off,' Cook called to her. 'Don't want anybody slipping.'

When she had finished the kitchen and pantry, Cook came to inspect them. She looked into the corners and, as seemingly they were satisfactory, she told Grace to wash the floors in the butler's pantry and in the cold pantry where the milk and cheese were kept, and also the wine cellar. 'Onny don't knock any of 'bottles or wipe 'dust off 'em, whatever you do,' she said. 'Just swab down 'floor.'

It was nine o'clock when she had finished, and the kitchen was bustling with maids preparing breakfast trays to take upstairs. 'Sit down and have a cup o' tea and some breakfast afore you go,' Cook said. 'Can you come again on Friday? I'll give you regular two mornings a week. The other maid can keep dust down during week if you'll come to do 'hard graft.'

Grace agreed that she would and the cook said that the housekeeper would pay her every Friday, seeing as she was a casual worker. 'If you want more work,' she said, 'you can try next door at 'shipping company. Masterson and Rayner. They're onny offices, there's nobody living there any more. 'Family moved out years ago, but I happen to know they need somebody to keep 'place clean. Tell 'em I sent you,' she added.

Grace finished her breakfast of bread and cold ham and another cup of hot strong tea. Although her hands were red and sore, she felt deliriously happy that she had obtained work and was promised more, and had the most unusual sensation of fullness in her stomach.

She took a deep satisfying breath as she went out of the door and glanced across to the bustling river. The sun was well up and although the wind was sharp, it was a bright morning. Silver ripples shimmered on the water and gulls screeched overhead. Ships were being unloaded at the staithe side and everywhere along the wooden planking there were piles of ropes and crates. Men shouted and called out instructions to each other.

She gave a little smile. I like this town, she thought. Even though I'm poor and we have to put up with the stink of blubber and seed oil and the burning stench from the charnel house, this is my town. I like the river being close by, even though some of it's a sewer, and the Humber estuary too, with its promises of other lands as it leads out to the sea. The sea. I've never seen the sea, but I can smell it even as I stand here.

She was turning away to leave the staithe side and go back into the High Street to try the building next door, when two men came into view, their heads down in earnest discussion. One was middle-aged, dressed in a black cloth coat and trousers, but hatless, and the other wore a grey overcoat with a grey top hat. When he raised his head, she saw it was Martin Newmarch.

They both looked across at her, and she gave a little dip of her knee and went on her way down the next staithe side to the building of Masterson and Rayner. There was a large yard with stables and empty waggons, but no-one about. She knocked on an open door but there was no response, so she climbed up an outside wooden staircase and knocked on a door at the top.

'Come in,' a man's harassed voice called, and she opened the door and said, 'I'm sorry to bother you, sir, but I'm looking for work and was advised to come here.'

A broad-set man in his mid thirties leaned back in his desk chair and laughed. 'I never thought I'd see 'day when a woman worked in shipping.'

He wasn't the owner, she decided, judging by his accent, though he was obviously in authority. 'No, sir,' she smiled. 'Cook next door at Emersons' recommended I come. I understand you need somebody to clean 'offices.'

'Yes. Can you start tomorrow morning? Half past five before 'place gets overrun with men?'

'Yes, sir. Don't you want to check with 'cook next door before I start?'

'No.' He grinned at her. He seemed to be a very cheerful fellow. 'I can generally tell somebody's character when I meet them, though I expect everybody tells you that you look more like a lady's maid than a scullion!'

'Yes,' she smiled again. 'They do.'

He nodded. 'My name's Hardwick. Robert Hardwick. I'm manager here, in charge of loading ships' stores. My family's worked here for donkey's years.'

'I see. Do I report to you, Mr Hardwick?'

He pursed his lips. 'I suppose so. There's no other cleaning staff here, they all seem to have vanished. Can you organize yourself? See what needs doing?' He rubbed his chin. 'I don't know how often you'd need to come in. Mebbe three mornings. Would that suit? And I'll pay you at the end of 'week?'

'Yes, thank you, Mr Hardwick. You can trust me,' she said, and hoped that he was more efficient in dealing with his men than he was with the female staff.

She was jubilant as she walked back down the High Street to return home. She calculated that with five mornings' work, she would be earning almost as much as she would have done with six full days at the mill.

She moved closer to the buildings as she heard the clatter of wheels behind her in the narrow road and a chaise went by. The driver raised his whip to her and she saw that it was Martin Newmarch again, heading towards the cotton

270

mill. The chaise rolled to a stop further up the street and she realized that he was waiting for her.

'Miss Sheppard.' He touched his hat. 'Can I give you a lift anywhere?'

'No, thank you, sir. I'm going home and enjoying the walk.'

He jumped down from his seat into the road. 'Have you found work?'

'Yes, sir. Five mornings a week.'

He raised his eyebrows. 'Good! Doing – ?'

'Cleaning, sir.' Why does he want to know? she wondered. Does he feel guilty? It's nothing to do with him.

'You can do better than that, Grace,' he said in a low voice.

'I have to eat, sir.' She gazed at him steadfastly.

'So, your afternoons are free?'

She felt a moment of panic. What was he going to suggest? Surely he wasn't like his brother, wanting to take a mill girl to his bed?

'I shall try for other work,' she said stiffly. 'Honest work.'

He nodded, his face serious. 'I would never imagine you doing anything other than honest work. It's just that – Miss Gregory and Mrs Westwood were asking about you. There was something they wished to discuss with you.'

'Oh!' She felt a great relief. She would have been so disappointed if he had suggested anything improper. He had always appeared to be worthy and honourable.

'Would you be willing to meet them? I could arrange a suitable place, perhaps a coffee house in the town? Miss Gregory lives in Hessle with her aunt, and Mrs Westwood, because of her present difficulties, is staying with Mr and Mrs Emerson.' He pointed down the street to the house where she had been working.

'I think you must be mistaken, Mr Newmarch! There can be nothing that those two ladies would have to say to me.' She almost laughed. Mrs Westwood having a discussion with a scullery maid from the house where she was a guest!

The traffic in the High Street was getting busier as they talked and other drivers were shouting at Martin Newmarch to move the chaise out of the way. He climbed up onto his seat. 'Please,' he said. 'Come up. I have to move the carriage and I haven't finished talking to you.'

She shook her head and started to walk on. 'I'm sorry, sir. But there's nothing they'd need to talk to me about.' And she slipped into one of the narrow entries where she knew he couldn't follow, and which would eventually, by means of cutting down alleys and courts, bring her out into Lowgate.

But he was waiting for her as she reached the top of Lowgate where the road widened. He had tied his horse to a post and was standing with his arms folded across his chest as she walked towards him.

'Miss Sheppard,' he said, taking off his top hat. 'They really do want to talk to you. They would like your opinion on certain issues.'

'Why?' she asked, and for some inexplicable reason tears smarted in her eyes as she realized how inadequate she was. 'I have no education.

The onny learning I had was at 'chapel school in Mason Street which my parents paid for two years until they could no longer afford it. What can I have to say to such as Miss Gregory or Mrs Westwood?'

'That is precisely why they want to talk to you.' He leaned towards her. 'Don't you realize, Grace, Miss Gregory and Mrs Westwood are forward-thinking women, but there are others who are totally ignorant of what happens outside their own circle. Less educated than you are, in fact,' he added softly.

He seems sincere, she considered. Though I never really thought him anything else. What should I do? I suppose I could go and find out.

She took a breath and exhaled. 'All right, Mr Newmarch. I'll listen to what they have to say. What about Thursday at twelve o'clock at 'coffee house in Queen Street?'

CHAPTER TWENTY-FOUR

On the Wednesday morning at Masterson
and Rayner's, Grace swept down the walls and
ceilings of two rooms, moved boxes to make
more floor space and washed the floors and
windows. There was a cooking range in a room
which had once been a kitchen, and she asked
Mr Hardwick if it could be lit on the mornings
when she came in to clean. He agreed that it
could and asked one of the stable lads to light it
and fill up a hod with coal. She searched in the
cupboards and found a kettle and a pan, filled
them from the pump in the yard and asked the
boy to make sure they were put on the fire
the next morning, so that she could have hot
water for cleaning as she did next door at the
Emersons'.

She had started at five thirty and was finished
by nine o'clock when the yard and offices
were bustling with men. When she saw their feet
tramping in and out of the building she knew
that there would be constant work for her. As
she left the premises an old-fashioned carriage
pulled in. The stable lad ran to open the door

and let down the step to allow an elderly man to descend. She dipped her knee as she passed. She guessed that this was the owner of the company, one of the Rayners, for the Masterson connection was no longer in evidence. He smiled at her and touched his beaver hat.

By Thursday she had a routine, and ventured upstairs to Mr Hardwick's office where he was at his desk and sitting in his overcoat, for there was no fire.

'Shall I light a fire, Mr Hardwick? It won't take me a minute to bring up some kindling and coal.'

He looked up from his paperwork in some surprise, as if he had forgotten she was there. 'Oh! Please. Has the lad forgotten to make it?'

She smiled and ran down the wooden steps and saw the stable lad crossing the yard. 'Will you take some coal up to Mr Hardwick's office? There's no fire made and it's freezing in there. Look sharp,' she added confidently and decided that it must be really quite enjoyable to have others do your bidding.

She washed her hands and face and hurried home, brushed her hair and tied it in a coil at the nape of her neck, changed her blouse for a clean one and then remembered that she had lent her best shawl to Ruby.

'Ruby!' She hammered on her door and on getting no reply, peered through the window and saw two motionless humps on the mattress. 'Ruby. Wake up!'

Ruby sat up and gazed at her, then signalled for her to go away. She was half asleep with her hair dishevelled.

'I need my shawl,' Grace implored through the glass. 'Be quick!'

Ruby opened the door. 'It's 'crack of dawn,' she complained. 'It's not a work day, is it?'

'Mebbe not for you, but I've done a day's work already,' Grace boasted triumphantly. 'It's gone ten o'clock! Why are you still in bed?'

'I'm worn out.' Ruby yawned and stretched sleepily. 'Ma's been awake all night again. Tossing and turning and wanting her loddy. I'm going to have to get a supply and give it to her when she's desperate.'

'Can you afford to?' Grace was astonished.

'Yes,' Ruby nodded. 'Though I'd rather spend 'money on summat else. But what else can I do?'

'I need my shawl,' Grace said urgently, conscious of time passing. 'I'm going to a meeting.'

Ruby fetched the shawl and handed it to her. 'At Dock Green?'

'No. I'll tell you about it later.' She wrapped the shawl around herself. 'I've got regular work,' she beamed. 'And I'll tell you about that too when I get back.'

She had hoped that Mr Newmarch would be at the coffee house too, for she felt she would be less nervous if he was there, having had previous conversations with him. Disappointingly he wasn't, but both ladies and another companion were already waiting for her at a table in a corner of the room.

Miss Gregory rose on seeing her enter, and waved to her to come across. She dipped her knee as Miss Gregory introduced her to the other young woman, whose name she said was Miss

Daisy Emerson. All three ladies were wearing hats and gloves, and plain though elegant outfits.

Miss Gregory indicated that she should be seated and asked if she would take a cup of chocolate or coffee. Grace shyly asked for chocolate, which was brought with a plate of sweet biscuits.

'Miss Sheppard! I asked Mr Newmarch if he would ask you to meet us,' Miss Gregory spoke first, 'because I heard you speak at Dock Green and was most impressed by your manner and confidence. I spoke on the same day, but I regret that what I had to say didn't have the same impact.'

Grace took a sip of chocolate and felt the sweet creamy richness run down her throat. 'But that's easily explained, Miss Gregory. That day at Dock Green the people there were ordinary working folk, or if they weren't working, then they wanted to be. They were more concerned about earning money to feed and clothe themselves than they were about giving 'women same rights as men,' which is what you were asking for.'

She took another sip of chocolate and licked her lips, then added with growing confidence, 'Where I live, women do have equal rights. They work 'same hours as their menfolk, when they can get work that is.' She hesitated, then said thoughtfully, 'Though they don't earn as much.'

'I understand you are no longer working at the mill,' Mrs Westwood remarked. 'Have you found other employment?'

Grace glanced at Miss Emerson. 'Yes, thank

you. I'm working at a house in High Street and at 'offices at Masterson and Rayner.'

'As an office worker?' Mrs Westwood persisted.

'As a scullery maid,' she replied and pondered on why they were questioning her.

'I understand that the cotton mill terminated your work because you were heard speaking at Dock Green,' Miss Emerson broke in.

'I don't think so, miss.' Grace was quick to refute this. 'Decline in 'cotton industry, so I understand.'

The three ladies smiled. 'Oh, well said,' Miss Gregory applauded. 'You have learned tact and diplomacy at a young age.'

'Mr Newmarch – Martin Newmarch, that is – told my father that you had been asked to leave because of your speech,' Miss Emerson murmured into her cup.

'Your father, miss?'

She nodded. She was a bright sparky young woman, younger than Miss Gregory, perhaps not much more than twenty. 'Emerson,' she said. 'He was formerly a director at the mill but resigned over a management disagreement. Did you not see him speaking with Mr Newmarch as you left our house on Tuesday?' She turned to Mrs Westwood. 'We discussed you at supper, did we not, Emma? That's why I came along today. I wanted to meet you. It's so good to meet someone as brave as you, who will say what they feel.'

'I'm not brave, Miss Emerson. Some might say that I was foolish to take that risk, especially when I need to work.'

'Did none of your fellow workers stand up for

you, Miss Sheppard?' Miss Gregory questioned curiously. 'I understand that you spoke up for them over a wages issue.'

'How could they, miss?' Grace thought of that day when the women had marched behind her when she had pleaded for their wages to be paid. 'They might have lost their own jobs.'

'Indeed they might.' Miss Gregory was thoughtful. 'And you must have to work extremely hard now to make up for the loss of your employment at the mill?'

Grace began to feel impatient. What did these ladies know of hard work? Why had they asked her here? She put her reddened chapped hands in front of them. 'These are my hands, able to work.' She flexed her fingers, which were slim and long. 'I'm strong, though I might not look it. Ladies.' She looked at them frankly and in turn. 'What do you want of me?'

Miss Gregory's eyebrows rose at her directness and then she started to explain. 'Very shortly, Mrs Westwood, Miss Emerson and myself are to join other similarly inclined women, to tour northern towns to proclaim the rights of women. As you are concerned about working children and the fact that they are taking the work from adults, and speak most eloquently and sympathetically on that issue, we would like you to join us.' She leaned towards Grace whilst the other two watched her intently. 'Please say that you will.'

Grace gave a nervous exclamation. 'How can I, Miss Gregory? I've got to work and I've no money for travelling.' And no clothes or boots to carry me, she thought. What are they thinking of? These ladies live in a different world from me.

'There would be no expense in travelling,' Miss Emerson chipped in. 'My father is providing a carriage.'

'I have no money or carriage either,' Miss Gregory sympathized, as if she was in the same predicament as Grace. 'And I intend to go.'

'And we will stay in the homes of ladies who are fervent about the cause,' Mrs Westwood said. 'We have an open invitation.'

'But I would have to give up work,' Grace insisted. 'And my mother and father need my money.'

They were silenced then, until Mrs Westwood asked, 'Would you like to speak to your parents first? I have met your mother and found her a very forward-thinking and intelligent woman. Perhaps she would prefer that you were doing something constructive with your life?'

Grace could make no answer to that. It was true that her mother did have many opinions which she was prepared to voice.

'And if you were thinking that you had nothing suitable to wear,' Miss Emerson added softly, 'for it is always the first thing that I think of when asked to go anywhere, why, I have many gowns that would fit you, for we are of a similar size.'

Grace glanced from one to another. They seemed sincere, but what could she say that would make a difference? Besides, things were supposed to be improving for working people. 'My father told me he had read in a newspaper that the Act of 1847, last year, laid down a ten-hour day and a fifty-eight-hour week for women and children over thirteen.' Her father had been scornful, she remembered.

'It did,' Miss Emerson agreed, 'and in '44 an Act was passed where children below that age should only work a six-and-a-half-hour day.' She sat back and folded her hands in her lap. 'And that is the reason why *my* father resigned from the board at the mill. There is a loophole, apparently, and factory and mill owners are flouting it.'

'I see.' Grace was dismayed. 'I didn't know.'

'That is why it is imperative that you come with us,' Miss Gregory implored. 'People need to be reminded of what their rights are.'

'But why me?' Grace looked at her from scared eyes.

'Because, my dear, they will believe you. They will recognize that you are speaking for them.'

'Yes,' Grace murmured, seeing the truth in that. 'Of course.' She chewed on her lip. 'Do I have to decide now?'

'Of course not.' Miss Gregory smiled and shook her head. 'It is most important that you give it considerable thought and speak to your parents about it, even though I'm sure you are capable of making up your own mind. But discuss it with them and if you decide to come with us, we shall be departing in about two weeks' time. We shall go to West Yorkshire, Preston and Oldham and be away for several weeks.'

'What shall I do, Ma?' Grace asked, after discussing it with her mother late that afternoon. 'Would it do any good?'

'Won't do any harm,' her mother replied thoughtfully. 'Except mebbe to you. You'd lose both jobs and they mebbe won't take you back.'

'Miss Emerson said that I'd be able to go back to work at their house if I still wanted to. She'd make sure that they took me back. But I'd probably lose my job at Masterson and Rayner. Which would be a pity, cos I like it there. There's nobody to tell me what to do, I can organize myself.'

'Aye, it's all very well Miss Emerson saying that you'd be tekken back,' her mother declared. 'But Cook might not want you back. She doesn't like unreliable workers and she rules 'kitchen, not Miss Emerson!'

'I'll ask Da what he thinks,' Grace decided, as she contemplated a decision which might change her life.

Her father had a story of his own to tell when he came home from the woodyard. 'I'd such a fright this morning,' he began. 'I was sweeping up 'yard and restacking some of 'timber, when I saw somebody come through 'gate. When I got a proper gander at him I realized it was Tom Hanson.' He indicated with his thumb across the court to the Hansons' house.

He sat down in his chair and exhaled. 'So! I thought that's it then, he's come back beggin' for labouring work and I'll be out on my neck!'

Grace stared and her mother put her hand to her mouth. This could be really bad news and might determine Grace's decision.

'Anyway,' he went on. 'I saw him go into gaffer's office and I could see them talking through 'window. I hung about for a bit and then they came out.' His face was suddenly wreathed in a grin. 'And then Hanson came over. He told me that he was coming back to help in 'training of apprentices. He said that even though he onny had one good hand, he could still show them how to measure and cut and mitre, and how to hone and polish.' He gave a huge sigh and briefly closed his eyes. 'I can't tell you what relief I felt.' His voice cracked as he continued. 'I don't think I could have come home if I'd been told I was finished.'

Lizzie briefly patted his shoulder and then turned to take the pan off the fire. Her voice too was subdued as she said, 'Tell your da, Grace, about what happened to you today.'

Grace related the outcome of her meeting with the three ladies, not giving any indication as to what her feelings were in the matter. The three of them then sat down at the table and ate their soup in silence.

When they had finished, her parents looked at each other and then at Grace. 'We think you should go,' her mother said.

'But – we haven't discussed it!' Grace exclaimed.

'We don't need to.' Her father was emphatic. 'Your ma and me agreed a long time ago that you don't get anywhere in life unless occasionally you tek a chance. And you're young enough to tek that chance. We're not any more, so you'd better go and fight for us and for them that come after.'

Grace felt a lump in her throat. 'It might not do any good,' she began.

'It mebbe won't,' her father agreed. 'But you'll not know unless you try.'

'Will you be able to manage without my wages?' Her eyes swam with tears. She had never been away from home or her parents.

'There'll be more for us to eat, won't there?' her father joked. 'We all know what a gannet you are!'

She gave a trembling smile. 'So I'll tell them, shall I? I said I'd meet Miss Emerson tomorrow to let them know.'

'Aye,' her mother said, and there was a gleam of pride in her eyes. 'You tell 'em.'

CHAPTER TWENTY-FIVE

'What do you mean, you're going away?' Ruby demanded when Grace told her of her plans. 'How can you go? What will I do? Who will I talk to?' She clutched Grace's arm. 'Please don't go, Grace. It's a mad idea.'

'But Ruby! You're seeing Mr Newmarch.' Grace dropped her voice, for they were in the Market Place on Saturday morning. 'You can talk to him. You won't need me and anyway it's only for a few weeks.'

Ruby gasped. 'Talk to him? I can't talk to him. He doesn't ever want to talk! He's so passionate, Grace. He said last night that I mustn't see anybody else, but only him.'

Grace felt uncomfortable; she didn't really want to hear about Edward Newmarch's passion.

'And don't ever say that I won't need you, Grace,' Ruby said vehemently. 'I'll allus need you. You're my best friend!'

'I know that,' Grace said gently. 'But I have to do this. Don't you remember when we said that we would support each other in whatever we decided to do?'

'Yes,' Ruby wailed. 'But I didn't think it meant that we should be parted. What'll I do without you, Grace?'

'You'll manage very well.' Grace was being as patient as possible. 'And at least you'll be still at home with everyone that you know, and I'll be alone with complete strangers.'

'Oh, Grace! Will they look down on you for being poor – those grand ladies? You must let them know that you are as good as they are in spite of having no learning or money! Here!' She felt in her pocket. 'Take these two shillings. Go on.' She saw Grace's eyes open wide. 'I've plenty.'

Grace shook her head. 'I don't need your money, Ruby, but thank you anyway. I've got my wages and I shall have next week's as well before I leave,' and she gave an involuntary shudder at the idea of using Edward Newmarch's money. 'I'm going to 'baths this afternoon,' she announced. 'Do you want to come?'

'Yes,' Ruby agreed eagerly. 'But let me pay, please, Grace.'

So Grace reluctantly agreed that Ruby should pay this time, but determined that she would give her the penny back at some stage. She was going later in the day to Miss Emerson's to try on some of her clothing, hence her bathing. I may be poor but she'll see that I'm clean, she decided. However, on presenting herself at the Emersons' back door as usual and being shown upstairs to Miss Emerson's room, she found one of the maids, Molly, whom she had met before, there to greet her.

Molly smiled at her. 'Hello, Grace. Miss Emerson said would I help you with these.' She pointed to the bed, which had gowns and petticoats laid upon it. 'What's happening?' She dropped her voice to a whisper. 'These are too good for a scullery maid!'

It wasn't said with animosity. Molly was merely stating a fact, and she was right. The gowns were much too good for a scullery maid. Though they were not fancy or elaborate, the cloth was costly, being velvet or silk, and the colours plain. Miss Emerson had also thought to include muffs and bonnets, and an umbrella.

Grace shot a look of dismay at Molly. 'I can't wear these,' she said. 'No-one would believe in anything I said, if I did,' and she quickly explained to the maid why she was here trying on these clothes.

'You're right,' Molly agreed. 'No-one would believe that you'd been a mill girl.' She examined Grace critically, up and down, and then smiled. 'You don't look like a mill girl anyway, even in your own clothes. You could be a proper lady, Grace, if you were dressed right and spoke like them upstairs.'

She searched amongst the gowns and brought out a plain grey wool one with a white lace collar. 'This is meant to have an overskirt and several petticoats,' she said. 'But if you wore it as it is, with just your shawl, it would look presentable and tidy without being too grand. Try it on,' she urged.

Grace slipped off her skirt and bodice and Molly handed her a crisp white petticoat to put underneath the dress. 'And what's this?' Grace picked up a garment in red flannel.

'It's another petty. Would you like to wear it? It'd keep you warm.'

'Oh yes, please!' Grace was delighted by the bright scarlet colour. 'It's 'colour of a poppy.' She put it on and swirled around. 'It's so daring,' she laughed.

Between them they chose the grey, and a similar gown in dark blue, for Molly insisted that she would need at least two if she was going to be away for several weeks. 'And I'll pack several petticoats as well,' she said, ' 'cos they get so grubby. What about pantaloons or drawers?' she murmured, casting a glance at Grace. 'Miss Emerson always wears them.'

Grace gasped and put her hand to her mouth to hide her amusement. 'I don't know,' she gurgled. 'I've never worn them!'

'Me neither,' Molly laughed. 'So we'll not bother wi' them.' She put to one side the two gowns, a selection of petticoats, including the red one, three pairs of stockings, a grey bonnet and an extra shawl. 'Miss Emerson will want to see what we've chosen,' she commented. 'And we'd better put in this cloak for travelling in. Oh, and these boots. Try them. See if they fit.'

Grace pulled on a pair of narrow-toed boots in the softest black leather and Molly laced them for her. 'Oh!' Grace exlaimed, as she felt their softness about her bare toes. 'What bliss. I shan't want to give them back!'

Molly sat back on her heels. 'Oh,' she said. 'I thought they were yours for keeps!'

Grace shook her head. 'No. Onny for borrow-ing.'

'Ruby!' Edward toyed with her hair, winding it around his fingers as she lay beside him.

'Mmm?' She turned towards him, knowing how he responded to the touch of her flesh on his. 'What?'

'I've something to tell you.' He nuzzled into her neck and put his arms around her. 'A surprise.'

'Is it a nice surprise? I don't like horrid ones.'

'Of course.' He nibbled at her ear. 'You will only ever have nice ones from now on.' He pulled her on top of him. 'I've found us some-where else instead of here.'

'But I like it here,' she pouted. The staff at the Vittoria were used to her now and nodded as she came through the doors and made her way upstairs to their usual room.

'Yes, so do I,' he agreed. 'But sooner or later I'm going to meet up with someone I know. There are men from my club who frequent this hotel.'

'Probably for 'same reason as we do,' she teased. She was becoming much bolder now that she realized just how passionate he was about her.

'That's as maybe,' he said brusquely. 'But I don't want to take the risk.'

She looked down at him. She knew that she made a pretty picture with her flushed cheeks and tousled hair. 'So where shall we meet?'

He sat up beside her and placed his hands

around her face. 'I'm taking a suite of rooms in Wright Street. There will be a woman to take care of the fires and the cleaning, and the shopping if you wish, and we shall be quite, quite private, with no-one to disturb us.'

'A set of rooms!' She was astounded. 'Where we shall live?'

'Where *you* will live, my darling. And where I can visit at any time.'

Her face dropped. 'You mean – for me to live on my own?'

He gave a sudden grin. 'You didn't think that I would live there too?'

'Well.' She was deflated. 'I hadn't thought that I would live by myself! I've never lived on my own.'

'But you won't be alone very often.' He became tender and stroked her throat and naked breasts. 'It will mean that I shall be able to come at any time when I'm free. I can come in a morning before I go to the mill, or slip out during the day. Or in the evening before – before I go home. We won't have to book a room in advance as we do now. You must come and look at the rooms. You will be delighted, I know.'

'You've chosen them already?' I've no say in the matter, she thought. I'm a kept woman. A mistress. And in spite of the money which she now had and the food which she ate in abundance, she didn't know why she felt a sudden lowness of spirits.

'Indeed I have. I'll show them to you on Monday, and you can collect your things and move in.'

Collect my things and move in, she pondered, as later that night she opened the door to their room in Middle Court, and saw her mother snoring on the mattress. What things? I have nothing! Only the clothes that I'm wearing. I have to think this over. What do I do about Ma? Can she live by herself? I haven't told Edward about her. Not that he would want to know, or care!

She took off her boots and lay down on the mattress beside her mother. Not once has he asked me if I have a family, a mother or father, brothers or sisters. Not once has he mentioned Grace, though he knew that we were always together and he must realize that she was finished at the mill. It seems that he is interested in nothing but his own pleasure.

But then that is what he is paying me for, and he pays me well, she considered. I've paid the rent. I've paid Jamie what I owed him. Not that he was very pleased. Jamie had been downright aggressive when she had handed over the money she had borrowed, and accused her of going behind his back and making her own arrangements with the man he had procured for her. She had denied it, but worried since, in case he should catch her in the lie.

At least if I'm living in Wright Street, which is not in Jamie's territory, he's not likely to find me out.

Wright Street was a better area than that in which she lived. It was close by the General Infirmary, the affluent Albion Street, and in proximity to the Public Rooms in Jarratt Street where surgeons, doctors and philosophers met for discussions and lectures. There were rooming houses in Wright Street where visiting lecturers and artists stayed, but it was also an area where businessmen and their families lived.

Ruby sighed and pulled the blanket over her head. She hadn't undressed, for the simple reason that she couldn't reach the buttons on the back of her gown. I'll worry about everything in 'morning, she thought sleepily, and tucked her hand under her cheek.

'I can't live on my own, Ruby,' her mother whined when she told her the next morning. 'How can I?'

'Then I won't go,' Ruby declared. 'I'll tell him I've to give him up. I'm not that bothered.'

Bessie was silenced. Then she asked, 'But what about my loddy? And my dinner?'

Ruby shrugged. 'It's one or 'other, Ma. You decide!'

'I'll have a think on it.' Bessie hunched herself on the mattress and sat silently. 'It'd be nice to have a chair to sit on, 'stead of mattress, now that we've got a fire,' she said, after a few minutes.

'But we won't have a fire, Ma,' Ruby said gloomily. 'Not if I give up my gentleman.' She had always been careful not to give Edward Newmarch's name to her mother, who would most certainly have dropped it into conversation with her cronies when she was in her cups.

'No fire?' She stared at Ruby. 'So does that mean no hot pie for dinner?'

Ruby nodded. 'It means we shall be just as we were afore, Ma.'

'No loddy and no dinner?'

'That's right.'

'Then I'll just have to manage 'best I can, Ruby.' Bessie sighed and put on a brave martyr's face. 'I can't have you giving up so much on my account. You'll come and see me, won't you?'

'Course I will. Every day. I'll bring you a hot dinner and—'

'And my loddy,' Bessie interrupted, her eyes bright and eager. 'Don't forget that.'

'I won't forget,' Ruby said wearily. 'I'll go to see Mr Cooke and pay for a regular dose.'

She arranged with Mr Cooke the apothecary to provide her mother with a daily dose of laudanum. One small bottle to last her all day. 'I can't make her take it a teaspoon at a time, Ruby,' he said. 'There are five hundred drops in this bottle, equivalent to five teaspoons or twenty grains of opium. If your mother chooses to take it all at once there's nothing I can do about it.'

'Just as long as you don't give her any more than that,' Ruby implored. 'She'll give you all kinds of reasons why she should have extra.'

He shrugged resignedly and Ruby paid him for a week's supply. She bought a sack of coal and some firewood and a small bag of potatoes in the hope that her mother might see fit to bake them in the hot coals, and she bought a second-hand blanket for the mattress and a warm shawl.

In a furniture-shop window there was an old rocking chair, and she wondered how much it was. The shop was closed, but she decided to come back the next day and enquire. Perhaps if I make Ma comfortable at home, she won't get into trouble. I won't leave her any money but I'll make sure she has plenty to eat.

On the Monday evening she went as arranged to the house in Wright Street. Edward Newmarch was already in the upstairs rooms waiting for her. 'So what do you think, Ruby? Will they suit?'

'Wonderful,' she breathed, her doubts melting away. There were comfortable leather chairs by the fire, a dining table and chairs by the window, rugs on the floor and in the bedroom, a large tester bed with cream hangings, a cane chair and a washstand with jug and bowl on it. These she looked at doubtfully, and wondered where the pump was to draw the water. I didn't notice a pump in the street, she pondered. Perhaps there's one in the yard, but she didn't wish to bother Edward with such trivialities and decided she would ask the woman downstairs, who was to do the cleaning and the washing.

'Ruby! Don't you have another gown to wear?' he asked as he unbuttoned her. 'You have worn this each time we have met and it's crumpled and shabby.'

'No!' she said. 'I bought this specially to meet you. I only have 'clothes I wore at 'mill.'

'Then I shall buy you some more, but I can't come with you to choose in case I'm recognized.' He ran his hands down her body. 'You look best without any clothes on at all, but I suppose you must wear them! But don't get cheap and tawdry like this red gown, change it for something feminine and fashionable.'

She nodded. She liked the red dress, but if that was what he wanted she would go tomorrow to Rena's, and she would ask Grace to go with her.

'You're so beautiful,' he said, as they lay together. 'If I had the talent to paint you, I would.'

'What!' Her eyes were wide. 'You mean naked,' she whispered.

He laughed. 'Yes, of course. Men do have portraits painted of their mistresses.'

She pulled the sheets up against her chin. 'I couldn't possibly do that,' she said, aghast at the thought. 'It wouldn't be right.'

'Oh, Ruby,' he murmured. 'You're priceless. So naive. It's what I love about you.'

After he'd left to go home, Ruby dressed again, damped down the fire in the hearth and wrapped her old shawl around her. She glanced around the room. Tomorrow, she thought. I'll come tomorrow. I'll get up early and I'll bring Daniel's stool, which is my only possession and is still at Grace's house. But I'll spend tonight at home with Ma.

CHAPTER TWENTY-SIX

'You're very preoccupied these days, Edward.' Martin and Edward were driving into Hull together. 'Is something troubling you?'

'Troubling me?' Edward grinned. 'Certainly not. Everything is fine.'

'You've been staying late in Hull,' Martin persisted. 'I would have thought you'd be spending time with May. There must be plans you need to discuss for your marriage.'

Edward's mouth drew downwards and he said sullenly, 'It's all in hand. May and her mother don't want any interference from me.'

'Even so,' Martin murmured, and noticed how his brother raised his whip and urged on the mare even though they were on the outskirts of Hull and there was congested traffic of waggons, carts and carriages. 'It has been mentioned that you don't seem to be very involved.'

'I said, it's in hand,' Edward repeated irritably. 'I'm spending time at the club,' he muttered. 'Making the most of my freedom.'

'You've got a mistress, haven't you?' Martin

asked bluntly. 'That's why you leave the office early and come home late.'

'Don't be ridiculous.' Edward turned and swore at an old woman who had scurried across the road in front of the chaise, causing him to pull on the reins. 'And what if I have? It has nothing to do with anyone else what I do.'

'For heaven's sake, Edward,' Martin burst out. 'You're to be married in a few weeks! It's no basis for a marriage. What if May found out? Or her father did?'

Edward said nothing, but as they approached the road leading to the mill he automatically looked down at the place where he used to see Ruby and her friend walking arm in arm.

He changed the subject. 'What happened to—' he almost said Ruby's friend, and checked himself just in time, 'those girls, the one who was sacked for speaking at Dock Green, and who always walked with her friend?'

Martin frowned. 'If you mean Grace Sheppard, the official reason for her leaving was the decline in the cotton industry! I know nothing about her friends, but I assume that she found other employment.' If Edward can lie, then so can I, he deliberated, and, in any case, he knew that his brother wouldn't be interested in Grace Sheppard's involvement with social issues.

'You must give her up,' he stated flatly as they entered the mill gates. 'This woman, whoever she is. It isn't fair to May. Your marriage is doomed if you don't.' He kept his eyes to the front, not looking at his brother. 'All right – if you needed to sow wild oats! But have done with her now.'

Edward too stared in front towards the river, not seeing the boy who was waiting to take the horse and chaise away to the stables. The morning sun gleamed on the normally murky water, tinting it to a burnished russet brown.

'I can't.' His voice was husky. 'I can't give her up. I'm totally obsessed by her. I think of her night and day.' He put his hands to his eyes. 'I want nothing more than to be with her.'

Martin gave a silent oath. What a mess! 'Then you must cancel the marriage with May Gregory,' he said. 'It's the only decent thing to do. But you'll be sued for breach of promise and be ruined.'

Edward turned and looked at his brother, his eyes dull and hooded as if he hadn't slept. He shook his head. 'I can't do that either.' His mouth slipped into a cynical lopsided grin. 'I must marry May. I need her money and her father's approval.' He blinked and his expression became lively again. 'Don't worry about me, old fellow.' He threw the reins to the boy who was patiently waiting. 'It should be rather fun leading two separate lives.'

Martin sat at his desk. He had a pounding headache. Things were not going well at the mill. The shareholders were becoming more and more demanding. They wanted better returns on their investments and were not concerned about the workers who must suffer because of it. But he was also shattered by Edward's behaviour. The wedding was merely four weeks away and he thought of the scandal that would ensue if Edward should choose to cancel it.

I wonder who she is? Not anyone we know, surely? The woman can't be marriageable, he considered. There's no money there, otherwise – He gave a grunt. He knew his brother so well. He would have no compunction in cancelling the marriage if it suited him to do so.

His mind flickered from one thing to another. To May Gregory, who was being so deceived, to her cousin Georgiana, who would be returning early from the ladies' tour of northern towns in order to be a witness at the marriage, as he was to be also.

His thoughts slipped to the morning they had departed. He had promised Georgiana that he would see them off, and he had arrived at the Emerson household and been shown into the drawing room. Daisy Emerson was there with Georgiana and they were waiting for Mrs Westwood and Grace to appear.

They were chatting perfunctorily about their journey and where they would stay, when the door opened and Mrs Westwood came into the room followed by Grace Sheppard. He bowed to Mrs Westwood and she inclined her head, and he turned to Grace to greet her also.

He was totally unprepared for the change in her and to cover his embarrassment, he gave her a formal bow. She was wearing a grey dress with a high white collar and her fair hair, which was parted in the centre, had been dressed and coiled about her ears, the style emphasizing her high cheekbones. There was, he pondered, an untutored serene elegance about her, but as she bent her knee to greet him and her skirt fell in folds about her feet, he caught a glimpse of scarlet petticoat.

He smiled at her then and considered that although she seemed so demure, that peek of scarlet showed a defiance. If these ladies think that they can use her for their own ends, I fear they will find they are mistaken, he thought. Grace Sheppard will not be told what to do by these organizing women. She will do what she wants.

'Miss Sheppard is worried that people will not listen to what she has to say about child labour if she is dressed in fine clothes,' Georgiana had remarked. 'She considers that they will not believe she has had the experience of which she speaks. What do you think, Mr Newmarch?'

Martin caught a look of entreaty in Grace's eyes and was struck, not so much by the steadfastness with which she gazed at him, but by the blueness of her eyes, accentuated by the silver-grey of her gown. 'I fear you are right, Miss Sheppard,' he had murmured, answering her directly although Georgiana had asked the question. 'No-one would believe, looking at you now, that as a child you crawled beneath the machinery at the mill to remove the dust and debris, as I know you must have done.'

'Thank you for your honesty, Mr Newmarch,' she had replied in a soft shy voice. 'And would you agree that it's not right for children to labour under such conditions?'

He hesitated and before he could answer, she had added, 'Even though these little bairns are willing, as I was, to add their coppers to 'family purse.'

He remembered that he had thought that she would do well, especially if she spoke in her natural voice without trying to ape the ladies she was with. People will understand what she is saying and believe in her, but not in those elegant garments.

He rubbed his forehead and sighing, shuffled some papers on his desk. But whether it will do any good, I have my doubts, he pondered. He had answered her question honestly, as he thought that she would want. 'I am a shareholder in an industry which condones these practices, Miss Sheppard,' he had told her. 'I believe in the ten-hour day, but I know that it isn't working. Mill and factory owners cannot afford to cut down the working hours, the machines must keep on turning and producing. Their livelihoods and the livelihood of those who work there depend on that continuity.'

She had seemed disappointed, he reflected, yet he had decided that it was right that she knew the truth. She would have many hard questions thrown at her. The public platform was not for the faint-hearted.

Grace was relieved that Molly was to journey with them to help dress the three ladies. The maid rode on top of the carriage next to the driver. Mr Emerson escorted them on their journey towards Wakefield and left them at the Woodman Inn, a coaching inn near Castleford where their escort the next day was to be the Reverend Rogerson.

His wife was to be their hostess during their stay in the West Riding.

Grace had been enthralled at the difference in the countryside as they journeyed out of the flatlands which surrounded the town of Hull, following the line of the Humber and the Ouse, towards the Aire and Calder river network. She had felt queasy as the carriage negotiated the bumpy roads in the hilly district of the West Riding of Yorkshire.

She saw the tall chimneys of factories and mills and the thick black pall of smoke and dust which hung over the mean narrow streets of the industrial mining towns. There was a constant rumbling and clattering of heavy machinery, and the wretchedness of poverty showed on the faces of the inhabitants. She saw the dark mountainous heaps with children and adults swarming over them, which Miss Gregory told her were not hills at all but piles of coal waste, and she could smell and taste soot and sulphur at the back of her throat.

Miss Emerson and Miss Gregory were very animated during supper and talked constantly of their journey, of whom they would meet, of the response to expect during their speech-making, and Grace gathered as she listened to them that this was as new an experience for them as it was for her.

'It was so very kind of Mr Newmarch to see us off,' Mrs Westwood remarked. 'He really does seem to believe in our cause, whereas so many gentlemen would consider that we would be better employed with our drawing or embroidery.'

So that is what ladies do in their spare time, Grace mused. I have often wondered.

'Mr Newmarch seems very taken with you, Miss Sheppard,' Miss Emerson commented. 'I felt that he explained the factory owners' position very clearly.'

Grace blushed. 'Mr Newmarch has always shown me consideration, Miss Emerson. He's always been very civil.'

'He is – you are quite right, Miss Sheppard,' Miss Gregory chipped in. 'Most civil, and he treats women as his equal.' She gave a sigh. 'It's a pity that he lacks a spark of vitality, though. He would be quite charming and—'

'Marriageable!' Miss Emerson laughed. 'Although I understand he is that already. He is the elder son, is he not? But I agree, he can sometimes appear to be rather grave and dull. But very dependable, nevertheless, or so my father says.'

Grace was shocked. How could they speak of a friend in such a manner, and especially in front of her?

'I understand his brother is to be married shortly?' Mrs Westwood addressed Georgiana Gregory. 'To a relative of yours?'

Georgiana nodded and wiped the corner of her mouth with a table napkin. 'To my cousin, May. She and Mr Newmarch have been affianced for some months, but my aunt, May's mother, wished them to have a spring wedding.'

Grace had been trying not to listen for she was perplexed by their casual gossip, but her attention was now caught by their conversation.

'Edward Newmarch is very handsome, isn't he? But I feel he might be liable to stray. Your cousin will have much to do to keep him at home!'

Edward Newmarch! To be married? Grace was dismayed at what she heard. Oh, poor Ruby! She can't know or she would have said. She'll be cast off and be back where she started! No. Worse than that, for she's become used to eating well and living in those lovely rooms, and paying her mother's rent. Oh, wicked man for giving her all that and then taking it away. And I'm so far away and can't warn her!

'Are you all right, Miss Sheppard? You have become rather pale.'

'I'm tired, Miss Gregory,' she replied. 'If you don't mind, I'd like to go to bed.' They agreed that she should and that they would shortly do the same. As she rose from the table, she asked politely, 'Do you think you could call me Grace? I've never been called Miss Sheppard, except by Mr Newmarch,' and she recalled that sometimes he called her Grace, when no-one else was listening. 'It doesn't really sound like me. I keep thinking that you're speaking to someone else.'

They all smiled, seeming to be quite relieved. 'Grace!' Mrs Westwood proclaimed. 'It's a lovely name. It suits you very well.'

Grace hesitated outside the dining-room door. It was an old inn with numerous small rooms and staircases and, as she paused to get her bearings, she heard Miss Gregory's voice saying, 'I'm a little worried about Mrs Rogerson's reaction to

Grace. She is so haughty and patronizing even though she is a devout Christian lady. I'm not sure if she will wish Grace to dine with us.'

Mrs Westwood's murmured reply registered disapproval, though Grace couldn't hear her actual words. But she was pleased that her unintentional eavesdropping had prepared her, and, as she mounted the narrow staircase, she knew what she had to do.

The Reverend Rogerson was polite towards her when introduced the next day, although he seemed to be puzzled by her accent and eventually asked if she was a native of Hull.

'Yes, sir,' she said shyly. 'Born and bred, like my ma and da.'

'Good and honest working people, are they?' he enquired probingly. 'I ask, because people who come to hear you will want to know your background.'

'Poor but honest, sir,' she said, gazing back at him. 'Whether they'd be considered good by others, I don't know, but they have been good parents to me.'

He nodded sagely. 'We can only speak of what we know, my dear, and you do right to be so frank.'

His wife, when Grace met her, was courteous, but only just, being more interested in Miss Gregory's views on the rights of women, yet expressing astonishment when she declared that women should be allowed to take part in politics and to vote. 'Those of us who are able must of course practise philanthropy, and teach that there is a better life through Christian religion and education, but few women, in my opinion, are able to understand the principles of politics.'

'Do you not consider, Mrs Rogerson,' asked Mrs Westwood, 'that you are intellectually as intelligent and capable of making decisions as your husband?'

The Reverend Rogerson had by this time retired to his library, and the question could be answered without fear of offence, but Mrs Rogerson appeared completely taken aback by it and was unable to reply coherently.

Grace sat quietly listening and absorbing, and not always understanding as Miss Emerson, Miss Gregory and Mrs Westwood quoted women such as Elizabeth Fry, whom she had heard of, Sarah Martin, whom she hadn't, and Lady Byron who had opened schools for pauper children.

'Begging your pardon,' she said in a low voice, during a brief break in the discussion. 'But – these ladies are not working women such as me. They've had an education so they can speak without fear of ridicule. The words which come out of my mouth won't be expressed in 'same way.'

Mrs Westwood leant towards her. 'You need not be afraid,' she said earnestly. 'We have heard you speak, and the reason you were asked to join us was because of your sincerity and eloquence. And,' she added, 'Sarah Martin, of whom we spoke, was not a rich woman. She was the daughter of a shopkeeper who became a prison visitor.'

'And', Miss Emerson intervened, 'working

women are beginning to speak publicly and support reforms. They became chartists and have denounced the Poor Law. Please, Grace,' she implored. 'You must speak. You are far more important than any one of us here.'

CHAPTER TWENTY-SEVEN

Grace asked if she might take supper in her room at the Rogersons' house. She thought it might save the ladies embarrassment in view of what she had overheard, and she explained to them that she needed to prepare herself for the next day when they were to attend the rally in Wakefield.

Molly was in the room next door, and she too was having her supper on a tray rather than eat in the kitchen with the Rogersons' staff. 'Let's eat together,' Grace suggested.

'Will anyone find out?' Molly asked anxiously.

'Does it matter?' Grace was surprised at the question.

'Well, you're one of 'ladies that I have to look after,' Molly explained seriously. 'Miss Emerson said so.'

'Oh!' Grace was astonished. 'But I can look after myself.'

'But I dressed your hair, didn't I?' Molly grinned. 'You couldn't have done it as well yourself.'

Grace nodded. 'No. I couldn't. But there'll be

no need for you to do it tomorrow.' She glanced at Molly. 'I have other ideas for tomorrow.'

The next morning she rose at six o'clock, poured the water from the jug on the washstand into the bowl and washed herself thoroughly. Then she brushed her hair and plaited it and dressed in her own clothes which she had brought with her. She wore a clean grey skirt, a white shirt, and wrapped her checked shawl around her shoulders.

When the maid knocked on the door at eight o'clock to bring her breakfast tray, her mouth dropped open as she saw Grace sitting by the window, looking out at the view of the gardens.

'Beg your pardon, miss. I didn't think you'd be up yet.'

'I'm usually up at this time.' Grace smiled. 'In fact I'm usually at work by six.'

The maid, who was very young and obviously confused by the situation, simply nodded, put down the tray on a side table and backed out of the room.

Grace stared at the tray. This surely couldn't all be for her? There were boiled eggs and ham, slices of thin bread, and a pat of golden butter in a silver dish. A dish of marmalade, a pot of tea, milk in a jug and a china plate with sliced lemon neatly arranged on it.

There was another knock on the door and Molly came in. She was dressed in black, with a white apron. 'You're wearing your own clothes!' she gasped. 'Whatever will Miss Emerson say?'

'I don't know,' Grace confessed. 'But I have to feel comfortable. This is the real me, Molly, and

309

if I'm to speak for working women, then I must look like one. Would you like some breakfast?' she asked. 'They must have made a mistake in 'kitchen. There's enough here for two or three.'

Molly looked at her. 'I've had mine already,' she said. 'And there's no mistake, Grace. This is how rich folk live. They waste so much food that could be given to 'poor folk if onny they'd think of it. Go on, eat up. You'll need your strength if you're going to face all them at 'rally. I've just heard in 'kitchen that there's hundreds expected.'

Other ladies joined the party after breakfast, all eager and excited at the prospect of what was to come. One or two were not in the class of Miss Emerson and Miss Gregory, but were better educated and more confident, Grace surmised, than she was herself. The Reverend Rogerson and his wife were not accompanying them at this stage, but were to come later after morning service, as the day was Sunday, though they were not expected to participate in the meeting. Some of the ladies had already attended church, Grace discovered, but no-one had said that she was obliged to do so.

Four carriages trundled off from the Rogersons' home and within half an hour they were entering the town of Wakefield. A platform had been erected in an open space off the Bull Ring and close by the cathedral, and some wooden seats and benches placed there.

One of the other ladies came up to Grace as she stood feeling isolated on the platform. 'So what do you do? Miss Sheppard, isn't it?'

'Grace,' she answered quietly. 'Grace Sheppard. I was a mill worker, but now I'm a maid of all work. I do anything I can to earn an honest living.'

The woman nodded. She was tall and imposing, plainly dressed and with a forthright and abrupt manner. 'And what axe do you have to grind?'

Grace stammered that she didn't know what she meant. That she was here to speak on behalf of children who had to work to add to the family earnings. The woman gave a wide smile. 'Good,' she said. 'Not here for yourself then, like some of these women?'

Grace noticed that she called them women and not ladies and was looking in the direction of Mrs Westwood and Miss Emerson. She hesitated for a moment, then explained. 'I suppose I'm also here for selfish purposes. I've lost my job at 'cotton mill because married women and children earn less money than me. But if I'm honest,' again she hesitated, wondering if she was being disloyal to Mr Newmarch, 'I also think I lost it because of speaking against children working and taking adult jobs.'

'That's more like it.' The woman took her hand and shook it in a brisk masculine fashion. 'My name is Mary Morris. I'm here to speak on women's rights, same as Miss Gregory over there. But we need a fresh young voice to speak up for working children who can't speak for themselves. You'll mention the wretched climbing boys, won't you? And the boys and girls who are sent to their deaths in the coal mines?'

Grace gazed at her. I am so ignorant of facts. Why am I here? I know nothing. What do I have to say? But there came into her head at the same time an image of Freddie, Ruby's brother, who had gone to be a chimney sweep's lad and who, Ruby and Bessie were convinced, was destined to be his own master. He won't, she thought miserably. He won't come back. We've been telling ourselves that he will, but he'll be broken or burnt and have the hand of death on him.

Tears came into her eyes. 'Yes,' she said in answer. 'I will.'

Mary Morris was the first to talk and introduced the other speakers, not all of whom were women, Grace was surprised to see. There were some men who wished to question the Factory Act, and others to complain of insanitary housing conditions.

Miss Gregory spoke on women's issues, followed by Mrs Westwood, and Grace wondered why Mary Morris had seemed to gaze disparagingly upon her. Mrs Westwood spoke of her children who, since they were over the age of seven, were within her husband's care. She was only able to visit them when he agreed to it. 'My children need me as their mother,' she pleaded. 'Why should they be deprived of my love and attention?'

'You shouldn't have left 'em, missus,' a woman shouted from the crowd. 'You should have put up wi' his blows for t'sake of thy bairns.'

Mrs Westwood shook her head. 'Someone has to take a stand. Is it right that women should be considered inferior to men and have no rights in their children's welfare?'

She spoke for ten minutes more in this vein and was given only a mild ovation for they were mainly working-class people in the crowd, who were not unduly concerned about the problems of middle-class women. The women there were not unused to a beating from their menfolk and accepted it as their lot, along with the exhausting struggle of daily living.

And then it was Grace's turn. She trembled as she stood in front of them. She had no notes to read from, as Mary Morris and some of the male speakers had. She tried to swallow but her throat was dry, so she took a deep breath and someone called out, 'Don't be shy, lass. We'll not bite thee.'

There was a ripple of laughter and Grace smiled and felt better. 'My name is Grace Sheppard,' she began and raised her voice. 'I ask you to forgive my nervousness but I'm not used to having so many people listen to what I have to say. My ma and da, they've allus listened to me, but I never thought that anybody else would be interested.' She took another deep breath. 'But perhaps you might be. I used to work in a cotton mill . . .'

She told them of her circumstances, much as she had done at Dock Green, of losing her job which she had had since she was nine years old, and of Freddie who had been sold to be a climbing boy. She didn't mention Ruby, for she realized now that she was speaking of different issues and Ruby was a grown woman and not a child. But she told of the dark morning when the little Irish girl had drowned in the river Hull as she went to work.

A tear trickled down her cheek as she remembered, and she brushed it away. She saw that some of the women who were sitting at the front of the crowd were wiping their eyes on their sleeves or shawls, and she realized that these people knew what she was talking about: they too had lived through the experiences of which she was speaking.

A woman got to her feet and came towards the platform. She was carrying what appeared to be a bundle of rags, but as she held up the bundle towards Grace, she saw that it was a child. 'Look,' she cried, holding out her arms. 'This is my bairn. Murdered in t'coal fields. Murdered, though he's not yet dead.'

Grace knelt down on the platform floor and put out her arms to take the child, but the mother wouldn't let him go. She shook her head and drew back the thin shawl which was over him. Grace saw the emaciated body of a young boy, his legs and back crooked and his spindly arms a mass of cuts and bruises. His face was yellow and skeletal and his bloodshot eyes, which he opened as his mother took off the shawl, were large in their sockets.

'Twelve years old, he is,' said his mother, and Grace drew in a breath, for she had thought him no more than six or seven. 'And won't reach his thirteenth birthday.'

The boy looked up at Grace and smiled, and reached up to touch her cheek with thin fingers. She smiled back and bent to kiss his forehead.

'God bless you, Miss Grace,' the woman whispered. 'Do what you can. It's too late for my lad, but there's many like him.'

Grace stood up. Her cheeks were wet with tears and she found that she couldn't speak any more. She put out her hands in supplication towards the crowd and then towards the boy and his mother. With a slight bow of her head she retreated to the back of the platform where the other speakers were clapping.

'Go forward, Grace,' Miss Gregory urged. 'They want you to.'

Grace looked up. The crowd were clapping and calling her name. 'Miss Grace! Miss Grace!' She stepped forward to the front of the platform and inclined her head and a cheer rang out.

'Well done, Grace,' Mary Morris said in an undertone. 'Very well done.'

As the applause died away, Miss Morris put up her hand. 'Miss Grace has given up her job of scrubbing floors to be with us for this tour. Would you be willing to spare a copper for her to give to her family, who will sorely miss her contribution?'

Grace shook her head. 'No,' she objected in a low voice. 'My ma and da wouldn't want that. They said that I should come.' But nevertheless she saw a hat going round and those who could afford it dropped in a coin.

When the hat came back it was full to the brim, mainly pennies and halfpennies, though there was the odd piece of silver shining through the copper. The woman and boy were still sitting at the front of the crowd and Grace watched them.

They were obviously very poor: the woman's dress was ragged and torn, she wore no shawl and Grace guessed that her only one was covering her son.

She took the hat from the man who had collected and thanked him, then, carefully balancing it with one hand, she took a penny from it and held it up for the crowd to see, and told the man to give the rest to the woman and boy.

'I have my youth and strength to survive,' she called out. 'I thank you so very much. I shall keep this coin for ever and will use it only if I'm at death's door.'

The applause once again erupted at her generous gesture and she retired to the back of the platform in some confusion.

The meeting concluded with a short prayer by the Reverend Rogerson and the singing of a hymn, led by his wife, and the crowd started to drift away.

'You must be exhausted, Grace!' Miss Emerson said. 'Will you be able to do the same again on Tuesday?'

'I'm not exhausted, Miss Emerson.' On the contrary she was buoyed up and exhilarated by the response she had received and was quite ready for the next part of the tour.

They departed that evening from the Rogersons' house. Both Mrs Rogerson and her husband were very warm and civil towards Grace and invited her to stay with them again, should she be in the area.

They travelled all of that week in the West

Riding of Yorkshire, visiting large towns such as Bradford, Barnsley and Huddersfield and other smaller towns and villages. Although the crowds were not as great as at Wakefield, the meetings being held during evenings, the response was very good and Grace became more confident.

'Tomorrow we move off into Lancashire,' Miss Gregory said to Grace after the Friday evening meeting in Halifax. 'A very long journey indeed to Preston, and I fear we will all be tired by Sunday. But it is particularly important that we visit that town.'

Some of the other ladies had left them to go their separate ways, but they were expecting to be joined by others once they reached Lancashire.

'Mrs Westwood and I will not be speaking in Preston, Grace,' Miss Gregory told her on their journey. 'You will be the only speaker from our group.'

'Oh!' Grace said. 'Why is that?'

'You will see, once we arrive, that the workers there have more pressing concerns than women's rights,' she explained. 'I haven't been there but I have read of the conditions in which the workers live.' She shook her head in disbelief. 'Can you imagine that whole families often live in one room and have to share a tap and privy with their neighbours!'

Grace gazed at her and would have smiled if she hadn't been so weary. I am not the only one to be in ignorance, she thought. These women know nothing. They have read of conditions but have not seen as I have seen or lived as I have lived. Mr Newmarch knows. When I took him to the Groves I could see that he was shocked. So why are we preaching to the workers? They know of their deprivations. It is the men in power who should be made aware of the poverty. Or do they know already and do nothing about it? And am I the one to remind them?

CHAPTER TWENTY-EIGHT

There was a feeling of unrest and disquiet in the town of Preston. Groups of workers were on strike over low pay and poor working conditions. Many were having meetings of their own, and, although the audience which came to hear Grace and the other speakers at various venues throughout the week was attentive, Grace felt that she was ineffective. Instead of telling them about her own working life she exhorted them to petition Parliament to act on the 1842 Report into Sanitary Conditions which was not yet being dealt with.

She had known nothing of this Act until one of the male speakers had taken her on one side, told her of its existence and asked her to mention it in her speech. 'I speak from experience, as many of you do,' she told the crowd. 'I live in a court of twelve houses with two rooms in each house and a family in each room. One privy and one water pump has to serve us all. We all know of 'night-soil men who come into our houses, we know of 'stinking muckgarths which explode every summer. And we know of children and adults who fall sick with disease because of it. We know of 'cholera which plagued our towns last summer and will do 'same this year.

'Tell 'local Medical Board of our plight. Tell the newspapers. Tell 'Members of Parliament. Bombard them with information on how we live. Do it now!'

She was flushed and excited when she had finished and as she stepped down from the platform, she was astonished to see Martin Newmarch sitting at the front of the hall next to Miss Gregory. He rose to his feet as she came to a stop in front of him.

'Miss Sheppard,' he bowed. 'Many congratulations. Such fervour. You certainly aroused your audience,' and it was true, for she had been given a standing ovation.

'She is known as Miss Grace now,' Miss Gregory interrupted. 'After Wakefield,' she smiled. 'The name seems to suit.'

'I have read of it,' Martin replied. 'There was an account of your speech in the *Packet*.'

'In the *Packet*?' Grace was astonished that the Hull newspaper should know of their meetings.

'Indeed,' he said. 'You are in the news at the moment – Miss Grace,' he added, his eyes crinkling with humour.

She was embarrassed. She hadn't wanted this. Yet perhaps it would do some good, make some changes for the better.

'Will you excuse me for a moment,' Miss Gregory said. 'I need to speak to Mrs Westwood before we go.'

Grace raised her eyebrows. Before we go

where? 'Are you here for 'rest of 'week, Mr Newmarch?' she asked as they made their way to the back of the hall where free refreshments were being served. 'We're here for two more days before moving on to Bolton and Oldham and then returning home.'

'No,' he said, and his gaze on her face seemed very piercing. 'Regretfully not. I have come only to escort Miss Gregory to her home. She is to attend her cousin's wedding to my brother next week and a carriage journey seemed to be the quickest option, rather than the train or waterway.'

'Mrs Westwood is also returning,' he added. 'I have brought her news of a crisis at home.'

He must be very fond of Miss Gregory to come all this way in order to escort her, she pondered. I wonder if they are promised to each other?

'I have come as a favour to Miss May Gregory,' he said by way of explanation. 'Georgiana will of course be almost related after the wedding, but I must confess', again his eyes sought hers, 'that I was curious as to how you – er, how the tour was progressing.'

'Very well, I think,' she replied. 'But 'workers of Lancashire have many difficulties which will take a long time to overcome, and,' she shook her head, 'nothing that I can say will help them.'

'Don't say that,' he interrupted quickly and clutched her arm. 'Many voices are needed, and yours is as effective as any.'

She gazed frankly at him, and he dropped his hand. 'And what of your voice, Mr Newmarch?'

she asked quietly. 'What do you have to say on these issues?'

'I do what I can.' He was hesitant in his reply. 'But my position at the mill makes it difficult to take sides.' He glanced around the room as if searching for a plausible answer. 'I try to put the workers' point of view to the management.'

She nodded, but felt disappointed that he wasn't willing to stand up on a platform and speak against poor working standards.

He must have seen the cast-down expression on her face or else felt the dissatisfaction and taken it as failure on his part, for he repeated in an urgent manner, 'I assure you, I do what I can!'

Miss Gregory and Mrs Westwood returned to them, and Mrs Westwood told Grace how sorry she was that she couldn't continue with the tour. 'But I must return home. It is most important that I do.' She appeared to be very distressed.

'There will be just you and Miss Emerson to represent us now,' Miss Gregory said, and Grace wondered at that, as Miss Emerson hadn't taken part in any of the speech-making, but had merely accompanied them and taken notes. 'But you will of course be escorted all the way.'

'If women want their rights and freedom, Miss Gregory,' Grace said thoughtfully, 'doesn't that mean that they should be free to travel alone without a gentleman to escort them?' She had wondered about this often whilst travelling, for every step of the way they had had a male escort, and it had seemed to her that it was often quite unnecessary.

Miss Gregory laughed. 'I often travel alone in

a chaise around Hull, but I wouldn't venture any further on my own. I can't imagine, Grace, that that day will ever come!'

'I beg your pardon, but I believe you are entirely wrong in that observation, Miss Gregory,' Martin Newmarch broke in. 'There will be – are – women who are quite independent,' and, as he glanced at each of them in turn, Grace knew that he was speaking of her. 'There will be women who have the strength of spirit to be self-reliant and liberated, and they will not need an Act of Parliament to grant them that freedom.'

Lizzie Sheppard pushed open her door and staggered into their room. She was doing her best to keep back tears. Tears of frustration, anger, and pain. She eased herself onto the bed and gingerly lay down. 'Oh!' She closed her eyes and grimaced. 'Oh! Dear God! What are we going to do? I'm finished. I can't go on!'

All day she had battled with the pain in her back and it had taken her twice as long as usual to do the waashing. The housekeeper and cook at the house she had been at were anxious for her to finish and leave, so that they could clear up after her and get on with their own chores. Usually there was nothing for them to do, as she was a clean worker and left everything as she had found it. But today she couldn't bend to wipe up the spilt water from the floor, and the cook had told her to go home and the scullery maid would do it.

'It's no good, Lizzie,' she had said. 'You're

going to have to look for other work and we're going to have to find another washer-woman.'

Lizzie reluctantly agreed and had made her painful way home. 'All that soaking and scrubbing, rinsing and wringing, it's finished me,' she grieved, as she lay on her bed. 'But what else can I do? I wish Grace was here to make me a cup o' tea. No. No, I don't! She's doing some good, I'll be bound. Why should she waste her life here as I've wasted mine? I could have done more, me and Bob both, but we've been worn down with 'daily grind of making ends meet. Keeping 'wolf from gate.'

Someone hammered on the door and she shouted to come in. 'It's onny me, Aunt Lizzie.' Ruby put her head round the door. 'Are you poorly?'

'Aye,' she said wearily. 'My back's gone again. I've had to come home.'

'Shall I make you a cup o' tea?'

She shook her head. 'There's no fire and there's onny a scraping o' leaves left. I'll wait 'till suppertime.'

'I've got some,' Ruby said eagerly. 'I bought Ma a kettle and a teapot and a bag of tea. I'll go and make you some.'

Ill-gotten gains, Lizzie thought as Ruby disappeared out of the door again, but beggars can't be choosers and I suppose 'lass wants to pay back what we've given her over the years. She hadn't seen much of Ruby since she had chosen a new way of life and Grace hadn't spoken about her much, knowing that her father disapproved.

She came back in five minutes with a pot of tea, milk in a cup and a biscuit. 'Kettle was already on 'fire,' she beamed, 'so it didn't take long. I don't know where Ma is. It's just as well I came when I did cos 'kettle would have boiled dry. I don't suppose you've seen her?'

Lizzie gingerly pulled herself up on the bed. 'No. I haven't. I'm allus out early in a morning.' She sniffed. 'Long afore she's out of bed!'

Ruby bit her lip. She knew that there was no love lost between the two women, though she didn't know why. 'Gone for her dose of loddy I expect,' she said diffidently.

She poured the tea and handed it to Lizzie, who thanked her gratefully. 'That's a lifesaver, Ruby. By, that's a good strong cup.'

Ruby nodded. She'd put in an extra few leaves as a treat. 'I don't suppose you know when Grace is coming back?' she asked.

Lizzie blew on the hot liquid. 'Another couple o' weeks, I think. She wasn't sure herself how long they'd be. Did you want her for owt special?'

Ruby shrugged. 'I'm lonely when she's not here,' she admitted. 'I miss her. I've nobody to talk to.'

'Aye, I miss her too,' Lizzie said. 'And I keep wondering what she's up to.'

'I'll make you a fire, shall I?' Ruby offered and looked round for the firewood. 'You've no coal?'

'No, onny wood, but there's plenty of that now that Mr Sheppard's at 'woodyard.'

Ruby delved into the sack which she thought contained firewood. 'This is not for burning!' she said, bringing out the wooden ship. 'This must be

Daniel's. Oh, it's beautiful!' She ran her fingers over the hull. 'We should make some sails.'

'That's what Grace said. She said she'd beg a bit o' canvas from 'sail maker. 'Firewood's in 'other sack.'

Lizzie dozed on the bed after Ruby had gone and was woken briefly by a sound of shouting outside, but then drifted off to sleep again. She was woken a second time when her husband came in. He expressed surprise at her being in bed.

'There's no supper ready,' she said. 'Feel in my apron pocket for some money and go and fetch a meat pie from 'baker's.'

'Are you badly again?' He sat on the edge of the bed and looked down at her. 'Will you be at work in 'morning?'

'No. I can't do it any more. And they'll not want me, I'm too slow. I'll find summat else to do.'

'Like what?' Bob got to his feet. 'There's nowt else you can do. You managed to mek 'fire anyway.'

'Ruby made it for me,' she said. 'And a pot o' tea.'

He grunted disparagingly. 'What did she want?'

'Onny to talk to Grace. Wanted to know when she was coming back.'

His face tightened. 'I don't want our Grace mixing wi' 'likes of her.'

'Don't be such a hypocrite, Bob Sheppard,' she hissed. 'Now get your coat back on and fetch that pie or there'll be nowt to eat tonight.'

Later, as they finished their supper in silence, they heard the sound of shouting in the court. 'Have a look through 'window,' Lizzie said. 'I heard a row going on earlier this afternoon.'

'It's Hanson,' he said, peering through the glass. 'Looks like 'bailiffs have come. They've taken a table out at any rate.'

'Can't have paid his rent then?' Lizzie shuddered. 'It's 'one thing I dread, being turned out into 'street.'

'He's coming across. Shall I let him in?'

'Aye, you'd better.'

'They've tekken me table.' Tom Hanson was distraught. 'I made that afore we was wed. I promised I'd pay arrears now I was in work but they wouldn't listen.'

'No, well, they wouldn't,' Lizzie said. 'They'll get a deal o' money for a table like that.'

'That they will, it's solid mahogany.' He ran his hands through his hair. 'I don't know what Mrs Hanson will say.'

'You think she'll come back then, do you?' Lizzie said bluntly.

He folded his arms across his chest and bent his head. 'Well. No. I don't think she will, to be honest. She said once that if ever she left she wouldn't come back.'

'So where do you think she's gone?' Bob Sheppard asked.

Tom Hanson pursed his lips and stared into the fire. 'To 'bottom of 'river, I shouldn't wonder. She was allus a dowly woman – given to melancholy, you know. She couldn't cope wi' being poor.' He sighed. 'I can't afford to keep 'house on, not on a labourer's wages.' He looked up at the two of them, who were watching him closely. 'There's both of you bringing money in, and your lass, so I expect you can just manage. But I can't, not on my own, and, besides, I'm no cook, I can't feed myself. Never done it, you see. So I'll have to find some cheap lodgings.'

'Sit down,' Lizzie said, indicating Grace's stool. Bob was in his usual chair and she was sitting on the bed. 'Listen to what I have to say.'

She outlined her dilemma, of her back and not being able to work as a washerwoman any more. He started to say he was sorry to hear that, but she stopped him. 'Our Grace is away at 'minute, so we don't have her wages, and when she comes back she won't have any work.'

She glanced at her husband. 'I don't know if this will work out or even if you'll agree, but 'way I see it, we've got a house here which will take another person living in. I'll be able to find work of some kind and I can still cook, as long as I've a fire. And I can keep 'house clean, provided I'm careful. What I suggest is, that you give up your house and come here to live with us. Share 'rent and give me summat for your board. You can bring your own bed and chair, and sell what you don't need. If we don't get on, then you can move out and find other lodgings.' She looked at them both. 'What do you think?'

'I don't know.' Her husband spoke first. 'We've never had anybody living with us afore. What about privacy?'

'We can rig up a curtain in 'corner and put 'other bed there.' Lizzie was ever practical and that was the first thing she had thought of. 'Besides,' she said, 'I don't think we can afford privacy any more.'

'Well, it sounds all right to me,' Hanson said. 'Bailiffs said they'd be back for other furniture next week, so I have to make my mind up. Yes,' he declared eagerly. 'If you're agreeable, Bob. We get on well enough at 'yard.'

So it was settled. He and Bob brought over his bed and bedding and two chairs, and Lizzie looked over Mrs Hanson's saucepans to see if they were better than hers, which they were, so he brought those too. 'See if you can sell 'rest of stuff in 'market tomorrow,' she told him. 'Then there'll be nowt left for bailiffs when they come.'

Bob shook his head and tried not to listen. He'd always been honest, but it seemed that the time had come when they couldn't afford honesty either.

CHAPTER TWENTY-NINE

Ruby dawdled back to Wright Street. She hadn't seen her mother, but she had left a box of groceries so that she would know that she had visited. I wish Grace was back, she pondered miserably. It's all very well having money in your purse but if there are no friends to talk to or have a laugh with, well, what's the point of anything?

She didn't think that Edward would come that evening. He had called at midday to see her, but hadn't stayed long. He seemed rather jittery and had paced about the room, but his passion was as fervent as ever and he had held her tightly and vowed that he would never let her go.

But when she turned into Wright Street, she saw a hansom cab outside the door of the house and knew that it would be him.

'Where have you been?' he demanded, greeting her from the top of the stairs. 'I've been here half an hour!'

'I'm sorry!' she stammered. 'I didn't think you would come again today. I've been to see my ma.'

'You should be here,' he complained. 'I need you.'

'So does my ma,' she answered quietly. 'I have to see her sometimes.'

He ushered her inside the room. 'I must come first, Ruby.' He put his arms around her and she felt smothered. 'That's why I took these rooms, so that you would always be here.'

'But I have to go out. I can't stay in all day! This is 'first time I haven't been here when you came,' she wheedled, for he seemed so very agitated. 'What is it?' she asked. 'What's 'matter?'

He clutched her face with his hands. 'Promise you won't ever leave me,' he urged. 'Promise!'

She laughed and drew him to a chair. She made him sit down and then sat on his knee. 'It should be 'other way round, shouldn't it? I should be making you promise. You're more likely to tire of me!'

'Never,' he vowed. 'Never. Never. Never!' He lifted her from his knee and started to walk backward and forward about the room. 'Ruby, I have something to tell you. That's why I want you to promise that you won't ever leave.' He turned swiftly and caught her to him. 'Say that you won't! I never thought that I would feel so passionately about someone. But since I first saw you at the mill I've been obsessed with you. I think about you day and night. I can't sleep. I can't work.'

She was flattered but also rather disturbed. She was beginning to feel trapped. Am I losing my freedom? If I ever had any, she mused.

'What is it you have to tell me?' She avoided giving him an answer.

He sat down again and put his head in his

hands. 'I don't want to lose you.' He looked up at her and she saw pain in his eyes. 'I'll give you anything you want. Jewels, money, whatever you want you can have, but please don't go away.'

'I'm not likely to leave, Edward,' she said softly. 'Where would I go? I came from nowhere and that's where I'd go back to, so why would I want to?' She looked around the pleasant room. The late evening sun was shining through the windows, casting a warm glow on the walls and furniture, not something she had ever seen in the dank and dark room in Middle Court. 'Tell me!'

'I'm getting married!'

'Oh!' She was surprised, yet it was inevitable, she supposed. 'Oh!' She sat down on a chair opposite and leaned towards him, putting out her hands. 'Edward!' she breathed and felt a faint sense of relief. She was often anxious when he was so passionate, afraid of becoming pregnant, and always washed herself thoroughly afterwards with vinegar and water. Perhaps he wouldn't be quite so demanding if he had a wife to please. 'When?'

'Next week,' he groaned. 'I have to marry her, Ruby. It's expected of me. She would sue me for breach of promise if I didn't.'

She didn't know what that meant, but it sounded very threatening. 'But of course you must if you've promised.' She tried to sound downhearted. 'She would be heartbroken if you didn't!'

'Heartbroken!' He gave a wry laugh. 'I don't

think so. Not May. She would think she was ill used, for it would ruin her reputation.'

'And in any case, you can't marry me, can you?' She looked at him from under her lowered lashes.

'Of course I can't!' He drew her to him, bending his head to kiss her throat. 'Even if it were possible I wouldn't want you as a wife, Ruby. Not when I can have you as my mistress.' He started to unbutton her gown, slipping it off her shoulders and running his hands over her naked breasts.

As she lay beside him on the feather bed, his head cradled beneath her arm and his cheek on her breast, she pondered her situation. He says I can have anything I want. Jewels, then, and I can sell them when he gets tired of me, which he will one day, or when his wife finds out what he's up to. Money. Yes! Then I can save to buy Freddie back and bring him home. She stroked Edward's cheek and he murmured in his sleep. Poor Edward. Having to marry someone he doesn't love, when he's so full of passion! I wonder what she's like? She'll be rich, I expect. That's why he's marrying her.

She had no illusions about Edward New-march's principles or motives, nor did her own conscience stir, for she had thought that she would only be meeting married men when she had agreed to join Jamie. Hadn't he told her that married men didn't lie with their wives except to conceive children?

Jamie! She felt anxious whenever she thought of him. She tried to avoid meeting him for he had been angry with her when she had paid him back what she owed, and he had demanded to know where she had got the money. She had told him to mind his own business and he had become threatening and warned her off his and his mother's area.

Edward stirred and said he would have to go. 'But I'll see you again before your wedding, won't I?' she asked softly. 'I couldn't bear it if I didn't.'

She smiled to herself as he groaned and buried his face in her hair, and whispered that of course she would. 'Every day,' he said, 'until then. And we shall be away for only a short time.'

'You might not want me after you've – been with your wife.' She let her mouth tremble.

He smiled and pulled her on top of him. 'I shall have to be careful that I don't shock her by expecting too much on our wedding night,' he said. 'Virgin ladies are so modest and delicate – and untried. They are unaware of what pleases a man.'

'But Edward,' she objected, digging her finger-nails into his shoulders and letting her hair tumble across his face, 'I was a virgin when I met you.'

He rolled her over and she saw by the look in his eyes that he wouldn't be going home yet. 'So you were, my darling Ruby. But you were not and never will be a lady.'

'So, Mother, will you miss me when I'm gone to be a married man?' Edward teased his mother as she fussed over the last-minute arrangements. 'You will only have Martin and he's such a sobersides.'

'He is not a sobersides at all,' his mother objected. 'He simply does not have your frivolous nature. Now, I wish to speak to you seriously.'

Edward groaned. 'Not a lecture, Mother. I have to go out.'

'That is exactly what I want to talk to you about.' His mother's cheeks flushed. 'I have asked your father to speak to you but he refuses, but I must have my say.' Mrs Newmarch, normally a placid woman who did not impose her views on anyone, was determined to tell her son of her feelings now.

'You spend far too much time at your club, Edward, and although it is perhaps excusable in a single young man, it will not look good if you continue in such a manner once you are married.'

Edward yawned. 'We have had this conversation before,' he began, but his mother interrupted.

'It has been commented on by Mrs Gregory,' she said firmly, 'that you have spent little time with Miss Gregory since you became affianced. The poor child is quite distressed and wonders if her married life is going to be lonely.'

'Then I shall go to see her now.' He rose to his feet. 'This very minute.'

'But they will not expect you,' she said in alarm. 'It will be most inconvenient if you call now whilst they are busy making arrangements for tomorrow.'

He bent and kissed her forehead. 'They must

335

take me as I am, Mother, and if I am to put May's mind at rest then I will do it now.'

He saddled up a mount and rode off towards Hessle to the Gregorys' house, situated not far from All Saints Church where he and May were to be married the next day. He greeted Mrs Gregory and asked if he might speak to May.

'It is not convenient, Mr Newmarch,' she demurred. 'May is having last-minute fittings to her gown.'

'I must see her,' he pleaded. 'I can't wait until tomorrow when we will be surrounded by so many people.'

Mrs Gregory relented. 'Oh, very well then – you young people,' she gushed. 'So impetuous!'

As May came into the room, he was struck by how pale and listless she looked, but for the bright spots of colour on her cheeks. He gave a slight bow, then drew her towards him. 'I just wanted to see you before the ceremony,' he whispered. 'There will not be a chance to speak to you alone.'

'Oh, Edward.' She clung to his arm. 'I have been so worried. I have seen so little of you, I feel as if I hardly know you.'

He gave her a smile. 'We shall get to know each other very well during our married life together, May, but we do not need to spend our whole time in each other's pocket. Men and women have different interests,' he said persuasively, 'which is how it should be, for then we shall have something to discuss when we meet at supper every evening.'

'Of course,' she agreed. 'I know I'm being very

336

silly and I know also that you will not spend too much time at your club once we are wed. Will you?' she added, and he thought he saw a look of determination in her expression, in spite of her girlish manner.

He kissed her cheek and reassured her, then left her to return to her dressmaker, whilst he, rather than going home, cantered swiftly into Hull to assuage his appetite and longing for Ruby.

The bright morning sun woke him the next day as it came through his window, and he groaned as he remembered his commitment. His marriage to May. The clock in the hall struck five and he rolled over in bed and put his head beneath the sheets. 'Damnation!' he muttered. 'How will I get through the day?' He lay for ten minutes, thinking that he wouldn't see Ruby for nearly two weeks and wondering how he could possibly bear not to be with her. 'The girl has possessed me,' he murmured. 'She's got under my skin so that I can't do without her.'

He sat up in bed, then swung his legs out. There's time, he thought. Plenty of time to ride into Hull and back, the ceremony isn't until twelve. He pulled off his nightshirt and rinsed his face and hands with the water still in the jug from the previous evening, then quickly dressed in shirt, trousers and jacket. He crept stealthily downstairs with his boots in his hand and let himself out of the front door.

The road was quiet apart from a few early morning traders making their way to the Hull market, and just after six o'clock he was putting the key in the door of the house in Wright Street and waking a sleepy Ruby.

'I just had to see you,' he murmured in her ear. 'I couldn't face the day without being with you. What am I to do, Ruby? I need you so much.'

They both fell asleep and were woken by the rattle of waggons and voices in the road outside. Edward sat up and looked at the clock on the wall. 'My God!' He jumped out of bed. 'It's ten thirty! The service is at twelve!'

Ruby was tempted, just for devilment, to call him back to bed. She knew that she could. If he could spend his wedding morning with her, she was very sure that she could ask for and be given anything she wanted. But she resisted and put her face up for a kiss.

'Oh, Ruby.' He closed his eyes as he bent over her. 'I'd give anything to spend the day with you.' He straightened up. 'But duty calls.' He emptied his pockets of money. 'There's not much there, but I'll make it up to you later.' He gave a grin. 'There'll be plenty of money after today.'

The house was in turmoil when he got back, for no-one knew where he had gone, only that his horse wasn't there. 'I was awake early,' he explained. 'So I went for a canter along the Humber bank. I forgot the time, that's all.' He shrugged and dashed upstairs to change into his morning suit.

'You went to see *her*, didn't you?' Martin said in a low voice as they climbed into the open landau which was to take them to church. 'Mother was having a fit! You're sailing too close to the wind, Edward. You'll be found out.'

Edward held his grey top hat on his knees and tapped it with his fingertips. He stuck his chin in the air, and didn't look at his brother as he replied. 'It'll be too late then, won't it? In half an hour's time I shall be a married man, and as a married man in my own household, I make the rules.'

Martin said nothing. There was nothing to say. Edward was quite right, he could do anything he wanted and his wife and children, if he had any, must obey him. He thought of Mrs Westwood, returned unwillingly to her brutal husband because her child was ill and fretting for her. He sighed. The campaigning women were right. It was an unjust world.

'You look beautiful, my dear.' Edward was very convivial as they celebrated at the wedding breakfast which was being held at the Gregorys' home. He had drunk several glasses of champagne and smiled benevolently, if not lovingly, at his new wife. He touched the sparkling jewels around her throat. 'And you're wearing my gift.' He thought of his promise to Ruby that she would have jewels. I'll buy her rubies, they will suit her vibrant personality. I mustn't think of her, he reminded himself hurriedly, or I shall want to dash away to see her.

Instead he bent to kiss his wife's cheek and murmured something in her ear. 'Edward!' She drew back, her cheeks colouring. 'There are people here!'

'Doesn't matter,' he slurred. 'You're my wife now.'

339

'We must still behave with propriety,' she insisted. 'Come.' She gave a bright smile and took his arm. 'We must circulate and speak with our guests.'

Georgiana Gregory chatted to various guests and then made her way across to Martin. 'You're looking very thoughtful,' she said. 'Not very merry for a wedding celebration.'

'Mm, well.' He gave a slight shrug. 'Marriage is a serious business, it's not all merrymaking.'

She raised her eyebrows. 'And do you think that your brother will take it seriously?'

'I don't know, to be perfectly frank with you, Georgiana. I don't know at all.'

'You are quite different, are you not – you and Edward?' She gazed thoughtfully across at Edward, whose eyes were straying around the room even as he spoke to guests. He saw her looking at him and gave a small bow. 'I wouldn't wager that he will be faithful,' she murmured. 'Whereas, if you made a commitment, then I'm sure you would always keep it. Does your offer to me still hold?' she added swiftly, and saw the startled look on his face.

'I – ' He took a deep breath. 'As you say, if I make a commitment, then I keep it. Of course it still holds.'

'It's just that – ' She gazed steadily at him. 'Well, it's a funny thing about a wedding ceremony – for women, anyway. It makes us feel that married life would be such bliss. Whereas, in reality,' she added slowly, 'we know very well that it isn't.'

It was late as the last of the guests took their

leave, and May, followed by her maid, went upstairs.

'Just one more drink,' Edward murmured as he took a glass from the tray which the footman held. 'Here, Martin,' he took another and handed it to him. 'You look as if you need cheering up.' He drained his glass. 'Then I must go up to my little wifey.'

Martin took a drink of wine. 'Not really for me to say,' he murmured. 'But – May is only young –'

'I know,' Edward's voice dropped, 'and inexperienced, and I'm a hot-blooded male.' He shook his head and looked down at the floor. 'Why do you think I went off this morning to visit Ruby? I desperately needed to see her, and I didn't want to frighten May on our first night together.'

Martin nodded, thinking that he was halfway to understanding his brother, and beginning to feel rather sorry for him.

'You probably will never experience a grand passion,' Edward went on. 'You're far too sensible. Well, neither did I think that I would, but I have – am doing, and I'm not sensible at all, and so I can't give her up.' He took a handkerchief from his pocket and blew his nose. 'I would die if she should leave me.'

Martin touched him on the shoulder. 'I'm sorry, old fellow. Really sorry. But you should have called the marriage off. It's not fair to May.'

'Couldn't do that,' Edward replied. 'She'd have ruined me. No, this way, we'll both be happy. May will have a husband who doesn't bother her overmuch, which is what every woman wants, and I'll have enough money to indulge my mistress and keep her happy.'

Martin watched Edward as he walked unsteadily up the stairs. He can't be right, he pondered. There surely can be love and passion within marriage without looking elsewhere for it? He thought of Georgiana's question of did his marriage offer still hold. Although he hadn't formally asked for her hand, but had only suggested that she should marry him in order to give her freedom from the restrictions of her family, nevertheless it was an offer as such, and he would of course keep it. He was fond of Georgiana, yet for some reason which he couldn't quite fathom, as he collected his coat from the footman at the door, he felt quite dispirited at the prospect.

Edward knocked on May's door and without waiting for an answer, he opened it. The maid was in the act of removing May's wedding gown over her head and Edward saw not May's face, which was covered by masses of skirt, but a wide crinoline overlayered with frilled petticoats.

The maid gave a small scream and dropped the skirt back over May's shoulders, revealing her flushed face.

'I beg your pardon,' he said, hiding a grin. 'I thought you would be finished.'

The maid gazed at him with her mouth open in dismay. 'No, sir. Sorry, sir.'

'Can I help you with that?' he said, moving closer. 'It looks extremely complicated.'

'No! No!' May shrieked. 'Please, go away. Come back in half an hour!'

'Half an hour! I'm damned if I will. I want my bed. Come on,' he said to the girl. 'Let's get this contraption off.'

The maid looked from one to the other, but whereas her mistress's face was distressed, her master's was determined, so once more she hauled the gown over May's head.

'It's not decent,' May's voice was muffled from beneath the gown. 'Edward, how can you?'

'God damn it, May, I'm your husband, that's how.' He winked at the maid as together they lifted it up and over May's head, and she lowered her eyes and hid a smile. They removed the layers of petticoats, Edward grumbling and exclaiming and May crying at the indignity of her husband seeing her like this. Finally she stamped her foot as they reached the last petticoat which hid the whalebone hoop and demanded that he leave the room.

Edward laughed and said he had never seen anything so ridiculous as women's fashion, and instead of leaving as he was asked, he picked up the pile of petticoats and the gown, bundled them into the maid's arms and ushered her out of the door. As she ran down the hall she gave a huge bubbling laugh.

May put her arms across her chest, even though she was still wearing a silk shift beneath the hoop. 'I am so ashamed, Edward.' Tears ran down her cheeks. 'How could you humiliate me in front of a servant?'

'Well, she must think it ridiculous to see you

wearing all this paraphernalia,' he argued, and turned her around to undo the ribbon which held the hoop. 'Come on, lift up your arms, or do you step out of it?'

'We need a chair to stand on,' she wailed. 'Fetch Dora back, please, Edward.'

'No,' he said. 'We can manage without her.' I've undressed Ruby often enough, he mused, and felt a great desire rushing through him as he thought of her compliant body. He swallowed hard and concentrated on unfastening the bands of whalebone.

'Stand on a chair, then.' May's bottom lip trembled. 'And lift it over my head.'

Edward roared with laughter at the notion, but he did as he was bid and swung the hoop over May's head, leaving her standing in her pantaloons and lace chemise, her arms crossed over her chest and her head lowered in embarrassment.

Edward stepped down from the chair and took hold of her arms, forcing them wide so that he could look at her. 'For heaven's sake, May,' he said softly. 'You're still covered from head to toe in clothing. I can't see a single part of your body, not even your feet.' He looked down at her feet which were encased in white silk stockings. 'Why are you so embarrassed?'

'It shouldn't be like this,' she sniffled. 'You should have come in when I was in my night attire and ready to receive you.'

'Ready to receive me?' he bellowed. 'What do you mean? That I'm only to come to your room with your approval? Must I ask permission to couple with you? What about desire, May? Have you given any thought to that?'

May's face blanched. 'How dare you use such language to me?' she whispered. 'And on our wedding night!'

'I can go elsewhere,' he said from between clenched teeth, 'if you do not wish to *receive* me. If tonight is not convenient to you.'

She started to cry, sobbing that she never thought that it would be like this, but he gazed at her stony-faced, then interrupted her to ask, 'Do you wish me to stay or not?'

She wiped her cheeks with her fingers, and taking a deep breath said as if reluctantly, 'I suppose you'd better. We'll get it over and done with.'

He swore beneath his breath. By God, but we will. Reaching towards her he roughly unfastened her chemise and threw it on the floor, then picked her up and carried her to the bed.

CHAPTER THIRTY

Grace arrived home late one midweek evening. The tour was considered to be a great success and many local and some national newspapers had given commentary on it. Their final town was Oldham; the group then split up and made their various ways home. Mary Morris had singled Grace out to offer her congratulations, and to remark that she was sure they would hear more of her. 'You are young,' she said, 'and you may feel that what we are fighting for will never come. But it will,' she asserted. 'One day the common people, and women too, will find a different life from the one we know now. Don't become downhearted.' Mary gazed steadily at her. 'Fight for what you believe in, and it will come.'

Grace travelled with Miss Emerson and Molly for the final part of the journey, and on arriving in Hull she asked if she could be put out of the carriage in the Market Place.

'Will you get a hansom?' Miss Emerson asked. She fumbled in her reticule. 'I have some change.'

'No. No, thank you.' Grace refused her offer. 'I'd like to walk home.'

'But it will soon be dark,' Miss Emerson objected. 'Will it be safe?'

Grace smiled. 'For me, yes,' she said. 'I have nothing that anyone would want.'

'You have your youth and beauty, are you not afraid of being attacked?'

Again Grace replied no. 'This is my home town, Miss Emerson. I know which areas are safe and which are not. Will you thank your father for me?' she asked. 'It was so kind of him to allow me to travel in his carriage.'

Miss Emerson opened her mouth to say something, but then seemed to think better of it and gave her a pleasant smile. 'Goodbye, Grace. It has been wonderful to have you with us. You have made such a difference.' As the carriage started to move off she suddenly called a halt. 'You have forgotten your travelling bag!'

'Those are your garments, Miss Emerson,' Grace told her. 'Molly said that she would launder them for me. I have my things here.' She showed her the package beneath her arm which contained her own clothes. 'I will return the clothes that I'm wearing tomorrow.'

'Oh, but there's no need.' Miss Emerson seemed embarrassed. 'You can keep them, really you can.'

Grace hesitated. She had taken rather a fancy to the grey dress that she was wearing, and the red petticoat. 'If you're sure? No, no, I won't take the others. Just this that I'm wearing. Thank you, you've been very kind.'

She walked slowly home, along the Market Place and Lowgate, skirting the Old Dock, where, as always, there was a great activity of labourers unloading ships which had come in on the evening tide along the Humber, through the narrow Old Harbour and into the dock. This is a town to be proud of, she thought. So much industry. Whaling, timber, corn, iron, wool. She saw a ship with its decks piled high with hides, another which was being laden with bales of wool to be taken abroad. A wealthy town, like Da says, onny with poor people.

She walked on towards Middle Court, cutting across Charlotte Street, Mason Street and Sykes Street, and was suddenly aware of how narrow the streets were, away from the main thorough-fare and bordering the river Hull. She saw people sitting on the doorsteps of their houses, for the evening was warm, and noted how they glanced at her as she passed. She nodded to some of them whom she knew by sight. Someone called out, 'It's Grace Sheppard, isn't it?' and she realized that by wearing different clothes she must look like a stranger to them. So this is why Miss Emerson was nervous, she pondered. I must seem to be better off than these people in their shabby garments. They don't know that I'm the same person in spite of my clothes.

The alleyway was dark and it stank of urine and animal matter. Did it always smell like this? she wondered. Was it always littered with debris? She held the skirt of her gown closer to her, away from the damp walls, and entered Middle Court. She had been so much looking forward to coming home, to seeing her ma and da, but she was overcome by the squalor of the court. Will I ever get used to it again? Her spirits dropped. Can I accept that this is how I will always live?

She slowly opened the door to their room and put her head inside. There was a low fire burning in the grate. Her mother and father were sitting at the table eating their supper, and she was surprised to see Mr Hanson seated with them. She waited a second, for she had opened the door so quietly that they hadn't heard her come in.

Then her mother looked up. 'Well, I never! Our bairn's come home at last.' She rose from the table and Grace frowned, for she saw the wince of pain on her mother's face.

'Ma! Da! Hello, Mr Hanson.' She was disappointed that he was there, for she wanted immediately to share the news of what she had been doing with her parents. Now it would be tempered because there was a stranger in the house. But perhaps he wouldn't be staying long. Then she saw the mattress on the floor and a thin curtain held up by string which stretched across from corner to corner.

Her mother gave her a kiss and, on seeing that Grace had noticed the mattress, explained, 'Mr Hanson's staying with us for a bit – as a lodger. I've had to give up work.'

Grace nodded and gave her mother's arm a squeeze of sympathy, then moved to kiss her father on his forehead. 'Welcome home, lass,' he said quietly. 'We've missed you.'

'Well.' Tom Hanson spoke up. Soup had

dribbled from his mouth and stained the whiskers on his chin. 'Prodigal daughter, eh! Hope you've been paid well while you've been away wi' them nobs. We read about you in 'Packet.'

'Will you have a drop o' soup, Grace?' Her mother gave her an anxious glance. 'There's some left.'

'No.' Grace shook her head. She wanted to cry. 'I had something at dinnertime. I'm not hungry.'

'By heck.' Tom Hanson pushed his seat back and wiped his mouth with the back of his hand. 'There's not many of us can say that.'

'You've eaten well enough while you've been here.' Lizzie's voice was sharp.

'Oh, I didn't mean owt, missus. Don't tek offence.'

'Then watch your tongue,' she said curtly.

'I'm off out,' he muttered. 'I'll be in later.'

Grace's mother pulled a face behind him as he left the house. She sat down again at the table. 'I'm beginning to rue 'day that I asked him to come,' she said angrily. 'He's that ignorant, has no manners or consideration for anybody but himself. There's no wonder his missus left home.'

They told Grace why they had asked him to stay. 'We knew his money would just tide us over until I can get some other work,' her mother said. 'But I can't apply for owt until my back is a bit better.'

'I'll be looking for a job in 'morning.' Grace's spirits dropped even lower. 'We'll manage, Ma, and then you can ask him to leave. I don't suppose he's had news of Daniel? And what about Ruby?' she asked. 'Have you seen her?'

'Aye, once or twice. She's been round here looking for you, wanting to know when you'd be back. But we've not heard owt about Daniel. But never mind about all of us. What about you? What about 'famous *Miss Grace*? Tell us what *she's* been up to!'

She found it strange talking about the past events, and it was almost as if she was speaking of someone else and not herself. She told them about the crowds at Wakefield, about the woman and the sick child, but not about the collection which she had given away. She had no need to be modest, however, for the news of her generosity had reached the *Packet* and her parents had read it.

'That was right good of you, Grace,' her father said. 'You'll allus find somebody worse off than yourself.'

Grace agreed that that was true. 'But had I known that you'd had to take in a lodger because I was away, I might have felt differently about it. I've been well fed,' she confessed, 'and I've slept in beds with cotton sheets and wool blankets, and a maid to bring me more breakfast than I could eat. But I haven't earned a penny. Only this one.' She took it out of her pocket and held it up for them to see. 'I hope I never have to use it.'

The next day, before going to look for work, she called on Ruby's mother. 'Will you tell Ruby I'm back, Bessie?' she asked.

Bessie was still in bed. A proper bed on legs which she said Ruby had bought for her. There wasn't a fire, but Grace noticed there was a sack of coal and a box of firewood by the hearth. There was also a chair and a table and on the table was a loaf of bread and a jug.

'Are you eating, Bessie? Are you managing to look after yourself?'

Bessie sat up. Her skin was sallow and her hair lank. 'Aye,' she said in a quavery voice. 'I manage, though I miss Ruby not being here, but she said I wouldn't have my loddy if she wasn't with her gentleman.'

There was a knock on the door and a child came in. She looked at Grace and then at Bessie, who nodded at her. The child took the loaf from the table and picked up the jug, which appeared to be empty, and went back out again. Bessie shuffled about on the bed and said almost apologetically, 'One of Mrs Blake's bairns. They don't get much to eat.'

How generous, Grace thought, but I wonder what she is doing with the jug? Fetching ale perhaps?

She left, reminding Bessie again to tell Ruby that she was back home, but as she turned out of the alley and into the street, there was Ruby walking towards her. They put out their arms and ran towards each other.

'I've read about you in 'paper,' Ruby said excitedly. 'Edward left it when he came one day, I don't think he'd read it cos he never mentioned you. He's away,' she said gleefully. 'He's just got married and has taken his wife on holiday for a few days, so I've got a bit of peace.'

'Are you not worried that he might not come

back to you now he's married?' Grace asked, and explained that she had already heard about the marriage from Miss Georgiana Gregory.

'I know that he will,' Ruby laughed. 'He came to me on his wedding morning and 'day after. He's besotted with me, Grace. Totally besotted!'

Then how could he marry someone else? Grace thought as she looked at Ruby, so beautiful with her dark hair and sparkling eyes. She looked so plump and well that she didn't wonder at Edward Newmarch falling in love with her.

'She's wealthy, of course,' Ruby said. 'And she doesn't want any of 'bedroom palaver. He'd quite a time with her on their wedding night, it seems. She's not taken with that sort of thing at all!'

Grace gave a gasp and covered her mouth with her hand. How dreadful that Edward Newmarch should discuss his wife with Ruby. She remembered the conversation that Miss Gregory and Miss Emerson had had about Martin Newmarch, as they mulled over his personality and marriage prospects. If that is how well-to-do folk behave, she thought to herself, then I'm glad that I don't belong with them.

'I'll just slip in and see Ma,' Ruby said, 'and then we'll go and have a cup of chocolate. That's what I've been doing,' she laughed. 'And that's why I'm getting fat!'

'I can't,' Grace said. 'I'm going to look for work. I've been to see your ma, she's still in bed.'

'Going to look for work? I thought that after all you'd done, people would be asking for you.'

Grace shook her head. 'No. Everything is as it

was and I need to earn a living. I've no money, Ruby. Nothing at all to live on and Mr Hanson is lodging with us. Ma wants him out.'

'He's mean,' Ruby said, 'and greedy. I don't know how they managed to have a son like Daniel.' She looked pensive. 'He should be home soon. Do you think he'll talk to me, Grace?'

'Why shouldn't he?' Grace was surprised at the question.

'You know – because I'm being kept by a gentleman.'

'Oh! I don't know.' Grace considered. 'Yes, of course he will.' She saw the anxious look on Ruby's face. 'You're fond of him, aren't you?'

Ruby put on a bright smile. 'Of course I am! Just as you are. He's our friend, isn't he? But you're the one he cares for, Grace. Make no mistake about that.'

Grace's job as a scullery maid at the Emersons' had been given to someone else, her mother had told her, and she wasn't sorry to hear of it. She didn't want to work where there was a chance of bumping into Miss Emerson and causing any awkwardness. But she was disappointed to find that the work at Masterson and Rayner's had gone.

'I'm sorry. Very sorry,' Mr Hardwick said to her. 'But this girl is very thorough, as you were, and it wouldn't be fair if she was asked to leave.'

Grace hastily agreed that it wouldn't. She wouldn't want to take the bread from someone else's table. She tried other places, shops of all kinds, factories, seed mills, offices, but everyone had a full contingent of workers. There had been a mass arrival of Irish people into Hull who were willing to work for coppers, and the employers were taking full advantage of them. So what else can I do? she thought despondently. I must find work of some kind or I'll be begging in the streets. How else can I earn money to live?

'Try for a housemaid or lady's maid,' her mother suggested the next day. 'Try and go up in 'world. You've got 'right manner.'

So she wore the grey dress and applied at several houses, but she hadn't had the experience, she was told, and some threw up their hands in horror that she hadn't any references, and so another day went by. By the end of the following week she was getting desperate. She was trying not to eat after she had heard Tom Hanson muttering that he hadn't expected to feed another mouth out of his wages.

Ruby offered to give or lend her money, but she refused. She couldn't turn away the box of groceries that Ruby brought in and left on the table, for she saw her mother's face light up when she saw the packet of tea and a bag of potatoes and onions. 'Don't tell your da where it came from,' she whispered after Ruby had gone. 'He'll not want to eat it.'

Grace sighed. She took after her father, she realized. They were both far too proud for their own good.

Then Tom Hanson came in on Saturday after work, sat down and ate his supper, and abruptly announced that he was leaving. He was taking lodgings with a widow in Sykes Street. 'You can keep them saucepans belonging my wife,' he said in an unaccustomed fit of generosity. 'And I'll sell 'mattress and chair, unless you want to buy 'em,' he told Grace's mother. 'And you've had money for this week's lodgings, so I've nowt to pay. I'll be off first thing in 'morning.'

Grace saw that her mother was deflated – they would only have her father's wages coming in now. Lizzie turned an eagle eye on Tom Hanson and told him he was a mean and greedy peazan and she would be glad to see the back of him.

After he had gone out, for he was a habitual drinker at one of the local inns, Grace sat on Daniel's stool and threw another piece of wood on the fire. It burned quickly, being dry, and sparks flew out onto the clipped rug. There must be something I can do, she worried. There must be some way of earning money. Or else – She stiffened as a thought occurred to her. I could apply to 'workhouse! Ma and Da can't keep me. I've no money and no livelihood. She looked up. Her mother was lying on the bed and her father was hunched in his chair staring into the flames.

She got up from the stool. 'I'm going out,' she declared. 'I feel like having a walk.'

'You've been walking all day, haven't you, looking for work?' her father asked.

She nodded and told a white lie. 'Yes, but I thought I might see if Ruby's about, just for a chat, you know!'

Her father looked at her suspiciously. 'A chat about what?'

She shrugged. 'Just things, Da.' She gazed at him steadily. 'Nothing much.'

She wrapped her shawl around her. 'I won't be too long.'

I'll just take a look, she decided as she walked towards Whitefriargate, one of the main shopping areas of Hull and where the workhouse was situated. The doors will be locked for the night anyway, though there'll be vagrants hanging around outside.

She stopped at the high wooden doors of the workhouse, which, as she had guessed, were locked. Vagrants and destitute people were sitting on the ground outside, waiting for the morning when they might apply for shelter.

Am I brave enough to ask? Could I stand the crush of poverty within those walls? A woman in thin clothes and shawl, with a mewling child pressed to her breast, looked up at Grace. Her eyes were dull and lifeless and Grace felt such pity for her. It's not fair! Outrage consumed her. It's not right! Tears filled her eyes. What have we been campaigning for? Do the Guardians of Hull come down here to see these people?

She felt a restraining hand on her shoulder and she jumped and put up her hand, ready to strike in defence. It was her father, who, uneasy at her going out late and thinking the worst, had followed her.

'Come on, lass.' His voice was choked. 'We're not ready for this yet.'

She turned to him and leaned her head on his chest. He put his arms around her and held her close, and she wept hot tears of anger, frustration and sorrow.

CHAPTER THIRTY-ONE

Jamie was furious with his mother. She hadn't come home until the early hours of the morning, and although he knew where she was and with whom, a grocer from nearby, he told her he'd been worried about her.

'Worried whether I'd be bringing some money home, more like,' she said sharply. 'Here.' She handed over her money bag which she always kept beneath her skirt. 'Is this what you want?'

Sullenly he took it from her, counted the contents and handed some coins back to her. 'You've been going to him more regular than you used to,' he said sarcastically. 'Working longer hours, is he?'

'I haven't been to his shop,' she muttered and her neck flushed. 'I've been to his house.'

Jamie stared at her. 'He took you home? Where's his wife?'

'Six foot under.' She stared back at him. 'She's been sick for a bit. She died a week ago.'

'I never heard!'

'Well, you don't hear everything! Didn't you notice his shop was shut for a couple o' days?'

He shook his head. 'So, that means he'll want you more often.' He rubbed his hands together. 'Good!'

'No,' she said and looked away. 'It doesn't mean that. He wants me to marry him.'

Jamie's mouth dropped open. 'Customers don't marry whores like you,' he gasped.

She turned to him in fury. 'Don't you speak to me like that!' she spat. 'I'm your mother, remember?'

'You're still a whore,' he shouted back. 'A street woman! And you'd be nowt without me. You'd be sleeping in 'gutter if I hadn't tekken you in hand!'

'Why, you dirty little pander!' She brought her hand up and slapped him across the face. 'What do you think folks think about us? A son procuring for his mother!'

He reached out and grabbed her by the throat, pushing her against the wall. 'I'm not bothered about what folks think,' he snarled. 'But what do I do if you marry him? Where's my living going to come from?'

She pushed him away. 'You'll have to find somebody else like you said you would,' she yelled. 'You were willing enough to drop me if it suited you! Anyway, there's plenty of young lasses about who've no money and no livelihood. Go and hang round 'workhouse. There's any amount of women in there who want to earn a copper!'

'So when's this wedding taking place?' His mouth curled into a sneer, but he was devastated. What would he do?

'Not yet,' she said, calming down. She took the

359

pins out of her hair and let it fall. 'He's got to wait a bit – out of respect for his wife.'

'You what! He's been fornicating wi' you all these years and now he has to wait – out of respect for his wife!' He gave a derisive snort. 'He's having you on! He'll not marry you, Nell. Why should he?'

She put out her left hand. On her third finger a ring sparkled. 'He's allus said he'd marry me if he was free,' she said quietly. 'But I never believed him. I allus thought it was bed talk.' She took a deep breath. 'But he does mean it. We get on, you see. He says I make him laugh.' She shrugged. 'And we're good together at 'other thing. So I said yes. It'll be at 'end of 'summer.

'Sorry, Jamie,' she added. 'But this is 'best chance I'll ever have. I'll have a nice little house and a steady income and I won't have to go out at night. Besides, I'm fond of him. He's been good to me.'

Jamie turned without speaking and slammed out of the door. He couldn't believe it. His mother getting married! Well, there'd be no room for him in that relationship. The grocer wouldn't want him hanging around, he'd shown his disapproval of him several times.

Other women? He ran those he knew through his mind. There was Grace, but she was far too pure and besides she was on some kind of crusade, so he'd heard. Ruby was out, and he was mad about that, he was sure that the man he'd arranged for her to meet was the one she was living with now. By rights I should be taking some of her earnings! He slouched to the top of the alley and put his hands in his coat pockets. His fingers touched the bag of raw opium which a drunken seaman had given him when he'd directed him to Leadenhall Square in search of a girl.

He broke off a piece and chewed it. He'd always been quick-witted. He just needed the right opportunity to come along. He'd know it when it did.

At the beginning of a week when Ruby had brought her a box of groceries, Bessie was in fine fettle. She ate dutifully as was expected of her and trotted down to Mr Cooke to collect her bottle of laudanum, nodding agreeably each time that he told her that it had to last the whole day. By the middle of the week she was craving for more than the small dose and forgetting to eat.

She had an arrangement with Mr Blake, who was being paid a shilling a week by Ruby to keep an eye on her. She gave the Blakes her bread which was collected from the baker every day and they brought her a jug of ale, which was in addition to the one which Ruby brought. Ruby knew nothing of this and Bessie had told the Blakes most emphatically that they were not to tell her. But the craving for more laudanum was intense and no matter how she pleaded, the apothecary would not let her have another bottle and she had no money to go elsewhere.

'Mrs Blake,' she called out one afternoon as Mrs Blake came cautiously down the stairs. She lived in constant worry of the discovery that they were living rent-free in the room upstairs.

'There's no fear of 'landlord coming,' Bessie had assured her previously. 'Our Ruby pays at 'rent office, every month.'

Now, as she called Mrs Blake in, she had a special favour to ask. 'I've dropped my bottle of loddy,' she grieved, putting on a downcast expression. 'Most of it spilt on 'floor. What am I to do? Apothecary won't give me any more.'

'Oh, Bessie, I don't know.' Mrs Blake always had an anxious look on her face, a frown which started at the top of her nose and ran down her cheekbones to her narrow chin. 'I'd buy some for you if I could, you know that I would. But I've no money, onny that shilling that Ruby gives to Mr Blake.'

'And have you spent it?' Bessie asked eagerly.

'Most of it.' Mrs Blake looked warily at Bessie. 'I think there's thruppence left.'

'Thruppence?' Bessie pursed her mouth. She could get a few pieces of raw opium for that. 'Mrs Blake,' she wheedled. 'How would you like to sleep in a proper bed?' She pointed to hers. 'Like this one.'

Mrs Blake gave a low snigger. 'Have pigs got wings?'

'If I was to lend you my bed for a night,' Bessie suggested, 'would you get me a tincture of loddy or threepennoth o' raw?'

'But where would you sleep, Bessie? There wouldn't be room for you to share wi' me and Mr Blake and 'bairns.'

'No!' Bessie laughed heartily at the idea and was encouraged that Mrs Blake hadn't said no. 'I'd sleep on 'chair, here by 'fire. There's allus a good blaze,' she added coaxingly. 'We've plenty o' firewood – and coal.'

Mrs Blake looked tempted. 'I'll ask Mr Blake. It'd be nice,' she said longingly.

'Well, ask him,' Bessie encouraged. 'And if he says yes, we could mebbe have an arrangement once or twice a week, say. Cos I must have me loddy, Mrs Blake. I'm desperate. Onny you're not to tell our Ruby!'

Mr Blake agreed to two pence for the loan of the bed. 'We might need that extra penny,' he said to his wife. 'And she can get a goodish piece o' raw for tuppence.' They were managing very well on the bread that Bessie was giving them every day, and they usually had a gulp of ale from the jug before taking it to her. They had also been given outdoor relief for the children. In the last week the Board of Guardians had supplied them with an ounce of tea, half a pound of sugar and a loaf of bread, and told them to apply again the following week.

So with the shilling that Ruby was giving them and the fact that they were living rent-free, and sleeping on Bessie's old mattress which they had hauled upstairs again, they reckoned that their fortune had changed for the better.

'Shall I fetch it for you?' Mrs Blake asked Bessie before handing over the coins. 'I can go quicker than you.'

'No, no. I can manage.' Bessie hurriedly pulled on her boots. 'I know a good grocer.' She also knew that Mrs Blake would be tempted to nibble a few crumbs of opium if she had it in her hand. 'I'll see if he won't let me have a bit o' baccy as well. Our Ruby spends plenty of money with him.'

She slipped her clay pipe into her pocket and scurried off, her black skirt flapping around her heels and her shawl pulled tightly around her head.

'Where you off to, Bessie?' A voice greeted her as she came out into the street, and she looked up at Jamie who was lounging against the wall.

'Nowt to do wi' you where I'm going.' She scowled at him.

He put his hand into his pocket and brought out a paper bag. 'I was going to offer you some of this,' he said. 'Just got it off a ship.'

She hesitated, then, curiosity getting the better of her, she stopped. 'What? What is it? Not some of that bad loddy like you sold me last time?'

'It wasn't bad, Bessie. Just stronger than you're used to. Here, try a bit o' this.' He broke off a few crumbs from the block in the bag.

Bessie peered into the bag. 'That must have cost you a bob or two,' she muttered. 'Business must be good. Your ma doing well, is she?' she asked cynically, but took the offering and popped it in her mouth and chewed. 'Are you selling?'

'I might,' he said. 'But onny to folks I know. This is good stuff. Worth a bit.'

'I'll buy a pennorth from you,' she said, and wondered how big a piece he would trade for a penny.

'A penny! It's worth more than that. It'd cost you a shilling down at 'grocers for this quality.'

She shrugged and turned away. 'Suit yourself! That's where I'm off to anyway.'

'Hang on a minute. Don't be so hasty, Bess.' He broke off a larger piece. 'You can have this for sixpence.'

'I haven't got sixpence! Tuppence is my limit.'

'Go on, then. Seeing as it's you,' he said reluctantly. 'Onny don't tell anybody what a bargain you got. I can't afford to let anybody else have it at that price.'

She took it from him and handed over the two pence and considered she had done a good deal. It was a bigger piece than she would have got from the grocer. Though she still needed to go there to wheedle some tobacco from him. She broke off a small piece and rolled it around her mouth. Yes, it was good, better than laudanum, which was often diluted.

'Come and have a glass of ale, Bessie,' Jamie offered. 'I'm just off for one.'

Bessie frowned. What was he after? 'I've no money left,' she muttered. 'Can't afford to pay,' but it would be nice, she thought. She'd finished off the jug which the Blakes had brought her, and Ruby wouldn't bring any more until the next morning.

'I'll buy you a glass,' he persuaded. 'I need a bit of advice, Bessie. From somebody mature and experienced like you.'

'Mmm.' She was flattered, but she didn't trust him. Still, a glass of ale was a glass of ale, and she didn't need to do more than listen to him.

He took her to the Tap and Barrel, which he said was his favourite watering hole. He sat her down at a table and called the landlord to bring a jug of ale and a rum each.

'What you after?' she asked, taking a long drink from the glass, and, crumbling a piece from the opium in her pocket, she slipped it under her tongue.

'I need your advice, Bessie. You've seen a bit of life, haven't you?'

'Huh,' she grunted. 'Not 'sort I'd want to boast about.' She shook her head to clear it and saw Jamie's hand push the glass of rum towards her.

'It's my ma, you see, Bessie. Nell.' He gazed piercingly at her. 'I'm getting a bit bothered about her.'

Bessie leaned forward and took the rum. She drank it down in one swallow, then followed it by a gulp of ale. 'Why's that then?' She screwed up her eyes then opened them wider, the better to see him. 'She's all right, ishn't she?' Her tongue and few teeth were not co-ordinating. 'She's getting on a bit to do what she's doing.' She shook her head again. 'She must be thirty-five, easy.'

He nodded and watched her. 'Thirty-six,' he agreed. 'You need to be young for 'game she's in. More like your Ruby's age.'

She wagged a finger at him. 'Don't mess wi' Ruby.' She picked up her glass and found it was empty, and he signalled to the landlord for another jug. 'She's doing all right is my Ruby. Got a nice gentleman.'

'Yes, I'd heard. What was his name again?'

Bessie blinked. Something told her he was probing, but she was feeling very light-headed

366

and couldn't concentrate. 'Don't know,' she mumbled and took another drink. 'She's never said.'

'Oh, but you must have some idea,' he persuaded. 'Fixed her up somewhere, has he? I hardly ever see her around these days.'

'Got a nice place,' she slurred. 'Doesn't have to live in Middle Court.' She nodded her head and smiled blissfully. 'Set up, she is, but she looks after her ma. Brings me groceries. Bought me a proper bed.'

'She's a good daughter,' Jamie agreed. 'Businessman, is he? Man of property?'

'Summat like that,' she said drowsily. 'Looks after her anyway. Comes to see her every day, 'cept this last week when he got married.'

'Ah! Got married, did he?' Jamie watched Bessie's head drop lower to her chest until it was almost level with the table. 'And comes every day, which means he must have some kind of business around 'town. Well, that's a start, I suppose.'

He got up from the table and looked down at Bessie. 'Sorry I can't stop, Bess. I have to be off.'

'You're not leaving her there, are you?' the landlord called.

Jamie shrugged. 'She's not my responsibility,' he said. 'She can't hold her ale.'

The landlord came over and peered at Bessie. 'She's had more than ale,' he said. 'You shouldn't have given her rum, Jamie. She's mebbe had a dose o' loddy, these old women can't do without it.'

'She's not wi' me,' Jamie asserted. 'We just came through 'door together. She persuaded me to buy her a drink. I thought I was doing her a favour.'

'But you know her, don't you? Bessie Robson! She lives round here.'

'Oh, aye. Everybody knows her, and her lovely daughter.' He was about to leave, then turned as if in afterthought. 'Have you, er, have you heard of any nob getting married lately? Somebody in business round here?'

The landlord shook his head. 'Weddings are not my line. Not much demand for 'em in this area.'

'I have,' a woman's voice called, and the landlord's wife came from behind the counter with a cloth in her hand. 'One of bosses from 'cotton mill. He's just got married to some bigwig's daughter.'

'Ah.' Jamie shook his head. 'Not 'same one then. Anyway I'll be off.'

'What about her?' The landlord pointed to Bessie, now snoring loudly.

'Like I say, she's not wi' me. But if I see her daughter I'll tell her to collect her. Cheerio!'

The landlord and his wife looked at each other as he went out. 'Damned pander!' she said. 'He's up to summat. What's he brought an old woman like Bessie in here for?'

The landlord snorted. 'Well, not for owt he's selling, and that's a fact. She's long past owt like that. Shout for 'lad to bring 'handcart round to 'front door, will you? We'll have to get her home afore dark.'

CHAPTER THIRTY-TWO

'Grace!' Ruby hammered on the door, then opened it. She had a huge grin on her face. 'Can I ask you a favour?'

Ruby crouched down beside her. There was no-one else in the house, but she lowered her voice. 'I'm going away tonight just for a couple of days!'

'Going away? Where?'

'To York!' she said breathlessly. 'I wanted to go to Scarborough, but Edward said his family's too well known to go there. They go every year, so we're going to York instead where he isn't known.'

'But – why? How? What about his wife?'

'She's visiting friends in 'Yorkshire Dales, so Edward says we can go away for 'weekend. He says he wants to show me things and walk with me and spend a whole day and night without having to rush away home!'

'Goodness.' Grace put down her sewing. 'He really is taken with you, isn't he?'

'Yes.' Ruby nodded. 'I'm afraid he is.' She held out her wrist. 'Look what he brought back for me from his honeymoon.' She was wearing a silver bracelet. 'He says he'll get me 'necklace to match when we go to York, he couldn't buy it before in case May noticed.'

Grace sighed. 'So what's 'favour?'

'Will you watch out for Ma? I've asked Mr Blake and given him some money to get her a few things, but I'd feel better if you were watching out for her as well.' She frowned. 'I think she's getting an extra dose of loddy from somebody. She was acting a bit strange 'other day.'

Grace nodded and wondered if she should tell Ruby of her mother's humiliating arrival home in a handcart one evening. But then she decided against it. 'I'll watch out for her,' she said, 'but sometimes she goes off and I wouldn't know where to look for her, except at 'Ship or Tap and Barrel.'

'I don't expect you to be her keeper, Grace,' Ruby reassured her. 'Ma's a law unto herself and if owt happened to her, I wouldn't blame you.' She bit her lip anxiously. 'Perhaps I shouldn't go.'

'Go,' Grace said. 'It'll be wonderful.' A yearning came into her eyes. 'I wouldn't have missed my journey to 'West Riding and Lancashire for anything.'

'Have you heard from any of them folk you were with? You know, them ladies or anybody?'

'No. Not from anybody.' She put her head down. It was very disappointing. She was sure that someone would have written, but no-one had, not even Miss Gregory, and she hadn't seen

370

Mr Newmarch's carriage either, even though she had passed the mill a few times.

'You haven't found any work yet?' It was a question put hesitantly.

She shook her head. That was why she was sewing. It was a last resort.

'I – erm.' Ruby hesitated. Grace was so proud.

'Don't think of it!' Grace said quickly. 'I don't want your money. Save it. You never know when you might need it.'

'Yes.' Ruby sighed. 'I'm saving up for Freddie. I've nearly got 'ten shillings Ma sold him for, but I know 'agent will want more than that, so as soon as I have a bit extra, I'll go and see him.'

'Wouldn't Mr Newmarch give you the money if you asked? Instead of buying you presents, I mean?'

'I haven't asked him,' she said. 'He never asks me about anybody belonging me. I don't think he would be interested. But he doesn't tell me about his family either.'

'You could try. If he wants to please you!'

Ruby smiled a little sadly. 'He's more interested in pleasing himself.' She pondered. 'But yes, perhaps whilst we're away I could ask him then.'

After she had gone, Grace picked up her sewing. Her fingers were sore for the canvas was stiff. She was making sails for the wooden ship which Daniel had given her for firewood. 'I'll have to ask Da which way to hang them,' she murmured. 'Then a final polish on the hull and it's ready.' She leant down and searched amongst a pile of pieces of cotton on the floor, then picked up one of the faceless peg dolls and proceeded to fashion a dress for it, topping it with a velvet shoulder cape.

Her mother came in whilst she was busy and Grace smiled up at her. 'Look,' she said, holding up the doll. 'Isn't she elegant?'

Her mother took it from her. 'You'll have to paint a big smile on her face. Where did you get 'fabric?'

'Rena's. I was passing and went in and asked her if she had any scraps she didn't want. She gave me a bag full and when I said I hadn't any money, she said I could pay her a penny for it when my ship came in.'

She picked up the sailing ship and fondly stroked it. 'And this is it,' she said softly. 'Here's my fortune.'

Her mother took off her shawl. 'Come on,' she said determinedly. 'Pass me a doll. I'll help you. Where are you going to sell them? Market Place?'

Grace nodded. 'Yes. I noticed when I was there last Saturday that there were quite a few families there. Some of them looked as if they might have a bit of money to spare for a toy for their bairns. So I'll go on Saturday. I just hope that it stays fine.'

The day was fine, bright and sunny, and Grace carried her stool to sit on and a tray to display her goods, which were carefully wrapped inside a cotton bag. As well as the dolls, she had made cotton and velvet hair bows, a patchwork bag and, with a piece of fur which she had found amongst the other materials, she had fashioned a child's muff. There was also a piece of lace which she had edged neatly and made into a collar.

She chose a place outside a grocer's shop opposite the Holy Trinity Church, where most of the market traders pitched their stalls. The grocer employed a man to call out to passers-by to buy guaranteed produce from him, rather than the market stallholders. Grace had noticed previously that he had a rich humorous patter, and people often stopped to listen, even though not always to buy, for the stall traders carried varied goods, many from abroad, which drew the crowds away from the regular shops.

She set out her tray with the dolls, the lace collar and the hair bows, and was amazed to find a small crowd quickly gathering. 'How much for this?' A man picked up a peg doll dressed in blue cotton.

'Six pence,' she said promptly.

'I'll have it,' he said, and picked up another in red velvet. 'Is this 'same price?'

'Ninepence for that one, 'material's more costly.' She put up the price as he hadn't hesitated over the first doll.

He took the two and she was jubilant. One shilling and threepence and she had only been trading for ten minutes.

A woman with two little girls bought bows for their hair, and asked the price of the fur muff and did she have two. 'I can get another for next week,' Grace said eagerly. 'They're one shilling and sixpence each.'

The woman declined to buy at that price, but Grace didn't reduce it; she was convinced that someone else would buy it. They did, and the lace collar too.

The tray was slowly emptying and she replaced the sold goods with others from the bag, and brought out the sailing ship. Her father had tied the sails to the mast and made lines and rigging with strands of cotton. She held it in her hand and sighed. She was reluctant to sell it, it was such a work of craftsmanship. But then recalling that Daniel had left it to be burnt and had no fondness for it, she decided that being the person he was, he wouldn't mind at all if she sold it in order to live.

Someone loomed over her. A gentleman, holding a small boy by the hand. He smiled. 'Good morning, Miss Sheppard,' he said pleasantly and tipped his hat. 'That's a very fine vessel.'

'Good morning, Mr Emerson.' She was extremely surprised to see him, but couldn't get up to greet him as she had the tray on her knee. She would never have expected to see him here. She would not have thought he would frequent somewhere like the Market Place.

'This is my grandson, Charles,' he said. 'Say good morning to Miss Sheppard, Charles.'

The child did, very politely, touching his hat as his grandfather had done.

'Charles is my eldest son's child,' Mr Emerson thought fit to inform her. 'He's on a visit here and he and I are having a little trot around the Market Place. We like to see what's going on, buy a few trinkets.' He smiled benevolently at the little boy and Grace guessed that he indulged him.

'May I look at the ship?' He held out his hand and Grace passed it to him. 'Beautiful!' he said. 'Perfectly made.'

'It is, sir,' she agreed. 'It was crafted by a friend of mine.'

'He has a real talent.' He turned it this way and that as he examined it. 'How much is he asking for it?'

She hesitated. She didn't know its worth. 'My friend didn't put a price on it, sir. Would five shillings seem excessive?'

'Five shillings!' He semed astonished and she thought she had asked too much. 'My dear Miss Sheppard. You are asking far too little. I would certainly give you half a sovereign for such a ship, but you may possibly get more if you tried.'

'Oh!' She was flabbergasted. More than half a sovereign! But then she considered. It would be nice to know where the ship had gone. She saw the little boy handle it carefully and look at his grandfather with eager eyes. Would Mr Emerson buy it for him or himself? 'I would be happy to let you have it for the amount you offer, Mr Emerson.'

He nodded. 'Then we'll settle.' He looked down at Charles. 'It shall be yours, Charles. But we will keep it at my home until you are a little older. It is too good to be a simple plaything which might get broken.'

The boy seemed disappointed, but his grandfather, examining the ship again, murmured, 'But I think it will sail, and so when I next visit you I'll bring it and we will try it on your father's pond,' at which Charles beamed and nodded his head.

They completed the transaction and Grace asked tentatively, 'Is Miss Emerson well?'

'Daisy! Oh dear yes, in excellent spirits.' He leant towards her. 'It seems that she is in love,' he whispered. 'Some young parson fellow she met in Oldham, he's asked permission to call.'

'Oh!' Grace did remember a clergyman speaking to Miss Emerson, but nothing pertinent was mentioned as far as she could remember. She murmured pleasantries and then asked, 'And Miss Gregory, have you heard if she is well?'

He gave a small frown. 'I believe she is away visiting at present with her cousin. Has no-one been in touch with you, Miss Sheppard? Has there been no communication of the results of your tour?'

No, she told him, but she really hadn't expected to hear anything.

He tutted and muttered that it was most reprehensible of Daisy. 'And so you will not have heard either that Mr Newmarch has been very ill?'

She clasped her hand to her throat. 'Oh! No,' she said in alarm. 'I had not. I'm so sorry. Is he – is he making a good recovery?'

'Slow. He has had a very bad fever. At first it was thought to be cholera, but fortunately it turned out not to be so, but nevertheless he has been very ill and I heard only yesterday that his father had also contracted a similar complaint and is very ill indeed.'

'How very worrying,' she said anxiously. 'I'm so

sorry. If you should see Mr Newmarch, perhaps –
would you be kind enough to pass on my good
wishes for a return to health?'

He gave her a sudden smile. 'Of course I will,
he will be most pleased to receive them. He holds
you in high esteem, Miss Sheppard.'

'Does he?' she said in surprise.

'Indeed he does.' He tapped his finger on
his mouth as if contemplating. 'I do beg your
pardon, and I mustn't keep you from your business, but,' he weaved his hand towards her tray
and the goods on it, 'do you do this regularly? I
haven't seen you here before.'

'This is 'first time, sir,' she confessed and a
blush suffused her pale cheeks.

'Forgive me if I am impertinent.' He gazed at
her intently. 'But do I assume that you have not
obtained work since your return from the tour?'

'I haven't, sir. There isn't much work about.'
She gave a wan smile. 'The mill won't have me
and word seems to have got about to other
factories that I'm an agitator. As soon as I give
my name it seems that they have a full quota of
workers!'

He shook his head in dismay. 'I'm so very
sorry. You must be feeling very let down?'

His eyes were full of concern for her plight,
but she replied, 'I'm not sorry that I went, Mr
Emerson, please don't think that I am, and Miss
Morris said to me that I might think that what we
were fighting for might never come.'

She tried to hide a sigh. She felt very tired and
listless and had quite often wondered if she had
done the right thing in giving up her work to

fight for what seemed to be a worthy cause. 'She said that we had to believe in what we were doing,' she told Mr Emerson. But it is hard to believe in principles, she thought, when hunger is knocking on your door.

He nodded gravely and took his leave of her and without knowing why, she felt sad to see him go. He's such a very kind man, she thought, and most considerate. The sort of gentleman who would be a good friend to his fellows.

She packed up in the afternoon for she had sold practically all of her goods, and went into the grocer's to buy tea with some of the money she had earned. 'Well, young lady,' the grocer said as he weighed out the leaves into a paper bag. 'Have you had a good day?'

She nodded. 'Yes, thank you, and thank you for letting me sit by your window.'

'That's all right,' he grinned. 'As long as you don't start selling butter or cheese on my doorstep, I shan't mind. Here.' He cut some cheese with a knife. 'Try that.'

She popped the thin slice into her mouth and immediately her taste buds started to tingle and her dry mouth to salivate. 'It's delicious,' she said weakly. 'I wish I could afford to buy some.'

'You've just sold that ship,' he said. 'You must have made some money on that?'

'Yes.' She felt a rush of relief and suddenly rather tearful. 'Now we can pay 'rent for next couple of weeks.'

She walked slowly home. She really was so very tired, her legs ached and as she swapped her stool from one hand to the other she saw how

thin and white her fingers were. Her mother had been making broth every day, but the ingredients were getting less and less and recently had consisted only of onions and potato with occasionally a carrot or handful of barley. Turnips, which were usually very cheap, were not in season as summer was coming on fast. Grace and her mother took only the broth and gave the vegetables to her father, who was the only one working and needed the strength.

'Here, Ma.' She managed a smile as she went in the house and handed over the bag of tea and the money she had earned. 'Let's celebrate our success and have a cup of tea.'

The expression on her mother's face was reward enough, though Grace thought she looked rather tearful. She put the kettle on the fire and took off her shawl, and it was only as she turned around that she noticed that the room seemed bigger, only it wasn't of course bigger, but emptier.

'Table!' she said in astonishment. 'Where's the table?'

'Pawned it,' her mother muttered. 'We haven't had a bit o' bread to eat all 'week. I'm sick to death of damned broth which is nowt but hot water.' She put her hand over her eyes and Grace was dismayed – her mother was always such a pillar of strength and fortitude. 'So I've pawned it,' she said in a choked voice. 'I borrowed a handcart and pushed it round to 'pawnbrokers. He gave me two shillings for it and I've bought bread and cheese and potatoes and beans.'

'I'll get it back.' Grace hastily reached for her

shawl again. 'You make 'tea and I'll run round now and pay him. What'll Da say!' She burst into tears. 'Ma! What sort of life is this? What was all that talk about? Those high ideals? Those equal rights for everyone? What a waste of time and energy!'

CHAPTER THIRTY-THREE

Bob Sheppard came in to find his wife and daughter in tears. 'It's onny a table,' he roared, on finding out the reason for the weeping.

'It's not just the table, Da,' Grace sobbed. 'It's having to get rid of it in order to eat that's wrong!'

'Aye, I know, lass.' He sat down on his chair. 'It's a good job it wasn't my chair that'd gone to 'knocking shop, or I should have had summat to say.'

He was attempting, they both knew, to put a bright face on the situation, even though he was quite aware that his wages wouldn't feed the three of them adequately and pay the rent. And the roof over their heads, in his opinion, was of major importance.

'I've summat to tell you,' he muttered, as Lizzie made the tea. 'Hanson was sent for this morning. They fished a woman out of 'Humber.'

They both looked up at him, dismay on their faces. 'Aye,' he nodded at their unspoken question. 'It was her. Mrs Hanson.'

'How did he tek it?' Lizzie asked in a low voice.

Bob shrugged. 'Said he'd been expecting it. She'd threatened him she'd do it one day if he didn't get a job.'

'And now he has got a job and she's not here to see it,' Lizzie murmured. 'What a life!'

They did a reckoning as they sat, subdued and barely speaking as they sipped their tea, and decided that with the money raised from the little sailing ship they could pay the rent for the next three weeks. 'That means that with what's left of Grace's money you can fetch 'table back, Lizzie, and with my wages we can buy some food, and even a jug of ale.' Bob Sheppard had taken charge when he realized how demoralized his wife and daughter were.

Grace was putting on her shawl again to slip round to the pawnbrokers with the two shillings, when someone knocked on the door. A man in baggy cotton trousers, a navy blue reefer jacket and with a bag over his shoulder, stood on the doorstep. 'Beggin' your pardon, miss, but I'm lookin' for Bessie Robson or her relations.'

'I'll take you,' Grace said. 'She lives further along.'

'Ah, but I've been there, somebody directed me, but there's nobody in. I can't make anybody hear.'

'We'll go back,' she said. 'She doesn't always answer 'door.' And, she thought, the Blakes will have barricaded themselves in, in case the rent man calls. She banged on Bessie's door and called her name, and looked through the window, but she wasn't there, although a fire burned in the grate.

Then she called out for Mr Blake, saying, 'It's onny me, Mr Blake. Grace Sheppard.'

The door opened a crack. 'Sorry, Grace,' Mr Blake muttered. 'But you can't be too careful. Bessie isn't in,' he said. 'She must have gone out first thing.'

'But her fire is lit,' Grace pointed out.

'Ah, yes!' The whites of his eyes were the only part of his face showing from behind the door. 'I lit it. I've been keeping it in for her for when she gets back.'

And having a warm by it as well, Grace thought, though she couldn't blame them for that. 'So where has she gone,' she asked, 'if she's been gone all day?'

Mr Blake peered round the door at the stranger with Grace and raised an eyebrow. 'Well, Ruby left her a bit o' money to buy some baccy. Not much, but Bessie had grumbled about being left without a penny to her name, so Ruby gave in and let her have a couple o' bob.'

Grace turned away. Bessie could be anywhere, but more than likely at one of the inns. 'I'm sorry,' she said to the stranger. 'Can I give her a message?'

The man hesitated. 'Are you a friend? It's very personal. Bad news, I'm afraid.'

'I am a friend. A friend of her daughter, Ruby.'

'And did you know her son?'

Grace put her hand to her mouth. 'Freddie? Something's happened to Freddie?' He shook his head. 'You mean Josh?'

'Aye,' he agreed. 'That's who I mean. Josh. We were shipmates. 'Fraid he's gone. Got washed overboard. I've brought his things.' He indicated the kitbag. 'There's a bit o' money as well, so I'd want a receipt. Where will I find his sister?'

'You won't. She's away. She won't be back until mebbe Monday.'

'I can't stay that long.' He fiddled with his thick beard. 'My ship sails tomorrow morning and I've to be on board tonight.'

'I'll sign for it if you'll trust me. My name is Grace Sheppard, but I've no reference that I can give you.'

'Grace Sheppard?' he said and looked at her quizzically. 'Where've I heard that name?'

She smiled. 'Nowhere! Why would you have heard my name?'

He stared at her. 'Well, I have.' He stroked his beard again, teasing it with his fingers. 'Some-where.' He raised his hand and pointed a finger at her. 'Got it! You were one of 'speakers at Wakefield!'

She gazed at him in astonishment. 'Yes, I was. How do you know? You were never there, a seaman of all people?'

He gave a grin. 'No, not me, but I've just been to see my sister and her family. She married a man from Wakefield. She'd been to hear some of 'speakers at 'Bull Ring and was full of news about this young woman who spoke, and who gave all of her collection away to a poor woman and her lad.'

Grace was embarrassed but also amazed that people were speaking about her. 'Come inside for a minute,' she said, conscious of Mr Blake listening behind Bessie's door, and led him towards her own door. 'Will you have a cup of tea?'

He refused the tea and handed over the kitbag and a brown packet, and, looking around the bare room, he declared, 'I'll write to my sister and tell her that you do live in poverty like you said you did. My sister believed every word you uttered, she said she had never been so moved by anybody before.' He put out his hand. 'Can I shake your hand? Our lass will be that proud when I tell her.'

'Proud! But why?'

'Why, because you believe in summat. Cos you're trying to right some wrongs.' He looked keenly at her and then at her parents. 'Don't give up, Grace. There's a lot of folks depending on you.'

Grace's eyes were full of tears as she bid the man goodbye. So the cause had been worthwhile after all, even though we're suffering now, me and Ma and Da. Miss Gregory and Miss Emerson have gone back to their comfortable homes and can reflect that they have done their best for the sake of women. Mrs Westwood, well, I don't know why she has gone back to her husband, but perhaps she found life unbearable without her children.

But as for me – She took a deep satisfying breath. My eyes are opened and I've found my voice, so I'll go back to Dock Green and anywhere else if I'm asked, and if I'm known as an agitator, well, so be it.

* * *

'I'd better go and look for Bessie,' Grace said after they'd eaten their supper. She had been back to Bessie's house several times but she wasn't there, and as she looked through the window had seen a sudden flurry of bodies as the Blake family rushed away from Bessie's fire. The weather wasn't cold, but the houses were damp and mouldy and a fire was very comforting. Mrs Blake had come to the window when she saw that it was Grace, and called that Bessie hadn't been home and Mr Blake had been out to look for her.

'Try Tap and Barrel,' her mother said wryly. 'That used to be her favourite place. Onny be back afore dark. It's Saturday and there'll be drunken men spending their wages and their wives and bairns waiting for 'em at 'inn door.'

'Yes, I won't be long.' Grace glanced at her father, half hoping he would offer to go with her, but he seemed rather morose and didn't look up as she went out. She heard her mother mutter something and her father say, 'Leave it be, woman!' in answer.

She looked in the hostelries around Sykes Street and Mason Street, but there were so many that it would have taken her all night to check them all. She cut down New George Street towards the river Hull where the mills and factories were situated, and where there was an even greater profusion of inns and alehouses. Going inside one of them she called out, 'Bessie Robson! Has anyone seen Bessie Robson?'

A man turned round. 'Aye, she's been here. Ask 'landlord.'

Grace pushed her way to the counter and was aggrieved to feel fingers pinching her as she passed and comments made on her person. 'Have you seen Bessie Robson?' she shouted above the din to a man in a stained apron behind the ale-brimming counter.

He nodded. 'She was here last night. Not seen her since.'

Grace was dismayed. Last night! Did that mean she hadn't been home? She then went on to the Tap and Barrel which she knew Bessie frequented, but she felt uneasy as it was getting dark and there were few street lights down by the river. Again she repeated her question to the landlord. 'Has Bessie Robson been here today?'

'All day,' he agreed. 'I had to ask her to leave at 'finish, her and her pal.'

'You won't know where she went?'

'Don't much care,' he said grimly. 'She was mekking a nuisance of herself, asking for loddy, beggin' for money from folk.'

'Who was she with?' she asked. 'You said she was with somebody.'

'Oh, aye. He sat there laughing at her, but he allus clears off if there's trouble brewing. Can't think why he comes with an old lass like her.'

Grace was puzzled. 'Wh— who are you talking about?'

He passed a tankard of ale to a man who was waiting, and then served a woman with a glass of neat gin. 'Why, Jamie, of course. She was with him last time and then he left her for us to send home. Are you her daughter? Cos if you are I'll tell you, I'll not have her in here again.'

She shook her head in denial and, as she turned to go out, a toothless old woman grabbed her skirt. 'Bessie set off for Whalebone,' she grinned, showing her gums. 'Said her lad might be there and he'd buy her some loddy.'

'Her lad?'

'Aye, the one that's a seaman. Treated her 'last time he was home.'

Well, he won't be treating her any more, Grace thought, and I'd better keep that money that his shipmate gave me, and give it to Ruby when she comes back. She tried to prise the old woman's hand from her skirt but she held it fast.

'Don't suppose you've any money to spare, have you, dearie? I'm that parched.' She looked eagerly at Grace. 'Drop o' loddy? Screw o' baccy?'

Grace shook her head at each question. She didn't feel distaste for the woman's craving, only sorry that she should be driven to it by the life she had led.

'Jamie gave her some raw,' the old woman said in a disgruntled tone. 'But he wouldn't give me any.'

'Raw opium?' Grace said.

'Aye, he'd got a bag of it. He and Bessie were sharing it.' Her lips curled downwards. 'It'll be 'finish of her.' She gave a loud cackle. 'She'll not get home tonight.'

Bessie had begged Ruby to give her some money. 'Don't want much,' she'd said. 'But I feel like a pauper without a penny in my pocket. I'd like to wander down to 'Market Place and buy a bit o' baccy or meet some of my old pals and

388

have a glass of ale.' She put on a wheedling voice. 'I know you've bought me some groceries but I don't want to be stuck in 'house all of 'time, specially now when weather's nice. And you'll be off enjoying yourself, I expect,' she'd added.

And because Ruby felt guilty at leaving her alone, she'd given in and handed her two six-pences. Bessie had looked down at them in her palm and said not a word, so Ruby added another sixpence.

'It's not that I don't want you to have it, Ma,' she said defensively. 'It's onny that I'm afraid of what you might spend it on, or what you might get up to.'

Bessie had laughed and put the money in her pocket. 'You forget, Ruby, I'm your ma. I allus used to look after you, and Josh and Freddie as well! I can look after myself.'

'Not when you've had a dose of loddy and a glass of ale, you can't, Ma.' But she hadn't asked her to promise she wouldn't buy any laudanum or opium and Bessie was glad of that, for her craving was intense. She had a gnawing in her stomach and a buzzing in her head which told her she needed something now.

When Ruby had gone, she seized the bottle of laudanum she had brought and took a long gulp. 'I'll be sensible,' she said out loud. 'Like I said I'd be. I'll have a bit o' breakfast.'

She took a bite out of the loaf and cut a slice of cheese, but the cheese was sharp and she spat it out and decided that she would ask the Blakes if they would swap it for opium. Ruby would have been sure to have given them money as she was to be away for a few days.

Mrs Blake was coming down the stairs and she shouted to her. 'Same arrangement, Mrs Blake? You can sleep in my bed tonight and there's a nice bit o' cheese if you'll get me three pennorth o' raw.'

'Your Ruby said we hadn't to get you any loddy,' Mrs Blake said nervously. 'Onny food if you want any. Milk or tea and that.'

Bessie pulled a face. 'Tea! Never drink it. No, our Ruby knows that! Get me a jug of ale and three pennorth o' raw. It's loddy she says I haven't to have. Can't trust 'grocers to mix it right, you see. They use too much morphine.' She patted her nose with her finger. 'But I mix a bit o' raw wi' baccy and it's a grand smoke and doesn't do any harm. It's not like eating it or drinking loddy.' She shook her head knowledgeably. 'Oh dear no. Not 'same at all.'

And Mrs Blake, being a gullible, artless sort of person, gave Bessie the benefit of the doubt and trotted off on her errand.

In the meantime Bessie ate the rest of the bread and took another gulp of laudanum from the bottleneck. When Mrs Blake returned with her shopping she felt pleasantly aware that it was a delightful sunny day, though a little bright. The door and window frame, the bed and table stood out distinctly, and Mrs Blake appeared to have two heads, both with distorted features.

'You poor thing,' she muttered. 'It must be awkward for you. I mean, how do you know which bonnet to wear? Not that I ever wear a bonnet. Used to wear my old man's cap, softened blows when he hit me.' She closed her eyes for a moment. 'Does he hit you? Your mister, I mean?'

Mrs Blake nodded and agreed that sometimes he did, and then ran upstairs to tell her husband that Bessie was going off her head.

'Did you get us some shopping as well as her?' he asked.

'Aye. I got three pennorth o' opium for Bessie, but took some out, and here's a bit of her baccy for you. She's far gone already so she'll not miss it, and we can have her bed again tonight.'

'And for next couple o' nights if Ruby's away with her gent.' Mr Blake gave his wife a nudge. 'If Bessie goes out this morning we'll light a fire and have a bit of a kip, shall we? Just you and me! Send bairns out beggin'. About time little blighters started earning their living.'

Bessie did go out and somehow lost the day, for she didn't go home and Saturday morning found her on the doorstep of the inn where she had spent the night. Several people had tried to shake her awake or nudged her with a foot, but she was quite oblivious. She had had several jugs of ale which she shared with whoever was at her table, someone bought her a couple of glasses of rum, and she had chewed or smoked all of her opium.

When she finally awoke her head was spinning, she had been sick and couldn't get to her feet. 'Where am I?' she croaked. 'Can somebody help me up?' But there was no-one about so she crawled up the steps on her hands and knees and hammered on the bottom of the door until someone came to open it.

'Clear off, Bessie.' The landlord looked down at her. 'It's six in 'morning. You should be home in bed.'

'Where do I live?' she asked. 'Do you know?'

'Aye, I do,' he grunted. 'Took you home last time but I'm not mekking a habit of it.'

She groaned and tried to get up from her knees and he bent down to haul her to her feet. 'Look,' he said, grabbing her as she swayed. 'You can come in and we'll mek you a cup o' tea, but then you must go home. Your family'll be worried about you.'

She screwed up her eyes and moaned with the pain in her body, feeling as if she'd been kicked. 'There's nobody at home. Our Ruby's gone off with her gentleman.'

'And left you on your own? An old woman like you?'

She looked at him through bleary eyes and said in a shocked startled voice, 'Am I an old woman? I didn't know that I was! Nobody told me. When did that happen?'

The landlord didn't answer. He was looking across the street at someone going past and he put two fingers between his teeth and gave a shrill whistle. 'Hey! Hey! Jamie. Come here, I want you.'

Bessie's legs wouldn't hold her and she sat down again on the doorstep. Through her muddled mind she heard two voices talking. 'You're out early,' said one, and the other agreed that he was. 'Just doing a bit of business,' he said.

'Can you tek her home? She'll not get back on her own.'

A face grinned down at her. 'Now then, Bessie. What you been up to?'

She shook her hand to waft him away, but the gesture was feeble and she felt his hands under her armpits as he heaved her to her feet. 'Don't want—' she began, but he pinched her cheeks between his thumb and fingers, and whispered in her ear, 'I know what you want, Bessie, and I've got it. Drop o' loddy, eh? Bit of raw? But first of all you and me are going to have a little chat about your Ruby.'

CHAPTER THIRTY-FOUR

Grace was on the point of giving up her search
for Bessie. Thick grey mist was drifting in from
the river, shrouding corners and making the
groups of people who were hanging around
the alehouses look sinister and threatening,
although as she approached she saw that most of
them were women and children. It was not an
area in which she felt safe after dark: the lodging
houses were derelict, yet housed occupants. The
streets were undrained and potholed, dogs
barked and men and women shouted and
shrieked.

Some street women were leaning on the
corners of buildings and they looked at Grace
with uninterested eyes as she passed. She
stopped to speak to one of them. 'Do you know
Bessie Robson?' she asked. 'Have you seen her?'

The woman shook her head. 'Don't ever see
anybody, dearie. It's 'best way.'

She moved on in the direction of home, but
on a sudden impulse she crossed the street
towards a narrow alleyway where a light was
showing from an open doorway of an alehouse,

and loud laughter coming from within. It was merely a room, but ale and beer were being served and it was packed with customers. She looked in the door but her spirits sank when she saw the roughness of the people who were inside. She turned away and as she did she saw a bundle of rags huddled in a corner, and she thought it moved.

A man pushed past her to go inside, then stopped and leered. 'Looking for customers, darling?' He moved towards her and she smelt a putrid breath of ale and onions, and an unwashed body.

She backed away. 'No. No. I'm – I'm looking for my ma.' She appealed to him. 'Could you – could you try and see who that is?' She pointed down at the corner. 'I daren't look.'

He coughed and hawked and pushed his boot into the bundle. 'Has she any money on her?'

'No. We don't have any money.'

'You could earn some.' Again he leered and grinned at her.

'Not tonight. I have to find her. She's sick.'

He bent down and pushed some of the black cloth aside. 'It's an old woman,' he said. 'Phew! If it's your ma, she's for 'knacker's yard.'

She peered down fearfully. It was Bessie. Her face gleamed a deathly white, her neck was stretched back and her mouth open.

'Cheerio, darling.' The man moved into the lighted doorway. 'Can't do owt for her, but let me know if you change your mind.'

Grace knelt down beside Bessie and touched her throat. It was cold but she thought she felt a tremor, though there seemed to be no breath in her. How can I get her home? I can't carry her. There was no possibility of calling for any help from the alehouse, not if the customers were of the ilk as the man who had just gone inside. Besides, she might be putting herself in danger.

I'll have to fetch Da, she decided, and taking off her shawl she wrapped it around Bessie's shoulders and set off at great speed towards home.

'Where've you been, bairn?' Her mother's face was anxious and her father was buttoning up his jacket as she burst through the door. 'Your da was just coming to look for you.'

'Bessie!' she panted. 'I've found her. She's – she's, I think she's alive but she's not moving. She's down an alley near 'river, but I can't lift her.' She looked from one to the other. 'I think she's been out since yesterday morning.'

'God in heaven,' her mother muttered. 'I allus knew it'd come to this.'

Grace's father looked at his wife. His face was expressionless and she stared back at him, her mouth working but not uttering a word.

It seemed to Grace that they had forgotten she was there as she stood trying to get her breath back and ease the stitch in her side, and she waited for one of them to speak.

It was her father who broke the silence, though Grace could hardly catch the words. 'For pity's sake, Lizzie,' he said softly. 'Have some mercy.'

Her mother swallowed, then said in a tight voice, 'You'd better go with your da and fetch her back here.' She looked at Grace. 'Take a blanket wi' you.' She took a blanket from the bed and handed it to her.

'No. You stop here, Grace,' her father countermanded. 'Tell me where she is and I'll fetch her.'

Grace told him where to find her and her father was furious. 'You should never have gone there on your own! It's a den of hell down there. Pimps and thieves. You were risking your life!'

'But I found her, didn't I?' Unusually, she retaliated. She had been scared, though she wouldn't admit it, and she decided not to tell of the man who tried to proposition her.

Bob Sheppard hurried towards the river. A light rain was falling and he put up his jacket collar and pulled his felt hat over his forehead. He knew where the streets were which Grace had described, though he wouldn't normally venture into them, not even in daylight. They were usually flooded with rainwater and the residents lived upstairs, for the lower floors were uninhabitable.

How did you come to be down here, Bessie? he wondered as he picked his way through debris. How did you come to this? Have you lost your senses altogether? Did the poppy finally get you?

He found her exactly where Grace had said. Trying not to attract the attention of the occupants of the alehouse, he crouched down at her side. 'Bessie,' he whispered. 'Bessie! Can you hear me?' He gently patted her face. 'It's me. Bob.'

There was a slight movement and a rasp from the back of her throat.

'Can you hear me?' There was an imperceptible nod of her head. 'I've come to take you home.' He wrapped the blanket around her and as he lifted her she cried out. 'Where do you hurt, Bessie? Can you tell me?'

She shook her head. 'Everywhere,' she moaned. 'Who is it, did you say?'

'Bob.' He looked at her in the light coming from the alehouse door, and hardly knew her. Her lips were swollen and she had a bruise beneath her left eye. 'Bob Sheppard.'

She gave a croak which sounded rather like a laugh. 'I've onny – ever known one Bob,' she rasped, her words coming out in grunts. 'So you don't have to tell me your other name.' She took a breath and said huskily, 'Does – Lizzie know you're here?'

'Aye,' he said softly. 'She told me to fetch you.'

'She's – forgiven us, then?'

'She forgave you a long time ago.' His voice dropped to a mere whisper. 'It's me she hasn't forgiven.'

She was no weight at all, and he cradled her in his arms and made his way back down the alley to the street.

'Somebody – said I was – an old woman,' she said breathlessly and he had to bend his head to hear her. 'I didn't know that I was.' She lifted a weary, listless hand as if it was carrying a great weight, and moved the blanket away from her face to touch his cheek with her fingers. Her eyes were half closed. 'Do you remember me, Bob – when I used to – inhabit a younger woman's skin?'

He stopped, and the lamplight shone down on her pale and wrinkled face. 'Aye, Bessie. I remember.' He nodded and said softly, 'I won't ever forget.'

'What happened, Ma?' Grace sat shivering by the fire. The running home had sapped her strength and she felt weak. Her mother sat on the edge of the bed and stared into space.

'What?' Lizzie shook herself from her reverie. 'When? You tell me.'

'No, I mean you and Bessie. You used to be friends. What happened?'

Her mother shook her head. 'Nowt. It was a long time ago.'

'Tell me,' Grace insisted. 'You should talk about it.'

Her mother gazed down at the floor. 'It's finished. Doesn't matter any more.'

'It matters to Da.'

Lizzie nodded slowly several times, then, sighing, said softly, 'Ah, well, that's my fault, you see. I made him suffer. I was vindictive and bitter.'

'About what?'

'Him and Bessie.' She looked across at her daughter. The room was dark, but the firelight was flickering on Grace's pale face and she could tell that she was upset. Either about Bessie or maybe something else. She had been quiet anyway since she had come back from her tour. Only the stranger's remarks today about her speech at Wakefield had given her some spirit back.

'Da and Bessie? Did they – did they – ?' Grace's question hung in the air.

'Bessie and me were friends,' her mother began. 'Good friends like you and Ruby, though I was allus anxious about her. Forever worried about what she might get up to. She used to act first and think after.'

'Just like Ruby,' Grace murmured.

'And then there was her habit. Her craving for her loddy. She's allus tekken it, since she was a babby. A lot of folks do.' Lizzie's face became pensive and Grace got up from her chair and sat next to her on the bed. 'Then there was Rex. He used to beat her when he was drunk which was most of 'time.'

It was the first time Grace had heard his name. Rex Robson, Bessie's husband, Ruby's father.

'She used to come to us when he was 'worse for drink and stay until he went to sleep or went out again.' Lizzie gave an ironic grunt. 'She allus had a black eye in those days. She used to joke about it, said it matched her black hair. She was beautiful. Just like Ruby is.'

She gave a deep, deep sigh. 'Then one day she came round here in a state, said he was smashing up 'furniture and threatening to kill her for spending his ale money on loddy. Onny – I wasn't in!'

She twisted her hands together, round and round as if she was wringing out washing. 'Just your da was here. He said she was desperate, terrified and weeping, and – I suppose he was just comforting her to begin with. But like I say, she was beautiful and – '

'It's all right, Ma,' Grace said softly. 'You don't have to say any more. I understand.'

'Do you?' Her mother turned to face her. 'No. You don't. You can't possibly. I was so jealous, you see, when I found out. If I'd been sensible I'd have known that it was nowt, that it would have died away. Your da wouldn't have left us. He wouldn't have left you, that's for certain. But I wasn't sensible and I never spoke to Bessie and I hardly spoke to your da, and I drove him towards her.'

She gave a little sob. 'And then he started taking opium. Bessie put him onto it, and I knew then if I didn't take that in hand, I'd lose him altogether. So I told him I was leaving and tekking you with me, that I'd beg in 'streets if need be.'

She patted Grace's hand. 'And so he came back.' Her voice trembled. 'Nobody'd think to look at us, poverty-stricken wretches that we are, that we were capable of love and passion. They wouldn't, would they?'

'No.' Grace whispered. 'Nobody would.' She felt terribly sad. 'But we suffer and hurt just as rich folk do. More, probably, for we've no comforts to distract us from our misery. I wonder', she said thoughtfully, 'if I will ever feel such love for someone?'

'You're onny young,' her mother said, 'and sometimes love grows slowly. Mebbe out of admiration or respect and not just because somebody is handsome.' She gave a winsome grin. 'I mean your da and me are not oil paintings, are we?'

She gazed at her. 'You must try to get out of here, Grace. This is a bottomless pit and there's no future for you. Go and do your speechifying again and see what opportunities it might bring.'

Tears glistened in Grace's eyes. She had been so full of hope, yet nothing had come of that fervent anticipation. Everyone she had been involved with had faded away. Miss Emerson was presumably locked into her own emotions, Miss Gregory taking a holiday. Mr Newmarch? Mr Newmarch! Mr Emerson had said he was ill, maybe that was why he hadn't been in contact. But then why should he? He had been considerate towards her, but why should she expect that consideration to continue? Yet she had felt disappointment at the silence.

'Grace?' her mother said. 'What are you thinking?'

'I was thinking of Mr Newmarch. I heard today that he was ill. I sent my good wishes, but perhaps – perhaps I should write to him?'

'Yes.' Lizzie nodded and looked keenly at her. 'Perhaps you should.'

A figure passed the window and they heard the sound of a boot on the outer door. Grace rushed to open it and let in her father, carrying Bessie. 'She's all in,' he panted. 'I don't know if she'll mek it. She's been beaten up by 'look of her and she's had her fill of summat. Opium or liquor or mebbe both.'

'Who would beat her up?' Grace cried. 'You can see she has nothing.'

'There's no knowing why people do what they do.' Her mother pulled back the covers on the bed. 'Put her down, Bob. Let's tek a look at her. She must have had summat that somebody wanted. A copper or two, a bit o' baccy. Who knows?'

Bessie cried out as he placed her down on the bed and Lizzie unwrapped the blanket that was around her. 'My shawl,' Grace said. 'Did you drop it? I put it over her when I came for you.'

Her father shook his head. 'There was no shawl when I found her. Somebody must have tekken it.'

Grace wanted to cry. Not over the loss of the shawl, but the cruelty of someone who would steal something from what appeared to be a dying woman.

'Get me a bowl of warm water, Grace,' her mother said quietly. 'I'll bathe her face. Somebody's given her a right smack.'

Bessie groaned as the warm rag touched her cheek. 'Who did this, Bessie?' Lizzie asked. 'Who smacked you one?'

'Didn't – tell him,' Bessie croaked. 'Nowt – to tell.'

They looked at each other. 'Who was it, Bessie?' Bob leaned towards her. 'I'll search him out.'

She half-opened her eyes. 'Watch out for Ruby,' she breathed, then gave a moaning wail. 'Loddy! I'm hurting. I need some loddy.'

CHAPTER THIRTY-FIVE

Ruby arrived fresh and exuberant in Middle Court on Monday morning. She had told Edward about Freddie and without a question he had given her money. He had also bought the necklace to match her bracelet, a new gown and a wool cloak with a shoulder cape fringed with fur. Though where I shall wear it I can't imagine, she'd thought as she'd whirled in front of the mirror in the fashionable York salon.

But as she opened the door to her mother's room she knew immediately that something was wrong. Her presence was missing, as was her blanket which she always rolled into a bundle, and her oldest shawl, which she would never part with, was gone from the back of a chair. There was a small fire burning in the hearth, though the sack of coal was gone.

'Perhaps Mr Blake lit 'fire for her, though it's not like him to be up so early,' she muttered, but then she looked around and saw objects which didn't belong to her mother. A child's worn boot beneath the bed, a sacking apron on the floor and a pipe in the hearth which was not Bessie's.

'Mr Blake! Mrs Blake! Where's my ma?'

'Oh, Ruby!' Mr Blake came to the top of the stairs, rubbing his eyes as if he had just awakened. 'What a time we've had with her!'

'Where is she?' Ruby demanded. 'Why isn't she at home?'

'She's with us.' Grace appeared behind her in the doorway. She'd seen Ruby pass their window. 'She's sick, Ruby. You'd better come.'

She explained briefly what had happened as they walked back to her house, and told her that she had gone to tell the Blakes where Bessie was and found the whole family tucked up in Bessie's bed.

'So I brought the coal home with me and left 'firewood. There was no food left. The Blakes must have eaten it.'

'And spent money I gave them,' Ruby said bitterly. 'They were supposed to be watching out for her!'

Grace opened her door. 'You said that your ma is a law to herself, Ruby, and she is. It's no use blaming 'Blakes or yourself either,' she added, for Ruby was starting to weep. 'And I expect that they couldn't resist 'chance of a comfortable night's sleep and a warm fire.'

Ruby nodded, and wiping her eyes went in to see her mother, who was lying in the middle of the Sheppards' bed. She looks so small and shrivelled, she thought. Lizzie had washed her face and smoothed her hair, but there was no disguising the ugly bruises below her eye and the cut on her mouth.

'Who would do this?' she whispered. 'Why

would anyone want to? She had nothing!'

'Somebody was asking her something,' Grace told her. 'She keeps saying that she didn't tell. What does it mean?'

'I don't know.' Ruby knelt by the bed and gently touched her mother's face. 'Ma! It's me. Ruby.'

Bessie's eyelids flickered; she half-opened her eyes and then closed them again.

'She's best left sleeping,' Lizzie said. 'When she wakes she's in pain.' She came and stood by the bed. 'I never thought that I'd say this, Ruby, but I think you're going to have to go to Mr Cooke and buy some laudanum.'

Ruby looked up. 'But you never – '

'No, I've never taken it, but your ma allus has and she can't do without it now.' She clenched her lips together. 'I'll come with you if you like and explain 'situation. He'll give her what she needs.'

Bessie stirred and moaned. They couldn't understand what she was saying, but she kept repeating the same mantra again and again. Ruby put her head close to her mother's. She frowned. 'I can't make it out. Loddy? Is that what you're saying, Ma?'

Bessie didn't answer, but lay still. Ruby rose to her feet. 'Shall we go now, Aunt Lizzie? To Mr Cooke's, I mean.' Her voice quivered. 'Whatever he gives her, it's not going to do her any harm, is it?'

'No, it's not,' Lizzie said bleakly. 'Harm was done long ago.'

Grace sat with Bessie whilst her mother and

Ruby went to the apothecary's. She was very tired, even though it was only mid-morning. She had lain on the floor last night with a blanket wrapped around her. Her mother had curled up at the bottom of Bessie's bed, whilst her father had nodded off in his chair. But none of them had slept. Bessie had kept them all awake with her shrieks and moans as she drifted in and out of nightmarish dreams.

'Pander!' she had shouted. 'Shan't tell,' she hissed. 'Give me my loddy,' she had cried pitifully, and Lizzie had gone to her and cradled her in her arms and wept with her.

Grace closed her eyes for a moment, then shook herself awake to find Bessie staring at her. She leant towards her. 'How are you feeling, Bessie?' she asked softly.

'Watch out for Ruby,' Bessie whispered hoarsely and her eyes were wild. 'Don't tell!'

'What shouldn't I tell?' Grace asked.

'Nothing,' she muttered. 'Tell him nothing.'

'I won't.' Grace indulged her. 'Ruby will be back in a minute. She's just gone to see Mr Cooke, she's bringing you some medicine to make you well.'

Bessie's eyes seemed to glaze and become vacant, then she mumbled, 'It was bad loddy.' She licked her dry lips. 'But I want it now. He said he'd give me some if I told him.'

'Told who what, Bessie?'

A sly grin came to her face. 'Won't tell,' she said and turned her head away.

Ruby brought food, and laudanum from Mr Cooke, who promised that he would come and see Bessie to assess her needs. It was then that Grace asked her to sit down, as there was something else she had to know.

She listened quietly to the news that Josh was drowned and then said, 'I've no feelings about him. He's been dead for a long time as far as I'm concerned. We'd never have seen him again anyway.'

She opened the packet which the seaman had brought and tipped out a substantial amount of money. 'You see,' she said, her mouth curling. 'He could have helped us out when we had nowt, but he didn't.' She pushed it all back into the packet and handed it to Lizzie. 'I don't want it. Keep it, Aunt Lizzie, and use it as you want. It belonged to Ma anyway, not to me.'

She left shortly afterwards and went back to Wright Street, for although Edward had spent the night there, she was expecting him to call at midday as usual when he slipped out from the mill. He arrived early, but left in a hurry and said that he had just been informed that his father was very ill and he must visit him at once.

'My mother is sick too,' Ruby ventured. 'Someone attacked her whilst I was away.'

He uttered an exclamation but didn't comment, then reached into his pocketbook and took out some money. 'Buy her what she needs, medicine or – get the doctor or somebody.' He kissed her goodbye and said he would see her the next day. 'May will be back this evening,' he said gloomily. 'So I'd better be there when she arrives.' Then he turned back and put his arms around her, saying, 'It was so wonderful to be with you for those few days, Ruby.'

She waved him goodbye from the window and felt a sense of relief that he wasn't coming back until the next day. For the rest of today at least she could concentrate on her mother's needs.

Martin stood by his bedroom window and watched as his brother drove his new chaise up the drive. Edward did not yet know how ill their father was. A message had been sent to his home on Friday, but his manservant had said that he was not expecting him until Monday as he was away on business. Martin was puzzled by this and couldn't understand why that would be so, but as he had been away from the company himself for the last few weeks he had deliberated that something crucial must have happened in his absence. He had therefore sent a further message to the mill to be given to him on his return.

But then, he pondered uneasily, May is away. Is Edward making the most of her absence, even so soon after his marriage? Has he not given up his mistress as I have urged him to do?

He walked slowly downstairs. The fever had left him feeling very weak. He had lost a great deal of weight and, as he paused to get his breath on reaching the bottom of the stairs, the maid opened the door to Edward.

'Good heavens,' Edward exclaimed. He had not seen Martin since he had become ill. 'Are you not any better? You look pretty rough.'

'Thank you for that,' Martin replied wearily. 'That's very encouraging.'

'What's this about Father?' Edward frowned. 'There was a message at the mill when I got there this morning.'

'Have you not been home yet? We left a note there on Friday for you to come as soon as possible.'

Edward stared straight at his brother and nonchalantly smoothed his sideburns. 'No,' he replied flatly, offering no explanation. 'I haven't been home.'

Martin swallowed. He hadn't the energy to argue with him, and especially not at this time. 'Father is critically ill,' he said. 'The doctor doesn't hold out much hope. Mother has been at his side since Friday evening.'

Edward's jaw dropped. 'Oh,' he muttered. 'I didn't know it was so bad.'

'No,' Martin said coldly. 'How could you?'

Edward glared at him. 'Don't give me that holier than thou attitude, Martin. You must have known who I was with, even if you didn't know where, and how was I to know that Father was ill?'

Martin turned away. 'No. I'm sorry. Of course you were not to know. It was unfortunate that it happened when you were away. But Mother needs our support now.'

'I'd better go up then.' Edward looked a little shamefaced. 'Try to make amends.'

Martin sat in his father's library. A fire had been lit at his request, as his father's papers needed to be attended to. His own illness had been slow in onset, beginning with a headache as he returned home with Miss Gregory and

Mrs Westwood, and then tiredness, until he had succumbed to a raging fever which had subsided leaving him exhausted. His father's illness had been swift and virulent and, in an older man, bound, said the sombre doctor who had attended them both, to have only one outcome.

He looked at the pile of envelopes waiting to be opened and tried to conjure up the energy to attend to them. His father had many business interests, shares, and investments in many companies, all of which were now Martin's responsibility as the elder son.

There was one envelope addressed to him personally and on opening it he found it to be from Emerson, who had heard of his father's illness, and was sending good wishes regarding his own continuing recovery.

'I met a mutual acquaintance,' he wrote. 'Miss Grace Sheppard. She was selling home-made goods in the Market Place, and, apart from a beautifully crafted ship which she said a friend had built, they were of poor quality, made, I surmise, from whatever she could lay her hands on without the expenditure of money. I fear we have neglected her very badly since the tour, for she has no work and apparently no means of support. She also looks quite thin and ill.

'In view of your present circumstances I will do what I can for her, and am this day putting pen to paper on her behalf as we discussed previously. She insists, however, that she does not regret her involvement in the tour, and on hearing of your illness showed great concern and begged that I send her good wishes for your speedy return to health.'

Martin put down the letter, all thoughts of working on his father's papers vanishing. I meant to communicate with her, he fretted, but I took too long in considering what reason I could give for my attention. The last thing I wanted was to appear patronizing, or worse – a knight errant! And then this dratted illness overtook me! And no-one else has had contact with her. Georgiana is away accompanying May, and Daisy Emerson is so wrapped up in herself she wouldn't think of sending a card or letter.

He was angry with himself and anxious at the same time. I trust she is not as destitute as Emerson implies. She must think that we have forgotten her. Used her, even! He got up from the desk and roamed about the room. And *nothing*, he deliberated, *nothing* could be further from the truth, for I think of her and her situation constantly.

Edward returned home that evening to await May's arrival, and Martin took his mother's place by his father's bedside. He sat in a chair with a blanket around him whilst a nurse constantly monitored his father's progress. At three o'clock in the morning she shook him awake from a light slumber and asked him to fetch his mother, as the time was nigh when his father would depart from this world to the next. He gazed dazedly at her as she whispered to him, and allowed her to push him gently out of the room and in the direction of his mother's.

Charles Newmarch's passing was peaceful,

more peaceful than his busy life had been, and Martin looked down at him and knew that he had inherited his mantle. His estate, his house, everything that his father owned would come to him apart from a bequest to his mother and Edward.

I am a man of substance, he reflected. I can now give up my position at the mill, for I have long been unhappy with the management of it, and can follow my true instincts. It will be expected that I shall marry in the conventional manner. Uneasily he thought of Georgiana, with whom he had a kind of understanding, and felt a heaviness of regret. But I shall not do what is expected of me. Not if I can avoid it without causing distress.

The next morning he received another letter from Emerson, not imparting any news, but accompanying an envelope which Emerson had been requested to forward. He looked at the enclosed envelope curiously. It was made of coarse brown paper and neatly stitched to seal it. His mother was in the room with him and he asked if he might borrow her sewing scissors to cut the stitches.

'What a singular thing to do,' she commented, passing her scissors. 'How very charming. Someone has taken the time and effort to make the receiving of the message so personal.'

'Indeed they have.' He removed the sheet of paper from its casing. It was tissue-thin and looked as if it had been cut from a piece which might have wrapped a gown or piece of clothing. He saw the neat but unformed writing and knew immediately who it was from. He folded it and put it into his waistcoat pocket to read when he was alone, and not when there were so many pressing things to attend to, as there were now. 'But I feel, Mother, that the sender has no means of obtaining writing paper and envelopes and so used whatever was available.'

She looked up from her own correspondence. 'Do you mean that they are not able to go out to obtain writing paper, or that they cannot afford to buy it?'

'The latter is what I mean.'

She considered, tapping her fingers to her mouth. She had prepared herself calmly and philosophically for her husband's death, and was now writing to inform personal friends of his demise, whilst Martin would send out official notifications. 'Someone so poor to use such initiative! It has to be a woman,' she declared, 'and it must be an important letter that such effort has been made in order to send it.'

She searched his face for clues, and, seeing that there were none, added, 'I sincerely trust that it is not a begging letter, for now you have come into your father's estate, you must be aware that you will receive many.'

'I am conscious of that, Mother,' he smiled. 'But as no-one outside our family circle yet knows of Father's death,' he touched his waistcoat pocket, 'then this letter cannot possibly be seeking charity. However, I do know who it is from, and without reading the contents, I am convinced that the sender is someone who has compassion within their heart and would far rather give than receive.'

His mother observed him gravely, and, in an appeased tone, replied, 'Then a rare creature indeed.'

CHAPTER THIRTY-SIX

Grace's father went to collect Bessie's mattress to bring home. 'I don't see why 'Blakes should have such comfort,' he grumbled. 'They're living rent-free in a room with a hearth and sleeping on somebody else's bed, whilst we're sleeping on 'floor!'

Mr Blake didn't say a word or offer to help him with it, though Mrs Blake showed a sad and reproachful expression as he carried the mattress out.

They left Bessie on their bed, for it didn't seem right to move her. Her condition was worsening – she wasn't eating, although Ruby was bringing in boiling fowl and pieces of bacon for Lizzie to add to the broth, but Bessie simply turned her head away when it was offered. Her nightmares increased and she sweated and shouted through-out the night, so that they were compelled to increase her doses of opium to quieten her as Mr Cooke instructed.

Ruby spent most of the daytime with her mother, and went back to Wright Street each evening. Edward didn't come until the Thursday morning, however, when he told her that his father had died, that the funeral was to be the next day and that he must spend time with his family for the rest of the week. 'I shall miss you, Ruby,' he said fervently. 'I can't bear not to be with you.'

She told him that her mother too was very sick and that the apothecary was treating her with opium.

He nodded. 'Finest thing,' he agreed. 'Take a drop of laudanum myself occasionally. Makes me feel good.'

'Please don't,' she begged. 'My mother is addicted to it.'

He laughed. 'Nonsense! It's perfectly all right, providing you're sensible about the dosage. You should try it, Ruby.'

She shook her head and silently reflected that her mother wasn't sensible and probably never had been. He left to go to the mill, but returned within the hour as she was preparing to visit her mother. She heard the slam of the cab door and the sound of his feet pounding up the stairs.

She opened the door to him. 'What's happened?' she said as she saw his agitated expression.

He propelled her inside the room. 'You tell me, Ruby! You tell me!' He took hold of her by the arms. 'Who have you been talking to? Who knows about us?'

She prised his fingers from her arms. 'You're hurting me,' she cried. 'What do you mean? Nobody knows.'

'Your friend! What's her name? She knows.'

'Grace?' She was nonplussed. 'Of course. But what – ?'

He ran his fingers through his hair. 'Somebody has put it around the mill that I have a mistress who used to be a mill girl. God damn it, Ruby,' he shouted. 'They even know your name!'

'Not from me, they don't,' she retaliated. 'Nor from Grace, she doesn't work there any more and besides she would never tell!'

'Well, somebody has told,' he said angrily. 'Somebody told the workers and they told the foremen. It went all around the mill before going to the office workers and the directors.'

She looked at him. His face was red, his eyes flashing. 'Are you ashamed of me?' She was angry and hurt. 'I thought that men in your position took a mistress because their wives don't like to –'

He paced the room. 'They do take a mistress, but usually from their own class,' he said distractedly. 'They don't have a long-standing relationship with a—' He stopped when he saw her stricken face. 'Ruby!' He gathered her to him. 'No! I'm not ashamed of you. You're wonderful just as you are, but you must realize what this would mean if it gets out to my family, and especially to May.'

'You mean that it wouldn't matter so much if your mistress was a lady?' Her voice trembled, but he didn't seem to notice.

'No, it wouldn't. People would think that I was a bit of a loose fish. A Lothario, but nothing more.'

'Whereas, with me,' she said in a hushed voice,

'they'd think you were playing in the dirt with a drab?'

He fell silent and with his arms around her, rested his head on hers. 'Yes,' he whispered after a moment. 'That is what they'd think.' He pulled away and looked down at her. 'Even though it isn't true.'

She sat down after he'd gone, for he was on his way home again, and pondered. I don't understand. Wives don't like to sleep with their husbands, but ladies from the same class become mistresses. It doesn't make sense.

She walked slowly to Middle Court. Was this the end? Would Edward now give her up? If his wife found out then he would have to. She sighed and muttered, 'Pity. I've got used to 'good life. It's nice not to have to worry about where 'next meal is coming from and to know that 'rent is paid.'

As she pursued her thoughts she remembered that the rent for her mother's room was overdue. It should have been paid on the Saturday she was away, but with the worry over Bessie she had neglected to go in to the rent office. Tomorrow, she thought. I'll go in first thing, I just might need to live there again.

'Your ma's asking for you.' Lizzie greeted her as she arrived at the door. 'She wants to tell you summat.'

'Oh,' Ruby breathed. 'She's talking then?'

'Aye,' Lizzie said. 'After a fashion. She's asking for you anyway, and for Freddie.'

But not for Josh, Ruby contemplated as she knelt at the side of her mother's bed. Well, that's just as well, for I won't tell her. No need to add to her misery.

'Ma,' she said softly. 'It's me. Ruby.'

Her mother opened her eyes. 'I never told,' she muttered. 'I told him nothing.'

'I don't understand, Ma. Who are you talking about?'

'Ssh!' her mother whispered. 'Can't tell. Don't know his name. I want Freddie,' she moaned. 'Bring him back. Ten shillings! Give him ten shillings.'

'I'll find him, Ma. I've got 'money.' Tears pricked Ruby's eyes as she feared it might be just too late for her mother and for Freddie. She rose to her feet and turned to Lizzie and Grace. 'I've got that agent's card back at Wright Street. I'm going to fetch it and find him. He's somewhere in Hull.' She tensed her lips. 'He said not to bother him except in an emergency.' Her voice broke. 'This is an emergency.'

'Shall I go?' Grace offered, but Ruby shook her head.

'I'll go,' Lizzie said. 'He'll listen to me!' Ruby hesitated. That was true. People did listen to Aunt Lizzie. She had a determination that most folk didn't like to cross.

'Go fetch his card with his address on, and I'll go,' Lizzie repeated. 'Then you can stop with your ma.'

Ruby hurried off. Her mind was confused and she was so afraid. Her mother was dying, she knew that now. Josh was dead, Freddie could be anywhere in the country and she didn't hold out much hope of finding him. Her shoulders heaved as she wept. I should have looked for him before. Why did I leave it until it was too late? And now Edward is angry with me over the gossip, and it's not my fault. It's not my fault! She brushed away angry tears. Who knew about us and why would they tell? What would they gain?

She heard in her head her mother's moaning insistence that she didn't tell. Didn't tell. Told him nothing. She stopped in her tracks. Told him nothing! She frowned. Where had she heard that before? Told who nothing?

A woman called to her, laughing. 'Hey, Ruby! Heard about your gentleman. Can you lend us a couple o' bob?'

She hurried on. Was this how it was going to be? Edward would leave her for sure if it was. He wouldn't want the indignity or the embarrassment, and then what would she do?

'I'll not tell him owt.' Her mother's voice came to her loud and clear, and Ruby stopped again and took a breath. Jamie! She'd told her mother not to tell Jamie that she was going again to meet the gentleman, and she had protested vehemently that she wouldn't. She put her hand to her head to control the throbbing. Was it Jamie who had been asking the questions, and why?

She ran up the stairs to her rooms, glad to be inside for she felt as if there were prying eyes staring at her. She sat down for a moment and tried to collect her thoughts. Jamie had tried several times to find out if Edward was the same man he had procured for her, but she had avoided him as much as possible. Ma doesn't know Edward's name, she pondered, or anything about him. But Jamie wouldn't know that she didn't. She gave a small sob. Not Jamie, who had been their neighbour and friend for so long? Surely he wouldn't be so cruel and vindictive as to bully and attack her mother?

'Bessie'll not last 'day out,' Grace's mother said in a low voice after Ruby had left. 'That's why it's best that Ruby stops with her.' She glanced at Grace, whose face had drained of colour. 'You're not well, bairn. Can you cope with death?'

'I don't know,' Grace said shakily. 'But I have before when the ferry went down. But I must stay with Ruby. She'll need comfort.'

Her mother nodded. 'That she will, and you're 'best person to give it, which is why I said I'd go to see 'agent in her place. Not that it'll do any good. He'll not know where Freddie is. Poor bairn will be lost for ever.'

When Ruby came back, she and Grace sat side by side, holding hands, whilst Lizzie went out on her futile errand. Mr Cooke had been and given Bessie a sedative which had calmed her, so that she was no longer thrashing around as she had been doing previously.

'I want to tell you something, Grace,' Ruby began in a low voice. 'I think Jamie did this to my ma.'

She outlined to a shocked Grace why she thought it was Jamie. 'Ma said he'd given her some bad laudanum once before, and I think that he gave her some more to find out about me and Edward.'

Grace gasped and told Ruby what the old woman in the inn had told her, that Jamie had given Bessie raw opium. 'She said he had a bag full and grumbled that he wouldn't give her any, but was giving it to Bessie.'

Ruby wept. 'I've no proof that he hit her, but I've seen his anger when he's provoked, and he wouldn't believe Ma if she'd told him that she knew nothing. But why would he want to know?'

'Because he's grieved that you won't work for him,' Grace said bitterly. 'And he's out to make trouble for you and Edward Newmarch. Perhaps Jamie thinks Edward will leave you stranded and you'll go back to him.'

Lizzie came back within a few minutes and glanced towards the bed. 'I've just heard some news,' she whispered. 'It's all over 'area. Jamie's ma, Nell, is going to be married – to a grocer! And Jamie, it seems, is hopping mad!'

The day drew slowly on. Lizzie had found the agent's house empty, and his neighbours uncommunicative, so was at a loss to know what to do next. She busied herself making broth out of marrowbones which she'd begged from the butcher, adding lentils and potatoes to thicken it. Grace's father came home and sat silently by the fire, and it was as if they were all holding their breath, waiting for something to happen.

'I have to go out,' Grace said at last. 'I feel as if I can't breathe. Ruby, are you coming? Just for five minutes to get some air?'

Ruby didn't answer, but only shook her head. Grace borrowed her mother's shawl, for hers was gone, stolen from Bessie's shoulders, and stepped outside.

The evening was warm and she realized as she went up the alley and into the street that it had been a sunny day, although in the houses of Middle Court, they hadn't noticed it. The warmth, however, had brought out all the smells of the neighbouring seed mills and glue factories, and the stench from the blubber and slaughter yards.

Grace's stomach heaved. Mostly she didn't notice the smells but sometimes in the summer it was so bad that she wanted to vomit. She walked slowly along, trying not to take a breath. The street was crowded with people coming home from work, and many were dawdling, glad to be outside in spite of the foul odours.

She leaned against a wall watching the crowd. She didn't want to walk far or to be out long, for she felt that Ruby was depending on her, but her attention was drawn to a small group down the street who were pointing at the ground where what looked like a small animal was stumbling. She could hear some of the people protesting, and some were bending down to it, reaching out their hands.

Curiously she walked towards them. Sometimes a pig escaped from a slaughterhouse cart, making a bid for freedom. But then people would laugh and give chase, and they were not doing that now. Perhaps it has been injured, she thought, run over by a dray or carriage. Or maybe it's a starving dog, for they were a frequent sight. The murmurings grew louder and she caught some of the words. 'Somebody do summat!' 'Somebody should fetch help.'

As she drew nearer her eyes opened wide. It wasn't an animal, but a child, crawling in the gutter and pushing away the helping hands which were reaching towards it. It could have been a girl or boy: the hair was long and unkempt and hung over the child's face. Its body was half naked, the shirt on its back ripped and torn and the skirt or trousers tattered, exposing raw and bleeding knees and bare feet.

'Who is it?' Grace asked a woman in the crowd.

'Don't know. Poor bairn.' The woman wiped her eyes. 'But he won't accept any help. Just keeps saying he's going home to his ma.'

Grace felt a sudden palpitation in her chest and a tightening of her throat. She squeezed her way through the crowd to see the child more clearly. He was crawling a pace at a time, his head hanging low. She bent down to look at the child's face. 'Freddie? Is it you?' She felt a rush of tears stream down her face. 'Freddie! Tell me that it's you!'

He looked up. His eyes were enormous in his thin face and she barely recognized him.

'Yes.' His voice was cracked and hoarse. 'It's Freddie. I'm going home to my ma.'

CHAPTER THIRTY-SEVEN

A man helped to pick him up and put him into Grace's arms. He offered to carry him home.

'No, thank you. He knows me, you see. He'll feel safe now. Won't you, Freddie?' She put her face close to his and murmured, 'I'll take you home to your ma, and to Ruby. They're waiting for you.' She was choked with tears. Please God, she thought. Let Bessie still be with us.

Though she felt frail and weak herself, somehow she found the strength to carry him. It's like carrying a bag of bones, she thought. Is he going to survive? She remembered the sick child from Wakefield and saw that Freddie had that same haunted expression, as if he was hovering between life and death.

She felt a burning anger building up inside her. I'll find the vigour from somewhere, she resolved, I'll stand firm to fight this terrible injustice, and I'll do it alone if no-one will help me. She staggered down the alley and into the court. 'We're here, Freddie,' she said breathlessly, but the child had closed his eyes. She kicked hard against the door and her father opened it hurriedly.

'What—!' He took a breath and turned towards the room. 'Ruby, quick.' He took Freddie from Grace's arms and carried him towards the bed, where a bewildered Ruby was standing with her arms outstretched. Together they laid Freddie next to Bessie.

'Ma,' Ruby's voice was choked with tears. 'Here's Freddie. He's come back like you asked.'

Bessie half-opened her eyes. 'You're a good lass,' she breathed, and Ruby lifted her mother's arm to put it around Freddie.

Lizzie put a blanket over him, then poured some broth into a cup, and taking a teaspoon she trickled a small amount of the liquid into Freddie's mouth. He ran his tongue around his lips and gave a dry swallow.

'Would you like some water?' she asked and when he nodded, she poured water from the kettle into another cup and spooned that into his mouth. He gave a half-smile and a sigh and snuggling closer to his mother, murmured something and fell asleep.

'Is he going to be all right?' Ruby watched him anxiously. 'I couldn't bear it if he should die.' She gazed at Grace, who was sitting in her father's chair with her head cradled in her hands. 'Where did you find him, Grace? Where was he?'

'He was crawling along 'street,' Grace said in a low voice. 'I don't know where he'd come from, but he'd found his way here somehow.' She shook her head despairingly. 'It's not right. It's just not right.'

The day after his father's funeral Martin drove into Hull to offer his resignation at the mill as manager, though retaining his shares and those of his father's which had been bequeathed to him. He had decided to do this so that he would have a voice at the shareholders' meetings. After he had concluded his business there and spoken briefly to Edward, who had been extremely morose since his father's death, he asked his driver to go into the High Street where he intended calling on Emerson.

He was shown into Emerson's library. The older man rose to greet him. 'Newmarch! Dear fellow! I am this very moment writing to you!' He indicated his desk, where writing materials were laid out. 'I have a letter here for Miss Sheppard from Miss Morris, who asks if I would forward it to her. I thought perhaps you might have her address – from when she worked at the mill, you know.'

'Miss Morris?' he queried. 'Ah! erm – yes, I think I might be able to obtain Miss Sheppard's address.' In fact he knew where Grace lived, although he had never visited the area. He had looked through the lists of employees' addresses specifically to find it, when she had led the delegation of women to obtain their wages. He had been curious at the time to know what kind of address she came from.

'I took it upon myself to write to her – Miss Morris,' Emerson explained, 'after I had seen

Miss Sheppard in the Market Place. You remember we had discussed the possibility that she might have some suggestions regarding that young lady. It seems such a waste of obvious intelligence. Besides which,' he rubbed his chin thoughtfully and gazed at Martin, 'I did think that she looked quite exhausted. She had that grey look of poverty which was not apparent previously.'

Martin felt his spirits sink. Was she not getting enough to eat? There were thousands of people out of work, mostly men, dock workers, factory workers, and this had a devastating effect: the women then became the breadwinners, and their low wages were insufficient to feed and clothe their families.

'Her parents were both working,' he murmured. 'But perhaps now they are not.'

'She would not, I think, accept charity?' Emerson queried, and Martin shook his head in response. 'I did pay more for the ship she was selling than I would normally have done, but I felt that she was in need of the money.'

'Perhaps I should deliver this letter myself.' Martin tapped it against his hand. 'Would it be – ' He looked at Emerson, whom he had always regarded as being wise. 'Would it be in order to do so, do you think? To search her out?'

Emerson smiled and raised his eyebrows. 'You are a good fellow, Newmarch, as well meaning and benevolent as anyone I know, but there are times when you hold back when you should go forward. Miss Sheppard will not be offended,

I am sure, if you call.' His smile widened. 'You will not need to leave your card or arrange a visit.'

'No.' Martin returned the smile. 'I'm sure you are right.' It's just that I'm afraid of what I might find, he pondered as he was shown out of the door.

What he found was a narrow dark court of twelve houses which led into an even narrower darker passageway, which in turn led into another court with a high brick wall at the end of it. There was no name on the wall indicating where he was, but this was where he was sent when requesting directions for Middle Court.

She can't surely live down here? There was no light, and he involuntarily glanced up to see only a thin oblong of blue sky between the buildings. It was humid, too, as if the air had been sucked out through that same oblong. He looked along the row of terraced houses, six on each side. One door and two windows, one at the top and one below. Some were boarded up; only one had curtains at the window.

So which house will it be? He hesitated, then chose the first one where he could see movement within the room. He rapped twice with his knuckles and waited. The door was opened by Grace, who gave a slight gasping breath as she saw him.

'Mr Newmarch!' She dipped her knee as he took off his hat. 'Sir! Why are you here?'

He swallowed hard. Emerson was right, she did look ill, so frail and slight with no colour to her cheeks. 'I – ' He was so taken aback by her appearance that he was lost for words or reason for his visit, though he remembered that he had come to deliver Miss Morris's letter. I think that is why I have come. Or did the letter prompt me to follow my original intentions of seeking her?

'Grace!' A woman's low voice called from within the room. 'Either bring 'caller in or go out, there's a draught from 'door.'

'Sorry!' She seemed to pull herself together, lifting her chin and gazing at him, with, he thought, a slight defiance in her blue eyes, so large in her thin face. 'Would you like to come in, Mr Newmarch? Though we have some worry and distress in our home at the moment.'

'Oh? Then I would not wish to trouble you, unless of course I can be of any assistance?'

She opened the door wider. 'Perhaps you can, though I doubt it. Please come in.'

He followed her into a small hallway from which rose narrow rickety uncarpeted stairs, and through another doorway into a downstairs room. He narrowed his eyes, for the room was dim. There was no light, not a lamp or candle, though a fire was burning in the hearth. A bed took up most of the space and in it he could see two people, or perhaps they were children, he thought, though I'm sure Grace's mother said that Grace was the only child and had no siblings.

Then he saw Grace's mother kneeling by the bed. She didn't get up, but nodded in acknowledgement of his presence. She was stroking the head of a child in the bed who was lying next to someone whose face he couldn't see, only white hair streaked with dark.

'Is someone sick?' he said in a low voice. 'Do you need a doctor?'

Lizzie Sheppard looked down at the child and gently stroked his cheek, then stood up. 'Aye, we do, Mr Newmarch, for this poor bairn, and somebody's gone to try and get one.' She turned towards the bed and said quietly, 'It's too late for his ma, though she's still gripping hold of life, but we hope to save her lad.'

He glanced around the room and saw the other mattress in the corner. 'Is this the only room you have? Have you no separate room for the sick?'

Grace's lips turned up, although he didn't feel that it was a smile, but something like derision. 'This room is where we live, eat and sleep, Mr Newmarch. The sick are our friends and neighbours whom we have taken into our care in their last desperate hours.' Her voice tightened and he saw her mouth tremble. 'We are fortunate that we are usually only three to a room, unlike those Irish we visited in the Groves. I'm sure you will remember several families housed in one room there?'

Martin gazed at her. There was something she was trying to convey to him. Some passion was building up inside her and she was trying to contain it. He glanced at her mother. She too was much thinner than when he had last met her.

'What is wrong with the child?' he asked. 'Has he caught some disease from his mother?'

Grace shook her head and again he saw that disdainful look. 'No, his mother's disease is self-inflicted. She has had such a wonderful life that she has ended it with opium. Her son was sold to a chimney sweep and he was so battered, bruised and burned that he climbed down from his last chimney in Nottingham and walked home.' She stared at his look of disbelief. 'He crawled through 'streets of Hull on his hands and knees.'

He saw her hands clasp and unclasp and she gave a small sob. She was wide-eyed and her mother glanced at her and murmured, 'Grace!'

'I can't bear it any longer,' she cried, and Martin took a step nearer and reached out his hand. 'It's just not fair.' She turned towards him and raised her voice. 'Why should poor folks be treated as if they were nothing? Why should they beg and prostitute themselves in order to eat?' She clenched her fists so hard that the knuckles showed white, and to his utter dismay she began to beat him on the chest. 'It's not fair! It's not fair.' She started to weep, and as he grasped her wrists he felt the bird-like bones and was seized with alarm at her fragility.

He caught her as she fell weeping and exhausted, and her mother rushed forward. 'I'm sorry, sir. Put her in her da's chair.'

He carried her to the only chair by the fire. She was so light that he panicked that in her frail state she might succumb to illness. 'A pillow! Have you a pillow?'

'No. We don't have such luxuries. My shawl.'

She took the shawl from her shoulders and rolled it up for a pillow which he placed at the back of Grace's head.

'A blanket?' He was almost afraid to ask.

She took a blanket from the bed and he wrapped it around Grace's lap. They both looked down at her as she lay with tears streaming from beneath her closed eyes, her body shaking with sobs.

'I'll make her some tea, that'll revive her.' Lizzie placed the kettle over the fire.

'When did Grace last eat?' Martin asked, then glancing at her, said, 'When did any of you last eat?'

'Last night at supper,' Lizzie admitted. 'Ruby brought us a piece of bacon and I made some broth.'

'Ruby?' he queried, something ticking in his memory.

She pointed to the bed. 'Bessie's daughter. Young Freddie's sister.'

'Is she living here too?'

Lizzie turned away. 'No. They have a house further down 'court, onny Ruby's not in it at 'moment. She's – she's living in at 'place of her employ, so to speak. I have to say, though, she's been good to her ma and to Freddie. It's her who's gone for 'doctor.'

Grace stirred and opened her eyes, wiping them with her fist, and Martin knelt down on the rug at her feet. 'Are you feeling any better?' he asked softly.

She had looked vacant for a moment, then blinked. 'Mr Newmarch,' she murmured.

434

'What – ?' Then her face cleared as she remembered. 'Oh,' she breathed. 'Did I – ?'

'Yes, you did, my girl.' Her mother put a few sparse leaves in the teapot and poured boiling water on them. 'You gave Mr Newmarch a right old beating. You'd best apologize.'

'There is no need.' Martin put his hand on Grace's shoulder and felt again the frailty of her bones. 'You are overwrought and unwell, and disturbed too, I imagine, by what has happened to your friends.'

She nodded, then said, 'I'm sorry nevertheless, if I offended you. It seemed as if – '

She turned her head away and he finished the sentence for her. 'As if I and people like me are to blame?'

'Yes,' she whispered and a tear trickled down her cheek. 'And yet I know that it isn't true. It's society who's to blame, not individuals.'

'Yet individuals must make a stand,' he asserted. 'It is an individual who builds houses like this and makes a profit out of filling it with as many people as possible.' He gazed at her. 'And I do remember our visit to the Groves. I haven't been able to get those people out of my mind.'

'Nor I,' she said softly. 'And there are so many more.'

The door opened and Ruby came in, but she was alone. 'Doctor says he'll come when he can.' Then she saw Martin Newmarch kneeling by Grace, and, startled, stopped what she was going to say next. 'Mr Newmarch!'

He stood up and looked at her, and was

435

struck by her look of well-being and vitality compared to Grace's. He gave a small bow of his head.

'This is my friend, Ruby,' Grace said. 'She used to work with me at 'cotton mill.'

Ruby? Realization flooded over him. Edward, in a slip of his tongue, had spoken of Ruby. So was she – ? He saw perception and apprehension dawning on Ruby's face, and the colour flooding her cheeks, as she faced her lover's brother and knew that he was aware of her.

'I'm sorry for your troubles,' he said quietly. 'I know of a local doctor, one who attends the mill when we need him. If you will permit me, I will go for him now and bring him back. What is actually wrong with your brother?'

Lizzie spoke up. 'I think he's got a fever. He's walked for miles, in heat and rain, and he's just exhausted, poor bairn. His bones are hot too, as if they're on fire.'

'Then he has the fever,' Martin said. 'For I have just recovered from it and that is exactly how I felt.' He turned to Grace. 'Do you feel well enough to come with me? My carriage is out in the street and you could explain the situation to the doctor. Would that be permissible, Mrs Sheppard?' he asked her mother, who nodded but made no answer as her eyes glanced searchingly at him and then at Grace.

Lizzie closed the door behind them and turned to Ruby, who was standing as if dumbstruck. 'He knows,' Ruby whispered. 'I could tell by 'way he looked at me. Edward must have told him my name.'

Lizzie put her hand to her chest. 'Edward? Who is Edward?'

'Edward Newmarch. His brother. He's the man I'm – ' Her face crumpled and she couldn't finish.

'His brother! God in heaven, do you think they're tarred wi' same brush?' Lizzie stared in horror at Ruby. 'We've just let our Grace go off wi' him in his carriage. What's her da going to say?'

CHAPTER THIRTY-EIGHT

'It's not 'same carriage,' Grace observed, as Martin Newmarch helped her inside the brougham.

'No, it was my father's.' He sat opposite her. 'He always preferred to be driven. He was not a good driver, was never in control of his horse. My father died last week,' he explained hesitantly. 'That is one of the reasons why I have not been in contact with you before, er – regarding the tour. That, and because I have been ill myself.'

'I'm so sorry,' she murmured, and added, 'Mr Emerson told me of your illness. I wrote – '

'Thank you,' he smiled. 'I received your letter. It was kind of you to be concerned.'

She seemed embarrassed. 'I'm sorry about what happened back at home.' She looked over her shoulder towards Middle Court. 'I don't know what made me act that way.'

He couldn't explain to her the strange sensation he had experienced, catching her flailing hands as she'd battered his chest, but he answered quietly, leaning towards her. 'You are very sensitive about the problems of others, Grace, but also you are not well. It seems to me that you haven't been getting enough to eat.'

'I've had just 'same as my ma,' she said defensively. 'Da has 'most food 'cos he has to work.' Her expression drooped. 'But he doesn't have enough. He's always very tired when he gets home. Though Ruby's been bringing in extra food since we've been looking after Bessie,' she added.

He had to try and suppress a smile as he wondered if Edward knew he was supporting another family as well as Ruby.

'I know about Edward and Ruby,' he said quietly, determined to tell Grace himself rather than Ruby say that he knew of the affair.

'Oh! But how?' She looked startled. 'Your brother, Mr Edward, insisted that Ruby should tell no-one, and she didn't, only me.' She gazed steadily at him. 'Except that someone else found out and all of 'cotton mill knows about them now.'

It was his turn to be startled. So that was why Edward was so touchy and morose! It wasn't because of his father's death at all, but because he had been found out! It would only be a matter of time now before the servants discovered it, if they didn't know already. Certainly Edward's manservant had had a knowing look on his face when he'd said that Edward had gone off *on business*.

And then it will come to May's attention. Hints of it will be dropped from her personal maid and then there'll be the devil to pay. From what little he knew of Edward's wife, he was convinced of that.

'Edward inadvertently let slip her name,' he explained. 'Though I had guessed that there was someone.'

'I'm so sorry,' Grace said in a hushed voice. 'I did beg Ruby not to. But she said there was no other option open to her.' Her mouth trembled, and he felt a protective sensation towards her. He gave a slight shudder. How dreadful if it had been Grace who had chosen that downward path.

'We are not their custodians, Grace,' he said. 'Though I cannot say that I approve, my brother and your friend must do what they will with their lives.'

'But we should advise, surely, if we think that way is doomed?' She paused. 'Though Ruby is lucky that Mr Newmarch thinks so highly of her. He made her promise that she wouldn't – she wouldn't see any other man. And she hasn't,' she added fervently. 'I know that she hasn't.'

So Edward really does care for the girl, Martin mused as the carriage drew up outside the doctor's house. I'm not sure if I don't find that more disturbing than if he was out wenching every night.

Dr Ellis listened gravely as Grace told him of Freddie and how in his ramblings they gathered that he had walked from Nottingham. He said that he'd heard there were many young chimney sweeps in Nottingham: the town was considered a good training ground for them, as there were so many narrow chimneys.

'Let's hope he hasn't developed scrofula,' he

said. 'For if he has, then there is nothing I can do for him.' He looked at Grace from over his spectacles and added, 'You are very pale, young woman. Are you not well either?'

'A little tired, sir. Nothing more.'

He made no comment on this and told Martin that he would visit the child in Middle Court immediately.

Martin handed Grace into the carriage, then said, 'Excuse me for a moment, I forgot to mention another matter to Dr Ellis,' and returned swiftly to the doctor's door before the maid closed it.

'Mr Newmarch,' she said on his return, 'you were caught up in a situation which you can't have expected, but you must have had another reason for your visit today. Was it in regard to the tour?'

He took a breath. He was concerned. On his return to the doctor he had asked if he would look again at Grace when he visited the house. Dr Ellis agreed that he would, adding that she appeared to be bloodless and in need of good food.

'Yes,' he said, in answer to her question. 'Initially I was coming to enquire if you had found employment after your travels, but when I called on Emerson, I heard that a letter had been delivered for you which he had been asked to forward. I offered to bring it as I was about to call on you anyway.' A smile hovered on his lips as he remembered Emerson's comments on his tardiness in going forward.

'A letter for me?' she said in astonishment.

'Why – who would write to me through Mr Emerson?'

'Miss Mary Morris.' He studied her face for the slightest hint of colour and noticed also that her hands, which had fluttered to her face, were white and thin. 'But I have no idea why.'

She waited. When he didn't hand over the letter, she clasped her fingers together and raised her eyebrows questioningly, and, with a sudden start, he put his hand into the inside pocket of his coat. 'I beg your pardon,' he said, and drew out an envelope.

The carriage drew up close to the alley leading to Middle Court. 'Do you mind if I read it now?' Grace asked. She turned the crisp white envelope over, remembering the shoddy paper and hand-made envelope she had used for the letter to Mr Newmarch, and felt ashamed. 'This is 'first letter I've ever received,' she murmured. 'And 'first one I've ever sent was to you after I heard you were ill.'

He marvelled at the fact and was delighted, yet tried not to show it. 'Then I will treasure it always,' he said softly. 'And consider it a gift.'

She shook her head. 'It was a poor thing, made from old paper.'

'I was thinking of the contents, not the wrapping.' He gazed steadily at her and saw a blush tinge her cheeks as she busied herself opening the envelope.

'This is 'right place, sir!' The coachie appeared at the door.

'Yes, thank you, but we will be one moment longer,' Martin said. He watched Grace's eyebrows raise higher as she read the letter, and she took a deep breath of astonishment.

'Mr Newmarch!' she said in some consternation. 'I shall need your advice on a matter. Miss Morris is asking something impossible.'

The doctor's black carriage drew up behind them and Grace tucked the letter into her skirt pocket. 'I must take him in,' she said hurriedly. 'He won't know which house it is.'

Martin handed her down and she thanked him. 'You've been very kind,' she said. 'Sending for 'doctor, I mean. I can't thank you enough.'

He nodded and put on his top hat. 'I have business to attend to but will come back in an hour,' he said. 'Perhaps you will tell me what diagnosis the doctor gives for the boy and his mother.'

She dipped her knee, and joining the doctor led him down the alleyway, where he fastidiously trod amongst the debris, to her house.

'First thing you must do', he said brusquely as he looked down at Freddie, 'is remove the mother to another bed. She's dying, but hanging onto life by taking succour from her son. We can do nothing for her, but we can perhaps save the boy.'

He looked at Ruby, who was weeping and wringing her hands. 'What should I do, Grace? My poor ma!'

'She's had her life,' Lizzie answered for Grace. 'And she's had her wish to see Freddie again. Besides, Bessie wouldn't want Freddie to die because of her.' Though he almost did, she muttered to herself.

The doctor removed the covers from Freddie and looked him over. 'Wash him all over with cool water,' he said, 'and I will give him a small dose of laudanum for his pain and the fever.'

He heard the gasp of disapproval from Lizzie Sheppard. 'A measured dose only,' he said, glancing at her. 'I will put you in charge of the medication if you disapprove of it, so there is no risk of him becoming addicted.'

'There'll be no fear of that, Doctor,' she said grimly. 'It's what's killing his mother.'

'It kills many,' he said. 'Or else renders them incapable of rational thought or action, and so they hurt themselves in other ways. But, nevertheless, used properly it has its uses.' He peered at Bessie. 'She's had a fall or injury to her face which must have rendered her insensible.' He shook his head. 'She has done well to live to old age.'

He unpacked his leather bag, taking a small bottle and carefully measuring a few drops of the contents into another, which he topped up with liquid from yet another, then shook vigorously. 'Move the mother to the other bed.' He pointed to the mattress in the corner of the room. 'Then wash the child as instructed, give him plenty of clean cool water to drink and a dose of this medication. Then give him another tomorrow morning. You'll see an improvement in a day or two.'

'Sir,' Grace said. 'Does he have any other disease, like the one you mentioned?'

'I don't know yet.' He delved into his bag again.

'I'll come back in a day or two and examine him thoroughly when he is over the fever.'

Ruby drew in a breath. 'Could you tell me what it will cost, Doctor?'

'It is attended to,' he said briefly. 'In some cases, I make no charge. Now, young lady.' He turned to Grace. 'You look to me as if you could do with a tonic. The best thing of course is good food. Eggs, milk, chicken and liver, and an occasional glass of red wine, but as I am sure those items are impossible,' he handed her a bottle of pink liquid, 'you must take this three times a day and eat as often as you can.'

He put on his hat and picked up his bag. 'I wish you good day.' He turned to Ruby as he went to the door. 'Take care of the boy. He should recover with good nursing.'

'Mr Newmarch!' Grace's mother exclaimed, after the doctor had gone. 'He must be paying.' She looked suspiciously at Grace. 'Why would he do that?'

Grace stared down at the bottle in her hand. She must look really ill for the doctor to notice, she thought. 'I don't know,' she said softly. Then she looked up. 'Yes I do. It's because he's a kind man. You've met him before, Ma. Surely you can tell?'

Her mother grunted. Glancing at Ruby, she said, 'Come on then, let's get your ma moved over onto 'other mattress like 'doctor says.'

'What's Mr Sheppard going to say?' Ruby asked fearfully as they lifted her mother out. 'There'll be nowhere for him to sleep.'

Lizzie heaved a big sigh. 'He'll sleep wi' me

and Freddie in this bed. We'll manage, and if your ma was taking energy from Freddie, then Freddie can tek ours by sleeping between us, though God knows I haven't got much left anyway. You'll have to sleep in 'chair, Grace. Grace!' she repeated when there was no response. 'Where are you, girl?'

'Yes.' Grace came out of her reverie. 'Yes, all right. I'll sleep in Da's chair. Can you and Ruby manage, Ma? I need to go out for a few minutes.'

'Out where?' her mother puzzled. 'Where you off to?'

'I won't be long.' She avoided answering the question and hurried out of the door.

'What's going on?' her mother asked Ruby. 'Is she going to meet Mr Newmarch, do you think? Why did he come calling anyway? He didn't say, did he?'

'No, he didn't.' Ruby covered her mother with a blanket and gazed sadly at her still form. She hadn't so much as flinched as they'd moved her. 'But you don't have to worry about him, Aunt Lizzie.' She looked across at the older woman and reassured her. 'He's a proper gentleman and not 'sort to risk his position or standing in society. He wouldn't tek that risk, not for folk like us. He's not like his brother Edward. He's far too sensible.'

Grace leaned on the wall at the top of the alley whilst she waited for Mr Newmarch's carriage to appear, and reread the letter from Miss Morris. I don't understand. Why would she ask this of me?

She looked up as someone slouched in front of her. It was Jamie. She stared straight at him but didn't speak, and he, in turn, lowered his eyes and merely nodded in greeting. Perhaps he realizes that we know about him and what we think he did, she mused, but then, would he care?

The carriage wheels rattled on the cobbles and the driver slowed as he saw her. She stood by the door as it opened. 'Mr Newmarch,' she said. 'I don't like to bother you, but I think I'm going to need your advice.'

Martin got out. 'We can speak here if you wish, or we can take a drive.'

Grace looked about her. Already people were glancing curiously at the brougham, not the kind of vehicle normally seen in this vicinity, with its leather hood and painted wheels and a liveried driver on top. Broken-down waggons with tired horses were the more usual transport. She saw a glimpse of Jamie as he hid in the alley watching, and she decided. 'Take a drive, please, if you don't mind.'

She handed him the letter as the carriage pulled away. 'Please read it, Mr Newmarch, and tell me that perhaps I have misunderstood Miss Morris's offer.'

He gazed at her quizzically. 'Why do you think you have misunderstood?'

'Read it, sir,' she urged. 'And then you will see. Miss Morris has asked if I would be willing to go and work with her as her assistant in a project she is planning.'

CHAPTER THIRTY-NINE

Bob Sheppard was later than usual arriving home from work. He was tired and sank down in his chair. The room was lit only by the light of the fire, and Bessie's occupation of the mattress on the floor went unnoticed. Lizzie handed him a cup of tea.

'I've been down to Albert Dock wi' a waggon-load o' timber,' he said wearily. 'That's why I'm late. There's a ship just come in. It's laden wi' passengers from Scandinavia all sailing to a new life in America.'

'Lucky for them,' his wife said laconically.

'Aye, and a mass of folks from Hull waiting to go on board. I reckon we might have tekken 'chance had we been younger.' He took a sip from his cup and then another, and looked down at the steaming brown liquid. 'Have we come into money or summat?' he asked. 'This isn't usual washed-out brand o' tea.'

'No, it isn't,' she said, busying herself with the pan on the fire, adding vegetables to it. 'So enjoy it while you can.'

He glanced towards the bed. 'How's 'lad been

today? He was right poorly last night.' Then, with a start, he asked, 'Where's Bessie?'

Lizzie nodded towards the mattress. 'We've had a time of it today, what wi' one thing and another. Doctor's been, courtesy o' Mr Newmarch. There's quite a tale to tell, so drink your tea and I'll give you 'gist of it.'

She told of Mr Newmarch calling though she didn't know why, and of Grace having some kind of fit and beating him about the chest. Of him going with Grace to fetch the doctor. 'Now she's gone out again on some errand and isn't back yet. Ruby's gone back to – wherever it is she goes,' she said. 'And in 'meantime a parcel's been delivered by 'grocer.' She went across to the table where a large cardboard box was sitting.

Bob got up from his chair. 'What's in it? Who sent it?'

She shrugged. 'It must have been Mr Newmarch that sent it. 'Doctor that came said that Grace needed food, that's why she's so pale and thin. Milk, eggs, cheese and suchlike and that's what's in 'box.' She opened the lid for him to see.

'It's charity,' he said bluntly. 'We can't accept that.'

'You've just enjoyed that cup o' tea, haven't you?' she asked brusquely. 'Have another cup and see if it tastes any different now you know I didn't buy it wi' our own money!' She hesitated, and then said, 'If I'm honest I've had my doubts about it, same as you. But our Grace is fading away, I can see it in her eyes. She's never had much fat on her and she's got even less now.' She rubbed her hand across her forehead. 'If she

449

should get consumption or some disease, I'd never—'

'All right. All right,' he said hastily. 'We'll accept it for Grace's sake, charity or not. But one box o' groceries isn't going to keep us going for ever.'

'No,' she replied. 'And that's why I'm going to ask around for some work. My back's a deal better than it was.'

He knew that wasn't true, but knew better than to argue with her. He sighed and went across to the bed where Freddie was sleeping. 'He seems easier,' he said. 'Looks a better colour. What about Bessie? What did 'quack say about her?'

'Nowt much,' she said quietly. 'Onny that she's dying and was tekking strength from Freddie.'

Bob glanced at her and moved across to look down at Bessie. Then he knelt at the side of the mattress and put his hand against her face. 'Gone,' he whispered. 'She's gone.'

He stood up and gave a shudder. Lizzie came over and stood next to him. 'Are you sure?' she asked softly. 'I'd never have thought she'd go quietly! She was breathing when Ruby was here.'

'She's not breathing now.' He bent his head and gave a deep sigh. 'Poor Bessie.' His voice cracked and she put her hand on his arm.

'Aye, poor lass,' she murmured.

'I'm sorry,' he muttered. 'It was a long time ago and I've never really said that I was sorry for 'grief I gave you over Bessie.' He put his arms around her. 'But I never would have left you, Lizzie. It was just – just a time of madness, that's all.'

She leant her head on his chest and sighed and didn't see the glisten as he blinked his eyes. 'It's all right,' she said softly. 'It's all forgotten now.'

The carriage drew up by the Vittoria Hotel and Grace and Martin got out and walked by the riverside. 'It would be a good opportunity for you, Grace,' Martin persuaded after hearing all her reasons why she shouldn't take up Miss Morris's offer.

'But I have no education, Mr Newmarch,' she cautioned. 'How could I possibly help her? I'm completely ignorant on so many subjects.'

'You can read and write and have a good mental understanding, and if I recall,' he said, 'in her letter, Miss Morris said that she would help you to improve on any skills which you might think you were lacking. Believe me,' he insisted, 'Miss Morris would not have asked you if she thought for one moment that you were not able to do whatever it is she asks of you. She does not suffer fools gladly.'

'No,' Grace reluctantly agreed as she remembered Miss Morris's formidable manner. 'That I can believe. But Wakefield is a long way from home,' she added weakly. 'And I don't know what Ma and Da would say about it.'

He turned to her. 'How old are you, Grace?'

'Nearly seventeen, sir.' She looked across at the Vittoria. 'Last year, me and Ruby celebrated our sixteenth birthdays with Daniel. He bought a glass of ale at 'Vittoria which we all shared. We said that it was 'best birthday we'd ever had.' She sighed. 'We were all so happy and excited at being grown-up. We didn't know what 'year would bring.'

'What did it bring?' he asked, watching her closely. 'And who is Daniel?'

'Ruby and me lost our jobs at 'mill and couldn't get any work. I went to Dock Green and spoke about injustice.' She bit her lips together. 'Ruby's ma sold Freddie to 'chimney sweep. My ma hurt her back and couldn't work. Then Ruby had to – ' she paused. 'Well, you know – and Daniel, he had to give up his apprenticeship and go to sea to earn money.' She gave a fleeting smile. 'He should be home soon. He said he would try to get back in time for our next birthdays.'

'He's a friend, then? This Daniel?'

'Yes. A good friend.' She nodded vaguely, her mind preoccupied. 'But in spite of everything, not having any work or money, I'm glad that I've been to those other towns, and seen how it isn't only us that's suffering. Other folks are deprived just 'same. Even worse, some of them, like that poor, wretched woman and her young son who had been down 'mine.'

She hadn't been able to get her and the boy out of her head. 'God bless you, Miss Grace,' the woman had said. 'Do what you can for others like him.'

'So what are you going to do about it, Grace?' he asked quietly. 'Are you going to let them go on suffering?'

She turned to him and stared. Was he reading her thoughts? 'Me? What can I do? I've no power to help them. I'm just a nobody. I don't know any important people.' She continued to gaze at him. His eyes are such a deep brown, she thought. Unfathomable. It's not possible to know what he's thinking.

'But you do, Mr Newmarch,' she said boldly. 'You know all 'right people. You could talk to them, tell them what's happening.'

'I can,' he agreed. 'And so can you. You're seventeen. A woman. Go to Miss Morris. Complete your education. Then you can tell those in power, as other men and women are doing, just what is happening, and you can relate from your own experiences and those of the people close to you.'

She felt weak with emotion. She wanted to, she hated the injustice of what was happening around her. But could she do it? Did she have the courage?

'How would I live?' she wavered. 'I couldn't expect Miss Morris to keep me for nothing.'

'I think you would find that Miss Morris would be prepared to keep you in return for your services.' His eyes were suddenly lively. 'She might even be prepared to pay you a small salary.'

'Oh!' Her doubts were crumbling, yet she still felt unsure of her own ability.

'Tell me, Grace,' he asked, 'why did you speak at Dock Green? Why did you deliberately take your stool, walk there on that miserable day, and stand up to speak?'

'Cos I was angry,' she said.

'Are you not angry now?'

'Yes,' she nodded. 'But I'm also very tired, and I don't think I've got 'energy to do it now.'

For a moment, alarm showed on his face, then he took her arm and said, 'I missed my midday meal today and I'm quite hungry. What would you say if I suggested we go into the Vittoria and have a pot of chocolate and a slice of cake, and continue our discussion in there?'

She had no option but to comply as he was steering her in that direction, and besides she was feeling faint and needed to sit down. She had had only a slice of bread this morning, and now, with the worry of Miss Morris's request, she felt quite light-headed.

There were few people in the hotel, and they were shown to a table by the window where they could see out to the Humber. Martin ordered a pot of chocolate for Grace and a glass of ale for himself. He also asked for fresh bread and slices of beef and ham, to be followed by apple tart and cheese.

'Eat up,' he said as Grace hesitated. 'I can't eat all of this myself.'

'Erm – Mr Newmarch. I have to ask you something.' She blushed and lowered her eyes. 'I hope that you won't take offence at what I'm going to say, but I – ' She took a deep breath. 'I'm so sorry.' Tears gathered in her eyes.

'What is it?' he said in concern. 'You can speak of what's troubling you. I promise I won't be offended.'

'It's just that – ' She didn't dare look at him but kept her eyes firmly on the table. 'When Ruby went to meet your brother, he brought her here to 'Vittoria and gave her food such as she'd never seen in her life before, and then, and then – '

454

She looked up and saw his lips twitch momentarily.

'Ah!' he said gravely. 'And you thought that maybe I – had the same evil intentions?' Damn, he thought as he saw doubt and confusion written on her face. 'Grace, I have done you a great disservice and I apologize profusely.'

Her eyes widened and her lips parted in dismay. So was that his intention after all?

'I should not have brought you here. I am so very sorry! I don't know what I was thinking of.' He banged his forehead with his fist and gave a vexed exclamation. 'A gentleman should never bring a young lady to such an establishment on her own. It is quite unthinkable. To meet you and a friend by chance in the foyer and invite you to partake of refreshment, is of course a different matter entirely. But to invite you particularly and alone, well, of course you would gain the wrong impression!'

She opened her mouth to say something, but he continued, still beating his head with his fist. 'Good heavens! If it had been Miss Gregory or Miss Emerson, why – they would be either drawing up a marriage contract or informing the world I am a philanderer!'

'Oh, but I never meant – ' She blushed even more and he thought how pretty she looked with colour in her cheeks. 'It was just with Ruby – '

He gave up teasing her, for he saw that she thought he was quite serious. 'It was different for Edward and Ruby,' he said gravely. 'Quite different, and you have nothing to fear from me.'

'I did know, really,' she confessed. 'But I'm

onny used to plain speaking.' She gave a sudden shy laugh. 'And as for making up a marriage contract! Well, we both know that couldn't happen!'

'Yes,' he said slowly. 'I suppose we do.' He leant towards her. 'But perhaps we can be friends? Like you and Daniel?'

'I don't know.' She began to toy with her fork on the plate. 'Daniel's 'same as me and Ruby. We're different from you, Mr Newmarch.'

'I see.' He sounded disappointed. 'But that shouldn't preclude us from being friends, should it? Or is Daniel special to you? Perhaps he wouldn't approve?' He watched her closely as he waited for her answer.

She broke a piece of bread and started to nibble at it. 'Ruby said – ' She lowered her eyes and gave a self-conscious smile. 'Ruby says he's sweet on me, but I don't know about that.'

'I'm sure that he is.' He took a long drink from his glass and returned the smile. 'Who wouldn't be, Grace? Who wouldn't be!'

She walked slowly down the alley towards Middle Court, leaving Martin Newmarch with the promise that she would give serious thought to Miss Morris's offer and discuss it with her parents. She felt quite bloated, as Mr Newmarch had insisted that she ate up heartily, whilst he only nibbled sparingly in spite of previously saying that he was hungry. I should have kept some of that beef for Da, she thought. I could have hidden it in my pocket if I'd thought of it.

A woman was coming from their door and Grace looked at her curiously. She was wearing a long white pinafore over her black dress, with a black shawl over her head. Grace didn't recognize her and wondered who she was and what she was doing there. The woman nodded and murmured something, then scurried away up the alley.

'Who was that?' she asked as she went in, and then stopped. Bessie was back in the big bed with Ruby kneeling at the side of it. Freddie was on the mattress on the floor and her mother was sitting by the fire staring into the flames. 'What's happened, Ruby?' She dropped her voice to a whisper. 'Your ma?'

'Dead!' Ruby said hoarsely. 'At last. I've been expecting it for so long and now it's come I can scarcely believe it.'

Grace knelt at the side of Ruby. 'I'm so sorry,' she murmured and glanced at the serene Bessie, with her wild hair combed and smooth. 'But she's at peace now.'

'It shouldn't have happened,' Ruby said fiercely. 'She brought it on herself. Laudanum's been 'death of her. She couldn't stop.' She rose from her knees, her eyes red and swollen. 'And I'm going to find Jamie. He's got a lot to answer for.'

Lizzie looked up and spoke in a low voice. 'He has, but he was onny giving her what she was craving. If she hadn't got it from him she'd have got it from somebody else. Your ma started wi' laudanum afore you were born, Ruby, so you can't blame Jamie. She took it to forget her troubles. To make life seem better than it was. Your father took it; they took it together, and

457

then when he left it was 'onny thing that gave her any comfort, well – ' She turned her head away and sighed. 'Most onny thing, anyway.'

'But Jamie hit her!' Ruby wept. 'He wanted to find out about me and Edward, to make trouble so that Edward would leave me and I'd go on 'streets like Jamie wants me to.'

I can't bear this, Grace brooded. There's got to be something better than this life. 'Where's Da?' she asked. 'I want to talk to him.' She couldn't talk to her mother with Ruby there, not when her friend was in such an irrational state. She had to handle things carefully, for Ruby would be sure to think that Grace was abandoning her if she told her she was thinking of going away.

'He went out when 'woman came to see to Bessie,' her mother said quietly. 'He's probably gone for a glass of ale.'

'I won't be long, Ruby. I have to ask Da something. Why don't you lie down and have a rest next to Freddie?' Grace suggested. 'He's going to depend on you now.'

A worried look replaced the misery in Ruby's eyes. 'Aye, he is. But where will he live if I'm to stay with Edward? He'll not want him at Wright Street, that's for sure.'

Grace tracked her father down at a nearby inn, one where Bessie had been a frequent drinker. But he wasn't drinking, he was going amongst the crowd with his hat in his hand, collecting money for a grave at the new General Cemetery for Bessie. 'Come on!' He shook the hat at tardy people who were unwilling to put their hands in their pockets. 'Bessie's entertained all of you often enough. You can surely spare a copper to put her in a decent grave. Trinity's full up and so is St Mary's.'

'Here.' A man put sixpence in the hat. 'I heard as they've shut all Hull graveyards. They're that full that folks is laid on top o' strangers wi' just a shovelful of earth on top of 'em.'

Grace shuddered and screwed up her face at the thought. It was true that there was a dreadful stench near the Holy Trinity churchyard because bodies were not dug in deep enough, and most people avoided walking too near for fear of what they might see.

'Is all finished at home?' her father muttered. 'Has laying-out woman gone?'

'Yes,' she said quietly. 'You can come home if you want to.'

He shook his head. 'Not yet. I'll go to some of 'other hostelries first. Besides,' he added, 'I'll not sleep tonight. Not wi' Bessie lying there.'

'I'll come with you, Da. I need to talk to you.' She looked up at him and thought how thin and grey he was. 'I'm thinking of leaving home.'

CHAPTER FORTY

The next day a constant stream of neighbours and acquaintances came to pay their respects to Bessie. She had been well known in the district and people were genuinely sorry that she had died. Lizzie allowed some of the more disreputable characters to stay only a few minutes to view Bessie and murmur their condolences, and then firmly showed them to the door. 'Funeral's tomorrow,' she said. 'You can follow 'coffin if you've a mind to.'

'I don't know what I'd have done without you, Aunt Lizzie,' Ruby wept. 'For you to let her stay here – '

'She could hardly have stopped at home,' Lizzie said ironically. 'Not with 'Blakes living in your house. Besides,' she murmured, 'I owe it to Bessie. We were friends once. Now then.' She became very brisk. 'Go swill your face under 'pump and get off to Wright Street. You've got your future to think of, and it's not here.'

Ruby stared at her. 'But', she said brokenly, 'you don't approve of how I'm living, and neither does Mr Sheppard.'

'No, I don't.' Lizzie was frank with her. 'But I can't think of any other way out of this hellhole. Go and see your gentleman, see if 'rumours have reached his wife.' She shook her head. 'Them grand folks do things different from us and it might not matter to them, but you need to know.'

'What about Freddie?' Ruby asked huskily, starting to cry again.

'He can't be moved anywhere yet.' Lizzie glanced at the mattress where the boy was sleeping peacefully. 'We'll think about what to do wi' Freddie when he's better.'

The rumours had reached May Newmarch. They had been circulating first in the kitchen and then been passed to the housemaids, and then to May's personal maid Dora, who whispered discreetly to another who attended a friend of May's. This friend, on learning of it, slyly suggested to May that if her husband was philandering with a mistress, she herself should take a lover with whom she could flirt and who would bring her flowers and trinkets.

'I don't understand,' May exclaimed. 'Edward wouldn't do that. We are only just married!'

Her friend smiled and patted her coiffure. 'I understand he has known her since before your marriage. It is a pity she is common,' she added. 'But don't worry about that,' she purred. 'So much better if he keeps to one who will satisfy him completely, and he will not therefore trouble you too often.'

May was furious and confronted Edward at the

first opportunity. 'How dare you!' she shrieked. 'Everyone knows, even the servants. Dora's cousin worked with her at the mill! I am so humiliated.'

'For heaven's sake, why?' he retaliated. 'She is nothing to you. You don't know her! You're not likely to meet.'

'Not her!' she screamed at him. 'I don't care about her. It's you! You married *me*. I thought you would be happy with me. I didn't know you would go chasing after some doxy!'

Edward viewed her with distaste. 'She is not a doxy,' he said coldly. 'She might be poor but she is – ' He paused. She is beautiful and adorable and she makes me laugh with her funny ways, and I never thought that I would fall in love with anyone, but I have. I've fallen in love with Ruby. 'She's a perfectly respectable young woman,' he continued.

'And you are using *my* money, *my* dowry to keep her!' she exclaimed, bursting into tears. 'I thought you loved me, but you don't, you just needed to be married!'

Quite true, he pondered. I needed the security of a good marriage, but I didn't expect this kind of conflict. I would have been better remaining a bachelor, except I didn't have sufficient money. He sighed a deep sigh. 'For heaven's sake, May! What a fuss. Why, what I spend on R— on this girl, wouldn't keep you in hairpins.'

She put her hand to her forehead and took a long sniffling breath. 'I have heard that other men do the same,' she concurred, 'but I thought you would be different.' She blew her nose on a

462

lacy handkerchief. 'Of course you will always have to hide her away. Because she's common, isn't she?' She toyed with the ribbons in her hair. 'She would shame you. You couldn't take her into company. I don't suppose she can even play the piano or sing!' She gave him a defiant glance. 'I suppose she is only good for one thing.'

'In bed? Is that what you mean?' He glared at her. 'And that's something you would know about, isn't it? So very welcoming, are you not?' He leaned towards her. 'Just suppose,' he said softly. 'Just suppose I said to you now, that we lock the door to keep the servants out, and we lie on the bed – '

She gave a gasp and clutched her throat. 'But it's daytime! It's only eleven o'clock in the morning.'

'So?' He advanced towards her. 'Does that matter? Have you anything else to do that is more important than keeping your husband happy?'

'But – ' She took a step backwards. 'That would be disgusting!'

'Would it?' He stopped and narrowed his eyes. 'And that, my darling wife, is why husbands go elsewhere.' He turned towards the door. 'Don't worry. I would hate to spoil your morning. And anyway, being in *your* bed at this time of day is the last thing I want!'

He took a horse from the stable, saddled it and rode off towards the river Humber. He hadn't intended visiting Ruby today, as she had told him that her mother was very sick and she had to sit with her. He had taken pleasure in comforting her, in murmuring in her ear and stroking her hair, and although she hadn't objected to undressing and lying with him on the bed, he had felt that her thoughts were elsewhere. To his own surprise at his unselfishness in not demanding from her, he had suggested that she dressed and went back to her mother.

But now he wanted to see her. He wanted to feel her body next to his, to hear her laugh, to listen to that gurgle of uninhibited glee, not a prissy simper or coy smile.

He trotted down to the river and on to the shingled foreshore by the Hessle haven. A stiff breeze was blowing and the sun glistened on the water. Coal barges, cutters and steamboats, a Dutch fluyt laden with timber were moving briskly in the breeze, their sails gleaming white, and he halted to watch them for a while. I'd like to sail away, he mused. He hadn't yet told May that he had given up his manager's position at the mill. Don't need to work any more. Didn't need to before, except that Father insisted. Good for our character, he always said. What utter tosh!

Presently he trotted on towards Hull, the mare's hooves scattering the shingle into a white spray, and his ill temper eased as the thought of Ruby embraced him.

Instead of crossing the town, however, he decided to ride down to the Humber dock to see what ships were in. Emerson has ships, he mused, and so has Joseph Rylands. Perhaps that's the business to be in. They're both wealthy men. But then, business means hard work and

464

I'm not so keen on that. Freedom, that's what I want. Freedom to please myself.

He could see the tall masts and furled sails of several ships in the dock, and as he rode towards them he saw a mass of passengers disembarking down the gangplank of one of them. Most of them were wearing thick coats and mufflers in spite of it being a summer's day, and he called to a group of people and asked where they were from. Some of them shook their heads as if not understanding, but one man drew apart and came up to him.

'Speak slowly please or I not understand.' He was a red-haired man with a thick beard and a heavy accent.

'Where are you from – and where are you going to?' Edward repeated.

'I am from Germany and I go wit' my family to America. Some of these peoples', he waved towards the crowd, 'come from Scandinavia, some from Belgium. They go also to America and Canada. A new life,' he nodded in emphasis. 'A better life.'

'Good luck then,' Edward said and murmured beneath his breath as he rode away towards the town, 'Lucky dog.'

'My poor darling,' he said when Ruby told him of her mother's death. 'Do you need money for the funeral? For a carriage?'

She was surprised at his sympathetic attitude when previously he had dismissed her mother's illness with a nonchalant shrug, but lately he had become more caring and tender and that had confused her. She knew how to cope with him when he was passionate and demanding in his desires, but was wary and suspicious of this other side of his personality.

'A carriage? No! We'll walk to 'graveyard,' she said, hiding a smile. 'But – ' Extra money would be good, she reconsidered. I could buy a box of groceries for Aunt Lizzie, like Martin Newmarch did, and she wondered wryly if Edward knew of his brother's involvement with Grace. Bet he doesn't, she thought.

She lowered her lashes, then lifted tearful eyes to him. 'But – yes, perhaps we could hire a cab, then I could take Freddie to Ma's grave. He's still very sick, he can't walk there.'

'Freddie?' he said vaguely, reaching for his pocketbook.

'My brother Freddie. You know, I told you about him.'

'Ah, yes! How much? A guinea? Two?'

'Whatever pleases you, Edward.' She didn't want to appear grasping. 'I'm very grateful, and it'll mean I can get Ma a proper coffin now.'

He looked up. 'A proper coffin? What do you mean?'

'Well, some of 'coffins are that thin that rats get into them as soon as they're put into 'ground. I can get a proper wooden one for half a guinea.'

He shuddered, and gave her another guinea to add to the two. 'Do whatever is necessary, Ruby – only don't tell me about it, please!'

He put his arms around her and said, 'I know you won't want to stay now, I understand that. But I need you, Ruby, I want you more and more. I can't do without you, do you hear what

466

I'm saying? I just need to see you. To be with you.'

'To make love to me?' she whispered, and stood on tiptoe to nuzzle his cheek. 'But I will stay now.' She was mindful of what Aunt Lizzie had said to her, to find out if his wife knew of their relationship. 'I want to stay,' she lied.

'Not just because I have given you money?' he questioned.

'Silly!' She started to unfasten his cravat and then the buttons on his shirt, and sliding her hands beneath the soft linen teased the hairs on his chest. 'Of course not.'

It was a very warm day and Ruby was glad that she had hired a cab to take the Sheppards, herself and Freddie to the new cemetery on the Spring Bank for her mother's burial, though they were rather squashed, and Freddie sat limp and tearful on Lizzie's knee with a blanket around him.

There was a crowd of people waiting to see them pass. Innkeepers and their wives were there, Mr Cooke the apothecary in his white coat, the grocer with Jamie's mother Nell beside him, though no sign of Jamie. Daren't show his face, Ruby deliberated, but I'll get him before long. As the cab drove slowly behind the cart which carried the coffin, some comments were heard on Bessie's final stylish journey and how it was paid for.

'I hope she likes it out here in 'country,' Ruby cried suddenly as they approached the tree-lined burial ground and its flower beds on the Spring

Bank. 'It's very quiet. Ma's a town person, she's used to a lot of folks around her!'

'Don't worry about it, Ruby,' Bob Sheppard murmured. 'At 'rate folks is dying off in Hull she'll not be short of company for long. Cemetery'll soon be filled up.'

Grace had sat quietly, not saying much on the journey to or from the cemetery. As they returned home, where Ruby had ordered ale and food from the grocer for them to note Bessie's passing, she was more than troubled as to how and when she could tell Ruby of her decision. I will tell her today, she thought. It's best that we get it over with, for she knew with an absolute certainty that Ruby would be upset at her news.

As they trooped in single file down the alley, Bob carrying Freddie, Lizzie next and Ruby and Grace following behind, they were assailed by shouts and screams coming from Middle Court. 'What's happening?' Grace peered over the top of Ruby's head. 'What's going on?'

'Bailiffs,' her father commented. 'They're turning 'Blakes out!'

'Oh!' Ruby, appalled, put her hands to her mouth. 'I forgot to pay 'rent. Oh no! They're tekking 'bed and table.'

'Your ma's bed and table,' Lizzie said. 'But we've got 'mattress so they're not getting much, cos Blakes have got nowt.'

'They've been living rent-free for months anyway,' Bob muttered. 'Scroungers, that's what they are.'

'But what could they do, Da?' Grace objected. 'Where could they go?'

468

'Workhouse,' her mother said quietly. 'That's where they'll go now. If workhouse will have them, that is.'

Ruby ran across to where the Blake family were huddled together, watching the bailiffs locking and boarding up the door. 'I'm so sorry,' she blurted out. 'So very sorry. I forgot to pay 'rent cos I was so worried over my ma and Freddie.'

Mrs Blake gazed at her with soulful eyes and whispered that her bairns would starve, but Mr Blake scratched his bristly chin thoughtfully and said, 'Well, Ruby, if you dash off to 'rent office now and pay what's owing, mebbe they'll call these bum-bailiffs off and we can go back in again.'

Ruby stared at him, her eyes wide. 'But it was my ma's house,' she said. 'I paid 'rent for her, not for you, even though you were living in it! And Ma's dead now.' Her voice rose and then broke. 'We've just this minute laid her in her grave! What use is 'house to her now?'

'Well,' he said flatly. 'What shall we do, Ruby? You've let us down. Really let us down.'

Bob Sheppard came over. 'On your way,' he said bluntly. 'Get your wife and bairns to 'workhouse. They'll get a bed and summat to eat and you can live off your wits like you've been doing for 'last few months. You've scrounged off Ruby pretending that you've been looking after Bessie and all 'time you've been looking after yourself. Go on,' he jerked his head towards the alleyway. 'Get on your way.'

'How could you, Da?' Grace asked later as they sat silently drinking tea, but eating little as none of them had any appetite. 'Those poor bairns.'

Her father was crouched in his chair with his chin in his hands. 'What else could be done?' he said harshly. 'Like it or not, workhouse is 'onny place left for them.' He straightened up, and picking up his cup from the table took a drink. 'Is it any worse than drinking tea given to us by a lass that's sold her body to pay for it?'

Ruby gave a sob and put her hand to her eyes. 'I didn't, Mr Sheppard! Not this time. Mr Newmarch asked me if I needed any money for Ma's funeral. He didn't expect owt in return, honest he didn't.'

Bob Sheppard was silent for a moment, then nodded. 'Aye, all right, lass. I'm sorry. I spoke out o' turn. I just get so – ' He turned his eyes towards Grace. 'So aggrieved.'

Grace caught her father's gaze and waited. She had discussed with her mother and father the implications of going away to Miss Morris, for this would be for a longer period than when she went on the tour into the west of Yorkshire and Lancashire. They both had insisted that she should go.

'So very aggrieved,' he repeated. 'On 'unfairness of life.' When he spoke next there was a catch in his voice. 'So, daughter. We're in a pit of darkness and despair. What are you going to do about it? How are you going to change our lives?'

Ruby gave a slight startled laugh and looked from Grace to her father and back again. 'Grace? How can Grace change owt?'

'I don't know,' Grace said slowly, and knew

that now was the time to tell Ruby. 'But I'm going to try, and even if I can't do much and I probably can't, at least I'll know that I've tried and will follow in 'footsteps of others who've also tried, and maybe,' she took a deep breath, 'somebody who comes after me will succeed.'

'What are you talking about, Grace?' Ruby demanded. 'You're talking in riddles!'

'I'm talking about injustice, Ruby,' Grace said passionately. 'I'm talking about poverty, and I'm talking about being educated which should be everybody's right.' She got up and went across the room to stand beside Ruby, who was sitting on the bed. Putting her hand on her shoulder, she said softly, 'Don't feel hurt or let down. I know that you'll feel alone, especially now since you've lost your ma. Just try to remember that I'm doing this for you and for me, and for Freddie and for everybody that we know who've been mistreated or ill-used just because they're poor.'

'What?' Ruby whispered. 'What are you going to do, Grace?'

'I'm going away,' she said. 'I'm leaving home and I'm leaving Hull, and I don't know when or if I'll be coming back.'

CHAPTER FORTY-ONE

Ruby didn't go back to Middle Court the next day or the day after. For why should I go? she thought miserably. There's no-one there who needs me. No ma waiting for me and Freddie is being looked after by Aunt Lizzie, better than I could care for him. Grace is going away and I don't want to think about that. She sat looking out of the window into Wright Street on the third morning and stifled a sob, forgetting momentarily that she was living in luxury compared with her life before Edward Newmarch came along.

But Grace was seeking her out. She hadn't visited the house in Wright Street although Ruby had told her the house number in case she should ever need her, and as Ruby looked out of the window she saw Grace walking along the street and looking up at the doors.

Ruby immediately felt a lifting of spirits and tapped on the glass. Grace lifted her head and smiled, and Ruby indicated for her to come up. She lifted her skirts and raced down the stairs and opened the door before Grace had even knocked.

'Oh, I'm so glad to see you, Grace. I've been so miserable.' Ruby turned to her as she led the way upstairs to her living room. 'Have you come to tell me that you're not going away?' she said eagerly.

'What? No!' Grace was astonished. 'I've come to tell you that Freddie wants to see you. He's upset, Ruby. His mother has died and his sister isn't visiting – he thinks you've gone away and left him!'

Ruby's eyes filled with tears. 'I couldn't bear to come, Grace. I feel as if I don't belong. Ma's not there. Our old house, slum that it is, is boarded up. You're going away and I might never see you again.' She burst into a fit of weeping.

'And yet you have all this.' Grace surveyed the room as she sat down. The waxed flowers in a glass dome, the embroidered cushions on the chairs, velvet curtains at the window, a bright fire in the hearth and pictures on the wall.

'But it's not mine, is it?' Ruby wiped her eyes. 'It's Edward's and if he wanted to he could turn me out into 'street, and I'd have nothing, even less than I had before.'

'Is he likely to do that?' Grace asked anxiously. 'From what you've said I thought he cared for you.'

'I think he does,' Ruby gulped. 'But I allus feel guilty when I'm with him. It's as if I'm playing a part. I'm pretending that this is what I want, but really it isn't.' A tear rolled down her cheek. 'I want someone to love me for what I am and for me to love him back!'

Grace didn't answer. She had always felt the

security of love from her parents, and although she thought that Bessie had loved Ruby and Freddie, her own needs, tempered by her addiction to opium, had always been paramount to theirs.

'Freddie loves you,' she said softly. 'And he needs you. And I love you, Ruby, you're my dearest friend. Just because I'm going away doesn't mean that I shall stop caring about you. But I want a better life too, I don't want to stay in Middle Court for 'rest of my days. I want a nice house to live in like this one, onny I don't want to do what you do to get it.'

'I know.' Ruby took Grace's proffered hand. 'I'm a selfish pig. But I shall miss you, Grace, just like I did 'last time.'

'Come on.' Grace rose from the chair. 'Put on your shawl and come to see Freddie. Or do you expect Mr Newmarch to call?'

Ruby shook her head and picked up a fine wool shawl and draped it about her shoulders. 'Later,' she said. 'His wife has found out about us so he comes when she's out visiting.' She glanced at herself in the mirror. 'Or *out calling* as he says.'

They walked arm in arm down Wright Street, crossing the bustling Charles Street and turning towards Sykes Street and the myriad courts and alleys which surrounded it. 'You see,' Ruby said, 'I know all of this. I know the folks who live here. I know what to expect of them and they know me. I'm comfortable with them.'

'You've forgotten,' Grace told her. 'You're looking at it sentimentally from 'comfort of your rooms in Wright Street.' She avoided calling it home, because she knew Ruby would object to that. 'You're seeing it from 'advantage of a full stomach, decent clothes on your back and leather on your feet. You're no longer cold and hungry and scratching around to find 'money to pay your rent before 'bailiffs come.'

Ruby didn't reply but walked with her head down as she pondered. Her shiny black button boots and layers of cotton petticoats peeped from beneath the hem of her blue muslin gown, and she compared them with Grace's shabby, worn boots and thin skirt.

'Am I right?' Grace asked. 'Or am I wrong?'

'You're different, aren't you, Grace?' Ruby didn't immediately reply to her question. 'From 'rest of us, I mean? I remember when you stood up for 'women at 'mill and confronted Martin Newmarch. I thought then how brave you were.'

Grace started to object, but Ruby insisted. 'Yes. You are,' she said. 'And yes, you are right. I haven't forgotten what it was like, but I've pushed it to 'back of my mind. I hated getting up on a dark morning to go to work for a pittance,' she said bitterly. 'I hated trying to make ends meet when I knew that I couldn't, and I hated it when Ma spent our money on loddy because it was 'onny way she could forget her miseries.'

She squeezed Grace's arm. 'Go then, Grace. Go and make it better for all of us.'

Grace laughed. 'I don't know yet what Miss Morris wants. She mebbe will ask 'impossible of me, but I'd like to go and find out. Mr Newmarch says that he'll take me to her if I decide to go. I've to let him know my decision – '

Her voice trailed away. The broad figure of a young man was striding in front of them. He was wearing wide cotton trousers and a thick wool jumper, and carried a canvas bag over his shoulder. 'Look,' she murmured. 'Ruby! It looks like—'

'It is!' Ruby shrieked. 'It is! Daniel! Daniel!'

The man turned around on hearing his name, and his sun-browned face beamed. The girls ran towards him and he put down his bag and held out his arms to enfold them. Ruby reached him first and started to cry again as he hugged her, and Grace's eyes sparkled as he put his arm around her. He stood back, holding them out at arm's length so that he could gaze at them.

'Look at you, Ruby,' he laughed. 'How lovely you look. As plump as a chicken! And Grace,' his laughter faded. 'Grace! You've been ill? You're so pale and thin!'

'No, not ill,' she answered quietly. 'But there's been a good deal happening since you went away, Daniel. We shall tell all. Come back for a cup of tea, we're just on our way home.'

'I will,' he said eagerly. 'That's where I was heading, to Middle Court to see Ma and Da.'

Both girls fell into a shocked silence, not knowing how to tell him about his mother. Then as he gazed at them, struck by their startled demeanour, Grace said quietly, 'They're not there. The room's been let to someone else. Your father's gone into lodgings.'

'And Ma? Where's she?' His face showed dismay. 'What's happened?'

Grace shook her head. 'I'm sorry, Daniel. It's

bad news. Your father came to us one day to say that she was missing. He lived with us for a while – he couldn't manage on his own. But then after he moved out – we heard, he told my da – I'm sorry,' she repeated. 'I'm afraid she's dead. They found her body in 'Humber.'

Daniel closed his eyes for a moment as he registered the news. 'No! I can't believe it! It's my fault. I should never have gone away. She relied on me.'

'You can't blame yourself,' Grace said softly, whilst Ruby put her hand in his to comfort him. 'It might well have happened even if you'd stayed. Your da said she was often unhappy.'

'Is Da working?' he asked quietly.

'He's back with his old employer,' Grace told him. 'I only know because my da works there as well.'

'I must go and see him.' Daniel picked up his bag. 'Find out what happened.'

'Won't you come back with us first?' Ruby implored. 'You've had a shock. I know what it's like.' She had a catch in her voice. 'I've just lost my ma too.'

'Later,' he said, his eyes lingering on her. 'I'm sorry.' Then he glanced at Grace. 'I never thought that there would be summat like this waiting for me. I've been so looking forward to seeing you both. I came back for your birthdays, you see!' he added.

'So you did, Daniel,' Grace murmured. 'So you did. And will you be staying?'

'I'll tell you my plans when I come back,' he said, and walked away with his head down.

Ruby waited for Daniel until she heard a church clock strike two. She had played with Freddie, who was cheerful and seemed much better, and then when he became tired she put him to bed on the mattress where he fell into a healthy sleep. Grace's mother had gone out shopping, although Grace suspected that she was searching for work rather than food.

'I must go,' Ruby said dejectedly. 'Edward will be coming. Tell Daniel I waited, won't you, onny – onny don't tell him where I've gone.' She looked anxiously at Grace. 'I'd rather tell him myself.'

'I won't tell him that,' Grace assured her. 'Not about you. I'll tell him that I'm going away.'

Ruby stared at her. 'But – will you still go?' She seemed astonished. 'What if he's staying? I mean – what if he's not going back to sea?'

'Why should it make a difference?' Now Grace was astonished in turn. 'Of course I'll still go.'

'He might want you to stay.' Ruby's mouth trembled. 'He was allus sweet on you, Grace.'

Grace considered for a moment, then said, 'I think he cared for us both, Ruby, not one more than the other.' She gazed at her friend. 'He'll have changed since he went away, just as we've both changed. We've all grown up. We want different things now.'

Ruby's eyes were wide and dark and moist. 'I don't.' Her voice was husky, and Grace knew, at last, why it was that Ruby was always so close to tears.

'Go on,' she said gently. 'I'll tell him that you'll be here tomorrow.' And I won't tell him, she mused, as she watched Ruby pass the window with her head bowed, I'll let him find out for himself, that you love him more than you will admit to, because you think that he loves me.

Ruby was so very confused in her emotions. Going back to Middle Court after an absence of only two days, she was appalled by the worsening conditions, at how putrid the stench from the privy was, at the rubbish piled up in the alley. As she looked towards the house that she and her mother had occupied, she saw that the planks across the door had been pulled off and that smoke was coming from the chimney.

Her emotions too were in turmoil after meeting Daniel. How can I tell him that I'm a rich man's mistress? That he keeps me in comfort because of what I do for him? She took a deep sobbing breath. He won't want to speak to me when he finds out, and yet I have to tell him. Explain why, before someone else does. Perhaps he's guessed! He said I was as plump as a chicken. Yes, of course I am, compared with Grace who is fading away before our eyes. I must bring her some food – and wine, that doctor said. Yes! That's what I must do. Build her up before she goes away. Suddenly, Grace's indisposition seemed to be the most important thing in the world.

She walked back along Charles Street looking in the shop windows, at the grocer's, the vegetable shop and the butcher's, and planned what she would buy. Tonight, she thought, after Edward has gone home, I'll come out and buy the things that Grace needs.

'Hey, Ruby!' A drunken voice hailed her and she turned around.

'Jamie! I want to talk to you.' Suddenly her anger erupted as she remembered her mother's bruised face after she had been brought back to the Sheppards' house, and she ran towards him. 'You killed my mother!'

'What! Me?' Jamie threw back his head and laughed. 'That loddy-tripper! She killed herself. Been killing herself for years!'

He took a small bottle out of his pocket and waved it in front of her nose. 'This is what did it, Ruby. Couldn't keep off it, could she?'

She prodded him in his chest and he staggered back. 'And you helped her!' she yelled. 'You gave her some bad loddy, stronger than she was used to. You tempted her, you devil, and all because you wanted to pay me back.'

He grabbed her hand and pulled her round a corner. 'Black Drop!' He glared at her and tightened his grip on her wrist. 'That's what I sold her and she begged me for more.'

'Raw! That's what you gave her!' She tried to push him away. 'Somebody saw you give it to her, then you hit her when she wouldn't tell you owt about me, and left her to die in that filthy alley!'

He laughed in her face. 'Well, I found out anyway. You're seeing Edward Newmarch from 'cotton mill! 'Same gent as I got for you. So by rights,' he tapped her face with a dirty finger, 'you should be paying me for all that lechery that you and him get up to.' He gave a smirk. 'But it won't last, my darling. Any time now his wife will find out that he's sleeping with a drab.'

She pulled free and slapped his face. Passers-by glanced towards them, but walked on when they saw what looked like a lovers' quarrel.

'Don't do that, Ruby,' he warned her menacingly. 'Don't ever do that again.' He pushed her against the wall. 'When you come back to work for me, you'll have to behave better than that. You'll have to be a good girl or—' His words were stopped in his throat as he was caught from behind by the scruff of his neck.

'Or what?' Daniel towered over him and roughly spun him round so that his back was against the wall where Ruby's had just been. 'What then, Jamie?'

'Nowt to do wi' you,' Jamie croaked. His face paled. 'It's between Ruby and me. We've got an arrangement.'

'No. No, we haven't,' Ruby cried, her eyes wild and feverish. 'He's a murderer. He killed my mother. He gave her opium so that – that – ' she took a deep sobbing breath, 'and he hit her and left her to die.'

Daniel's grip tightened around Jamie's throat. 'Is this true? Do I send for a constable?'

'Ask her! Ask her why!' In spite of Daniel's strangling grasp, Jamie still managed a leer. 'Ask this whore what she gets up to.'

Daniel's fist smashed somewhere between Jamie's nose and mouth, crashing his head back against the wall. 'Ah!' Jamie spat out blood, and putting his hand to his face spat a tooth into his palm. 'You – whelp!' He hurled himself against Daniel, but his opponent was taller and bigger than him and simply held him at arm's length.

'Don't come near her again,' Daniel warned. 'And if I find it's true about Ruby's mother, then you'll lose all your other teeth.' He opened his hands, freeing Jamie. 'Go on. Clear off before I change my mind and break your nose into 'bargain.'

Jamie stumbled away. 'Her ma was a drunken opium-ridden old hag,' he shouted defiantly. 'Mine's a whore, and yours, well, she drowned herself, didn't she.' He tripped in his haste and almost fell. 'Mothers!' he yelled. 'Who'd have 'em!'

CHAPTER FORTY-TWO

Daniel walked Ruby towards Wright Street. She was shaky and upset, but she told him that she had arranged to meet a friend there. He nodded thoughtfully but didn't comment.

'I shall be all right now, thank you,' she said as they came to the top of the street. She was nervous of meeting Edward whilst she was walking with Daniel, but even more apprehensive of Daniel seeing Edward, especially after Jamie had called her a whore. 'I'll come to Grace's house later. Perhaps,' she gazed up at him anxiously, 'perhaps I'll see you there?' He didn't know and she didn't want to tell him that she no longer had a home in Middle Court.

He nodded and looked down at her, then lifted his head and followed the progress of a chaise down the street. 'Perhaps you will.'

Ruby didn't dare to look around to see if Daniel was still watching her, for it was Edward's chaise which was pulling up outside the house and he was driving it. He tied the horse's reins to a lamp post and waited for her.

'Where have you been, Ruby?' he asked. He seemed very sombre.

'Shopping,' she said brightly and smiled up at him. 'I've been naughty, spending your money on fripperies.'

'So where are they?' He put his hand on her shoulder. 'Can't I see?'

'I've – I've ordered them. Onny a few trinkets,' she lied.

'*Only*,' he corrected. 'Not onny. I keep telling you.'

'Sorry,' she shrugged. 'I keep forgetting.'

He led the way upstairs and kept hold of her hand. 'And where else have you been?' He glanced around the sitting room: the fire was low. 'You haven't just been shopping!'

'I've been to see Freddie,' she confessed. 'Grace came to look for me. She said that Freddie was fretting because he hadn't seen me.'

'She came here?' Edward questioned. 'You told her where you lived?'

'I had to,' she said defensively. 'I told her ages ago where I was, when my ma was ill – in case I was needed.' She looked at him apprehensively. 'She hasn't been here before.'

He was wearing a grey frock coat and top hat which he took off and threw onto a chair. He unfastened his waistcoat buttons, loosened his neckcloth and sat down. She watched him curiously. This wasn't his usual mode of behaviour.

'Come here.' He reached out to her and pulled her onto his knee. 'I want to talk to you.'

She blinked. 'What about?'

'About you and me.'

She stroked his cheek and smoothed his side-burns. Was he going to tell her that this was the end of their arrangement? That he could no longer see her now that his wife knew about them? How will I manage? she despaired. I have no home to go back to, no work. What will I do?

Some of the anxiety must have shown on her face because he pulled her towards him and kissed her. 'Don't look so serious,' he smiled. 'It's nothing dreadful.' He paused. 'It could be very exciting.'

She waited. The only thing that had been exciting in her life lately had been Daniel coming back. She thought of his dark tousled hair and his beaming smile as he had greeted her and Grace earlier in the day, and of how she wanted to put her arms around him when she saw his distress on hearing of his mother's death. And she also thought of how he had arrived in the nick of time as Jamie had cornered her.

Edward trailed his fingers along her neck-line. 'I've been thinking,' he began, and she immediately became nervous. He wasn't here to think. She had told Grace that he never talked to her. He only ever wanted the pleasure of her body. 'I told you that my wife had found out about us?'

She nodded, and wondered if she should tell him that it was Jamie who had spread the gossip.

'She made a terrible fuss and I can't think why. So many men take a mistress.'

She flushed. 'Does she think I'm a drab?'

He pursed his lips. 'Probably! She said that it

was a pity that you were common and that I'd never be able to take you anywhere socially.'

Ruby felt ashamed and yet angry too. How could this woman form an opinion of her when she hadn't even met her? And anyway, I wouldn't want to be in the company of such people, not even Edward or his friends. I know where I belong, she decided. I don't want to move up the social ladder even if I could.

'And of course she's right,' Edward continued. 'In this country people are hidebound by the class they are born into. For instance if I was at home I couldn't throw my things onto a chair as I have done now. The servants would be scurrying to pick them up and May would think I had lost leave of my senses.'

He picked her up and carried her into the bedroom, swung around and then threw her onto the bed where she bounced. 'Nor could I do that to my wife,' he laughed. 'She would be quite affronted.'

'Have you tried?' she asked breathlessly.

'Good heavens, no!'

'So what did you want to talk to me about?' she said, as he pulled off her boots and ran his hands up her bare legs.

'Nor would she ever dream of being without stockings or corsets and the million other items of clothing that fashionable women wear,' he breathed, his eyes becoming glazed, so she knew there would be no conversation for a while.

But she was mistaken, for as he slowly undressed her, he gazed down at her nakedness and gently kissing her breasts and running his

486

hands over her body, he murmured, 'I love you, Ruby! I never in my wildest dreams thought that I would love anybody. I'm not the loving kind, but I adore you and I want to be with you and I'm willing to sacrifice everything to be with you. Even my wife and my home!'

She sat up with a start, but he pushed her back onto the bed again. 'I want you to come with me,' he said, gazing down at her. 'We'll start a new life in another country. A country where there are no rules about what we should do and with whom. A country where we would have the freedom to be ourselves.'

'Where is this country?' she asked in a small breathless voice. 'And how? How can we?'

'America! Or Canada,' he beamed. 'I saw some people getting off a ship in Humber Dock only the other day. They were from Europe and on their way to another life. A better life.'

She gazed at him open-mouthed. Was he off his head? What about Freddie? What about leaving Grace? And Daniel? And do I really want to be with Edward for the rest of my life?

She swallowed. 'What would we live on?' she asked weakly. 'You haven't ever been poor, you wouldn't know how to manage. What sort of work would you do?'

'I wouldn't need to work, not to begin with.' He lay down beside her and clasped his hands behind his head. 'I have sufficient money from May's dowry for us to live on for a few years, and I've heard that there are rumours of gold in America. Perhaps I'd buy a piece of land, employ some miners and dig for gold.'

She would have laughed if he hadn't appeared so serious, and then the implication hit her. 'But how would your wife live if you took her money?'

'It's not her money,' he said sharply. 'It's mine! She has nothing that doesn't belong to me. Besides,' he added, 'her father has plenty. He'd make sure that she didn't go without. She'd have to move out of the house of course, I couldn't be keeping her there. She'd be buying all kinds of things out of spite if I left her and I'd be liable for her debts. Not that I'd be around to pay them,' he mused. 'And she'd soon run out of credit.'

Ruby was aghast. She hadn't always listened to Grace when she had talked about the ladies who were with her on the tour. But wasn't that what they had been campaigning about? Equal rights for women as for men. Could she, in all honesty, go with Edward knowing that he had left his wife virtually penniless? She has done nothing to me, she thought penitently. And yet I have probably hurt her, even without intending to.

'What about Freddie?' she asked. 'He'd have to come.'

He frowned. 'Freddie? Who is this Freddie? Oh! Your brother, you mean. How old is he?'

'Nine. I couldn't leave him!'

Edward shook his head. 'I'd rather not. He'd get in the way. We could send him to school somewhere, or wouldn't your friend look after him if we paid her – what's her name?'

'Grace,' she said slowly. 'No, she won't be here.'

'School then, for a couple of years, then he

could start work as an apprentice or something,' he murmured vaguely. 'Or get a passage out to you when he was old enough.'

Ruby got up from the bed and started to dress. 'I don't know,' she said. 'I'll have to think about it.'

'What do you mean?' He stared at her in astonishment. 'What is there to think about? This is a chance in a lifetime for us! It means we can be together.'

She turned towards him and gave him a brilliant smile. 'You've just tekken 'wind out of my sails,' she said. 'That's all.'

He smiled back at her. 'I know I said that we could be ourselves, but you could create a different persona for yourself. You would be my wife – well almost, no-one would know that you were not, but you would need to alter your speech, put on a little style – a little *la-di-da*, you know!'

'Of course,' she agreed. 'I wouldn't want you to be ashamed of me. We wouldn't want anyone to guess that I was only a kept woman.'

A slight crease narrowed his eyes, as if he didn't know whether or not she was joking. But he didn't say anything more about it until he left, when he said that he would make enquiries at the docks about passages out.

She watched him as usual from the bedroom window and waved as he drove off, flourishing his whip as he went and with a huge smile on his face. She turned away. What am I to do? How can I go with him? How do I know that I can trust him never to leave me alone in a strange country? If he can abandon his lawful wife, surely then he could also leave me! He says he loves me, but does he? Does he love me enough? And most of all, do I love him? She lay down on the soft feather bed and buried her head in the pillow. No, she reflected. I don't. I love someone else.

Daniel walked slowly back to Middle Court. He had watched the driver descend from the chaise, tie his horse to a lamp post and, with his hand familiarly on Ruby's shoulder, lead her into a house. He was a gentleman of quality, judging by his mode of dress and the embellishments on the handsome vehicle. He had wanted to stay, to verify how long the man was in the house, but some kind of common decency made him turn away. He also felt quite sick and angry at the thought of what might be happening behind those walls.

He knocked on the door of the Sheppards' house. Grace opened it and invited him in.

'You look tired, Daniel,' she said. 'Come and sit down. Did you find your father?'

He nodded and greeted Grace's mother, who was crouched over a bucket peeling potatoes. 'Yes. He told me that he and Ma had had a blazing row and she said that she was going and not coming back.' He didn't add that his father hadn't been overjoyed to see him, nor that he'd said he was glad to see the last of the dowly old woman. 'He's found lodgings with a widow.'

Lizzie Sheppard gave a grunt, and, wiping her hands on a piece of rag, said that she was slipping out for a minute. Daniel glanced at

Grace as she went out and gave a wry grin. 'Is your mother being diplomatic?' he asked. 'She has no liking for my father.'

'She probably thinks we want to talk,' Grace said. 'Which we do. I've got things to tell you.'

'And I've things to tell you.' He hesitated. 'And things to ask you too. I've just seen Ruby.'

'Yes, and – ?' Grace's expression remained calm and impassive.

'I saw her first with Jamie. I'm afraid I gave him a bloody nose because of what he said about her – and then I saw her with somebody else.' He stopped and looked away. 'It didn't take a great deal of imagination to know what was going on.'

'She was going to tell you herself, Daniel. She wanted to explain why. But you must have suspected?' Grace responded. 'You knew how things were when you left! We hadn't any work and Ruby must have hinted at what she was going to do.'

'She did,' he interrupted. His mouth turned down and a frown furrowed his forehead. 'And I've tried not to think of it all 'time I've been away. Then when I saw you both together, you looking so pale and frail and Ruby so – '

'Plump and beautiful?' She gave a sad smile. 'She might well have finished up in 'workhouse or on 'streets if it hadn't been for Mr Newmarch.'

'You didn't,' he said angrily. 'So why should Ruby?'

'Because I had my ma and da to support me. Even though it's been hard for them too, we pulled together. Ruby never had that!' she said in defence of her friend. 'She's supported her mother and Freddie for years.'

There was a movement from the mattress in the corner as Freddie heard his name, and Daniel noticed him for the first time.

'He's not well,' Grace explained, 'although he's on 'mend now.' Her voice dropped to a whisper. 'Bessie died of opium poisoning and Ruby blames Jamie.'

Daniel frowned, then his face cleared. 'So that was what 'fuss was about! Jamie was in a right old state too.'

'No wonder.' Grace's mother came into the room and caught the tail end of the conversation. 'I've just heard that Jamie's mother, Nell, married her grocer yesterday. Jamie's been given his marching orders and told not to bother his ma, nor show his face in 'shop! He's out of a job,' she said with some satisfaction. 'He'll have to try for proper work, just like 'rest of us.'

'Ma's got work again,' Grace told Daniel. 'Even though her back is still bad.' She smiled at her mother. 'But I hope I can soon support her and she can give it up.'

'You've got work? Doing what?' Daniel asked.

Grace reached for the shawl which she and her mother shared since her own had been stolen. 'Let's go for a walk,' she suggested. 'I need some air. Then I'll tell you all about it.'

CHAPTER FORTY-THREE

'It's a wonderful opportunity, Grace,' Daniel said when she had told him of the tour she had been on, and Miss Morris's offer. They leaned on a railing overlooking the dock in the centre of the town. 'It'll change your life.' He glanced at her and she thought how sad he seemed. 'I'll miss you, though,' he said. 'We might not see you again, or at least not often.'

'I don't know.' She didn't attempt to deny it. 'I can't see into 'future. But of course I'll come back. Ma and Da will be here, and Ruby.' She sighed. 'I worry about Ruby. She needs somebody to look after her.' She stole a sly look at him. 'She'll always need somebody she can trust.'

His face took on a sulky expression. 'She's got somebody to look after her, hasn't she? This Newmarch gent! He's set her up in a house, hasn't he? She's not living in Middle Court, anybody with half an eye can see that! She'll be well set up. She'll not need you or me any more!'

'Don't be angry, Daniel,' she said softly, guessing why he was so angry. 'I'd hoped that you would remain her friend when I was away.' Her voice dropped even further. 'I hadn't realized that you'd rather she'd starved to death or gone to 'workhouse, instead of doing what she's doing. You're just like my father,' she added, poker-faced. 'He's totally prejudiced against fallen women, too. And yet I know that he's not without flaws.'

Daniel gasped. 'I don't think that, Grace! I don't! I do understand why Ruby took this path, and I'd rather she was with just that one man than out on 'streets earning her living! It's just that – ' He put his hand to his forehead. 'Well, I've come home, brimming with ideas about what I was going to do. I wanted to share them with you and Ruby. Now I hear that Ma's dead, you're going away and Ruby is – is – ' He stopped and took a breath. 'My life is shattered,' he muttered. 'I need somebody too, just like Ruby does. I discovered that when I was at sea. I need to share with somebody special.'

'What are your ideas?' she asked. 'Are you not going back to sea?'

'No.' He shook his head. 'I realized that it's not 'life for me, though I've earned good money. It was after we'd collected 'timber to bring back that I noticed there were short bits of wood lying around on 'dock side. I asked 'captain if I could collect them to make some trinkets. He said that I could and when I wasn't on watch, I whittled some things.' He shrugged. 'You know, like that stuff in 'sack that I gave you for burning.'

Grace smiled. Here was yet another story she had to tell. Daniel didn't know that his wooden toys had saved them from near-starvation.

'So I made a couple of dolls and gave them to 'bosun for his bairns,' he continued, 'and then I made a ship which 'captain said he'd like to buy from me. He gave me five bob for it. I think I could probably have asked for more, except that he knew I'd got 'wood for free. So,' his face broke into a grin, which was more like the Daniel of old, 'I decided that with 'money that I've saved from voyage, I could rent a workshop and make toys and sell them in 'Market Place. I reckon that folks would buy them.'

Grace turned to him, her eyes bright and enthusiastic. 'I know for a fact that they would, Daniel. But you need somebody to help you, somebody to dress the dolls, to paint 'ships and hang 'sails, and to sell them.'

His grin faded. 'Who? You're going away, Ma's gone. And Ruby – ?' He shook his head and looked thoroughly dejected. 'She wouldn't want to. She doesn't need to. Why would she?'

When Grace arrived back home a large parcel was waiting for her. It had been brought, her mother said, by someone called Molly. 'She said she was Miss Emerson's maid.' Her mother had been impressed by Molly's manner and dress. 'She was very neat and tidy and said to say good luck to you.'

'That was nice of her,' Grace murmured. 'But what's in 'parcel? Something from Miss Emerson?'

She undid the string and pulled away the brown paper to find a selection of clothing and footwear, some of which Grace recognized: she had borrowed them when she went on the tour. Other garments looked as if they were new. Inside the parcel was a letter written on perfumed paper.

'Dear Miss Grace,' the letter began. 'I have just heard a whisper that you are going away to help Miss Morris with a social project, and it struck me that perhaps the enclosed garments might be of use to you. Please do not be offended by the offering, for I will explain that by accepting them, you would be obliging and relieving me of the necessity of giving them away to others, who might not appreciate them. You see, I am shortly to be married to my dear country parson, and the mode of dress required for my new role will be quite different from the one with which I am familiar in my father's house.

'I hope that I shall have the pleasure of your company once you are settled with Miss Morris, for Mr Nicholson's living is in a nearby parish and so we will be neighbours. Mr Martin Newmarch has also promised that he will call on us when time permits.

'I remain yours sincerely,
Daisy Emerson.'

'Goodness, Ma! What do you think? Should I accept them?' Grace held up a rose silk gown in front of her.

Her mother sat down on the bed. 'Well! Were you thinking of going in 'rags you're wearing now?' Her face creased into an expression which might have been either pain or happiness. 'I'd been worrying over how we'd dress you if – when you went, though I know you've got that grey one that Miss Emerson gave you. Try it on,' she said eagerly. 'Go on, afore your father gets home and calls it charity.'

Grace tried on the dress and the petticoats that went beneath it, and was laughingly holding up a pair of cotton drawers for her mother's inspection, when someone knocked. She quickly hid that garment beneath the blanket and with a smile on her face went to open the door.

'Mr Newmarch!' She dipped her knee and invited him in. He gave a small bow to her mother, who stood up and nodded her head in acknowledgement.

'I came', his eyes glanced over her, 'to ask if you have given thought to Miss Morris's offer?'

'Yes,' she said. 'I would like to take advantage of her kindness.'

'Good!' He gave a swift smile and she thought how handsome he was when he wasn't in serious repose. 'I hoped that you would, and to that end I brought the necessary requirements to reply.' He held up a portable writing case and opened it to reveal compartments holding pen and ink, paper and envelopes.

His face crinkled into another smile to which she responded, as she remembered the paper she had used when writing to him. 'If you would like to write it now, it will be my pleasure to post it for you – in case you change your mind!'

'She won't change her mind, Mr Newmarch,' her mother replied for her. 'Her father and me will see to that. Go on, Grace, sit down and write as Mr Newmarch says.'

497

Grace sat in her father's chair and her gown ballooned around her.

'You have a new gown, Grace,' Martin said. 'The colour is most becoming, if you will permit me to say so.'

She looked up and smiled. 'Miss Emerson – she sent me a parcel of clothing! She's heard already of Miss Morris's offer. It's very kind of her.'

'Ah, yes!' he said. 'Of course. She will have to dress more soberly as a parson's wife.'

Lizzie Sheppard raised her eyebrows slightly and said, 'So will they be suitable for Grace as an assistant to this lady – Miss Morris?'

He cast his eyes over the parcel of clothing strewn across the table. He shook his head. 'I really don't know, Mrs Sheppard. I know nothing of fashion, but I'm sure that Miss Morris will say if they are not. She is a force to be reckoned with. A woman who will speak her mind.' He looked squarely at her. 'If you will forgive my impertinence, someone not wholly unlike yourself.'

She pursed her lips and nodded. 'That's all right then. We don't want our Grace to be spoilt and get ideas above her station, even though she must learn to know her own worth.' She gazed at him questioningly. 'Shall we lose her, do you think, Mr Newmarch?'

Grace looked up in consternation at the question put about her, and heard Martin Newmarch say quietly, 'Again I must answer honestly that I don't know. Perhaps you will. But that will be your sacrifice for the common good. Will it be hard for you?'

'Aye,' Lizzie replied with a catch in her voice. 'It will. But we'll manage.'

Daniel had obtained lodgings in a house in Percy Street, which crossed the bottom of Wright Street, and after talking to Grace he went back there for supper. But his appetite was poor and his thoughts were in turmoil, for it seemed that, if he wanted to start up in business as a toymaker, he would have to do it alone. Stupid of me, he thought. Why did I imagine that Grace and Ruby would be waiting for my return, ready to fall in with my plans? They have their own lives to lead, livings to earn, and times have been hard, much worse than when I left.

He put on his jacket again and went out for a walk to clear his confused head and rethink his plans. He crossed into the town, skirting the town dock and walking down the long Lowgate, passing the church of the Holy Trinity and the butcher's shambles. He went on towards the river front where he had been with Grace and Ruby to celebrate their birthdays. He leaned on the railing and looked 'down at the swirling choppy water, thinking of his mother. Well, at least she was found and identified, he pondered. Not like that poor woman they found upstairs in our house. Why was Ma so desperate? It was my fault for leaving. She was very angry when I told her I was going.

'Give you a penny for 'em,' a small voice breathed next to him.

He turned. 'Ruby! What you doing here?'

Ruby gave a deep sigh and leaned on the

railing beside him, not looking into the water, but with her back to it, looking across to the Vittoria Hotel. 'Reminiscing,' she said quietly. 'Thinking about 'best day of my life.' She turned to him and smiled, a sad smile which didn't light up her face but which made her seem wistful and vulnerable. 'Last year on my birthday we came here, you and me and Grace.'

He turned around and looked across at the solid four-storey building. 'I do remember, Ruby. It was a special day for me too.'

'Was it?' Her mouth trembled. 'Why was it special to you?'

He looked down at her and took hold of both her hands in his. 'Because,' he said softly, 'I was with two very special people. Two people that I care about.'

Her eyes filled with tears, which ran slowly down her cheeks. 'We don't have much in life, do we, Daniel? Being poor,' she said huskily. 'So it's important that we cling to what we care about – and, and I'd hate to think that you'll stop caring just because of what you might hear about me.'

She took another shuddering breath. 'I have to tell you, that 'name that Jamie called me – is true.' She blinked away her tears and continued, her voice shaky. 'I was desperate. I hadn't paid 'rent, I'd lost my job, and then Jamie lent me money and persuaded me that he could find me work, like he did for his ma. I agreed and 'first man he took me to was Mr Newmarch – onny, onny –'

She was embarrassed to tell him, but with an effort she went on, whilst Daniel continued to gaze down at her with his soft grey eyes. 'Onny nowt happened. He recognized me, you see, from the mill, and he didn't want to stay there in 'place that Jamie had taken us to. So he found somewhere else.' She didn't mention the Vittoria Hotel, it was far too painful. 'And so I cut Jamie out, which made him mad at me. I never went with anybody else, onny Mr Newmarch.'

'Do you care for him?' Daniel asked quietly. 'Does he make you happy?'

'Happy? No!' She shook her head. 'I'm well fed, I've got money and nice clothes, but I can't be seen with him, and my old life has gone. I'm caged. I live in luxury, but I'm caged.'

'And would you like to fly out of that cage?' he asked hopefully.

She hesitated. That was the crux of the matter, wasn't it? Should she take the risk and sail off to another country with Edward, leaving everyone she cared for, and not knowing what lay in front of her? Or should she stay and drift back into the old life of poverty and uncertainty?

'I have 'chance,' she said. 'He's asked me to go to America with him. Start a new life, where it won't matter that I'm not of his class. I'd be his wife in all but name.'

'You mean that he won't marry you?' His face drained of colour, but his eyes flashed and his voice was hard.

'Can't.' Her voice was low. 'He's married already.'

'You mean that he'd run away with you and leave his wife behind?' And when she nodded in response, he muttered, 'Blackguard!'

He turned round again and stared down into the water. It was deep, in full tide, surging against the river wall, the spray splashing his face. The pull of it seemed to draw him, and he caught his breath. Had it enticed his mother when she saw whatever dreams she had shatter, as his were shattering now?

'Daniel?' Ruby said in a small voice. 'I'm sorry! I said to Grace that you wouldn't want to be my friend when you found out.'

'Does Grace think you should go with him?' He didn't look at her, but continued to stare into the water.

'Grace? She doesn't know. He onny asked me today. No – I meant when you found out that I'd been kept.'

'He onny asked you today!' he exclaimed. 'And have you said that you'll go with him?'

'No. I told him I'd think about it. I've to think about Freddie. I can't leave him, Daniel,' she said tearfully. 'How can I? Poor bairn's already had a terrible time, climbing up chimneys and then losing Ma.'

'So would you stay if somebody else made you a proposal?' His face seemed brighter and he searched her face for an answer.

'Somebody else? What kind of proposal?' Her lips parted, and she ran the tip of her tongue over them as her quickening breath dried them.

'Not money or jewels!' He caught her hands again and drew her towards him. 'But 'promise of honesty and being faithful, and love,' he added softly.

She blinked. 'But – I thought that you loved Grace?' Her voice quavered and broke. 'You was allus sweet on her.'

He smiled. 'I love Grace still, but differently, and I might have been sweet on her once, she seemed so fragile and vulnerable as if she needed taking care of. But she doesn't. And a year ago I was young, just as we all were. We've all grown up, Ruby.'

'That's what Grace said.' Again Ruby's eyes brimmed with tears.

He bent to kiss her wet cheek. 'It seems to me that you need somebody to kiss away them tears that you're allus shedding.'

'If I was with you, Daniel, I wouldn't cry.' She moved closer to him. 'I've allus loved you, but I thought you were meant for Grace.'

'No.' He put his arms around her and held her close. 'Grace is not for me. Besides, I'd hold her back, she's meant for somebody cleverer and better than me.'

She objected. 'There's nobody better than you,' she said. 'You're 'most handsome, nicest man I've known.'

'And you told me that you'd onny known one,' he teased gently.

Ruby looked up at him. 'Does it matter?' she whispered.

'I'd rather have been 'first,' he admitted, and put his head against hers. 'But I met some girls whilst I was away, so I reckon we're even. What matters is that I love you, Ruby. I loved both of you before I went away, but when I came back and saw you, you looked so lovely, and when you ran towards me with your arms wide open to greet me, I just knew.'

She squeezed him tight, and kissed him. 'Come on,' she said softly. 'Let's go back to Middle Court and tell Grace. She'll be so happy for us.'

CHAPTER FORTY-FOUR

'My dear, don't upset yourself.' Georgiana Gregory did her best to console her cousin May, who was in floods of tears over her husband's indiscretions. Georgiana privately thought that it was only what she had expected.

'Some men find other women irresistible, in spite of having a pretty wife.' Rake! she fumed. Spending May's money on a mistress!

'I thought he loved me,' May sobbed. 'I never thought that he would look at anyone else.'

'Really! Then I think you were rather naive, my dear. Men don't often marry for love, though some probably grow to love their wives eventually.' And women marry because they think they should, they think they will have a better status, she contemplated, which of course is nonsense. Unless they are marrying into position and wealth, which May hasn't.

She patted May's hand. 'If you really do love him,' she said, 'then we are going to have to think of some way to win him back from this woman, whoever she is.'

'She's a common mill girl,' May wailed. 'She's not even one of us.'

'So much the better,' Georgiana commented dryly. 'If she was one of us, then everyone would know of it and think it serious. As it is, people who do hear of it will think it's just a little fling – playing in the dirt, which is what all boys like to do.' She gave May another pat on the hand and said brightly, 'You're going to have to consider his tastes and pander to them. Imagine', she said coyly, 'what he might do with a common mill girl.'

May gasped. 'I couldn't possibly! Georgiana, how could you suggest it?'

Georgiana shrugged. Really, May was quite tiresome, and she began to reflect that it was no wonder that Edward had gone off. 'I am not suggesting anything, May. How could I, being a single woman? All I am saying is, use your imagination. Read some romantic novels and try to tempt him back.'

May ceased her crying and wiped her eyes, being careful not to rub them and make them red. 'He did say once – ' She stopped and closed her eyes for a second. 'Well, it was quite disgusting and improper, but I could tell you.'

'Please don't!' Georgiana said hastily. 'There are some things between a man and wife that shouldn't be discussed with others.'

'Well,' May considered, 'I can tell you, I think,' and continued in spite of Georgiana's objections. 'It was the morning I found out about her. We quarrelled and I was angry and said to Edward that she was probably only good at one thing, and he said, what if he— that if he suggested that we lock the bedroom door to keep the servants out, what would I say?' She stared wide-eyed at her cousin.

'Mmm.' Georgiana nodded and raised her eyebrows. 'And you said – ?'

'Georgiana!' May flushed. 'What did you expect me to say? I said no, of course! It was eleven o'clock in the morning!'

My goodness! Things are worse than I thought. Georgiana pondered. Has her mother told her nothing? Georgiana hadn't had a mother to tell her anything, but had discovered at a very young age that there were ways of finding out.

'Time has no meaning in the art of love,' she said softly. 'You must be prepared at all times to follow an impulse, either yours or your husband's.'

'How do you know?' May was shocked at her unmarried cousin's apparent knowledge.

'I have read about it,' Georgiana said briefly. 'And you must do the same and be prepared to act. Now,' she said briskly. 'You have told me that Edward hates the crinoline, so when he comes home he must find you in some soft floating gown, without stays or hoop, perhaps even without stockings. As if in fact you were almost ready for bed.' She felt herself grow hot. 'The rest is up to you, May. I can tell you nothing more.'

May with much misgiving did as her cousin had suggested, though curious as to which books Georgiana had read. May's reading material contained heroines who constantly swooned and heroes who galloped around on white chargers and rescued distressed maidens. None told of bedroom scenes.

But when Edward arrived home he seemed agitated over something. His cheeks were flushed and after supper he got up from the table and said he was going to have a ride along the riverbank. 'Pity you're not dressed, May,' he said, as he opened the door. 'You could have come with me.'

Ruby waited anxiously all the next morning for Edward to come, and when his chaise pulled up outside her heart was hammering so hard she was sure that he would hear it. She heard him take the stairs two at a time and he burst through the door. 'I've got the tickets! There's a ship sailing in ten days.' He picked her up and whirled her around. 'And we'll be on it.'

She shook her head and struggled to get out of his grasp. 'I'm not coming, Edward. I can't.'

He gave a brief laugh. 'What do you mean? Of course you're coming.' He put his hand in his pocket and brought out a folder. 'Look, here they are. Two first-class tickets and one for my valet, Allen. We travel from Hull to London and then across the— You're not serious?' He stopped in midflow as he saw her downcast expression. 'Is this because of your brother? All right, for God's sake, we'll take him! But I'm no good with children, I'll tell you now.'

'I – don't want to go,' she said nervously. 'I'm not 'sort of person for adventure. I wouldn't feel safe away from home.'

'Ridiculous!' he bellowed, then, offhand, stated, 'Well, I've bought the tickets so you have to go.'

'No I don't! It's not as if we're married and I have to do what you say.' She was astounded at her own audaciousness, and so was he.

'What's this?' His eyes narrowed and he said viciously, 'If I'm not here to keep you you'll go back to the gutter. Back to poverty!'

'I know.' She looked at him with shame in her eyes. 'I'm grateful to you, Edward. You're right, you did rescue me from 'gutter, and I'll never forget that. But I can't go. I belong here. In Hull. It's a place that I know, with people that I care about.'

'Huh! It doesn't care about you,' he blustered. 'And the people *you* know can't help you. Not one jot!'

He argued, he wheedled, then he said that he was going home and that he would be back the next day to hear that she had changed her mind when she realized the opportunity she was missing. 'I shall be giving up the lease on this place, so think about that,' he warned.

She let him go and then thought that he hadn't even kissed her, let alone wanted to take her to bed. She was glad of that for she had no desire for him, not now that she was committed to her beloved Daniel, who had said he would be waiting for her later in the day.

The next morning she laid out on the bed the jewels he had given her, and when he arrived she told him she was leaving. He looked at her in horror, dropped to his knees at her feet and begged her not to. 'I love you, Ruby! I've told you that. I want us to be together. I'll always look after you. You mustn't think that I won't!'

She shook her head and planted a kiss on his forehead. 'I'm sorry, Edward. It's over. I know that I'm the loser, but I can't go with you.'

He ranted at her and took her by the shoulders and shook her, then apologized profusely and begged her to forgive him. 'I can't bear it.' He sat on the bed and put his head in his hands. Then he looked up. 'There's someone else, isn't there? You've found some other man to keep you? Who is he?' He rose to his feet and thundered, 'Tell me who he is!'

'No. No,' she stammered in her lie. 'There's no-one else. But I've got 'chance of a job. In a toyshop.'

'In a toyshop?' He burst into cynical laughter. 'A shop girl! Hah, if that's the height of your ambition, Ruby, I wish you well in it. A shop girl!' He put his hands on her shoulders and stared down at her. 'Well, I'm still going. With or without you. The ship sails on the sixteenth. Be there.'

'Take your wife,' she suggested. 'It'd be a new life for her.'

'Take May! You haven't met her! She wouldn't survive a week with all those rough immigrants and prospectors. She's pink and white and pretty, and no backbone!'

He turned to the door. 'Are you sure there's no-one else?' and when she shook her head, he said, 'You once said that I'd be the one to leave you, not the other way around! I don't understand you, Ruby. You can have anything you want if you come with me.' He glanced at the jewellery on the bed. 'Keep those,' he said brusquely. 'They're only baubles anyway, gewgaws.'

She looked down at the jewels. Gewgaws! And I thought they were valuable. She ran them through her fingers. Did he think that was all I was worth?

She left that evening, packing the clothes and jewels into a cumbersome parcel. I might wear them again one day, she thought. But if not, then I'll sell them to Rena. She picked up her stool, the only thing that was truly hers, and left, not even looking back for one last time. She felt a lightness of spirit flow over her. Now, she thought, I can really be me.

A letter came from Miss Morris by return of post addressed to Martin Newmarch. In it she asked if he would be so kind as to make the necessary arrangements for Miss Grace to travel as soon as possible. 'I send this request to you,' she wrote, 'as I gather from your letter that you will be accompanying her. I'm sure I need not remind you, dear sir, that she is a young maiden and in this instance will also require a female companion.'

He smiled as he read it and wondered at the complexities of womanhood as they strove for independence yet were also wary of their reputations. 'Mother.' He looked in at her sitting room, where she was sewing. 'How would you like a jaunt into West Yorkshire? Say, this weekend?'

'Certainly,' she agreed. 'So what scheme are you planning now?'

'No scheme,' he answered. 'But I need you to accompany a single young woman. I don't wish to compromise her.'

'Oh?' She looked up with interest. 'Is she eligible?'

He laughed. 'No, she is not, and she would be most confused if she thought that she was being protected or considered vulnerable.'

'So are you the one who is at risk?'

He paused for a moment. 'Possibly,' he murmured, and a fleeting smile touched his lips. 'Quite possibly.'

It was raining when he called on Grace that afternoon, and the courts and alley were flooded. He cursed silently, then rolled his trousers halfway up his shins, splashed through the water and knocked on the door. Grace put her hand over her mouth and her eyes twinkled when she saw him. Then she apologized. 'I'm so sorry,' she said, with a laugh in her voice as she invited him in. There was a pan of water boiling on the fire and he stood in the small steamy room, feeling ridiculous with his top hat in his hands and his trousers rolled up. 'We're so used to getting wet, you see.' She pointed down at her skirt hem, which was wet and dirty. Her feet were bare and a pair of muddy boots were drying by the fire.

How can people keep clean? he wondered. It just isn't possible when they have to live in such conditions, and yet Grace has told me that they are much better off than many others.

'I've received a letter from Miss Morris,' he

said. 'She would like you to go to her as soon as possible. Would Saturday be a suitable day for you to travel?'

'Oh! Yes. Oh!' She appeared flummoxed. 'It's 'day after tomorrow. So soon!'

'If it's not convenient,' he began.

'Oh, no! Any day is as good as another, Mr Newmarch. It's just that suddenly my life is about to change and I don't know if I'm prepared for it – I don't mean packing or anything like that, for I have very little except for what Miss Emerson has given me.'

He saw her eyes glisten as she went on, 'It's just – leaving Ma and Da and wondering if they'll be all right.'

'Ah,' he said. 'I did wish to speak to them about something. A scheme, as my mother would call it. She will be accompanying us, by the way,' he added. 'She's calling on friends in West Yorkshire.'

'Please, won't you sit down?' Grace asked. 'Ma won't be long. She's taken Freddie to 'apothecary for some cough mixture.'

'Is he no better?' he asked.

'Oh, yes,' she beamed. 'Thanks to you, Mr Newmarch, he is. Just a slight cough, that's all.'

She offered him tea, which he refused, and then he told her that he had resigned from the cotton mill as he had now taken over his father's business interests, and also had ideas of his own to fulfil. She asked him about Miss Gregory, and he replied that he had not seen her for some time as she had been accompanying her cousin on various outings. They had lapsed into silence when the door blew open and Grace's mother almost fell in, with Freddie on her back.

'Beg your pardon, Mr Newmarch,' she said breathlessly. 'But Freddie couldn't walk all 'way. He's still a bit weak.' Freddie slid down and she stretched and grimaced, one hand on her back.

'Mrs Sheppard.' Martin stood up. 'I've come to ask if Grace can travel to Miss Morris's on Saturday? It's short notice, I realize, but Miss Morris is most anxious for her to start straight away.'

Grace and her mother looked at each other. 'So – so it's 'time of parting,' Lizzie said softly. 'So soon! Aye, well, so be it!' She looked around the room. 'It'll not be 'same without her.'

'It may not be the same anyway, Mrs Sheppard,' Martin replied. 'May I be so bold as to ask if you have a regular work commitment?'

'Huh!' She gave a wry laugh. 'Folks like us don't have owt regular, Mr Newmarch. Nothing we can rely on anyway.'

'Ah!' He rubbed his nose as if considering. 'Well, I was wondering if you might be interested in a proposition?'

'Oh, aye!' She looked at him suspiciously. 'And what might that be?'

'I'm planning a charitable project. My late father and I discussed an idea which unfortunately, because of my illness and then his, resulting in his untimely death, had to be abandoned. I intend, however, to take it up again.'

Her expression gave nothing away, yet he felt he had her interest.

'There are, as I'm sure you are aware, many

refuges in this town, apart from the workhouse, which cater for the poor.'

She nodded. 'Aye. Almshouses! There's Weaver's in Dagger Lane and 'Charterhouse, but they're all full up and some onny take in certain folks, like mariners' widows or religious people.'

'Exactly,' he agreed. 'Well, I have in mind to establish a sanctuary which will accept elderly couples, who, at the end of their lives and unable to work or maintain themselves, are forced into the workhouse. In spite of a clause in the Poor Law Act which says they may share a room, they are usually separated there.'

'Mr Sheppard and me would like to stay in a place like that,' Lizzie said eagerly. 'It's not right when couples have shared a life that they should be forced apart at 'end of it.'

He smiled at her enthusiasm. 'I wasn't thinking of you applying to live there, Mrs Sheppard.' He saw the disappointment on her face and hastily added, 'My father left an endowment, and a property is under offer now. It is on the outskirts of town, but not so far that the residents feel isolated. There will be a small garden where they can walk or sit, and a quiet room.

'We shall need a suitable matron to run the house. Someone who is able to supervise staff and ensure that the residents as well as the governing Board of Trustees are satisfied.' He paused. 'I would be pleased to put your name forward if it would interest you, Mrs Sheppard. And Mr Sheppard of course, for we should also require a porter.'

'And – and where would we live, Mr New-march?' She asked the question in a low breathless voice.

'I'm afraid you would have to leave Middle Court, Mrs Sheppard!' His eyes glinted with ironic humour. 'You would have to live in. There would be a private apartment available to you.'

Lizzie closed her eyes for a second, and when she opened them she looked at Grace, who was smiling broadly. 'Praise the Lord,' she said softly, her voice breaking as she spoke. 'Our ship's come in! I'll start packing now.'

CHAPTER FORTY-FIVE

'Goodbye, Ma. Bye, Da.' Grace kissed them in turn as Martin Newmarch held the carriage door open for her. 'Ruby!' She gave Ruby a hug and turned to Daniel. 'Take care of each other.' She gave Daniel a hug too, then bent down to Freddie. 'Give me a kiss, Freddie.'

After she had wished them all goodbye, she stepped into the carriage where Mrs Newmarch was already seated, then turning she whispered in a choked voice, 'I'll miss you all so much.'

'Cheerio, Grace. Best o' luck,' the grocer called to her from across the street and his wife Nell waved too. 'So long, Grace.' The baker, with his face floury and his white cap askew, shouted, 'You'll do well, lass. We allus knew you was a cut above 'rest of us.'

It seemed that the whole neighbourhood had heard that she was leaving the district and had come out to wish her good luck. Others had seen the fine carriage waiting out in the street and curiosity had drawn them closer, so that there was quite a crowd gathered around.

Mr Cooke the apothecary stood watching from

his doorway, and a young flower seller who lived nearby called out, 'Don't forget us, will you, Grace? Come back and see us one day.'

Grace glanced at Martin Newmarch and said, 'Can you spare another minute, sir?'

He nodded and she stepped down again and went to speak to several people in the crowd, thanking them for their good wishes. 'I won't forget any of you,' she said to the flower seller. 'It's because of all of you that I'm going. I'll do my best for all of us.'

She sat down opposite Mrs Newmarch and waved through the window as the carriage pulled away, and then took out a handkerchief and blew her nose.

'What a very brave young lady you are,' Mrs Newmarch said. 'Leaving a home where you are so obviously well loved and respected.'

Grace wiped away a tear. 'There's nothing to detract us, ma'am,' she croaked. 'We onny have each other. No riches to fall out over. We have to pull together or else we go down.'

Martin, who was sitting next to his mother and had been watching Grace as she spoke, asked, 'Erm – your friend, I forget her name – is she living back in Middle Court?'

'For the time being she's staying with my parents,' Grace said, knowing full well that he hadn't forgotten Ruby's name, but didn't want his mother to hear it. 'Until she gets married.'

'Married?' His eyebrows shot up.

'To Daniel. I told you about Daniel,' she said, and Mrs Newmarch looked from one to another in amazement at the familiarity between them.

'But I thought that he – ' he began.

'When he came home from sea he realized that he loved her, and she's always loved him.'

'And are you happy about that?' Martin asked, his eyes searching hers as if in concern. He said again, 'I thought that he – !'

'Very happy,' she smiled. 'They're quite right for each other.'

'And the other unfortunate affair?'

'Is over, apparently,' she confided. 'I understand the man is going away.'

'Who – who are we talking about?' Mrs Newmarch leaned forward with an eager countenance. 'I am most intrigued. What an exciting life you do lead!'

Grace was about to deny it, when Martin put in quickly and positively, 'Not as exciting as the one she is about to follow, Mother.' He gazed at Grace and she was riveted by the profound contemplation in his expression. 'The world is waiting for you, Miss Grace.'

Edward didn't visit Wright Street for two days but decided that he would let Ruby wallow in anxiety, for he thought she was sure to have changed her mind when she realized what an opportunity she would be missing.

Instead he mentally checked his wardrobe as he ascertained what he would need for the journey and his new life. Then he told his man-servant Robert Allen, whom he had asked to travel with him and who had eagerly agreed, to clean the clothes he required and pack as discreetly as possible without the other servants knowing.

When he did arrive at the rooms in Wright Street, he found them empty of their occupant, save for a lingering scent of her. On enquiring of the housekeeper she told him that Ruby had left one evening. 'She told me that you were giving up 'lease, sir!'

'So where does she live? Do you know?' he said sharply.

She gazed at him with a puzzled expression. 'Why here, sir! This is where she lived. I never asked her where she come from. None o' my business.'

He stormed out and travelled on foot up and down the streets nearby, but he really had no idea where he should look. He had never enquired about her former life. He only knew of her dead mother and her brother Freddie, whose name surprisingly he at last remembered. 'Not much to go on,' he muttered. 'I wonder, I wonder if I could find that other fellow? The one who brought us together. Now what was his name?'

But he couldn't remember it and, although he went in some of the inns and hostelries, he didn't see anyone he recognized. She had that friend at the mill, he considered, as he thought round and round the possibilities. Martin had some contact with her. He might know where they lived. He even considered enquiring of the address from the mill, but after the gossip which had ensued from there, he declined to become a laughing stock again.

I'll ask Martin! He knows already that I have a mistress, so there is nothing to hide. But Martin and their mother were away from home, he was told when calling, and wouldn't be back until Tuesday evening. But we sail on Saturday, he despaired. I must find her. Then he decided that Ruby was teasing him. She will be waiting, of course! She will be on the dock side with that mischievous smile on her face. I know her so well! She loves her clothes and jewels. How could she not be there? Still he walked the streets day and night, and although he stopped and asked people if they knew of a dark-haired young woman by the name of Ruby, and some nodded and said yes they did, none knew, or were telling, where she lived. Ruby, it seemed, had simply disappeared.

On the evening before the ship was due to sail, Edward asked his valet to put the trunk and valises into the carriage under cover of darkness, take them down to the dock and place them in safe storage. 'Then come back,' he said, 'and we'll leave during the morning.' As if, he ruminated, as if I was going about my normal day.

By this time, Robert Allen had deduced that Mrs Edward Newmarch would not be travelling with them, but that his master's mistress would be. He could not, however, being the man he was, resist making the odd remark in the servants' quarters about the great opportunities that were waiting in the New World for those who were willing to take a chance.

Edward wrote a letter to his mother regretting that he hadn't said goodbye, but promising to write as soon as he could. Then he wrote to May saying that he was leaving for a new life and apologizing for his failure as a husband.

'It is with great guilt that I realize what a grave error I made in marrying, and one day when I have made my fortune, I will return your dowry. I regret that you will not be able to stay in the house, as funds will not allow it, but I am quite sure that your father will take better care of you than I ever could.'

He then made a plea for clemency and forgiveness. 'I cannot explain to you the passion that I have within me, and to stay with you would only sow bitterness in both our hearts, bring us to hate each other and harm your reputation, and, my dear May, I would not wish that to happen for I think of you fondly. I sail today, the 16th, and ask, as my ship leaves the shore, that you try to forgive me and think of me with compassion.

'I remain your affectionate, though faithless husband. Edward Newmarch.'

He sealed the letter. 'There,' he murmured dispassionately. 'That should do it.'

'Aunt Lizzie!' Ruby said on the afternoon of the 16th. 'Would you think I was very foolish if I went down to the dock to see the ship set sail?'

Lizzie considered. 'Would you feel happier if you knew he had left these shores and hadn't decided to stay after all?'

'In a way,' Ruby replied. 'But also I feel that perhaps I owe it to Edward to say a proper goodbye. Because, you know, I just left 'house in Wright Street and didn't leave him a note or anything. And he did give me clothes and food and shelter.'

Lizzie cast her a look of disdain. 'For which you paid in kind, girl. Don't forget that! He didn't give you those things for nowt, did he?'

'No,' Ruby admitted. 'But that doesn't seem important now. Not to me anyway.' She considered, then said thoughtfully, 'But I think he cares for me. He said he did, at least. He was allus saying how much he loved me.'

'Was he?' Lizzie murmured. 'That's an awkward one, considering how he's a married man. Well, it's up to you, Ruby. Onny be careful. He might be persuasive and you might find yourself sailing, whether or not you want to.'

'Oh, I don't want to.' Ruby gave a smiling sigh. 'All I want is to be with Daniel. But to have a fresh start I'll go and wish Edward God speed.'

Lizzie watched her go, and whilst being a shrewd and sagacious woman, she was also discerning, and remembering the tenderness and artlessness of youth, she put on her shawl and went to look for Daniel.

The luggage was in the hold, the carriage sent back to Hessle with the driver, and Robert Allen was on board checking that Mr Newmarch's cabin was in good order.

Edward paced the quayside. There were hundreds of people milling around. Some travelling, some come to see relatives off, and many foreigners who had left the ship to stretch their legs on shore and savour the delights of

Hull, before setting off on the epic voyage which would change their lives irrevocably.

What if she doesn't come? Will I still go? He was beginning to have doubts. He was not normally an adventurous man; he liked his creature comforts, which was why he had asked his valet if he would come. I have to go, he thought, everything is on board, and besides I've left May the letter. I can't not go now. I should look so foolish. He imagined May reading the letter and shrieking, then fainting, then sending the servants for her parents and Georgiana to comfort her, and of how his name would be infamous. He gave a wry grin. They would never expect it of me. They'll be in total disarray. But Ruby, my darling girl, where are you? His stomach churned with anxiety. Hurry or it will be too late!

'Edward! Edward!'

He turned quickly. There she was, hastening towards him. He ran to her and gathered her into his arms. 'Oh, Ruby, I thought you were never coming! But where's your luggage? Your trunk?'

She gazed at him in bewilderment. 'But I told you, Edward, that I wasn't coming.' She shook her head. 'I told you that I couldn't.'

'What? But that's nonsense!' he said tersely. 'You must come. I have the tickets. I want you to come. You must!' He grabbed her arms urgently. 'Never mind, we can buy what you need when we get to London. I can't go without you, Ruby. There'd be no sense in my going alone.'

They were jostled together by people making

their way on board. There was a queue of immigrants on the gangboard, and others leaning over the side of the ship waving farewell to those standing on shore.

'I can't, Edward.' She clutched at his coat, her knuckles white. 'I can't leave. I told you, I belong here in this town.'

He stared at her. 'And even though I have told you that I love you?' he said softly, his eyes misting. 'Even though I've left my wife and home to be with you, it doesn't make any difference?'

She shook her head, her emotions making it impossible to speak as she realized how he was hurting and that his love for her was genuine.

'There is someone else, isn't there?' he asked quietly. 'You wouldn't stay if there wasn't. What is he? A rich man or a poor one?'

'A poor one,' she confessed. 'I've allus loved him. Since before I met you.'

'And would you have come with me if he hadn't been there?'

'No,' she admitted huskily. 'I wouldn't. I'm sorry, Edward, but we're worlds apart, you and me, and eventually the love that you say you have for me would disappear. You'd become ashamed of 'way I speak, of 'way I am. You said once—' Her voice broke. 'You said that I could never ever be a lady.'

He held her close in contrition.

'And it's true,' she whispered. 'Perfectly true, and I would have hated it if you were ashamed of me. I would have tried to change myself, to be 'person you thought you wanted me to be. And then,' she added, drawing away from his grasp, 'it wouldn't be me any more. The Ruby that you once loved would be lost.'

She saw misery in his eyes, and he swallowed hard before speaking. 'You are probably right, Ruby. I wanted to possess you, to shape you into the perfect woman, which if I had only looked beyond my own selfish desires, I would have realized you are anyway.'

'No, Edward.' She gave a gentle smile and reached up to kiss his cheek. 'I'm not. I'm full o' flaws and weaknesses.'

'And your poor man accepts those, does he?' he asked, knowing, if he was honest with himself, that he could not.

'Yes,' she said. 'He does.'

He nodded and glanced towards the ship. The seamen were preparing to sail and the last few straggling passengers were being urged on board. Robert Allen was leaning over the bulwarks waving urgently for him to hurry, and watching them on shore were three other people. Daniel, May and Martin.

Edward kissed her for the last time and she saw tears glisten in his eyes. 'I know that I'm not the man you love, Ruby,' he said softly. 'But never forget that I'll always love you. I will always remember you as you are and how happy you made me. Nothing will ever destroy that memory. But I can't stay on these shores knowing that you are here and belonging to someone else.'

He walked away, his head and shoulders bowed as he climbed the gangboard without looking back. Ruby stood with her hand clutched to her mouth, trying to fight back the tears. He reached the deck and then he disappeared, not staying to watch the departure as the ship broke anchor and pulled away from its mooring to the accompaniment of cheers from the passengers and those left behind.

Young seamen up on the yards looked down, some raising an arm in farewell as the sails unfurled and the vessel eased its way out of the dock towards the river. Daniel came forward and put his arm around Ruby's shoulder. 'He's gone then,' he said quietly. 'Was there any trouble?'

'No,' she choked. 'No trouble at all.'

'I'm sorry, May.' Martin took his sister-in-law's arm as they turned away from the quay. 'I blame myself. I should have talked to him more.'

'You wouldn't have stopped him,' May said pensively and turned one last time to watch the departing ship. 'He loved her, didn't he? He wanted her to go with him, and yet she didn't!' She looked up at Martin. 'Why didn't she, do you think? There can be nothing for her here, being the kind of person that she is.'

Martin glanced towards the two figures walking arm in arm out of the quay towards the town. 'I think', he said with quiet admiration, 'that it's precisely because she's the kind of person she is, that she's staying.'

CHAPTER FORTY-SIX

The first thing that Miss Morris did when Grace arrived at her home on the outskirts of Wakefield was to put her on a diet of liver, beef, eggs and cream. 'You're fading away, young woman, and I can't have that. You'll never have a lot of fat on you, but I need you fit and healthy, we have a lot of work in front of us.' She insisted that Grace had breakfast in bed each morning and then took a walk around the garden for air and exercise.

Twice a week in the first three weeks, she ordered the carriage and they drove up into the hills and then got out and walked. Grace felt the blood coursing through her veins and in better health than she had ever been.

In the fourth week she tentatively asked Miss Morris what it was she wanted her to do and why she had brought her here.

'Did Mr Newmarch not say?' Miss Morris expressed surprise. 'How very odd, when it was he who planted the idea in the first place!'

Grace wrinkled her brow. She was sure that Mr Newmarch had said he didn't know what Miss

Morris wanted of her. Or at least, she considered, he hadn't suggested that he knew.

'Did he?' she queried.

'Mmm. Sometime when we were on the tour,' Miss Morris said vaguely. 'I can't remember exactly. Well, we are to begin a project, my dear,' she went on briskly. 'But first of all, so that you feel quite confident, I am obtaining a tutor for you to brush up your written language. We shall read some books and then we shall talk.'

Grace smiled. She would enjoy that. Her mother and father had improved her reading ability since she left school by giving her newspapers to read, but they could not afford books. 'And what shall we talk about, Miss Morris?' she asked.

'Why, women's matters, of course. Marriage, children, work, politics. All the things that women are interested in.' She leaned towards Grace. They were enjoying a cup of tea after having been out walking. 'All the subjects that concern women, yet, in the eyes of men, are no concern of women.'

She popped a piece of buttered scone into her mouth. 'That's what we are going to talk about.' She scooped up a spot of butter from her top lip with her tongue, and Grace smiled again. She had smiled a great deal since coming to stay with Miss Morris. She liked her a lot. She was original and unconventional with forthright opinions, saying what she meant, but never unkindly.

'Like on the tour?' Grace asked. 'Women's rights?'

'That's it exactly.' Miss Morris poured more

tea. She hardly ever waited for a maid to come and serve them. 'But very particular women. Not women like Mrs Westwood, who capitulated to her brutal husband, or Miss Gregory, both of whom are intelligent enough and have influence enough to fight for themselves if only they would make more effort. You and I are going to talk about the women who are unable, because of lack of money and resources, to help themselves. Women who live in poverty, but who would fight for their rights if they had someone behind them.'

Grace nodded and sipped her tea. My mother would have done that, she thought, if she hadn't been worn out trying to earn a crust.

'And then!' Miss Morris leaned back in her chair and gave a gentle belch. 'And then, when we have finished reading and talking, you and I, Grace, are going to write a book.'

Grace sat forward, slopping her tea into the saucer. 'Write a book!' she laughed. 'How can *I* write a book? I've barely read one, let alone know how to write one!'

'You see, you are improving already!' Miss Morris said approvingly. 'You are questioning what you think is impossible. Do you think it impossible?'

'I suppose it depends on what the book is about,' she acknowledged after a moment's thought.

'It will be about the women we will be discussing. Women in poverty. Which is why you are here, Grace. And,' she continued, 'I think we might call it *The Enlightenment of Women in Poverty*.'

Grace considered, then said slowly, 'The women in poverty that I know are already enlightened. They've seen the light but it's beyond their reach.' Then she added, 'When I was on 'tour, I heard the other ladies speaking of *emancipation*, and when I got home I asked my father what it meant.'

'And was he able to tell you?' Miss Morris asked gently.

'Oh yes,' she said earnestly. 'My father can explain almost anything. He said it meant freedom, or setting free.' She took a breath and, her eyes gleaming, said eagerly, 'Could we call the book *The Emancipation of Women in Poverty*?'

Miss Morris gave her a wide smile and reached to ring the bell at the side of the fireplace. 'It may be early, my dear Grace, but I think this calls for a celebratory glass of sherry.'

The maid brought in the decanter and glasses and poured the sherry. 'Top them up, girl,' Miss Morris admonished. 'You might not know it but we're drinking your health.' She raised her glass and Grace did the same to make the toast. 'To *The Emancipation of Women in Poverty*.'

They were almost two years in the writing of it, and, in the meantime, Martin Newmarch visited every two or three months and Grace discussed with him the project of the book. They walked in the garden if it was fine, or, if it was cold or wet, sat by the fire in the small sitting room which Miss Morris had given her in order to study. He noted her growing air of confidence, her easy manner, due no doubt to the influence of Miss

Morris's informality. She had a quiet elegance of dress, and her fine complexion, which had always been pale, now had a touch of colour. Her fair hair was dressed in coils about her ears or in a neat chignon at the nape of her slender neck.

Daisy Emerson, now Mrs Nicholson, also called regularly, although Miss Morris was inclined to be otherwise engaged when she visited and left Grace to be the hostess.

'She's so very woolly-headed,' she declared. 'But I suppose very fitting for a parson's wife, for she can chatter to her husband's parishioners without any effort whatsoever.'

'But she came on the tour,' Grace declared, for she had a liking for the pleasant-mannered Mrs Nicholson. 'She has interests in other matters apart from local!'

Miss Morris glanced sideways at Grace and humphed, but said no more. Grace, however, was intrigued by Miss Morris's opinion of Daisy Nicholson, and the next time she visited asked her outright what had been her main interest in travelling on the tour with the other ladies.

'My parents have always treated me in the same equal manner as my brothers,' she said, 'and we have always discussed politics at home. But essentially I am very lazy and would not have gone on the tour if my father had not persuaded me. As it is,' she smiled complacently, 'I am extremely pleased that I did, otherwise I would not have met my dear country parson.'

'So why did your father persuade you if you didn't have the inclination yourself, Mrs Nicholson?'

'Oh, do call me Daisy, my dear Grace!' she exclaimed, taking a sip of tea. 'Why? Oh, because of you! Martin Newmarch insisted that you should have a companion and asked Father to ask me if I would go too.' She gave a wicked smile. 'I told you at the time, didn't I, that he was very taken with you!'

Grace blushed and repeated what she had said on the tour, that Mr Newmarch had always treated her with consideration, but Daisy simply raised her eyebrows and gave her a knowing look, then told her that she had heard gossip that Georgiana Gregory was emigrating abroad. 'I do believe that she is weary of playing nursemaid to May Newmarch since Edward left her. She is going, I hear, to seek her own fortune rather than relying on her uncle's.'

'Alone?' Grace asked in astonishment. 'Miss Morris will be most impressed!'

'With just a maid, so I understand.'

Grace visited home three times during the first year. Martin Newmarch collected her and brought her back and they travelled alone, for she had told him quite firmly and frankly, looking into his amused dark eyes, that she was not in need of a female companion. She had no reputation to think of, she said, nor one to lose. 'Besides which,' she continued guilelessly, 'I've travelled with you in a carriage before, if you remember. And I do trust you.' And he thanked her for the compliment and said that he certainly did remember, and wasn't likely to forget.

She asked him was it true that Georgiana Gregory was travelling abroad with only a maid, and he confirmed it. 'She came to ask my advice,' he said. 'She felt stifled by May's demands for companionship and constant whining about being abandoned by Edward.'

'Miss Gregory once said that she didn't think there would ever come a day when women would travel alone.' Grace glanced at him, for she recalled his answer on that particular day. 'And now she is to do it!'

He nodded. 'And I believe I said that there would always be women who would have the strength of spirit to be self-reliant and liberated. It seems that Miss Gregory had taken that remark to heart.'

What he didn't tell Grace was that at the meeting with Georgiana, she had told him that she couldn't seriously consider his earlier offer of marriage, for she felt that he had made it only in a light-hearted jocular manner. When he made no further declaration of intent, she had lifted her chin purposefully and told him that she had decided to take her life in her own hands and sail for the New World. He had expressed his admiration for her courage, and with a lightening of his spirits he had bid her goodbye for the last time.

On one of Grace's visits she saw her parents ensconced in their new apartment in the alms-house, and noticed how they both seemed to have grown in stature now that they had position and authority. Her mother had suggested various ideas to the Board which would improve the welfare of the residents, and these had been approved. Her father had given up his labouring work in the timber yard, for he found there was plenty to do in his new employment. He had a better head for figures than his wife and so took on the task of keeping accounts and book-keeping, freeing her to attend to the daily requirements of the residents.

Grace had also visited Ruby and Daniel in their rooms above the workshop where Daniel made toys and small items of furniture, such as footstools and tea caddies. 'They're selling really well, Grace,' Ruby said enthusiastically. 'And folks come to 'door to ask if he'll make sailing ships and dolls for them, and Freddie is helping him. We'll put him to an apprenticeship when he's old enough.'

'I'm so glad for you.' Grace gave her a hug. 'And you look so well, Ruby. As plump as a chicken,' she added jokingly.

Ruby's eyes gleamed and she glanced at Daniel. 'We can tell now, can't we, Daniel? We've been waiting for you, Grace. We've not told anybody else yet. We're expecting a babby. And if it's a girl we'll call her Grace after you.'

'So I'm mekking a crib.' Daniel looked as pleased and happy as Ruby. 'And a little table and chair.'

During one of their visits in the second year, as they drove back into the West Riding, Grace was pensive and wistful and Martin asked if something was troubling her. 'No,' she said. 'But each time I come back, I realize how I miss the people I've left behind and all 'familiar places. I miss the hustle and bustle of the town though I would never ever want to live back in Middle Court!'

'I should think not! But there's no reason why you shouldn't come back once you and Miss Morris have finished the book,' he said. 'You'll be asked to lecture, I expect, and that could take you all over the country, but you could make your home here in Hull, and be near your family and friends.'

'Asked to lecture?' Startled, she looked at him, holding his gaze, and he suddenly caught his breath.

'You will be in demand, Grace,' he murmured. 'The book will cause controversy and you will be asked for your opinion on matters relating to it.'

'But, surely Miss Morris will – '

'No. It's essentially your book. I haven't read it, but Miss Morris tells me that it is you who is writing it. You are the one who has seen poverty and degradation at first hand and risen above it. You have seen child labour and also experienced it. Your thoughts and opinions are going into the book and Mary Morris says that she is merely the adviser on various matters of politics and law.'

He looked earnestly at her. 'I said, didn't I, that the world was waiting for Miss Grace? Women in poverty will rejoice that there is a voice speaking for them.'

'But,' her face showed apprehension, 'I'm not ready for that.'

'You will be,' he assured her.

'I can't do it alone,' she protested.

'You don't have to,' he resolved.

'You planned all of this, didn't you?' she asked slowly and frankly. 'Right from 'beginning?'

He admitted that he had. 'It started when you took me into the Groves and I saw how people were living. They had no means of escaping from that terrible life and I felt so frustrated, and guilty too, that I had so much and they so little.' He moved from his seat opposite and came to sit beside her. He took hold of her hands and looked down at them.

'But it was when you spoke up for the women at the mill who had been given notice, but not their wages, that I started to think that you were someone rather special.'

He smiled and looked at her to find her gazing at him, her eyes tenderly searching his face as if she was seeing him for the first time. 'But I have to say that I was in awe of you, which is why I didn't offer you more work at the mill.'

'In awe of me?' she breathed.

'Yes.' He stroked her fingers. 'I felt that you would cause me great trouble. Which you have!'

'How?' she whispered. 'How have I caused you trouble? You were the one who arranged for me to meet Miss Gregory and Mrs Westwood. And,' she admonished, and he took pleasure in her naturalness and lack of reserve with him, 'Daisy Nicholson said that it was only because you asked her to be my companion, that she came on the tour!'

'Ah!' he laughed. 'So the truth is out! I did. At least I asked her father, who, like me, believes in equality. Not just for women but for all people.'

'So – have I been protected all along?' she asked quietly, as if cast down.

'No,' he assured her, most decisively. 'You

have not! What you have done you have done by yourself. You had the will to succeed, whereas you could have refused or turned away. Don't forget,' he added, 'you were alone when you were without work, and hungry, and yet you had the strength of spirit to survive!' He gave a deep sigh and murmured, 'I neglected you then, Grace, because of my own circumstances, and could so easily have lost you.' He touched her cheek, which had a faint blush on it. 'I don't know what I would have done then.'

She said nothing, but she put her hand over his.

'I saw my brother's face as he walked away from Ruby to board the ship,' he said softly. 'I saw the anguish and despair, and, for the first time ever, I understood his feelings. He looked totally lost and abandoned. Which is how I would have felt if anything had happened to you through my neglect.'

'He had said that he loved her,' Grace murmured, her voice beginning to tremble.

'Yes, I understand that now. And I realized how two people from totally different backgrounds can come to love each other.'

'Except that Ruby didn't love Edward,' she breathed and couldn't pull away from the tender expression in his eyes which told her that he wasn't speaking of Ruby and Edward. 'She refused him because she loved Daniel.'

'And I thought that you and Daniel – ' he began.

'No.' She gave a gentle smile. 'Daniel was always my friend, my dear friend, just as Ruby is.'

'And I?' he asked, as the carriage drew up the hill towards Miss Morris's house. 'May I be a dear friend too?'

She squeezed his hand. 'When I first came to Miss Morris's, she asked me if I thought a certain thing was impossible, and I discovered that it wasn't.'

He lifted her hand to his lips as she said softly, 'I think that it's quite possible that we could be more than dear friends, Martin, if that is what we wish.'

'And I do wish it, my dearest Grace. I can see no obstacle in our way if that is what we both desire.'

She leaned towards him to receive his kiss. 'My mother once told me that love can sometimes grow slowly, maybe out of admiration and respect.'

He drew her closer, and she nestled into his arms. 'Your mother, Grace, like so many women, is very wise. But what will she say, and indeed what will your father say, when I tell them that I love their daughter? That I have always loved their daughter!'

She kissed him and as the coach came to a halt and the driver opened the door, they drew apart. She smiled happily and replied, 'They will say that in the matter of the heart, everyone gets what they deserve.'

THE END

FAR FROM HOME
by Val Wood

When Georgiana and her maid, Kitty, make the long sea-journey from their native East Yorkshire to America, they are seeking a new life of freedom. But in New York, Georgiana encounters an imposter posing as Edward Newmarch, her cousin's womanising husband, who has abandoned his wife and fled to America. Edward himself seems to have vanished.

Meanwhile Edward, having escaped from a disastrous marriage in England, is now running from a bigamous union with the daughter of a wealthy plantation owner. His flight takes him through Mississippi swamps, across arid desert and mountain ranges towards the gold fields of California. As Georgiana and Kitty journey to the hidden valley of gold, and Edward tries to flee his enemies, the dangers and passions of this new country and its people threaten to overwhelm them.

By the author of *The Hungry Tide*, winner of the Catherine Cookson Prize for fiction, and also *Annie, Children of the Tide, The Romany Girl, Emily, Going Home, Rosa's Island* and *The Doorstep Girls*.

9780552150322

EMILY
by Val Wood

From shame and imprisonment to a new life . . .

Emily was only five years old when she was sent
away from her Ma and Da and her brother Joe to
go and live with old Granny Edwards. Growing up
to be a loving and hard-working child, she goes
into service at the age of twelve at the house of
Roger Francis, whose connections with Emily's
own family prove to be closer than she could ever
have imagined. Roger's daughter Deborah takes a
fancy to Emily, and when she moves away to
another household in Hull Emily finds that her
new employer's son, Hugo, is to marry Deborah.
But Hugo, too, has become obsessed with Emily;
he dishonours her and betrays her, bringing her to
the very depths of ruin.

Imprisoned, tried and transported to Australia,
her life seems finished – until she is reunited with
the one man who can save her from her misery and
bring her wealth and happiness.

9780552147408

GOING HOME
by Val Wood

For Amelia and her brothers and sisters, the grim past which their mother Emily has endured seems very far away. A striking and independent young woman, studying to be a teacher in York, Amelia is looking for a purpose in life, and hopes especially to become acquainted with the two young gentlemen who have travelled all the way from Australia to meet her family. Ralph Hawkins, bringing with him his friend Jack – a handsome half-aboriginal Australian – has come to Yorkshire to look for his roots. He finds Amelia, whose tangled family history is inextricably bound up with his.

Ralph Hawkins's whole world was turned upside down when he learned that he had been adopted by the couple he had always called his parents. In his quest to find his real mother, he uncovers some cruel and unpleasant truths, before at last realizing where his true destiny lies.

9780552148450

THE ROMANY GIRL
By Val Wood

Polly Anna could not remember her father, and after her mother died, in poverty, when Polly Anna was just three, the workhouse was the only place for her. Helped by Jonty, a young misfit who became her best friend, she ran away with the fairground folk and became a horserider and acrobat – · travelling to Bartholomew Fair, Nottingham Goose Fair and Hull Fair. Her friends became the circus people and the gypsies, and her home the caravans and tents of the travellers.

Meanwhile, in a great house in the Yorkshire Wolds, old Mrs Winthrop had never given up hope of finding her daughter, who eloped with a handsome Romany and was never seen again. Her young neighbour Richard Crossley set out to find the missing daughter, and discovered the colourful world of the fairs and the gypsies. He also discovered Polly Anna – once the waif from the workhouse, and now a fully-fledged *Romani Chi* – the Romany girl.

9780552146401

RICH GIRL, POOR GIRL
by Val Wood

Christmas 1860

A waif from the slums and a poor little rich girl

Polly, living in grinding poverty, loses her mother in childbirth and finds herself alone on the streets of Hull.

Rosalie, brought up in affluence and comfort on the other side of town, loses her own mother in similar circumstances and on the same day.

Polly takes a job as scullery maid in Rosalie's lonely house, and the two girls form an unlikely friendship. Travelling to the North Yorkshire Moors they discover a new kind of life and find tragedy and joy in equal measure.

By the author of the first Catherine Cookson Prize for fiction

9780552156806